D. W. BRADBRIDGE

A Soldier of Substance

www.dwbradbridge.com

First edition

© 2014 D. W. Bradbridge

Published by Valebridge Publications Ltd,
PO Box 320, Crewe, Cheshire CW2 6WY

Cover design by Electric Reads
Cover image (soldiers) used with thanks to Cliff Astles

Typeset for print by Electric Reads
www.electricreads.com

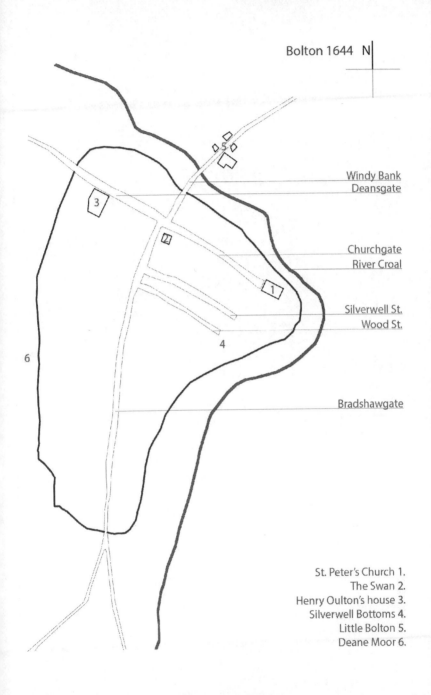

Bolton 1644   N

Windy Bank
Deansgate

Churchgate
River Croal

Silverwell St.
Wood St.

Bradshawgate

St. Peter's Church 1.
The Swan 2.
Henry Oulton's house 3.
Silverwell Bottoms 4.
Little Bolton 5.
Deane Moor 6.

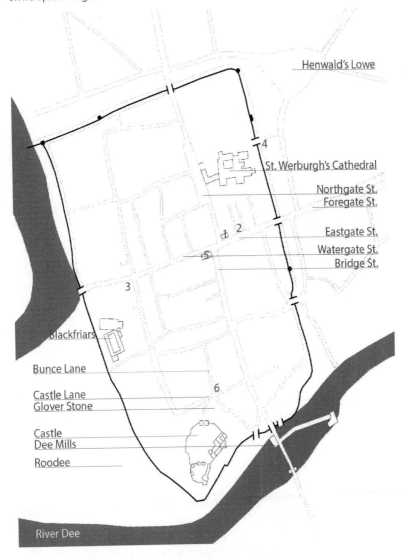

1. William Seaman's house
2. The Boot
3. The Earl of Derby's house
4. The Kaleyard Gate
5. Chester Cross and the Pentice
6. The Spread Eagle

Henwald's Lowe

4

St. Werburgh's Cathedral

Northgate St.
Foregate St.

2

Eastgate St.
Watergate St.
Bridge St.

3

Blackfriars

Bunce Lane

Castle Lane
Glover Stone

6

Castle
Dee Mills

Roodee

River Dee

Key Characters

In Nantwich:

Daniel Cheswis Wich house owner, cheese merchant, and reluctant constable of Nantwich

Elizabeth Brett Daniel's sweetheart

Ralph Brett Elizabeth's son from her first marriage

Cecilia Padgett Daniel's housekeeper

Amy Padgett Cecilia's granddaughter

Jack Wade Daniel's apprentice

Alexander Clowes Chandler, bellman, and Daniel's best friend

Marjery Clowes Alexander's wife

Simon Cheswis	Daniel's headstrong younger brother
Rose Bailey	Simon's sweetheart
George Simkins	Shoemaker and master of Simon Cheswis
Arthur Sawyer	Constable
Jack and Robert Skinner	Brothers to Daniel's former apprentice, James Skinner
Ezekiel Green	Nantwich's court clerk
Sir William Brereton	Commander of parliamentary forces in Cheshire
Colonel Thomas Croxton	Deputy lieutenant and responsible for the payment of Brereton's army
Colonel George Booth	Nantwich garrison commander

In Chester and around:

Thomas Corbett　　　Landlord of The Boot, a
　　　　　　　　　　　　tavern-cum-bawdy house

Charles Corbett　　　Thomas' son

Annie　　　　　　　　Madam of the brothel in
　　　　　　　　　　　　The Boot

Roisin Byrne　　　　A whore

James Skinner　　　　Daniel's ex-apprentice,
　　　　　　　　　　　　kidnapped by the royalists
　　　　　　　　　　　　at the Battle of Nantwich

Jem Bressy　　　　　Royalist spy. Skinner's
　　　　　　　　　　　　captor

William Seaman　　　Cheese and general goods
　　　　　　　　　　　　merchant

Isabel Seaman　　　　William's wife

Katherine Seaman　　William's sister

Roberts　　　　　　Footman in William
　　　　　　　　　　　　Seaman's household

John Gibbons	A servant
Martha Woodcock	A cook / housekeeper
Captain Edward Chisnall	(See also under royalist forces at Lathom) Royalist officer. Messenger to the Earl of Derby
Francis Gamull	Chester merchant and commander of the town guard
Robert Whitby	Merchant and close relative of Gamull
Jack Taylor	A glover
William Ainsworth	A divinity lecturer and preacher
Samuel Challinor	Blacksmith and farrier at Mickle Trafford
Randle Holmes	Mayor of Chester
James Stanley	Seventh Earl of Derby

In Ormskirk and around:

John Bootle Brother of William Bootle

Jane Bootle John's wife

Marc Le Croix A Frenchman, and cousin to the Seaman family

Beatrice Le Croix Marc's half sister

Jenny Reade A young girl, daughter of Mary Reade, a midwife, who died under torture after being caught smuggling messages into Lathom House

Old Isaac A drunkard

William Nutt Vicar of Ormskirk

Inside Lathom House:

Lady Charlotte de Tremouille Countess of Derby

Reverend Samuel Rutter	Private chaplain and close confidant of the Lady Charlotte
William Farrington	Advisor to the Lady Charlotte
Captain William Farmer	Major of the House. In charge of the garrison
Captain Edward Chisnall	(See under Chester) Royalist officer
Captain Henry Ogle	Royalist officer
Captain Edward Rawsthorne	Royalist Officer
Captain Molyneux Ratcliffe	Royalist Officer
Captain Richard Fox	Royalist officer
Ensign Edward Halsall	Junior officer
Broome	Chief Steward

Parliamentary Forces at Lathom:

Sir Thomas Fairfax Initially in charge of the siege, previously in charge of the parliamentary army at the Battle of Nantwich

Colonel Alexander Rigby Siege commander and MP for Wigan. Sworn enemy of the Earl of Derby

Colonel Ralph Assheton Parliamentary commander

Colonel John Moore Parliamentary commander

Colonel Peter Egerton Parliamentary commander

Colonel Richard Holland Head of the Parliamentary Committee in Manchester

Major Thomas Morgan Welshman, in charge of the artillery at Lathom

Browne Chief Engineer to Colonel Rigby

Major Edward Robinson	Parliamentary officer
Captain William Bootle	Parliamentary officer, exporter within Lord Derby's household and advisor to Rigby on the interior of Lathom House.
Captain John Ashurst	Parliamentary officer
Captain George Sharples	Parliamentary officer
Captain Duddell	Parliamentary officer
Captain Richard Davie	Parliamentary officer
Captain William Dandie	Parliamentary officer
Lieutenant Dandie	William Dandie's son
Lieutenant Lawrence Seaman	Parliamentary officer and son of William Seaman

In Newark:

Colonel Henry Tillier — Royalist commander of green-coated foot regiment (also at Bolton)

Sir John Meldrum — Commander of parliamentary forces at Newark

Major John Lilburne — Well-known political activist and writer – a parliamentary officer at Newark

In Bolton:

Henry Oulton — A wealthy merchant

Horrocks — Oulton's steward

Colonel Shuttleworth — Parliamentary Commander of Horse

Prince Rupert of The Rhine — Much-feared cavalry commander in charge of the royalist forces at Bolton

Colonel Henry Warren	Royalist infantry commander. Had previously been present at Nantwich
Sir Thomas Tyldesley	Royalist commander in charge of red-coated regiment of foot
Colonel Robert Broughton	Royalist commander in command of green-coated infantry regiment

Where they raised midst sap and siege
The banners of their rightful liege
At their she-captain's call
Who, miracle of womankind,
Lent mettle to the meanest hind
That mann'd her castle wall.
Discourse of the Warr in Lancashire, p xiii – E.
Robinson and W. Beamont, Chatham Society, 1864

On Saturday December 6th after the house was up,
there came letters to the Speaker of the Commons'
House of the surrender of Lathom House in
Lancashire, belonging to the Earl of Derby, which his
lady, the Comtesse of Derby, in proving herself of the
two a better souldier, hath above these two years kept
in opposition to our forces.
The Perfect Diurnall, December 8th, 1645

Chapter 1

Ormskirk, Lancashire – Friday April 26ᵗʰ, 1644

*T*he Frenchman was woken from fitful slumber by the sound of gunfire. Or at least, that's what it seemed like to his tired and blunted senses.

In the confines of the dismal, poorly-lit cellar, which had become the centre of his universe, he had grown so used to silence that the sharp report of the pistol had come as something of a shock, jolting him awake as though he had been poked with a sharp stick. True, he had occasionally heard the distant boom of cannon fire, which told him he was still close to Lathom, but the noise which had just assaulted his eardrums was something different. A bone-rattling crack, so close at hand that it seemed to reverberate through his very being, shaking him free from the stupor brought on by the interminable days of monotony. Despite the sudden and rude awakening, it was a welcome sound, for it told him he was still alive.

"Merde alors, qu'est-ce qui se passe?" he rasped, the words catching in his parched throat. Blinking rapidly, *he puffed out his cheeks and stumbled unsteadily to his feet. "C'est bien quelqu'un qui vient pour me tuer, n'est-ce pas?"*

In truth, he had little idea where he was or how he had got there. He remembered, a long time ago it seemed now, the convivial atmosphere in the tavern and the company of the small group of soldiers from the siege, who had teased him because of his accent. Swiss, they had thought, for he had told them he was from Geneva. After all, to be a Frenchman in England was to run the risk of being held for a papist. It was only partially untrue, for his adopted home town of Bolton had become known as "the Geneva of the North." He also remembered the smiles of the comely serving wench who had given him the eye and from whom he had hoped to receive a warm and willing reception later that evening. But after that, he remembered nothing.

He had woken to find himself stripped to his shirt and breeches, robbed of his coin, and sprawled on the floor of this godforsaken prison. At first, he had been tied with shackles to the wall, but after a couple of days, his captor, who always took great care to keep his face hidden with a scarf, had relented, freeing him from his bonds on the understanding that the prisoner was to stand back against the far wall whenever he entered the cell.

Not that he was there often. Once a day, watery-looking pottage or mouldy cheese and bread had been slipped unceremoniously through the door; but that was all he saw of his gaoler. Indeed, for the last two days, no-one had been to see him at all. Fortunately, the room contained an old, decrepit-looking barrel full of brackish water and a wooden ladle, which had stopped him dying of thirst, but he was desperately hungry and was beginning to wonder whether he would ever get out alive. Sliding over to the door, he counted the notches that he had gouged out of the wood with the end of one of the shackles that he had managed to rip out of the wall. Fifty-two. He had been incarcerated for almost two months. What a mistake it had been to leave Bolton.

Looking back, it had seemed like a good idea at the time. The town where he had spent his teenage years had taught him to speak fluent English, but, having survived a concerted royalist attack little more than a year ago, it had been becoming a dangerous place to live, especially for a Frenchman with the kind of jet black hair and olive skin that tended to get you mistaken for a Spaniard.

Those with suspicious minds in that Puritan stronghold had already marked him out as a closet papist, so when it became clear that the Englishman who had brought him up was in fact dying, he had grasped the opportunity to visit his cousins in Ormskirk with open arms. He had been told that the people in West Lancashire adhered more to the old faith than they did in Bolton and that being French would not pose so much of a problem. After all, Lady Derby herself was a Frenchwoman, albeit of Protestant faith. Nonetheless, he had taken no chances. He had arrived at his cousins' house in sombre Puritan garb. It was ironic, he reflected, that his new black doublet had been stolen, and his plain white shirt was now a filthy shade of grey.

He was being kept in a cellar – that much he had worked out – for the metal grille located just below the ceiling in one corner of the room, his only source of light, was just above ground level. He knew this because, one day, he had seen a pair of boots walk past; not the simple boots of a farm worker, but high quality bucket-top boots that might be worn by an army officer.

He knew that the cellar had been used for storing grain at some point, for the stone floor was littered with kernels. He also knew it was facing south-west, because on bright days, the room would be filled with a warm amber glow for twenty minutes in the evening. He looked forward to such days and had taken to bathing in the sun's rays for as long as the sunlight lasted and until the room was once more pitched into semi-darkness.

The Frenchman looked up at the grille, and thought he could perceive a slight lightening of the sky, which indicated that dawn was breaking. Alert now, he put his ear to the door. He thought he could hear raised voices above him, but couldn't be sure. He looked around the room and wondered if there was any way he could position himself to hear better. It sounded like the voices were coming from a room directly above the grille. The Frenchman thought about it for a moment and smiled. If he could re-position the water barrel and climb up so he could put his ear close to the grille, he might be able to ascertain what was going on.

Wiping the sweat from his hands, he gripped the rim of the barrel and heaved with all his strength. The result was spectacular. The rotting wood of the barrel split with a loud crack, spilling water over the stone floor in a swirling torrent and depositing the Frenchman onto his back, a moment before the barrel, now nearly empty, flipped over onto its side and landed across his legs. The Frenchman howled in pain and frustration.

Suddenly, there was a second bang up above, like that which had woken him, followed by a door slamming and the sound of feet retreating at speed. The Frenchman wheeled round to see a pair of boots flashing past the grille in the half light. He couldn't be sure, but they looked like the same pair of bucket-top boots he had seen before.

It was then that he realised that, although the voices above had ceased, the ominous sound of footsteps could be heard descending the steps to the wooden door of the cellar.

Groaning, the Frenchman rubbed his shins and pulled himself gingerly to his feet. Grabbing one of the timbers from the barrel as a makeshift weapon, he hobbled over to the door and positioned himself behind it just as the key started to rattle in the lock.

"Bon," he said to himself. "C'est ma seule chance. Je devrais en profiter." It was better to die trying to escape than to perish in this miserable hole.

As the door opened, he had just enough time to register the fact that he was at a disadvantage of four-to-one before launching himself into the fray, with two months of pent-up aggression.

Chapter 2

Three months earlier.

Nantwich – Thursday February 1ˢᵗ, 1644

It had never occurred to me that the role I played in solving the series of grim murders that had taken place in Nantwich during the freezing winter of 1643-44 would mark me out as anything more than a mere petty constable. I had certainly never considered the possibility that simply doing my duty would result in me being known as 'Sir William Brereton's man'. But if you were to ask me to identify the day when my life truly changed forever, then it would have to be the day that we cleared out the church.

During the week following Sir Thomas Fairfax's victory, St Mary's, the magnificent sandstone edifice which dominated Nantwich's main square, had been used as a makeshift prison to house the two hundred and fifty officers, a hundred and twenty women, and fifteen hundred common soldiers taken captive on the battlefield at Acton. Understandably, this had been much to the annoyance of the town's recently installed

29

Puritan minister, Joshua Welch, who had been mortified at the prospect of hordes of papists desecrating the interior of his church. Not only that; St Mary's was the town's only designated place of worship, and so Welch had been forced to preach his twice-daily sermons in Townsend House on Welsh Row, in the gallery of The Crown, and in Lady Norton's house on Beam Street. Welch was not best pleased, and it showed.

"It is a mortal sin to permit such foul acts of beastliness in the Lord's House," he had preached. "God has been much dishonoured by these wicked acts of debauchery. Is it not just that these men will be incarcerated? They will now have ample time to contemplate God's judgement on their sins."

When Welch claimed back his church on the morning of February 1st, nobody dared tell him that many of those removed from the aisles that morning had been persuaded to turn their coat and now served both King *and* Parliament.

I was no adherent to the type of hot Puritanism advocated by Welch, but I could not disagree with his outrage, for the interior of the church, once the prisoners had been cleared out, was a wretched and heartbreaking sight to behold.

Human detritus was everywhere. Soiled mats and bosses were littered in the aisles and strewn across the floor in between the pews. All would need to be removed and burned, and the seats would need to be made clean and washed. The walls, meanwhile, were covered in writing and streaked with urine. Worst of all, for everything else could be cleaned, the stone pillars lining the aisles had been defaced with crude carvings by the prisoners.

"By God's light!" I exclaimed, as I surveyed the devastation that morning in the company of Arthur Sawyer. "The place smells like a farmyard."

My fellow constable scratched his bulbous nose and turned over one of the mats tentatively with his foot. A rat squeaked and scuttled off under one of the pews.

"Aye, you're right," agreed Sawyer, a look of distaste spreading across his pock-marked features, "but what do you expect from a bunch of cankerous Irish arseholes such as those who were kept here?"

Such comments were no more than I should have expected from my colleague, of whose general ignorance I had long been convinced. Nevertheless, I could not let the comment pass unchallenged.

"Most of the men kept here were good Cheshire men, as you well know," I said, trying hard to mask my irritation. "Either that or Welshmen. And where else should they have been kept, do you suppose?"

"Me, I would have put them in a bloody big pen in the middle of Tinkers Croft," replied Sawyer. "The bastards had already spent a month living in fields. Another few days would have made no difference. This place looks like a herd of cattle has passed through it.

Treating them as such would have been no more than they deserved."

It was a view shared by many others in Nantwich, I had to concede, but I was increasingly forming the opinion that there was no right or wrong in this conflict, at least as far as the common man was concerned. Those who bore the greatest responsibility for the rivers of blood that had already flowed in our kingdom (namely our intransigent king, who thought himself elected by God, and his power-hungry parliament) seemed bent on a course which could only end in calamity.

I had little time for Sawyer's views at the best of times, and even less on a day like today, so I muttered an excuse and, brush in hand, made my way over towards the south transept. This was the part of St Mary's where the women prisoners had been kept, and, as you might expect, it was in rather a better state of repair than the rest of the church.

I found James Skinner's brothers, Jack and Robert, there, loading up a wooden hand cart with debris. I couldn't help thinking that the Skinners were ideally suited to such a task, for, like their younger brother, they wore constant hangdog expressions that gave them a downcast aura, often mistaken for indolence. Today their demeanour was even more woebegone than usual, although they lifted their heads and nodded to me as I approached.

"Goody, good een, Master Cheswis," said the eldest,

as he deposited an armful of filthy-looking rushes into the cart.

"Good, morning, Jack," I said, acknowledging the local greeting. "How are you faring?"

"We've been in better fashion, sir, if the truth be told," said Jack, wiping his hands on his breeches. "We're all missing Jim, you know – his mam especially. He might be a gallas young bugger, but it's mortal hard imagining him in the hands of those malignants in Chester. If I thought we had any chance of success we'd be after doing something about it ourselves."

I looked at the brothers and gave them what I hoped was a sympathetic smile. If there's one thing I didn't doubt, it was the Skinner brothers' loyalty to their kinfolk. However, I had to agree with Jack's assessment of the situation. Recruited into Byron's army and held firmly behind the city walls in Chester, he was unlikely to be easy to extricate. I was about to say as much when the younger brother, Robert, cut in with the words I had been dreading.

"Master Cheswis, you did promise us that you would help us bring Jim back home," he said. "Leastways, can you not advise how we might achieve that?"

I groaned inwardly. Why did I end up being responsible for the fortunes of so many people? It would be the downfall of me. Mrs Padgett, in her henpecking way, had advised me well when she told me to think of myself a little more often. And yet

Robert was right. Quite apart from the fact that I owed James Skinner my life after he had saved me from being shot by Nathaniel Hulse the previous month, I had given my word; and that, to my mind, was a bond that was unbreakable.

I had no idea how I was going to rescue Skinner, but I was saved from having to outline the extent of the difficulties in achieving such a thing by the arrival on the scene of a slightly breathless Ezekiel Green, the town's bright-eyed young court clerk, who had clearly been sent over from the courthouse on the other side of the square to seek me out.

"M-Master Cheswis, sir," he stuttered. "You are to come to the Booth Hall. Sir William Brereton's orders. Your presence is required with regards to an urgent matter."

I gave Green a searching look and tried to assess the situation. With the town still swarming with Brereton's men, as well as a sizeable contingent of soldiers from Lancashire, I had thought I might be allowed a few days grace before being summoned by Brereton. It was more likely, I considered, that this was a minor security issue that the Deputy Lieutenants wished to discuss with me, so I told Ezekiel I would be along presently, once I had finished my business in the church.

"No, sir," said Ezekiel, a little more abruptly than I thought was necessary. "You are to come immediately, I'm afraid. I am under instructions to bring you there."

I put down my brush and sighed. "Very well, "I said. "I will come, but at the risk of offending you, if I am required to attend with such haste, why are they sending a junior clerk to fetch me?"

Ezekiel reddened and shuffled his feet uncomfortably. "I *am* sorry, sir, but I have come with Colonel Thomas Croxton. He is waiting by the porch for you. He didn't want to get his shoes dirty. It is Sir William himself who wishes to see you."

I looked askance at Ezekiel and realised I had little option but to comply. Thomas Croxton was one of the Deputy Lieutenants considered to be closest to Sir William Brereton and therefore not a man to be ignored. As a military man, he also happened to be responsible for organising the payment of Brereton's army. I must admit to a certain degree of unease as I wondered what it was exactly that he wanted with me.

I turned to Jack and Robert. "Do not worry about Jim," I said. "Leave it with me. I will think of a solution, I promise." With that, I left my brush leaning against the Skinners' hand cart and motioned for Ezekiel to lead me to where Croxton was waiting.

Chapter 3

I found Thomas Croxton just inside the main porch of the church, staring at the thin covering of powdery snow that was swirling across the cobbles on the square. His arms were wrapped around his shoulders to protect himself against the cold, for the brief spring-like weather that had accompanied the lifting of the siege of Nantwich had been but a brief respite from the icy clutches of winter. Croxton, a young colonel, who had worked his way up under Brereton's command, was a short man with thin, piercing eyes and a reputation for a no-nonsense approach to running the finances of Brereton's army. He wore a plain black coat and breeches with gold trimmings, bucket-top boots and a black, wide-brimmed hat – sombre garments in the Dutch style, but just enough colour to display the arrogance of an officer who knew he was on the way up. He straightened himself rapidly when he realised I had arrived on the scene, and gestured in the direction of the courthouse.

"Ah, Constable Cheswis," he said. "You are a difficult

man to track down. We have a meeting of considerable import and your presence is required."

I looked at Croxton and mumbled an apology. "I was not informed of any meeting, Colonel," I said, truthfully. "I understood the Deputy Lieutenants were not due to assemble until next week."

Croxton smiled inscrutably and, holding one hand to his hat to prevent it being blown away by a sudden gust of wind, pointed to the group of people stood by the entrance to the courthouse. "That's right," he said, "but they have already met this morning, and their services are no longer required for today. It is a quite different committee which desires the pleasure of your presence."

Nonplussed, I glanced over at the crowd of people milling around outside the courthouse, and saw that Croxton was telling the truth. Amongst the crowd were most of the Deputy Lieutenants, including Colonel George Booth, the young garrison commander, who was wearing an expression of barely concealed rage and talking in an animated fashion with a representative selection of the county's ruling elite, including Booth's own grandfather, Baronet Delamere (also called George Booth), as well as Philip Mainwaring of Peover and Roger Wilbraham of Dorfold House.

I felt a sudden pang of unease and shot Croxton a quizzical look. "What vexes the colonel?" I asked. "He is not usually so heckle-tempered."

Croxton said nothing but gestured towards the door of the courthouse.

"All will become clear," he said, mysteriously.

I was not so sure.

My first surprise on entering the building was the sight of Alexander Clowes and my younger brother Simon, who were both perched on a bench outside the door to the main committee room, which was guarded by two burly sergeants. Simon looked up and shrugged, pulling his fingers nervously through his long mane of blond hair. Alexander sat motionless, a worried look on his face.

"Wait here," said Croxton, disappearing into the committee room. Thirty seconds later, he re-emerged and motioned for us to enter. "Sir William will see you now," he said, following us back into the chamber and closing the door behind him.

I had been in the courthouse's committee room many times before, as it was used regularly by the Deputy Lieutenants to conduct their business, and Arthur Sawyer and I had grown accustomed to being summoned there. It was a long, thin chamber, with wooden wall-panelling lit by candles housed in a row of sconces along the wall. In the middle of the room was a long oak table, at the head of which I recognised the thin, pinched features of Sir William Brereton. With him were four men, none of whom I knew.

Brereton was a slight man, whose sober dress, long

face, and pointed beard accentuated the aura of severity he had cultivated for himself. It had not always been so. I had heard tell that, as a younger man, he had been both well-travelled and open-minded, with an interest in exotic souvenirs, unusual business ventures, and a particular willingness to understand and learn from all kinds of religion, a far cry from the radical and ambitious politician that he had become. He rose to his feet as we entered and gave us an even smile.

"Good morrow, gentlemen," he said. "Pray be seated. It is indeed a pleasure to welcome a group of such promising intelligencers as yourselves."

Simon and I exchanged glances. This was not beginning well. "Intelligencers, Sir William?" I ventured.

Brereton stroked his moustache thoughtfully. "Why of course, Master Cheswis. Colonel Booth informs me that the three of you have been rather active during my absence in Wales. He speaks most highly of you, I should add, and my sources indicate that the Cheswis brothers have already gained some notoriety as a thorn in the side of His Majesty's forces in Cheshire."

"I did not realise we had become so famous, sir," I said. "I suspect notoriety sought us out rather than it being borne of any desire on our part."

"That may be the case for some of you," said Brereton, casting a sideways glance at Simon, who shuffled uncomfortably in his seat. "You may well have become intelligencers by default, or at worst by self-appointment, but you cannot deny that you have all shown a certain aptitude for the task. It occurs to me that such a talent should be placed on a more formal footing."

"Sir?"

"I will be happy to explain," said Brereton, "but first I have been somewhat remiss in failing to introduce my colleagues. Tomorrow I shall be travelling to London to try and raise support from Parliament to bolster our resources in Cheshire. Whilst I am gone, military affairs will be placed in the hands of an interim committee. You are looking at that committee now. Colonel Croxton, of course, you already know."

The four other men, who until now had said nothing, introduced themselves in turn as John Bromhall, William Marbury, William Massie, and Robert Venables. Although I did not know these men personally, their names were all familiar as local gentry who had obtained senior military appointments within Brereton's army.

No wonder Colonel Booth was angry, I mused. As Brereton's social superior, he would have expected himself to have been placed in command of military matters in Brereton's absence, not a young colonel from the middling gentry, elevated above his station because of his support for Sir William. Brereton had obviously created this new committee for his own benefit.

"But what about the Deputy Lieutenants, Sir William?" I interjected. "Surely they are in control of the local militia?"

"I don't think this is about the local trained bands, Daniel," cut in Simon. "The Deputy Lieutenants are only responsible for the maintenance of the bands of those hundreds in East Cheshire, which are not under royalist control. Sir William is talking about a committee to manage the wider army. If I'm not mistaken, we are here because he wishes to recruit us into the service of the main field army."

Brereton rocked back in his chair and clapped his hands in apparent delight.

"Ha!" he boomed. "You are nothing if not astute, young man. You will be of great service to our cause."

"But we failed, Sir William," countered Simon. "The documents we aimed to secure for Parliament were lost in the River Weaver, two of my companions were killed, and one of your soldiers needlessly lost his leg trying to defend us. I would hardly call that a success."

Brereton smiled patiently. "That is certainly true," he acknowledged, "but you and your brother showed great courage, and you managed to identify and nullify one of Lord Byron's most prominent spies. As for your bellman friend here, he doesn't say much, but he's discreet, loyal, and he is more than useful in a fight. You make an effective team."

"Do I understand you correctly, Sir William?" I interjected, trying hard to mask the feeling of disquiet that was beginning to creep over me. "You wish to recruit us as intelligencers?"

"Indeed. I am told that you have the kind of intuition and perceptiveness necessary for this kind of work. Your brother, on the other hand, has a level of bravado and commitment that may well make him suitable for more specialised work later on. However, for the time being, you will work as a team of three. Whilst I am in London you will be under the command of Colonel Croxton and will report directly to this committee."

I glanced at Simon and realised from the strange expression on his face that this was exactly the kind of work that my brother was cut out for. Alexander and I, however, had different priorities to consider.

"Sir," I said, "we are all three civilians. I presume you have good reasons why we would wish to accept your invitation?" This I said more in hope than expectation, for I could not imagine how a man like Brereton would have failed to ensure that the offer he was making was impossible for us to refuse.

"You presume right, Master Cheswis," he said, through a thin smile. "Let us begin with you. You have been a constable now for how long exactly?"

"Since the Michaelmas Court Leet in sixteen forty-two. I think you know this, sir." I realised that my tone was bordering on impertinence, but if Brereton was irked by this, he showed little sign of it.

"So you have already done several months beyond the usual one year's service?"

"Yes. As you know, elections have been postponed until such a time as the political situation has been assuaged somewhat."

"Which, as you will be aware, may be some time," stated Brereton. "This war will not be won in the short term."

"What is your point, Sir William?" I asked.

Brereton smiled and rose to his feet. "I have it on good authority that you would value being able to relinquish your duties-"

"Of course, I have two businesses to run and an adopted family to keep."

"And a new sweetheart, so I hear, who would no doubt be grateful of the opportunity of spending more time with you."

I was not surprised that Brereton knew about my relationship with Elizabeth Brett. Colonel Booth would no doubt have kept him informed about her role in the events that had led to the death of Hugh Furnival and the loss of the King's correspondence in the flooded River Weaver.

"That is so, sir," I said, my shoulders sinking as I realised what was coming next.

"This will not be a full-time engagement, Master Cheswis," he said. "You will only be required from

43

time to time, as the need arises. Join us and I will make sure that a new constable is found forthwith."

I was left with little option. The implication was clear. Refuse and Sir William would make sure I was burdened with the role for as long as he saw fit. I sighed and nodded almost imperceptibly, but Brereton had already moved on to Simon, strolling slowly round the table and laying his hand on his shoulder.

"As for you, young man," he said. "I suspect you will be less difficult to persuade than your brother, but I have an incentive that may suit you nevertheless. I understand that you are a follower of 'Freeborn' John Lilburne; that you have some sympathies with his political views."

Simon looked up, puzzled. "I have read his works, sir," he said.

"Quite so," said Brereton. "Lilburne is currently a major in Colonel King's regiment over at Newark. How would it be if, after a suitable period of time, I was to arrange for you to be transferred to Major Lilburne's command?"

Simon sat bolt upright. "You can do that, sir?"

Brereton patted Simon gently on the shoulder. "Of course I can," he said. "Think about it."

"That needs little thought, sir," said Simon. "I accept, of course. But what about Alexander? He is a family man. The life of an intelligencer will not be for him."

"That will be for him to decide," said Brereton. "I

do, of course, have something for our taciturn bellman too. Mr Marbury, if you please…"

At the prompt, William Marbury, a tall, lank gentleman with an unsmiling, narrow mouth and a pointed chin, got to his feet and retrieved a small candle from the mantelpiece above the fireplace, placing it in the centre of the table. At the same time, the man who had introduced himself as Bromhall produced a taper and lit it from one of the sconces before lighting the candle on the table.

"One of yours, Mr Clowes?" asked Brereton, with an air of fake nonchalance.

"I-I imagine so, Sir William," replied Alexander, his eyebrows arching upwards in surprise. "There are but two chandlers in Nantwich. There is a fair chance that this was made by me."

"Just so. And I imagine that you would prefer to keep it this way?"

"What do you mean, sir?"

Brereton leaned across the table and gave Alexander a hard look. "It's just that I have received a petition from a young chandler from Chester, a godly young man, who has been driven from his home town for his beliefs. He would settle here, but I have explained to him there is little room for another chandler and that he would be better served by relocating himself and his family to Manchester. I have asked Colonel Holland, the Governor of Manchester, who is in Nantwich this

45

week, to secure a permit for him to trade there."

Alexander bit his bottom lip thoughtfully and cleared his throat. "Then I have to thank you, sir," he said, "but I am also the town bellman. How am I to fulfil my duties to the town, if I am serving you?"

Brereton waved his hand in dismissal. "I have thought of that," he replied. "Mr Marbury has a young sergeant from Whitchurch in his troop who comes from a family of bellringers. I have it on good authority that the young man in question would relish the opportunity to become the bellman here."

Alexander stiffened, the colour draining slowly from his face. "But, Sir William," he implored. "Do not do this to me. My family has held the position of bellman for generations."

"And so it shall remain, Mr Clowes," said Brereton, in placatory tones. "I have made it clear to Mr Marbury that his man will serve as interim bellman only in the event of your absence. You need not concern yourself." There followed a few seconds silence while Brereton allowed the implications of what he had said to sink in. It was Thomas Croxton who broke the spell.

"Well, I think that concludes our business, gentlemen," he proclaimed. "It's all settled, then. You shall be hearing from me in due course. Is there anything else that you require from us?"

There were many times in the following months when I bitterly regretted what I said next, that I should have kept my counsel. However, an idea occurred to me that offered the opportunity to kill two birds with one stone.

The previous Sunday, I had kept my promise to Thomas Steele, the Chester cheese merchant and erstwhile Governor of Beeston Castle. There was little I could do to prevent his execution the following day for his perceived cowardice in surrendering the castle he had held to Thomas Sandford's small band of firelocks without a fight, but I could, at least, offer the man some words of comfort. I did not reveal the treachery of his brother-in-law, Hugh Furnival, for I did not want to burden Steele with feelings of hatred in his final hours. Instead, we talked about the previous week's battle and eventually about our mutual interest in the cheese business. It was then that Steele gave me the name of one William Seaman, a merchant from Chester, who would, he said, help me achieve my ambition of introducing the wonders of Cheshire cheese to the people of London. If I could only get access to Chester, I would not only have the opportunity to speak to Seaman, but would also be free to seek out James Skinner, with a view to working out a way to return him to his family.

"Can you get me a permit to visit Chester?" I asked. "I have some business I wish to carry out there." I knew as soon as I opened my mouth that I had made a mistake, because Brereton's eyes opened wide, and he looked at me with renewed interest.

"Chester?" he said. "There may be something you can do for me there. It may take a little while for our people in Chester to secure a trader's pass for you, but I will see what I can arrange."

And with that, we were ushered out into the street.

On reflection, I was pleased that I would get the opportunity to keep my pledge to the Skinner brothers, but I slept uneasily that night. I realised that my career as an intelligencer was not over. On the contrary. It had only just begun.

Chapter 4

Once Brereton had departed for London, life in Nantwich gradually began to return to normal. Although we had been immensely grateful for their intervention, the soldiers from Lancashire were threatening to overburden the town, and so it was with no little relief that we watched them march off in the direction of Manchester with Sir Thomas Fairfax at their head, his personal cornet fluttering in the breeze.

In the meantime, the mood of the townsfolk began to lighten as people became aware that Byron's army was well and truly on the back foot. Crewe Hall and Doddington Hall were both retaken by Colonel Booth and his garrison forces in early February, making the surrounding countryside significantly safer, so much so, in fact, that I was able to ride out to Hunsterson to retrieve the cheese and broken cart that I had been forced to abandon after Skinner and I had been attacked by Hugh Furnival's thugs six weeks previously. The market also began to return to normal as farmers and traders from the nearby villages once more began to throng our narrow streets. Arthur Sawyer and I were kept busy, as were the town's ale-tasters and leave-lookers, whilst the gaunt, hollow-cheeked figure of Andrew Hopwood, the town bailiff, was a regular sight, feeding a steady stream of drunkards and vagrants through the gaol on Pillory Street. Even the weather slowly improved, bitter snow and ice eventually giving way to the blustery showers of early spring.

One evening in mid-February, I was disturbed from my dinner by the arrival of a lone rider from Shrewsbury, who presented himself at my house on Pepper Street. The man, dressed unostentatiously in servants' attire, rode a tired-looking black gelding, which had the appearance of an animal rented for the purpose of the ride. However, I was more interested in the bay mare being led alongside him, which whickered in recognition as I emerged into the street.

I was overjoyed. I had wondered whether I would ever see my beloved Demeter again. I had missed her greatly since lending her to Alice Furnival for the purpose of escaping the clutches of those who would imprison her for treachery, but Alice, true to her word, had sent her back.

"I kept her fed and looked after proper, just as my mistress ordered," said the rider, a muscular man in his middle years with greying hair and protruding teeth, who introduced himself as a groom in Alice's household. "She's a proper mare, that one, sir, if you don't mind me saying so. You're lucky to have her."

"You're in the right of it, for sure," I agreed, as Demeter nuzzled my neck. I was somewhat taken aback, as I had not realised that the Furnivals had done so well for themselves as to be able to afford a stables of their own, but I thanked the groom and invited him inside for some food and ale. I was generally loath to share Mrs Padgett's veal and ham pie with anyone, but it would have been churlish to send the man on his way hungry.

"How fares your mistress?" I asked, once the groom was settled.

"Fair to middling, sir," replied the groom. "She misses my master, that is clear, but she busies herself with the care of her children. She asked me to give you this," he added. Reaching inside a leather bag, he pulled out a small pouch full of coin and a sealed letter.

"Enough to cover the rental for your mare for a month," he explained, through a mouthful of pie. I had not expected to be paid for the loan of Demeter, but I was more interested in the letter. I tore open the seal and began to read;

> *Dear Daniel,*
>   *There are no words I can write which can sufficiently express the sorrow I feel and the guilt which I bear for my part in the events of these past weeks. I do not deserve the*

forgiveness and understanding which you have shown to me despite the hurt I have caused. Please accept my heartfelt thanks for all your help.

Yours in friendship,
Alice

And that was it. Nothing else. I don't know what else I expected, if the truth be told. Certainly not a belated declaration of love, nor was I anticipating a grovelling apology, even after nearly ending up being killed on her account, for I knew that her loyalty to her king and her husband would always far outweigh any vestige of feeling she once held for me.

Pursing my lips, I folded the letter and placed it on the mantelpiece. Once the groom left, I would toss it on the fire, but not until then, of course. Suddenly, as if he were intentionally trying to make things worse, the groom spoke again.

"I don't know what happened between you and Mistress Furnival, sir, but she holds you in great regard. You must have been a great friend of my master."

"Aye," I said, smiling ruefully. "I suppose you could say we shared a common interest."

***

Although the visit of Alice's groom was unsettling, it did carry the benefit of drawing a firm line under my relationship with my first love, and, when placed against the other positive things happening in my life at that time, the episode soon faded into insignificance.

One of the most gratifying changes was the gradually improving health of Jack Wade, the young soldier who had lost his leg helping Alexander and myself chase Hugh and Alice Furnival across the Cheshire countryside. Overcome by guilt, I had taken him into my household to allow him to recuperate, and offered him a position as an apprentice once his wounds were healed. Although the constant sound of his flat Birmingham vowels made me wish for peace and quiet occasionally, his good-natured exchanges with Mrs Padgett, with whom he got on famously, added to the atmosphere of the house, lightening the mood and adding a certain vibrancy to everyone's step...except his own, of course. Despite the loss of his leg, Jack was showing remarkable resilience. Within a couple of weeks of January's battle, he had already been clumping around the house on crutches and lending a hand with the market stall on Saturdays. Once his stump began to be less painful, we paid a visit to a carpenter, who fashioned a wooden leg for him, held in place by leather straps.

By the end of February, he was able to help with the scheduled kindling in my wich house on Great Wood Street. Although he was in no fit state to manoeuvre the heavy barrows of salt around the storeroom, he proved himself to be an eager student of the walling process, spending the whole four days of the kindling with Gilbert Robinson, my head waller, learning how to mix the correct portions of cows' blood, egg-white, and ale with the brine in each of the six leads at the different stages of the process. John and Ann Davenport also helped with the kindling, as did their daughter Martha, all three refusing any kind of consideration for their help; their way, I imagined, of showing gratitude for my help in clearing John's name the previous month.

The biggest change in my life, however, was Elizabeth Brett, the young widow with whom I had fallen in love and to whom I had pledged my future. Having solved the murder of her husband, Ralph, I had expected little more from her than her thanks. I had certainly not thought it possible that I would once again be able to feel the otherworldly sense of euphoria that I had experienced with Alice all those years ago in the fields around Barthomley, but there was something about the honey-coloured lustre of Elizabeth's hair, the tone of her voice, and the line of that strange scar on her forehead that had the power to reduce me to a feckless halfwit. More than once during these curiously peaceful February days, Alexander was forced to tell me to remove the stupid grin from my face, for fear of being taken for an imbecile.

Mrs Padgett, once she realised Elizabeth posed no threat to her livelihood, also appeared to approve of the relationship, and, as February wore on, Elizabeth began to spend more time during the day at my house on Pepper Street. It was a rare pleasure to return home at lunchtime to find all three of the women in my life waiting for me; including Amy, Mrs Padgett's granddaughter, who had taken an immediate shine to young Ralph, Elizabeth's son, parading him around town as if he were a new toy.

For appearance's sake, I decided not to move into Elizabeth's more substantial house on Beam Street, at least not immediately, for it was too soon after Ralph Brett's untimely death for such a liaison to be deemed right and proper. But it did not stop us from making plans for the future. We talked of a summer wedding, of setting up home in Beam Street but retaining Mrs Padgett as our housekeeper. Jack Wade and Mrs Padgett would be allowed to continue living in the Pepper Street house, which I wished to retain, not least because it came with the best possible pitch on market day.

Meanwhile, Elizabeth sold the mercer's business she had inherited to Gilbert Kinshaw. The overweight merchant, like all predators, did not waste time in securing his prey, and the transaction was completed within a couple of weeks, which was just as well, because neither Elizabeth nor I knew where to start with regards to sorting out her husband's affairs. There was a stock of fabric and numerous books detailing purchases and sales, but, as Elizabeth had already agreed a price with Kinshaw, she just left him to it. I felt sure Elizabeth was being fleeced, but I had neither the knowledge nor inclination to prove it. After all, the money Elizabeth received for the business was still a tidy sum by any standards.

Elizabeth offered to buy a new horse for me to replace my dead carthorse, Goodwyn, and expressed an interest in learning to make cheese, so as to boost the amount of cheese available to sell. She even suggested that once we were married, we should use her money to buy a herd of milking cows and add them to my brother George's herd in Barthomley, but I stopped short of accepting that and told Elizabeth to save her money until times were more secure.

Of course, during this time, my joy at how things were turning out was constantly tempered by the knowledge that I could, at any time, be called upon by Croxton to serve Parliament's cause in some as yet unexplained capacity. As you might expect, when I finally got round to telling Elizabeth about it, she was somewhat less than pleased. At first, I thought I had got away with it, for when I broached the subject, Elizabeth said nothing. However, when I returned home from patrolling the earthworks the following evening, I realised that a reckoning was due, for perched in front of my fireplace were Marjery Clowes and Rose Bailey, while their respective partners, Alexander and Simon,

56

sat behind them on the stairs, both wearing worried frowns. I saw immediately that neither man had got around to telling their partners about our meeting with Brereton either.

Elizabeth was stood by the kitchen door, with her arms wrapped protectively around her waist, and when she saw me her face crumpled. I saw from the streaks on her face that she had been crying.

"How could you do this to me, Daniel?" she sobbed. "I have just got used to losing one husband. I have no wish to lose another. Do you think so little of me? I had held you to be a better man than that."

"And what do you suppose gives you the right to involve Alexander?" spat Marjery, her voice shaking with anger. "He has responsibilities, you know. We have two children to consider. You almost got my husband killed at Dorfold Hall, and now you plan to swan off together in the name of this cursed parliament, running the risk of being marked out as traitors."

"We have no choice, Elizabeth," I said. I explained the ultimatum that Brereton had given us. "It's for our future. One task, that is all, I swear," I said, but even as I opened my mouth I realised I could make no such promise.

Meanwhile, Rose Bailey merely sat morosely, wrapping strands of auburn hair around her fingers, saying nothing. It was clear that she already knew that Simon would not be able to resist the temptation to go to Newark, regardless of the conditions set by Brereton.

I turned myself back to Elizabeth and saw the hurt in her face. "What is it you wish us to do?" I asked, addressing all three of them.

"There is little you *can* do," conceded Elizabeth. "You have made your pledge to Brereton, but one thing is certain. There will be no wedding until this obligation has been fulfilled and you are free from any debt to Brereton. After that, if you are still alive, your commitment is to Ralph and me, do I make myself understood?"

I swallowed and nodded meekly. "Perfectly," I said. I would have done anything for Elizabeth at that moment. I would not have blamed her if she had returned to Beam Street that day and shut me out of her life forever, but she had chosen me, and at that moment I realised that my life belonged irrevocably to her.

Chapter 5

It would have been wholly understandable had I expunged the details of my conversation with Sir William Brereton from the forefront of my mind, for during the rest of February I heard not one thing from Thomas Croxton. However, experience had taught me the dangers of being lulled into a false sense of security, and so, when, one bright Monday in early March, I was accosted on my way to my wich house by Ezekiel Green, I knew what was coming.

"Colonel Croxton would see you at two o'clock this afternoon in his quarters at The Lamb," announced the young clerk, apologetically. "He asked that you make sure your brother and Mr Clowes are in attendance also."

I nodded my assent and waited for Ezekiel to get his breath back, for he had spotted me crossing the square from a distance and had come chasing after me across the cobbles.

"Any idea what this is about, Ezekiel?" I asked, eventually.

"No, sir," he replied. "I'm not privy to that information, but I do know that during the last two days, messengers have arrived both from Sir William in London and from Sir Thomas Fairfax at Lathom House."

"Lathom House?" I exclaimed, with surprise. Lathom was located near Ormskirk in Lancashire and was the family seat of James Stanley, the Earl of Derby, one of the King's most prominent supporters in the North of England. "What is Sir Thomas doing there, I wonder? I would have expected him to be heading back to Yorkshire just as soon as the roads across the Pennines become passable."

"That I cannot answer, sir," said Ezekiel. "Perhaps Colonel Croxton will be able to clarify matters this afternoon."

Of course, that was exactly what Croxton did, but what Ezekiel could not possibly have surmised was exactly how complicated my life was about to become.

***

The Lamb, a large coaching house located at the end of Hospital Street nearest the square, had served as the headquarters of the parliamentary garrison for nearly a year and been transformed beyond recognition by the soldiers' occupation. The whole building had been surrounded by a thick earthen wall to protect it from attack, and several of the ground floor rooms were in constant use by the garrison officers tasked with organising the day-to-day defence of the town. It was in one of those rooms that Simon, Alexander, and I found Thomas Croxton later that afternoon, his head buried in what looked like a pile of financial documents.

"Ah, gentlemen," he said, blinking as his eyes adjusted focus. "Do come in. Take a seat. The garrison accounts are making my head spin, so your arrival is most opportune." He signalled to a serving wench, who deposited tankards of ale on the table before sliding out of the room and closing the door behind her.

"Come and take some ale with me," said Croxton, taking a deep swig from one of the tankards. "I have an assignment for you. Let us drink to its success."

Simon and Alexander reached for their tankards greedily but I left mine on the table. "Perhaps you'd better tell us what that assignment is first," I suggested. "This wouldn't be anything to do with Lathom House, perchance?"

Croxton's face froze momentarily, but then broke into a broad smile. "Ah, yes. Young Ezekiel Green listens well," he acknowledged. "He will go far one of these days, although he still has one or two things to learn about the art of discretion. You're right. I admit it. Sir Thomas Fairfax has requested Sir William Brereton to release you to him so you can attend him at Lathom House, where he wishes you to assist him in a matter of some import. Sir William has agreed to that request."

I looked at Croxton in bemusement. "What services

could we possibly provide to Sir Thomas at Lathom House?" I asked, "apart from supplying him with salt, cheese, candles, and shoes, of course. I fail to see how we can be of help."

"All in good time," smiled Croxton. "Let me explain. Lathom House, as I'm sure you well know, is a huge fortified manor house, perhaps the largest in the kingdom, and it has been under pressure for some time now to surrender itself up to Parliament. However, Lady Charlotte de Tremouille, otherwise known as the Countess of Derby, is still in residence there, and is protected by a committed and well-trained garrison. Her ladyship has shown no inclination to accede to our wishes.

"Last week, however, the Committee in Manchester ordered Sir Thomas to march upon Lathom and seek its submission. This is significant because it is the first time that an attempt to seek the surrender of the garrison has received the official backing of Parliament."

"And has that made any difference?" asked Alexander, between mouthfuls of ale.

"Not one iota," admitted Croxton. "Lady Derby is made of sterner stuff than that. Sir Thomas is now preparing to besiege the house. Of biggest concern, though, is the fact that Lady Derby appears to be aware of everything that is happening outside the house. She knows what movements our forces are making, and she knows what discussions are being made at the highest level of Parliamentary command. We suspect, therefore, that there is a spy within our ranks, probably someone high up within the forces of one of our senior commanders: Alexander Rigby, Ralph Assheton, or John Moore. Your job is to unmask the identity of the infiltrator."

All three of us sat quietly for a moment, trying to digest the information Croxton had given us.

"Christ's Robes, Colonel," exclaimed Simon. "You would entrust that to us?"

"Not my decision," said Croxton, with a dismissive wave of the hand, "but Sir William appears to have faith in you. You will leave tomorrow."

"Tomorrow?" I blurted out. "But what about our businesses? We can't just leave them."

"Everything has been arranged," said Croxton. "We have people in place who can look after your affairs until you return: chandlers, briners, shoemakers. You name it. We have plenty of people with those skills within our forces. You would be surprised."

I had to admit that Croxton was right. Rising slowly to my feet, I strolled over to the window and looked out. The earthworks barely ten feet from the window shut out much of the light in the room, but over the top of the mound of earth I could just see the top of the octagonal bell tower of St Mary's. How long would it be before I heard those bells again, I wondered? I shuddered to think.

"Very well," I said, at length. "What's the plan?"

"Well, initially, you will not be going to Lathom," said Croxton, breezily. "According to your wishes, I have obtained passes for you to go to Chester. There you will be able to complete the personal business you wished to carry out. All I ask is that you avoid getting arrested, because we need you to carry out some work for us while you are there – a quid pro quo, if you like."

"I wouldn't expect it any other way," I said, sourly.

"Good, I knew you would understand. This is what we need you to do. You will be the guests of the landlord of a new tavern on Eastgate called 'The Boot'. His name is Corbett, and he is a trusted informer of ours. He will keep you safe. He has several people working for him, who are gathering information on the Earl of Derby, who is currently residing at his town house there. We know that messages are regularly being passed from Lathom to the earl, and Corbett's people have been monitoring this. Your task is to gather a report on this activity from Corbett and deliver it to Sir Thomas Fairfax at Lathom."

"And that's all?"

"Yes," said Croxton, "but there's one thing you should know. In order to protect your identities, you will be travelling under cover, as a family of shoemakers. We assumed that in a large garrison town there would be plenty of demand for good boots, so you'll be taking George Simkins' cart and selling his stock. Two of you are, of course, already brothers and so will pass as such. You, Clowes, look nothing like your friends, so you will have to act the part of their brother-in-law.

I stepped over towards Simon, whose face had turned a delicate shade of pink. "You knew about this, Simon?" I asked, surprised.

My brother shrugged. "No option," he said, simply. "I could hardly refuse, could I? And Simkins was more than happy to sell a cartload of his stock to the colonel. I swear I knew nothing about Lathom, though."

In exasperation, I turned my attention back to Croxton, who was watching us with a mixture of interest and amusement.

"This seems to be an incredible amount of trouble to go to in order to capture one fortified house and a small garrison," I pointed out. "What's the importance of Lathom, exactly?"

"Lancashire is the most popish county in the kingdom," explained Croxton, "so there are many people that support the King in the belief that he would be more tolerant to their religion. His wife, after all, is of the Roman faith. There are those, of course, who say that the main actions of this war are being played out elsewhere – in Yorkshire, in the South-West, around Oxford; but Lancashire is far from being just a sideshow. If we were to leave Lancashire to the royalists, that would give them the opportunity to set up a base and get supplies in through Liverpool. The

Committee considers the taking of Lathom House to be of both strategic and symbolic value."

"I see," I said. I stopped and considered Croxton's proposal for a moment. If this was truly the way to relieve myself of the need to carry out my constabulary duties on a long-term basis, then surely the risk was worth taking. The only uncertainty was the length of time needed to carry out the proposed duties at Lathom House. I saw a light at the end of the tunnel, and at that moment, as if to mirror my thoughts, the sun broke through the clouds next to the church tower and flooded the room with sunlight.

"And how long do you anticipate this assignment will last?" I asked, a naive question really, for I already knew the answer.

Croxton gave me a look that filled me with foreboding. "That depends entirely on you, Master Cheswis," he said. "Entirely on you."

Chapter 6

Chester – Tuesday March 5th, 1644

The village of Boughton, on the outskirts of Chester, was not as I remembered it. I had passed by here two years previously, during the time when I still had occasion to report to the high sheriff. At that time, Boughton was a sleepy, tree-lined place, the last port of call before entering the growing urban sprawl of Chester itself.

Now the village was little more than an empty shell, a ramshackle jumble of ruins. The blackened remains of cottages burned to the ground stood starkly against an unobstructed horizon. Debris from chopped down trees and hedges, levelled so as not to afford any shelter to those who might wish to attack the town, lay strewn along the side of the muddy, deeply rutted road. Even the attractive little chapel and the stone barn set against it had been pulled down. It was difficult to imagine that people had once lived here, tended gardens and farmed the land. Boughton would one day be rebuilt, no doubt, but for the time being it was an uncomfortable reminder of the devastation that war can bring to the countryside.

The road into Chester had also changed significantly since my last visit, for it was now blocked by an imposing-looking turnpike, flanked by earth walls topped with palisades and storm poles. In front of the earthworks was a wide pit, stretching as far as the eye could see, filled with sharpened stakes that were part-covered by brushwood. It was as well that Croxton had managed to secure passes for us, I mused, for finding a way into the town otherwise would have been impossible.

My attention was momentarily drawn away from Chester's defences by the sound of Simon cursing loudly as he manoeuvred George Simkins' cart around the ruts in the roadway, so as to avoid getting stuck. During the winter, the frozen ground had kept the road passable, but the subsequent thaw had reduced the route, in places, to a quagmire, and we needed to make several detours to ensure our journey was not brought to a premature end. The cart was piled high with boots and shoes and covered with a tarpaulin to protect it against the elements. Alexander and I rode alongside, occasionally stopping to help Simon point the cart in the right direction. For my part, I was pleased to be able to ride once more on Demeter's back, for over the years we had grown used to one another, her good-natured pliability making for a more comfortable ride.

As we drew closer to the turnpike, muskets began

to appear above the palisades, and two soldiers in red uniforms appeared at the gateway. Both were brandishing halberds.

"Halt!" said one of them, gruffly. "Your papers, if you please."

I reached inside my coat and extracted our passes, which the soldier inspected carefully.

"What's in the cart?" he asked, "and which one of you is which?"

Pulling back the tarpaulin carefully, I showed the soldier our stock of boots. "I'm Daniel Simkins," I said. "Accompanying me are my brother, Simon, and my brother-in-law, Alexander Smith."

The soldier sniffed, seemingly unimpressed. Pulling out one of the boots, he inspected it closely, running his finger along the stitching. "These are just what we need," he added. "Many of the poor buggers in here who've come over from Ireland are still walking around with holes in their boots. You'll do good trade on the market with these. Even better if you seek out one of the quartermasters."

"So we can pass?"

"Aye, I've not seen you before, but the Simkins name is well known enough here. You must be related to George Simkins. He used to come here to market regularly before the war started. How does he fare?"

"His back ails him," I said, "but otherwise he fares passably well." I was grateful to Croxton that he had made us learn our stories well before leaving Nantwich. We were aware that George Simkins was well known in Chester and, in order to make our story more believable, Croxton had arranged that we masquerade as his sons, rather than invent other assumed names.

The guard sniffed again, handed us back our papers, and waved us through. Behind the outworks, the scene was more familiar – a mile of gardens and elegant merchants' houses leading up to the Eastgate. Once past The Mount at Dee Lane End, the view opened up to reveal the length of the river as far as the city walls, its banks lined with water mills and tanners' houses. In the foreground, the vista was dominated by the prominent spire of St John's Church. As we approached the imposing twin-towered gateway which marked the entrance to the city, we stopped at one of a row of coaching houses which lined the road, in order to leave our cart and horses, for we had been forewarned of a lack of stabling at The Boot. An ostler appeared as we dismounted, and took hold of Demeter's reins.

"Ye'll be bonesore from the ride, no doubt. Will ye be needing accommodation too?" he asked.

"Not today," I replied, "we already have rooms – at The Boot. You can find us there if need be."

The ostler raised a quizzical eyebrow and smirked. "The Boot?" he said. "Good luck with that. You'll find many a sightly wench within those walls, but there's not usually much sleeping done in that place. Feel free to come back here if you need a good night's rest!"

The reason for the ostler's amusement soon became apparent as we entered The Boot, a compact-looking establishment located on the first floor of one of the rows, fifty yards from the cross.

"It's a bloody whorehouse!" exclaimed Alexander, eyeing the number of men accompanied by young, scantily clad women. "Croxton has seen fit to house us in a brothel! If Marjery should find out about this-"

"Quiet," snapped Simon. "There's no need for her to know. This is perfect. We will be less conspicuous in a place like this."

We had barely stepped in through the door when we were approached by a confident-looking youth with shoulder-length brown hair, who had spotted the pair of boots each of us was carrying.

"Would those be Nantwich boots, sirs?" he asked, his round, moonlike face betraying the flicker of a smile.

"Aye, nothing but the best for Lord Byron and his men," I replied, giving the pre-arranged response.

"Then I bid you welcome, gentlemen," said the youth. "My name is Charles Corbett. I am Thomas Corbett's son. If you'd care to follow me, we have vacated one of the chambers upstairs for you. There is only one truckle bed, I'm afraid, but I have provided mats for your men. I hope they will be comfortable enough."

The youth led us up a flight of stairs to an L-shaped

landing, which revealed a row of rooms on the left, the right hand side initially offering a view out onto the street. We were shown into the room at the end of the corridor, away from the street.

"Easiest escape route," explained Corbett. "There are some steps immediately outside the window, which lead to a courtyard at the rear of the house. You're free to come and go as you please, but take care to enter and leave the chamber one at a time. We don't want to attract attention to your presence. I will attend you again later." With that he left us and disappeared back down the corridor.

"Well, I don't know about you," said Simon, throwing his saddlebag into the corner of the room and heading for the door, "but I don't intend to sit in this room all evening. I will see you downstairs."

He had barely been gone five minutes when a quiet knock sounded at the door. Alexander opened it to reveal a stocky, balding man with a paunch, who introduced himself as Thomas Corbett, the landlord.

"I understood there to be three of you," he said, with a slight look of puzzlement on his face.

"There are," I said. "My brother could not keep himself away from the attractions of your fine ale. He is to be found downstairs. You have news for us for Sir Thomas Fairfax, I believe."

"I do," said Corbett, producing a leather pouch from underneath his shirt. "Guard it well. If you move the bed slightly to one side, you will find there is a loose floorboard. You can hide it there until it is time for you to leave. You plan to stay long with us?"

"Two days at most," I said. "We must attend tomorrow's market and dispose of a cartload of boots, but I also have some personal business of my own to attend to."

"You should have no problem with the boots," said Corbett. "Since Lord Byron returned in defeat, he suffers so much from lack of money, he cannot make provision for his soldiers. As many as seventeen hundred foot have recently landed from Ireland, and many are in sore need of new footwear. They rely in part on the townsfolk to keep them adequately clothed."

"The town is crowded then?" I asked.

"Full to the brim. Soldiers are lodged in houses at the townsfolk's expenses. They are hungry, bored, and unruly. It is perhaps as well that Prince Rupert himself will be here soon. No doubt he will call for many of those here to be sent on to Shrewsbury."

"Rupert is coming here?" I said. "That I would like to see."

"Aye, within the week, or so I hear. But you'd best make yourselves scarce before then, otherwise you might find yourselves pressed into his service."

I nodded my thanks and took the pouch from Corbett.

"Forgive my intrusion," said Corbett, "but you said you had personal business too?"

"Yes. Firstly, I must locate a cheesemonger called William Seaman, with whom I hope to do business."

"That is easy," said Corbett. "Seaman's shop is less than fifty yards from here. Just follow this row along towards the cross, through the Dark Row, and you will find his premises among the buttershops. And secondly?"

"I am searching for a young soldier called Skinner. He was my apprentice and was taken captive during the battle at Nantwich. I assume he has been forced into the service of Lord Byron. I would locate him and return him to his family."

"That might prove more difficult," admitted the landlord, "but most of Byron's foot soldiers who escaped from Nantwich are billeted in Gloverstone, down by the castle."

I thanked Corbett for his help and excused him so he could go about his business in the tavern. After secreting the pouch under the floorboards as instructed, Alexander and I left the room separately, arranging to meet by the stallboards in front of the tavern. Simon was nowhere to be found and, as neither of us had the inclination to dine in a whorehouse, we took a stroll through the rows with a view to finding something to eat.

It was now early evening and the streets were teeming with people. The Cornmarket Row on the other side of Eastgate was quiet, but some of the undercrofts at street level were busy, and the covered walkways in front of them were crowded with cooks serving all manner of food. Turning left out of The Boot, we passed through Cooks Row, nearly colliding with people transporting food out onto the stallboards on the other side of the first floor walkways outside their shops. Beyond that was the Bakers Row, where the atmosphere was infused with the aroma of yeast and freshly baked bread.

It was the first time that Alexander had been to Chester, and he was fascinated by the row system, which I had been told was unique to the town. The ground floor premises, mostly set slightly below street level, were set back from the street and used largely for storage. In front of them was a covered walkway often used by street vendors. The storey above this overlapped the ground floor walkway, creating the 'row' itself, which stretched in front of more shop premises and taverns. The stallboards were on the outer edge of the first floor walkway and used by the shop owners to display their wares. Nobody seemed to know for sure why the rows were created, although I had a suspicion that it had something to do with protecting the populace from the filth that was strewn along the main streets. The main thoroughfare, covered in horse dung, mud, and food waste, was separated from the shop fronts by drainage channels on either side of the street. Access to the shop fronts was provided by iron grids positioned at intervals along the length of the street.

After waking to the end of Eastgate, Alexander and I settled on a tavern called The Mitre, located on the corner of the street which led to the cathedral. There we ate a satisfying meal of bacon and potatoes before returning to our lodgings.

As we entered The Boot, we spotted Simon through a haze of tobacco smoke, sat in a corner with an auburn-haired Irish girl on his knee. The girl, who bore a striking resemblance to Rose Bailey, was introduced as Roisin. The significance of the name was not lost on me.

"Is one rose not enough for you, brother?" I demanded, stiffly. Simon was too drunk to be embarrassed by my comments, so I simply said, "Just make sure you're ready for market in the morning, that's all."

Simon said nothing beyond grinning inanely and waving his tankard at us, so Alexander and I left him to his carousing and retired to our chamber for a night of fitful sleep and constant disturbance.

Chapter 7

We were woken at the crack of dawn by the sound of Charles Corbett depositing a trencher of bread and butter on the floor, together with two tankards of small beer.

"Time to make ready for the market, Mr Simkins," he said. "Once you've eaten, I will help you recover your horse and cart. Your brother, I suspect, will take a little longer to rouse."

I rubbed my fists into my eyes wearily and scanned the room. Simon, as I suspected, was not there.

"There's no need for concern," said Corbett. "He is in one of the other chambers with Roisin."

I nodded in the bleary-eyed manner only a man who has had less than three hours sleep can manage, and stumbled to my feet. Despite having been kept awake for half the night by the unsavoury sounds of the bawdy house, I was not too tired to register the fact that young Corbett had addressed me by my assumed name. Croxton had evidently felt it safer to hide our true identities even from our allies. At least that way, we could not be easily betrayed.

I angrily tore off a piece of bread and shoved it into my mouth, whilst giving Alexander a gentle poke in the ribs with my foot; for he, too, was having trouble waking up. I was furious with Simon, not just for getting drunk, although that was bad enough, as doing such a thing in the middle of Chester put all our lives at risk, but for his betrayal of Rose Bailey, who I knew loved Simon with a passion. What disturbed me most was the confirmation that, whilst Simon would not think twice about putting his life on the line for the causes he believed in, consideration for the thoughts and well-being of those who loved him were very low on his list of priorities.

I half-expected him to be still asleep when Corbett, Alexander, and I returned an hour later with our cartload of boots, but I found him standing waiting for us on the roadside, with a sheepish look on his face. I had already decided that words would be superfluous that morning, so I merely thanked Corbett for his services, watched the young man disappear up the steps into the row, and motioned for Simon to jump on the back of the cart.

We drove the remaining fifty yards down Eastgate, as far as Chester Cross, and then turned left into Bridge Street, which was the centre of the clothing trade in Chester. Mercers' Row stretched all the way down the left hand side of the street, as far as the Dee

Bridge, while in the centre of the street, stallholders had already begun to set up their pitches for the flax and linen market. On the right hand side of the street was the Corvisers' Row, where all the shoemakers were located and where we had been allocated a pitch for the day.

We were shown to a small area under one of the walkways, where we busied ourselves with setting up a table to display our wares. Meanwhile, Simon unhitched the carthorse, making sure that the back of the cart was pointing in towards the walkway, so that anyone passing along the covered thoroughfare could see our goods being displayed on both sides as they passed through. The street was teeming with traders, most of whom had come into town from miles around, the lilting tones of Welsh mixing with the slower, more even speech of Cheshire folk.

Once we were satisfied with our pitch, Simon made off to trade with Simkins' shoemaker contacts in the rows and, as soon as I was satisfied that Alexander could cope with the passing trade unaided, I left him and made my way back towards the cross, for I had business of my own to conduct.

At the cross, I skirted past the Pentice, the timber building attached to the end of St Peters Church, which was being used to store the arms of the Chester trained bands. Avoiding the small group of redcoats guarding the building, I crossed the end of Northgate, climbed the steps on the north side of Eastgate, and emerged into Buttershops Row.

***

William Seaman was the owner of the second of the houses that made up the row of butter and cheese shops that lined this side of Eastgate. His shop front was fairly unassuming, as, like most of the buildings along the street, the house, at row level, had been divided into four narrow lock-up stores, which had been let to other shop holders. Whole cheeses and tubs of butter were laid out on the stallboards on the outer side of the walkway, where a young lad with a Welsh accent, presumably Seaman's apprentice, was busy cutting one of the full cream cheeses into smaller pieces with a cheese wire.

I was directed into the narrow storeroom, no more than six feet wide, where I found a nervous-looking woman in her thirties, with a long nose and pale complexion, who introduced herself as Katherine Seaman.

"My brother is upstairs, attending to the paperwork for a shipment of goods bound for France," she explained. "He received your letter and has been expecting you. I will fetch him for you now." The woman disappeared through a door in the back of the shop and up a flight of stairs, leaving me to inspect the interior of the storeroom.

Although the stallboards in the front of the shop

carried only local produce, it was clear that Seaman had interests in a much wider range of goods. Barrels of French wine lined the walls, and the room smelled strongly of spices. I also spotted two barrels of sack, half a dozen small crates of oranges, and on a table in the corner of the room, my attention was drawn to some strange-looking cheeses that I had not seen before. I picked one up and noted that its dark brown rind was marked with a curious tooth-shaped pattern.

"Manchego cheese from the plains of La Mancha in Central Spain," explained a voice behind me. "The pattern comes from the grass baskets in which they press the curd."

I wheeled round and was met by the smiling visage of a greying, middle-aged man, his generous mouth betraying a set of uneven, but otherwise healthy-looking teeth.

"You have Spanish cheese, Mr Seaman?" I asked, intrigued.

"Certainly, but only in small quantities, as they are expensive to transport, and not many can afford such luxury," said Seaman. "Won't you try some?" The merchant took a knife and cut off a small piece of the pale yellow cheese, which I tasted. The flavour was well-rounded, with a buttery, slightly nutty texture, and an aftertaste I could not quite place.

"Sheep's cheese," explained the merchant. "Quite unlike our own Cheshire cheese."

I nodded. "Most unusual. And you say you import all this stuff?" I added, pointing to the crates of wine and fruit.

"Indeed. I ship fabrics and calf skins to Saint Jean de Luz in France, a port near the Spanish border, and return with French wine, fruits, and spices. The oranges and cheese are transported over from Spain."

"I see. And the cheese transports well?"

"Certainly. Manchego can be aged for anything up to two years. But tell me," he said, changing the subject. "You are not here to discuss the merits of Spanish cheese. You knew my friend Thomas Steele, I understand."

"I did," I admitted, "although only in the last few days of his life. I am one of the town constables in Nantwich. I visited him in gaol after his arrest. We shared a common interest in the cheese business. You knew him well, I think?"

"I had not seen Thomas for two years," said Seaman, gravely, "not since he decided to cast his lot with Parliament. I fear a soldier's life was not for him. A constable, you say? I wondered how you had managed to secure a travel pass."

I forced a smile and quickly changed the subject, for Seaman had no idea that I had travelled under an assumed name. "It is my ambition to transport our Cheshire cheese to London," I said. "I've heard tell there is a market for it in the capital. Captain Steele said you might be able to help."

Seaman sniffed and popped another piece of cheese into his mouth. "Once this war is over, it should be possible to ship cheese by sea into London," he said. "But, of course, shipping anything to London from here is quite impossible under present conditions. Apart from which, I've a feeling that for the foreseeable future, we shall be needing all the cheese we can find for our own consumption."

At that moment, our discussion was interrupted by a clean-shaven, athletically built officer, who entered the store with a confident gait and was immediately recognised by Seaman, who stepped forward and shook his hand effusively.

"Captain Chisnall!" he said. "It has been some time. Welcome back to Chester. What news from Lathom?"

"Lathom is to be besieged," said the officer, guardedly, eyeing me with suspicion. "I am here to convey the news to his lordship and must return tomorrow. In the meantime, the earl's steward wishes to order some cheese, wine, and other goods, so I thought I would pay my respects."

I looked up sharply at the mention of Lathom House, and realised I was in the presence of one of the officers charged with defending Lathom from Sir Thomas Fairfax's attentions. Seaman, meanwhile, had noticed Chisnall's demeanour and quickly introduced me.

"Master Cheswis is a fellow cheese merchant from

Nantwich," he explained. In truth, I was still little more than a minor shopkeeper, but I was happy for Seaman to exaggerate my status.

"Captain Edward Chisnall from Chorley," said the officer, offering his hand, which I took.

"I have relations, who live in Ormskirk, near Lathom House," explained Seaman. "I have known Captain Chisnall for some time."

"What brings a Nantwich man to Chester?" asked Chisnall, giving me a searching look that filled me with unease. "That town is a hotbed for rebels."

"I cannot help the town where I live, sir," I said, carefully, "but business does not respect the barriers laid down by politics."

Chisnall smiled evenly. "Maybe," he said, "but perhaps politics are now setting barriers that cannot be surmounted. Do I take it you support Brereton and his traitorous minions?"

"I am loyal to my king," I replied, avoiding the direct question, and was grateful when Seaman stepped in.

"I will instruct my boy to deliver his lordship's order this afternoon, if you would care to leave it with me," he said.

Chisnall nodded and turned to leave. However, at that precise moment, Katherine Seaman reappeared at the foot of the stairs and gave a gasp of surprise. I turned to look at her and was discomfited to note that she had put her hand over her mouth, and her face was almost white.

"Whatever is the matter, Katherine?" said Seaman, helping her to a stool. I looked back at the door and saw that Chisnall had already disappeared into the crowds.

"It's nothing," said Katherine, after a few moments hesitation. Although her voice was weak, the colour slowly began to return to her cheeks. "I just came over faint for a moment. I'll be alright in a minute."

"Perhaps I should leave," I suggested, eyeing Katherine with curiosity. "I don't wish to intrude."

"You're not intruding," said Seaman, "but perhaps it would be better if you returned this evening. You are welcome to dine with my wife and I. We have some other guests coming, so you would be most welcome. And our housekeeper is an excellent cook," he added, by way of reassurance.

Thanking Seaman for his hospitality, I arranged to return at 7 o'clock that evening and left my host to attend to his sister.

Chapter 8

Chester – Wednesday March 6th, 1644

The independent enclave of Gloverstone appeared strangely quiet as I approached along Castle Street. The ramshackle collection of leather workshops and run-down tenements seemed somewhat incongruous set against the solid backdrop of the castle, which stood sentinel over Chester's poorest quarter. Along the ramparts, several redcoats could be seen, casting their eyes watchfully over the town, along Skinners' Row, and across the River Dee to the burned and ruined remains of Handbridge, razed to the ground several months previously on the orders of the city's governor.

Drops of sweat prickled uncomfortably on my neck. It was dangerous enough travelling under false identities to the very heart of royalist Chester, without venturing unaccompanied outside the city liberties into a neighbourhood of such ill repute. Developed as a centre where leather workers who were non-guild members could trade freely and without hindrance, Gloverstone had, over the years, developed a reputation for attracting the worst of Chester's criminal and vagrant classes. I felt unseen eyes on my back as I progressed down the street towards the Spread Eagle tavern, and my hand moved involuntarily closer to the inside of my coat, where I kept the wooden club which I had brought with me specifically for circumstances such as this.

In truth, I had little choice but to brave the alleyways of Gloverstone alone, for no sooner had I returned to the Corvisers' Row and our cartload of boots than Alexander had drawn my attention to an unkempt and breathless young street boy, who had emerged from the throng and was waving a piece of paper at me.

"Master Simkins, sir?" enquired the boy. "I have a message for you."

I took the paper with curiosity and, after handing the youth a couple of coins, unfolded the message to reveal a few hastily scribbled words.

GLOVERSTONE

SPREAD EAGLE

NOW

COME ALONE

SIMON

"Tell me," I said to the boy. "The Spread Eagle. Is that far from here?"

"No, sir," answered the boy, slowly regaining his breath. "I have just come from there. Follow Bridge

Street almost as far as the river. Then turn right at St Olave's Church and walk towards the castle. You'll find the tavern on the right. The gentleman who gave me that note is sat in a corner to the left of the main hearth."

The Spread Eagle, located on the corner of Castle Street and Bunce Street, was a large, sprawling building, which exuded an air of dilapidation, plaster crumbling from filthy walls stained brown with years of tobacco smoke and spilled ale. The atmosphere inside was lively enough though, and, unlike the rest of Gloverstone, it was full to bursting with off-duty soldiers. The sickly stench of tobacco and male sweat filled my nostrils as I entered the taproom. Simon caught my eye from the corner of the room and beckoned me over.

"Take a look over your shoulder by the window," he whispered, pushing a beaker of ale in my direction, "but don't make it obvious."

I nodded and, taking a long, grateful draught, turned round and nearly fell off my stool. Sat among a group of men playing dice and wearing the distinctive green coat of many in the tavern, was the instantly recognisable figure of James Skinner. I gasped with surprise, but Simon had already gripped my wrist in warning.

"Say nothing," he hissed. "There are eyes and ears everywhere. He knows we are here. We are going to drink our beer peacefully and unobtrusively and then we are going to leave without looking in his direction. Are we clear?"

I nodded and raised my beaker in salute to my brother, before draining it in a single gulp.

Simon paid the serving wench, who winked at us in a manner which I found somewhat disconcerting, and then, trying to remain inconspicuous, we pushed our way through the crowd and back out onto the street.

"This way," said Simon, indicating a narrow gap between two tenements on the opposite side of the street. We picked our way in between the buildings and round a corner until we stopped by the back entrance to a glover's workshop. Scraps of discarded leather lay in an open crate by the wall. Meanwhile, a dog, scavenging among the detritus left to rot in the street, looked up at us insolently and growled.

"Now what?" I asked, casting my eyes nervously up and down the alleyway.

"Have patience, brother," said Simon. "He will come."

As we waited, an old man shuffled by and eyed us suspiciously from beneath the rim of his hat. Presently, though, we heard the sound of footsteps echoing on the cobbles, and James Skinner emerged from around the corner, beaming from ear to ear.

"Master Cheswis," he exclaimed. "It is a surprise to find you in Chester. I did not realise you had business here."

"I usually don't," I said, looking at Simon, who gave me a mystified shrug of the shoulders. "It is not every day that I am asked to risk my life in order to rescue my apprentice."

"Rescue, sir?"

"Of course. Your brothers worry for your wellbeing. It is they who asked us to come here."

"I see." Skinner fell silent for a moment and pursed his lips. It was just for a second, but the hesitation did not escape my notice. There was something different about Skinner compared to the last time I saw him. He was still a gangly youth, but there was something more animated about his demeanour, and his skin had acquired a healthy pink glow that had been missing before. It suddenly occurred to me that Skinner did not care a jot whether he fought for the King or for Parliament. He was too young to comprehend the politics behind the war, and he was too busy enjoying the life of a soldier.

"They are treating you well, I see," I ventured.

"Yes, sir," said Skinner. "Food isn't plentiful, but there is enough, and although clothing is in short supply, I have acquired a new tunic. I am a musketeer in Sir Henry Tiller's regiment," he explained, showing off the new coat he was wearing.

"And Jem Bressy?" I asked. "What about him?"

"Bressy has other concerns," said Skinner. "I rarely

see anything of him, but he has not treated me badly. He sees my value as a marksman."

"I hate to interrupt," cut in Simon, who was nervously scanning both ends of the alleyway, "but we don't have time for this. It is too dangerous here. Listen carefully," he urged, addressing Skinner directly. "We have come to take you back to Nantwich. This is what I need you to do. After we have finished talking, go back to your friends in the tavern and do not reveal where you have been. Tomorrow morning at ten o'clock, we will meet again at this precise spot. There is a reason for bringing you here, and that is because I have purchased a cartload of gloves and tanned leather to take back to Nantwich. Tomorrow morning we will load the cart here and you will conceal yourself under the leather until we are out through the turnpike at Boughton. Understood?"

Skinner and I both nodded, but I noted with consternation that there was a certain degree of hesitancy in Skinner's response, and I began to wonder how I would begin to explain it to his brothers if my erstwhile apprentice chose to remain in Chester and fight against Parliament. But there was little time for negative thoughts of that kind. Simon and I bid Skinner farewell until the morrow, and with as much haste as we could muster without drawing undue attention to ourselves, we headed back towards the reassuring anonymity of Bridge Street.

Chapter 9

Chester – Wednesday March 6th, 1644

That evening, I left Simon and Alexander to sample the delights of Chester's many taverns and alehouses, under the strict proviso that they did not draw attention to themselves by becoming too drunk. Meanwhile, I prepared myself for my dinner appointment with William Seaman and his intimate circle of friends, an event which I was beginning to view with considerable apprehension, not least because it meant appearing in public under my real name, when my trader's pass said I was a shoemaker called Simkins.

In truth, I did not know what to expect from the evening, and, to add to my misery, I realised that the attire I had brought with me was woefully inadequate for socialising in polite company. Fortunately, Thomas Corbett offered me the use of a fine cobalt-coloured doublet with gold braiding and slashed arms buttoned up to the armpits. The sleeves were a little short, and my lack of a paunch left more room in the garment than

I would have liked, but, coupled with my own breeches and one of the best pairs of boots from Simkins' stock, it served its purpose.

When I arrived at Seaman's residence, I was mildly surprised to find that the interior of the house was substantially larger than it looked from the outside. Accessed via a wooden alleyway and a steep flight of stairs, which emerged at row level, the Seamans' living quarters occupied the whole of the top floor of the building. It was not quite the same as the impressive merchants' houses, which stood outside the city walls on Foregate Street, but it was nonetheless large enough to suggest that Seaman was a businessman of considerable standing within Chester. I was invited upstairs by a curly-haired footman with a pronounced limp, who led me into a dimly lit ante-room, where several people were already assembled.

"Ah, Cheswis!" exclaimed Seaman, as I entered the room. "Come and sample some of this sack. The very best produce from Jerez in Spain." Seaman was already displaying an air of jauntiness, which suggested that he had already sampled rather more drink than was advisable at this stage of the evening. I accepted a glass, gratefully, from a servant and took a sip of the sweet-smelling liquid as I was introduced to each of the guests in turn.

Seaman's wife, whose name was Isabel, was a surprisingly tall woman, whose height was offset by a quiet and unassuming air. She had long dark hair tied back under her coif and fine, sculptured features – no great beauty, but not unattractive in her own way. She had been in deep conversation with Katherine, who, I was perturbed to see, still looked nervous and as pale as a sheet. She allowed herself to be re-introduced to me by Seaman, but I was somewhat taken aback at a certain frostiness in her tone. At first, I thought she might have taken umbrage to something I had said that morning, but after a few moments I was intrigued to note that her icy manner was directed not at me but at her brother, who, it appeared, was oblivious to her ire, having already turned away to talk to the equally sour-faced Edward Chisnall, who was still studying me with an air of cautious distrust.

Of the other two guests, one was a well-groomed man with a pointed beard, in his early forties, who introduced himself as Robert Whitby. Dressed somewhat ostentatiously in a bright red satin doublet with a white lace collar of the highest quality, matching red breeches, and high-heeled boots, he cut an impressive figure. He was accompanied by a much younger woman: his wife, whose name he did not condescend to give me, but who gave me the sort of reserved smile typical of those not used to being allowed a prominent role in proceedings.

"Mr Whitby is here as a representative of Francis Gamull, with whom I share a number of business interests," explained Seaman.

I observed Whitby with a certain degree of curiosity. Francis Gamull, I knew, hailed from the most powerful merchant family in Chester, which, for the past twenty years, had controlled much of the import and export trade in the city. Gamull himself owned several of the Dee Mills down by the river, and he had served the city both as mayor and as a Member of the Long Parliament in 1640, as well as being responsible for the establishment of the town guard in 1643.

"You are well connected, sir," I commented, trying to look impressed.

"My uncle, Edward Whitby, was the third husband of Francis Gamull's mother," explained Whitby. "Our families have common interests going back many years." Whitby, I noticed, spoke with a slight lisp, and his upper lip curled upwards when he spoke, lending his features a look of aloofness.

"Francis Gamull and I have collaborated in the export of calf-skins to France and Spain for many years," interrupted Seaman, waving his sack glass in the air. "No doubt if circumstances were different, Francis would be in attendance this evening, for we have recent business successes to celebrate."

Whitby frowned, and I got the distinct feeling that Seaman had spoken out of turn.

"Francis is still in Oxford, attending His Majesty King Charles' legitimate Parliament," said Whitby, "but we can expect him back soon, for the King has expressed his wish that Francis succeeds Sir Nicholas Byron as governor of this place, following Sir Nicholas's unfortunate capture at Ellesmere."

"And what are the chances of that happening?" I asked.

Whitby sniffed thoughtfully and stared into the depths of his glass. "In truth, sir, about as likely as Puritan psalm singing in a bawdy house. No one would like Francis to become governor more than me, but he has too many opponents with axes to grind. That traitorous roundhead scoundrel Brereton and his lackey Edwards have a lot to answer for with their lies and politicking. Anyway, Prince Rupert will be here soon, and he will no doubt make sure that John – Lord Byron – is installed as Governor."

"You may well be right, Mr Whitby," I agreed. I knew the story well. William Edwards was a Puritan merchant, who for many years, had battled against the Gamulls, accusing them of negotiating monopolistic trading agreements in the interests of themselves rather than those of the city. Edwards had no doubt poisoned the minds of many of the inhabitants of Chester against the Gamulls. When war broke out in 1642, Edwards had also been one of Sir William Brereton's chief collaborators in beating the drum for Parliament. Brereton had subsequently been ejected from Chester and had been lucky to escape in one piece – unlike his

Chester residence, the old St Mary's nunnery, which had been ransacked and destroyed. It was no wonder that Brereton had often given the impression that he wished to bring Chester to its knees.

At that moment, we were all called to the table, and it quickly became apparent that William Seaman had spared no expense that evening. Our host's housekeeper had excelled herself. We were first treated to a magnificent carp pie baked with nutmeg, raisins, and lemon, followed by a shoulder of mutton with oysters and finally an orange pudding, cooked, I presumed, with some of the oranges I had seen in Seaman's storeroom.

I found Robert Whitby to be excellent company, as was Seaman, sustained no doubt by the copious volumes of good Gascon wine he was consuming. Isabel Seaman also proved to be a loquacious host, showing an impressive knowledge of local politics. Even the initially taciturn Edward Chisnall eventually loosened up, waxing lyrical on the benevolence of the Stanley family and the earl's loyalty to the Crown. The only people who remained quiet were Whitby's wife, who seemed afraid to express an opinion on anything, and Katherine Seaman, who sat with a face like stone, merely playing with her food; not that I found this disconcerting at all. After an hour of congenial company from the majority of those present, the evening seemed almost perfect. I should have known better.

The first sign that something was wrong was when Katherine Seaman suddenly pronounced that she was feeling faint and would like to take some fresh air. Robert Whitby got out of his seat and offered to escort her downstairs into the courtyard at the rear of the house. He returned five minutes later, announcing that Katherine had asked to be left alone, but that he had made sure that she was sat safely on a wooden bench in the corner of the courtyard with some cheese and a glass of wine.

Ten minutes later, we were disturbed by the footman, who delivered a message addressed to Edward Chisnall. The letter bore a seal depicting an eagle and child, immediately recognisable as that of the Earl of Derby. Chisnall tore open the letter and blanched when he saw the contents.

"I'm afraid I must excuse myself," he said. "It is difficult to tear myself away from the good cheer and companionship that we have enjoyed this evening, but I must leave for Lathom immediately. The Council of War in Manchester has decreed that Lathom must be subjugated and acquired for Parliament. Lord Fairfax rides as we speak."

There was a murmur of shock from all around the table, but everyone immediately got to their feet and wished Chisnall a safe journey. As he shook my hand he gave me another searching look, which conveyed the fact that, despite the evening's conviviality, he still did not trust me.

With only five of us left around the table and the food all gone, it seemed as though the evening was about to break up, and so it would have done were it not for what happened next.

Just as the Whitbys were preparing to leave, there was a gentle knock at the door, and the footman appeared.

"Master Seaman," he said, apologetically. "May I trouble you for a moment, sir? A word in private, if I may."

Seaman looked at the footman for a moment and, with a look of exasperation, threw his napkin on the table and strode out of the room. After a few moments, I heard a loud exclamation from the ante-chamber, which made me think for a moment that Seaman was arguing with his footman. However, a few seconds later the door opened again and Seaman appeared, a grave look on his face.

"Guests," he announced. "I'm afraid you must excuse me for a few moments. I have an urgent matter to attend to. I won't be long. Isabel, if you would be so kind as to entertain Mr and Mrs Whitby in my absence, I will return presently." Then, addressing me, he added, "Master Cheswis, I require your advice. Would you join me, please?"

Puzzled, I got to my feet and followed Seaman to

where the footman was waiting, his hands clasped together in agitation. I looked at the expression of anxiety on Seaman's face and a feeling of disquiet began to overtake me.

"She's downstairs in the courtyard, sir," said the footman. "You'd better follow me." With a halting gait, he led us through Seaman's steam-filled kitchens, where the smell of cooked oranges and baking fought gamely with the lingering aroma of gutted fish.

Limping out through a side corridor, the footman took us out into the sharp evening air and down a flight of stairs, which opened out into an internal courtyard. In one corner stood a compact stable block and an area for storing wood. In the other was a small table on top of which sat a small plate with some bread and cheese and a glass of wine, some of which had been disturbed and spilled on the floor.

Next to this was a wooden bench, on which was sprawled the dead body of Katherine Seaman. Her face, a mask of horror, stared upwards towards the gable end of the house, her eyes red and vacant. Small globules of spittle had formed around her mouth, and her neck was swathed in a mass of blood. On the cobbles next to her foot lay a discarded cheese wire.

"By our lady…" began Seaman, rubbing the back of his neck in anguish. "Katherine!" He stepped forward, but I held him gently by the wrist.

"Don't touch the body," I warned. "At least not yet.

We need to find a constable."

"I thought you *were* one," responded Seaman, his voice rising a notch.

"You are shocked and not thinking straight, Mr Seaman," I said, somewhat defensively. "I'm not a *Chester* constable. We need to report this death to a local officer. I would not have thought I needed to explain this to you."

Seaman halted for a moment and gave me a glassy stare before nodding apologetically. Taking a deep breath, he turned to his footman.

"Tell me, Roberts," he said. "Who found the body?"

"John Gibbons, sir," replied the footman. "He were out here throwing away food scraps into the ashpit, at least so he says."

"I see. Would you be so good as to fetch him? And while you're at it, ask Martha to come down too."

Roberts turned on his heels and limped obediently back upstairs towards the kitchens, leaving Seaman and I alone with the cadaver.

"I would have thought that it would be in your interest to delay the intervention of a constable as long as possible," said Seaman, matter-of-factly. "You will almost certainly be asked to remain in Chester as a witness. Is that not something that you would wish to avoid?" The merchant looked at me fixedly for a few moments, giving me time to fully comprehend the significance of what he was saying.

"You mean…?"

"Of course, man! Do you take me for a fool? Do you think I have not considered how a Nantwich man – and the town constable to boot – manages to get a pass to visit Chester in times such as these? You have already made clear you had an association with Thomas Steele, himself a parliamentarian. Not only that, you are not alone in Chester; something you did not tell me. I saw you walk past here this afternoon with two other men and an empty cart. My guess is you have other business here in Chester in addition to your dealings with me. Am I right?"

I shrugged and nodded in resignation. "I had no idea I had been so transparent. What do you plan to do about it?"

"Absolutely nothing, of course. I am also for Parliament, which is to your good fortune. Indeed, I already have one son who has given his life for the cause. He died on the field at Kineton Fight. The other serves under Sir Alexander Rigby. Ironically enough, he is probably among those setting up siege works at Lathom."

I gazed at Seaman in open-mouthed surprise. "I had no idea," I said again.

"Well, you wouldn't," said Seaman, "and stop awning at me like an imbecile," he added. "It's quite simple, really. It does not pay to be in open support of Parliament in Chester. Look at what happened to Brereton and Edwards. I have my livelihood to protect, and many of my business partners like Francis Gamull are strong and loyal supporters of the King. But let us discuss this later. We will have to call a constable, certainly, but our priority is to gather enough information to keep the local constable busy and to keep him from jumping to conclusions, in order to give you the opportunity to get away tomorrow. Let us focus on the matter at hand."

Seaman was in the right of it, of course; of that there was no doubt. But still, I couldn't fathom how a man, having to face up to the brutal murder of his sister in his own house, could behave so calmly and logically. I quickly pulled myself together and looked around the yard for clues as to how the murderer could have got in.

"There is just one entrance to this courtyard," ventured Seaman, reading my mind. "It leads out the back towards the cathedral precincts."

I walked over to the solid wooden gate and saw that it was secured by two solid bolts.

"Locked," said Seaman, thoughtfully. "So we know that the murderer did not come in this way."

"Not necessarily," I said. "He could have been let in by Katherine."

"But the door is locked. How do you account for his escape? He couldn't have locked the door from the outside on the way out."

"True," I conceded, "but it is not beyond the capabilities of a fit man to climb the gate."

"Sure, but why would he do that?" demanded Seaman.

"I don't know," I admitted. "Perhaps he wanted to incriminate somebody within the house."

At that moment, I heard sounds on the steps above me, and Roberts re-appeared, followed closely by the servant, John Gibbons, a slightly built man in his late thirties with angular features and a receding hairline. His face was white with shock, save for his eyes, which were red, as though he had been weeping. Behind him was a round-faced woman, who introduced herself as Martha Woodcock. She gasped and put her hand over her mouth when she saw the body.

"Mr Gibbons, is it?" I asked, addressing the servant, who was standing quietly, his head bowed.

"Yes, sir," said the man, barely daring to look at me.

"I understand you found the body," I said. "What can you tell me about it?"

Gibbons and Martha Woodcock exchanged glances, and I thought I caught a hint of a nod from the housekeeper.

"We were in the kitchen," said Gibbons, "Martha an' I, an' we thought we heard a commotion outside. Some banging, like, an' I could 'ave sworn I heard a scream. I thought nothing of it, but I were already on my way to throw out the food scraps. It were then that

104

I saw Mistress Katherine an' the murdering whoreson bastard who did this. He were halfway over the gate."

I looked at Seaman, who nodded at me as if to confirm the legitimacy of my theory.

"You saw the murderer?" I asked.

"Aye, I did. Leastways I saw someone escaping over the gate. Withering great fellow he was too."

"But you didn't see him actually committing the murder?"

Gibbons frowned and looked at me in puzzlement. "What are you getting at, sir? I saw him escaping. It were him alright."

"And did you try to stop him?" I asked.

"I ran towards him but he were too quick. Over the gate like a flash he was."

"A scranny little sod like Gibbons would have had no chance, if he was as big as he says," cut in Roberts.

"At least I tried," said Gibbons. "As for a cripple like thee-"

"Aye, alright," said Roberts, "but what were you doing down there, anyway? You could have cleared up the food scraps later. Don't tell me you were after talking to Mistress Katherine again?"

Gibbons stiffened, and his face turned a vivid shade of red. "You've no right!" he spat, suddenly lunging at the footman. I had been watching this exchange with interest, but now Seaman and I sprang into action and dragged Gibbons away before he could reach Roberts.

"Would one of you care to tell me what this is all about?" I demanded.

"Had a soft spot for her, didn't he?" breathed Roberts, straightening his collar and trying to regain his composure. "He was always trying to talk to her. Thought he had a chance, he did."

"I think I can vouch for that theory," cut in Seaman. "Katherine always felt Mr Gibbons carried a torch for her."

"But I would never have hurt her," said Gibbons, an element of fear entering into his voice. "I was in love with her."

I nodded and turned my attention to Martha Woodcock, who was sniffing into a handkerchief. "What about you, mistress?" I asked. "Did you see any of this?"

"No sir," said Martha. "It's as John said. We heard noises up here and John went down with the scraps, but I never saw nothing myself."

"And how long did it take for Mr Gibbons to return after he left the kitchen?"

"About five minutes or so," said the housekeeper.

Gibbons saw where the conversation was heading and his features turned a peculiar shade of grey. "But I just stood with her," he said. "I swear that's the truth. I just couldn't bring myself to leave her."

I studied Gibbons carefully and tried to make sense of his demeanour. He was now shaking violently and clutching his arms around his chest, both symptoms of shock. He could easily have made an approach to Katherine, I mused, and murdered her in a frenzy brought on by rejection, but something told me he was telling the truth.

I strode over to the bench on which Katherine Seaman's body was still sprawled and picked up the cheese wire by her foot.

"Does this cheese wire belong to the kitchen, Mrs Woodcock?" I asked. The housekeeper studied the bloody object with evident distaste and shrugged.

"I couldn't say, sir," she said. "It looks like ours, alright, but they all look the same to me. Mr Seaman uses similar ones in the shop. What I do know is that we lost ours the other day. We've been using a knife to cut cheese in the meantime."

"I see," said Seaman. "So the cheese wire could have been brought down by Gibbons, or by Whitby when he accompanied Katherine to the courtyard, or by Katherine herself, or by someone else, as yet unknown, who had the express intention of murdering Katherine with it."

"Precisely," I agreed. "Mr Seaman, it's about time we called a constable. I believe Mr and Mrs Whitby were just about to leave. Perhaps we could ask them to call a constable on their way home. If they are needed to act as witnesses, I'm sure they can make themselves available at a later date. In the meantime, please give

Mr Gibbons a cup of wine to calm his nerves, but make sure he goes nowhere."

Once Gibbons had been set down in the kitchen under the care of Mrs Woodcock and the watchful eye of Roberts, Seaman and I broke the dreadful news to Isabel Seaman and the Whitbys, all three of whom reacted, as expected, with utter shock. Whitby was the most practical, and after a suitable break to compose themselves, he and his wife left in search of a constable, leaving me in the dining chamber with Seaman and his wife.

"Tell me," I said, "your sister seemed preoccupied all day today. Was she usually so highly strung?"

"No," replied Seaman, shifting uncomfortably in his chair. "Although, I grant you, she was in an unusual mood today."

"Have you any idea why that might be?"

"She said nothing to me."

"What about Edward Chisnall? I noticed your sister's reaction when he turned up in your store this afternoon. She looked like she'd seen somebody who had come back from the dead."

"I couldn't say," said Seaman. "Chisnall is an officer in the garrison at Lathom House, and Katherine was in Ormskirk herself only a matter of days ago. She may have seen him then and been surprised that he had also travelled to Chester."

"Maybe," I said, unconvinced. "So what is your

connection to Ormskirk exactly?"

"We used to live there," said Seaman. "Actually, my family originally hails from Bolton, but we moved to Ormskirk as children. My sister, Jane, married a local man and still lives there, but Katherine and I moved away when we came of age. It was Jane and her husband who Katherine was visiting recently. Chisnall, incidentally, is also a local man, and we have known him for a number of years."

I thought about this for a moment. Chisnall, I realised, had left the Seaman house before Katherine had been found, giving him plenty of time to have gone round the back of the building and entered through the back gate. Katherine also knew Chisnall, so may have been persuaded to open the gate for him. Was there, perhaps, some connection between Chisnall and Katherine that I hadn't been told about? If so, I was determined to get to the bottom of it.

I then changed my attention to the question of William Seaman's business dealings and his connection with the likes of Francis Gamull and Robert Whitby.

"You were celebrating the conclusion of a business deal with Francis Gamull today," I ventured. "It must have been an important deal because you went to some expense."

Seaman frowned and exchanged a quick glance with his wife. "Why do you ask?" he said, guardedly.

"Pay no attention to me," I said, dismissively.

"I'm just curious. Your sister seemed to be vexed by something you'd done this evening. I wondered if there was a connection?"

Isabel Seaman, who had been quiet up to this point, touched her husband on the arm to get his attention. "I think you'd better explain to Mr Cheswis," she said. "It will be for the best."

Seaman pursed his lips in irritation and poured himself another cup of wine. "Very well," he said. "Katherine did not approve of the contract I had struck with Francis Gamull. I suppose I had better explain. My mother, who is now no longer alive, was the daughter of a wealthy merchant from Bolton called Henry Oulton. Henry, my grandfather, who is now in his eighties, made his fortune selling calf-skins to the Spanish and established a trading post in the town of Saint Jean de Luz near the Spanish border, the same town I told you about yesterday. This business was, for many years, run by my uncle, and after him by my cousin, but both are now dead. For many years, I had used this business as the French import post for Francis Gamull's calf-skins, importing wines and other goods in the opposite direction. You saw some of the produce we import this afternoon. Following my cousin's death, I have now become the sole heir to Henry Oulton's fortune, including the import business. My grandfather, who has retained control of the business over the years, is now ailing, and Francis

Gamull has expressed an interest in purchasing the business. I have signed a contract to sell that business to the Gamulls once I inherit, and Francis Gamull has made a pre-payment against that contract. Katherine thought I should not have signed that agreement, although I can't think why."

"And Robert Whitby? Where does he fit in?"

"Nowhere, really. When Francis Gamull's father, Thomas, died many years ago, his mother married Edward Whitby, who died in sixteen thirty-nine. Francis's mother retains control of her husband's assets for her lifetime, after which everything passes to Robert. Over the last few years, Francis and Robert have developed a mutual understanding on a number of issues. Neither of them are fools."

I scratched my chin in deep thought and tried to take stock of what I had seen. There were several people who could have killed Katherine Seaman. Chisnall was certainly one, as were Whitby and any of the three servants. But what about Francis Gamull, a man powerful enough to arrange for others to carry out such a task for him? How did he fit in, and was there something that William Seaman was not telling me? My curiosity had been awakened, and, despite the feeling that I was running the danger of becoming embroiled in something far more dangerous than I could imagine, I said the one thing that would guarantee my further involvement.

"I shall be travelling to Ormskirk myself tomorrow," I said, "perhaps I can carry this news to your son and your sister and make some discreet enquiries while I am there? If your son is serving under Rigby, I should have no trouble locating him."

Seaman looked me in the eye for a moment, and then his face broke into a conspiratorial grin.

"I knew there was something more to you than meets the eye," he chuckled. "If you are prepared to do that for me, then I would be immensely grateful, but I think you had better be on your way before the constable arrives. Am I right in thinking Daniel Cheswis is not the name on your pass?"

I inclined my head in acknowledgement.

"Then in that case the constable will never find you," said Seaman. "I think you know what to do."

I certainly did. I shook Seaman heartily by the hand and, thanking his wife for the hospitality, marched purposefully through the kitchen, descended the steps into the courtyard, and unlocked the gate. Finally, after taking one last look at Katherine Seaman's prone and bloody corpse, I slipped out into the street and merged silently into the crowds opposite the cathedral.

Chapter 10

Chester – Thursday March 7th, 1644

I slept fitfully that night, my dreams punctuated by alternating visions of Katherine Seaman's staring, lifeless face, and a huge manchego cheese being slit from top to bottom by a cheese wire, its rind oozing red blood where it had been cut. I awoke bathed in sweat, to find Alexander and Simon sat on their mats, dressed and ready to leave.

This was no surprise in itself, for I had returned to The Boot the previous evening to discover that both my friend and my brother had come back early from their evening exploring the city's various hostelries.

"Best to avoid getting fou drunk, Daniel," Simon had explained, a little too self-righteously for my liking. "We have work to do tomorrow. We need our wits about us." With that, he had fallen asleep on the floor, snoring like a horse, and leaving me to relate the story of Katherine Seaman's murder to Alexander, who listened to my experiences with increasing incredulity.

"Let me get this straight," he said. "Your friend, a secret parliamentarian sympathiser, is the heir to a

113

large mansion in Bolton and a considerable fortune, including multiple trading interests in France and Spain, and he has effectively sold part of his inheritance *before* his grandfather's death?"

"So it would seem," I agreed.

"And the one person who knows about this, his sister, is murdered whilst he dines with you in his own house and in the presence of several other people who may have an interest in the grandfather's death."

"Indeed. Robert Whitby, Edward Chisnall, and the servant, John Gibbons, all had motives and the opportunity to commit the murder."

"Not forgetting Seaman himself."

"True," I admitted, "although Seaman was with me the whole evening, apart from when he went with the footman, Roberts, to view the body. If Seaman is involved, then so must both Roberts and Gibbons be. Think about it. Roberts would have had to have collected Seaman specifically so he could go and commit the murder, and Gibbons would have to be lying about having seen the murderer escaping over the gate."

"Correct. An unlikely scenario, I admit, but Seaman certainly had the motive."

"That's also true," I conceded.

"And what is more, there appears to have been a significant and unexplained connection with Lathom House. Seaman has a son and a sister both within easy reach of Lathom, not to mention the suspect, Chisnall, who is an officer in the garrison there."

I nodded thoughtfully. Identifying the murderer was certainly no straightforward matter. It was then that I noticed a curious look on my friend's face, a look of anticipation that I had not seen since January, before Edward Yardley had paid with his life for the murders of William Tench and Will Butters, and before Hugh Furnival had been swallowed up by the raging waters of the River Weaver in full spate.

"It seems we have another murder to solve," said Alexander, with relish. "You seem to have a talent for seeking them out."

In all honesty, when I was sat in Seaman's drawing room, I had also felt animated at the challenge of seeking out the perpetrator of this foul crime, my enthusiasm stimulated, no doubt, by the potency of my host's fine wine. But the burden of this unsolicited responsibility was already beginning to weigh down on my shoulders and, in the cold light of day, I saw it for what it was: an unwelcome and unnecessary complication.

I swung my legs over the edge of the room's only bed, thankful that, as the most senior of our party, I had not had to sleep on a mat on the floor, and stared, bleary-eyed, at the wall.

At that moment, there was a gentle knock at the door, and Thomas Corbett appeared, with some bread, cheese, small beer, and a pitcher of fresh water drawn from the nearest well. I took a large cup of water and swallowed it gratefully, for my mouth was dry as a bone and still tasted of the wine I had drunk the previous evening.

Corbett then produced a small linen pouch and coughed politely to attract our attention. Putting his hand in the pouch, he extracted three small wax balls which he laid on the table by the bed.

"As you are leaving today, I need to give you these," he said, gravely. "One for each of you. Guard them with your lives. Each ball contains a small piece of paper with a message encrypted in cipher. They must be delivered without delay to Sir Thomas Fairfax when you arrive at Lathom. Hide them well, but if you are arrested, swallow them without hesitation. They must not fall into the hands of the royalists."

I looked doubtfully at the inconsequential-looking brown balls. They were certainly small, though, if the truth be told, they looked like they might need some chewing if one were to avoid choking on them. I imagined they would carry the tiniest morsel of paper inscribed with a number cipher to save space.

I picked up one of the balls and hid it within the lining of my coat. Alexander and Simon did likewise.

We ate a quick breakfast before thanking Corbett for his hospitality and making our way through the Eastgate to the coaching house on Foregate Street, where our horses were being stabled. After paying our dues and giving instructions to the ostler to look after Demeter and Alexander's horse until we returned later that morning, we hitched up the cart and drove it slowly back into the city, past the Pentice, and down Bridge Street to the glover's yard in Gloverstone, where we had been the day before.

The owner, a broad-shouldered man with greying hair and a full, silver-coloured beard, signalled to us to back the cart into his yard, where we commenced loading it with crates filled with gloves, which we positioned at the back of the cart, leaving a gap big enough for Skinner to scramble into and remain concealed. Over the top of the space left for Skinner, we positioned several layers of tanned leather, completing the illusion of a totally full cart. All we needed now was to find my erstwhile apprentice, secrete him underneath the pile of goods, and negotiate both the city gates and the turnpike at Boughton without being stopped.

Simon paid the glover and drove the cart back towards the entrance to the alleyway opposite The Spread Eagle, the wheels scraping loudly on the cobbles as it meandered its way over the uneven surface. Alexander and I emerged on foot behind the cart and glanced nervously down Castle Street, towards a dilapidated tenement block fifty yards away, which we had been told was the building where Skinner and much of his regiment were billeted.

Despite the hour, the street was relatively deserted. A couple of goodwives stood nattering by a row of houses on the other side of the road, and half a dozen local traders had opened up shop fronts on the Gloverstone side of the street, but other than that, there was little activity. Alexander and I walked a few yards towards the tenement block and were relieved to see the scrawny figure of Skinner emerge from a side entrance. He took a quick look up and down the street, adjusted his green Montero cap, and walked quickly towards us.

"Quick, get into the cart and get behind the crates at the back," I hissed.

Skinner nodded, and was just about to clamber in amongst the sheets of leather, when I saw something which made me place a hand on his shoulder and tell him to wait. Fifty yards away, two redcoat soldiers from the town guard had emerged from an alleyway and were looking meaningfully in our direction. On the other side of the street, two more had appeared through the front of one of the trader's stores, pushing the protesting shopkeeper roughly aside. I spun around and saw that a group of several more were also approaching us from the direction of St Olave's. Among them was the instantly recognisable figure of Jem Bressy.

Simon had also spotted Bressy and had jumped

down from the front of the cart, howling in pain as he twisted his ankle on the cobbles. Struggling to his feet, he limped to the rear of the cart and disappeared back down the alleyway towards the glover's workshop. I only had a split-second to decide on a course of action, so I did the first thing which came into my head.

"Hit me now," I ordered. "Make it look good and run like the wind."

Skinner looked over his shoulder and, spotting Bressy, immediately understood my meaning. He took a wide arching swing with his right arm, which caught me flush on the side of the head, making my ears ring as though I were in the bell tower at St Mary's. He then charged headlong towards Bressy with his hands in the air, shouting, "Parliament spies! Stop them!"

I thought I was about to pass out, but Alexander grabbed me forcefully by the left arm and dragged me instinctively up Bunce Lane, a heavily rutted side road, which led north from Castle Street and was the only apparent escape route not blocked by redcoats. I quickly calculated that if we were able to evade our pursuers by heading north past the rows of workers' cottages that stretched out before us, we would eventually be able to double back to the right and make our way to Bridge Street and from there along Eastgate Street and Foregate Street, to where our horses waited for us.

However, no sooner had we begun to run, than a flash

of red careered out of one of the yards on my left and caught me full in the midriff, sending me sprawling into the road. Winded, I looked up through mud-filled eyes to see a burly redcoat cursing as he struggled with his pistol.

Alexander, grabbed a stake from a pile of wood lying by the entrance to a carpenter's workshop and swung it violently at the soldier's legs. I heard a sickening crack and a deafening scream as the stake caught the redcoat on the side of the knee, and he crumpled into a heap on the floor.

I pulled myself to my feet and charged after Alexander, voices following us up the lane to our rear. I risked a look over my shoulder and caught the sight of Bressy and his row of musketeers crouching in readiness to fire.

"Into the garden!" I screamed at Alexander, and dived over a low wall as a musket ball flew over my shoulder, the sharp report of the volley of shots snapping loudly at my ears. My friend landed in a heap five yards in front of me, and at first I thought he had been shot, but he pulled himself to his feet in wide-eyed panic and was just about to jump back into the street when his attention was distracted by the sight of a female figure standing inside the doorway of the garden's attendant cottage, signalling frantically for us to head through a side gate into the backlands. With a start, I realised I was looking at Roisin, the auburn-haired

Irish whore with whom Simon had been carousing two days previously. Today, she was dressed more soberly, in plain brown, with a white coif on her head.

I looked back at Alexander and saw that he was already making his way towards the gate. I had no time to consider what the girl was doing there, so I simply leapt after Alexander, nearly tripping over a pile of firewood which blocked the path down the side of the house, and scattering half a dozen hens, which clucked loudly in complaint at the disturbance. A couple of seconds later, the back door of the cottage flew open and the girl appeared.

"But why-" I began, only to be interrupted by the girl's urgent tones.

"Quickly; go through the fence at the end of our yard and through the paddock beyond to the houses in the distance. If you can pass through there you come to the monastic lands of the old Black Friars monastery. Once there, if you start to the north, you can make your way onto Watergate Street and back up to the cross."

I nodded. "But what about Simon? He vanished into Gloverstone."

A momentary look of concern passed over the girl's face, but it quickly disappeared, and she pursed her lips in determination.

"If he has any sense, he will have gone back to Jack Taylor, the glover. He will be safe there until the soldiers have gone. Now go while you still can."

We needed no second bidding. I clasped Roisin's hands quickly in thanks before sprinting after Alexander towards the end of the garden. As I did so, I thought I caught the sound of angry voices and persistent banging on the front of the house, but I did not look back. Hoisting myself over the fence at the end of the garden, I dropped gratefully into the field beyond and ran for my life.

***

Once we were certain that we were no longer being followed, we halted by a low stone wall to regain our breath. I noticed for the first time that Alexander was still carrying the wooden stake with which he had scythed down the unfortunate redcoat. The white, neatly sawed wood was stained red with the soldier's blood.

"What now?" asked Alexander, wiping the sweat from his brow.

I looked over the wall and realised we were standing by the remains of the Dominican friary known as Black Friars. Behind the sorry-looking ruins of the church and the pits used for smelting the lead from the monastery's roof and windows was the meadow known as the Roodee, and beyond that the River Dee. To the north I could see the black and white gabled mansion that was the Chester home of the Earl of Derby, near to which stood the customs house and a row of other impressive properties lining the south side of Watergate Street.

"The first thing we do is dispose of that piece of wood," I said. "If anything is certain to draw attention to us, it is that."

Alexander looked at me with a blank expression, and I realised that he had also forgotten he was carrying the stake. I took it from him and threw it over the stone wall, into the field beyond.

"We walk over there," I said, pointing to the Earl of Derby's mansion, "and then we try and make our way through the crowds back out through the Eastgate."

"But what about Simon? We can't leave him here."

"We must," I said. "It pains me to say so, but we must hope Simon finds a way out of here by himself. Remember, Bressy and his men followed us, not him. With luck, he will get clean away." In truth, I was trying to persuade myself of something of which I was by no means confident, but one thing I had learned about my brother over the course of the past three months was that he was endowed with a great deal more resourcefulness than I had previously thought possible, and if the glover and the red-haired Irish girl were on his side, then perhaps he had a fighting chance to escape the search party that would inevitably be sent into Gloverstone to seek him out.

The walk back into the centre of Chester seemed interminable. It was less than a mile, but it was a nervous walk, our eyes constantly on the lookout for those who might wish to arrest us. Our hearts jumped every time a red or green-coated soldier came into view, but to our relief, none approached us. As we walked up Watergate Street towards the Pentice, the crowds grew busier and we were able to melt into the general throng more effectively. Once we reached the beginning of the rows, we mounted the steps to the first level and weaved our way through the stores, along the walkways, between the stallboards and the street; more cover, I imagined, from anyone looking out for us at street level.

Once we reached St Peter's Church, we descended to the street again, crossed in front of the Pentice, and climbed the steps once more on the north side of Eastgate Street, passing through the Buttershops Row, past Seaman's house, through Dark Row, and emerging in front of The Boot.

Thomas Corbett was stood in front of the tavern, sweeping the stallboards with a stiff brush, and he eyed us quizzically as we approached. I quickly explained to him in hushed tones what had happened.

"Christ's Robes, man," he exclaimed, his features contorted in anger. "What did you think you were doing? I wondered what was going on. You have put us all in danger. Take a look over there."

I cast my eyes over the balcony into the street, and my heart sank. Stationed at twenty yard intervals along the side of the street was a row of redcoats scouring the crowds as they passed. Immediately opposite me I recognised the jet black hair of Jem Bressy, who was organising the soldiers in line, and I realised that we must have been recognised and followed back from The Spread Eagle the day before – that was when this hunt had truly begun, unbeknownst to us.

To my dismay, Bressy chose that precise moment to glance upwards, and he caught my eye. Frowning, he immediately gestured to those soldiers closest to him and began to march across the street in our direction.

"By Jesu," growled Corbett, "can't you be more discreet? Now you've done it. Quick, get inside." With an angry shove, he hustled us both inside the doorway and across the tap-room, where his son and the most senior of his girls, a buxom, dark-haired woman called Annie, were busy cleaning the tables. Both looked up in alarm at the urgency of our approach and immediately stopped what they were doing.

"Quick, we have been exposed," said Thomas Corbett, with urgency. "You know what to do."

Charles Corbett nodded, dropped his brush, and disappeared up the stairs to the corridor which led to the rooms at the back of the building. Annie grabbed my wrist and led me towards the back of the tap-room.

"Follow me," she said, bursting through a door into the small courtyard separating the two parts of the house. Alexander and I looked, helplessly, at each other as I was dragged after her. At first I thought Annie was taking us to Corbett's private quarters, but she stopped by a solid wooden structure built against the outside wall of the building.

"In there," she ordered. Without hesitation, we did as she asked, allowing Annie to follow us and lock the door behind her. It was then that I noticed the smell and realised where we were. Annie, Alexander, and I were locked in the privy.

Chapter 11

Lathom House – Thursday March 7th, 1644

*S*amuel Rutter stood atop the Chapel Tower at Lathom House and watched the sun rise slowly above the trees in the Tawd Valley. As it cast its warming rays across the ground, the chill mists of early March began to dissipate, revealing the sharp zig-zag of the trench, which was working its way inexorably around the southern side of the house like a giant mole tunnel.

Rutter scratched his balding pate and pulled his black cloak tighter around his portly frame, contemplating the sight, which filled his field of vision. As the personal chaplain to the Earl and Countess of Derby, he would shortly need to ring the bells for his morning service. First, though, he needed to see what Fairfax and his band of rebels had been up to overnight. His mistress, the countess, Lady Charlotte de Tremouille, would expect at least that of him.

Rutter strained his eyes through the mist to the east and cursed silently to himself, for the curve of the ground in that direction meant that he could not see what the parliamentarian forces were doing. He could only imagine that the base camp for the siege works was being completed in the valley, for it was not only invisible to those inside Lathom House, but out of musket range as well. Rutter could hear the incessant chatter of what he imagined were hundreds of soldiers, but he could not see a thing.

This was not true of the lines of trenches that were beginning to encircle the house, though. Labourers had been toiling throughout the night, protecting themselves with baskets and hurdles from any musketeers on the battlements who felt inclined to attempt a shot at them in the darkness of the night. Now, as dawn broke and they became more vulnerable, the last of the men could be seen scurrying away out of musket range, back to the safety of the main siege works.

Rutter briefly considered climbing the much taller Eagle Tower in order to gain a better view, but he knew the floor of the valley was invisible from there too. It was an irritation, but one that he bore gratefully, for he knew that the shape of the slope rising from the valley made it impossible for any cannon to fire effectively at the house's walls. Any shot would simply fly straight over the top of the house or, at worst, hit the top of the battlements, where only minimal structural damage could be caused.

The cleric shook his head and chuckled to himself. He did not fear a siege and artillery bombardment by the parliamentarian forces, for the defences at Lathom

House were good. Thirty foot high walls, six feet thick, with banks of turves piled up behind them. The walls, in turn, were surrounded by a moat and an outer fence of timber palisades. The only way the house was vulnerable was if Fairfax carried out a direct attack with overwhelming force, but Rutter smiled to himself with satisfaction. It looked as though the roundheads did not have that in mind. The fools were playing straight into his hands.

Suddenly, Rutter was disturbed from his reverie by the familiar footsteps of Broome, Lady Derby's long-serving steward, who emerged at the top of the spiral staircase, wearing a look of mild irritation.

"You are a difficult man to find, Reverend," he announced, in a tone of mock rebuke. "Her ladyship wishes to consult with you."

"You will often find me here at this time of the morning, Mr Broome," said Rutter, with more tolerance than he felt inclined to give. "I find it the perfect place for a little quiet contemplation – the best way to face up to whatever tribulations the day might bring, I think."

Broome, a tall, spindly man, whose comportment displayed a level of grace and bearing which belied his raw-boned build, gazed over the crenellations, into the mid-distance, and raised his hand to shield his eyes from the morning sun.

"Aye, sir, especially on a day like today, I should

imagine. What's Black Tom got in mind, do you reckon?"

"If God is merciful, then let us hope we are in for a siege. We have enough victuals to last us for months."

"And you think Fairfax has fallen for that?"

Rutter smiled assuredly. "Fairfax is no fool," he admitted, "but his minions are not so bright, and that will give us time. Once a course has been set, it will not be so easy to change direction, mark my words. And that, I'll wager, will give the King enough time to send reinforcements. He will surely not wish for Lancashire to be completely overrun by the rebels. Indeed, Captain Chisnall tells us that the earl has already written to Prince Rupert for help."

"And so long as Fairfax and his main commanders are here, they cannot be elsewhere, so our small garrison will play its part in maintaining his Majesty's interests in the North, I presume?"

"Precisely," grinned Rutter, clapping the steward on the back. "Now let us see what her ladyship requires."

"You'll find her in the drawing room next to the Great Hall," said Rutter. "She is with Mr Farrington."

Rutter trotted down the stone steps and crossed the inner courtyard, passing by the entrance to the Eagle Tower, the imposing stone structure which dominated Lathom. Adjacent to it stood the striking brick building with plaster and lathe upper stories which formed the main house, holding the Great Hall, the Banqueting

130

Hall, and Lady Charlotte's own living quarters, as well as those of her main guests and the garrison officers. As he entered the main building, Rutter paused to acknowledge the presence of the six men descending the steps, who he knew would be entrusted with the defence of the house and therefore everyone's lives. Six captains in all, they were led by the Major of the House, William Farmer, a ruddy-faced Scotsman with many years' experience in the low countries, who saluted Rutter as he passed him. Following him were the other five captains: Ogle, Ratcliffe, Rawsthorne, Fox, and Chisnall, the latter having just returned from attending his lordship, the Earl of Derby, in Chester.

The other five officers ignored the cleric, but he could tell from their demeanour that they too had just met with Lady Charlotte and had been left in no doubt where their duties lay.

The drawing room next to the Great Hall was a bright east-facing chamber, which caught the morning sun. With its wooden cross-beamed ceiling and oak wall panelling, it was one of the best-appointed rooms in the house. The Stanley coat of arms was positioned prominently above the fireplace, and a tapestry displaying the eagle and child legend of the earl's family hung from the wall. It was not surprising that Lady Derby lost no opportunity to use the room as a means of reminding friends and foes alike of the status of her husband's family.

It was just as well that she did, mused Rutter, for much of Lathom House was beginning to show its age. The huge complex was far too large to be run efficiently, and the many disused parts of the house, much of which was affected by damp, no longer provided comfortable accommodation. The days were long gone when the house was able to receive 'two kings, their trains and all,' as the old ballad went. The earl and Lady Derby, he knew, preferred their residences at Knowsley and on the Isle of Man, but Lathom offered the one thing these could not offer: a defensible position that was worthy of any castle.

Rutter found Lady Derby standing by the window, alongside a slim, distinguished-looking gentleman in his fifties. Lady Derby appeared in a pensive mood, contemplating the scene in the inner courtyard, where Captain Rawsthorne was distributing powder and shot in advance of a change of watch on the battlements and towers. The sun highlighted the countess's large eyes and full, almost fleshy features, making light of her thick eyebrows and making her look younger than her forty-four years. Recognising his presence, she gave Rutter a contemplative smile and bade him take a seat on one of two ornate oak settles arranged around a low table in the middle of the room.

"Gamekeepers and fowlers," she said, turning to again watch Rawsthorne's group of marksmen, as they made their way, one by one, to their positions. "You *know, Samuel, sometimes I wonder whether I have the right to demand that these brave men risk their lives for this place, but I cannot allow my husband's birthright to be surrendered without a fight."*

"Do not doubt yourself, my lady," said William Farrington of Worden, the man standing by her side. "This place has been under siege for nine months already. You have been confined to your house and gardens, but that abominable churl Rigby is no closer to achieving his aims. Have faith, my lady. Just because Fairfax and Holland have decreed that you must surrender Lathom, it does not mean that anything will change. We must stand firm."

Rutter nodded enthusiastically in agreement. Farrington knew what he was talking about. Having served as High Sheriff of Lancashire only eight years previously, and more recently as one of the King's Commissioners of Array, the grey-haired and moustachioed Farrington was held in high regard by the countess. He had come to Lathom House seeking a source of refuge from parliamentary action and was now, alongside Rutter himself, Lady Derby's key advisor in tactical matters.

"Mr Farrington is right, my lady," affirmed Rutter. "Rigby and his men have been busy digging holes in the ground these past days. It does not take a genius to work out what is being planned out there. I cannot be certain, but I would hazard a guess that Fairfax has

decided upon a siege. We should thank the Lord for that. May I ask what it is that concerns your ladyship?"

"Only that I have received no news from our secret friend. There has been no sign of him for the past week." The countess spoke with the flowery yet nasal tones of her French homeland. Although it was eighteen years since she had married James Stanley, the then Lord Strange, she had not lost the accent which Rutter felt defined much of her being; haughty and not averse to using self-dramatisation to get her way, yet stubbornly proud and loyal to those who were loyal to her.

"I think he will contact us when he has more news to impart," said Rutter, carefully. "It is safest if we do not attempt to contact him directly. His identity is best protected if only your ladyship, Mr Farrington, and I are aware of his recruitment to our cause. In any case, he is probably too busy digging with the rest of them."

A hint of a smile touched the corner of Farrington's mouth, causing his moustache to twitch slightly. "It appears that your efforts to deceive that rebel captain, Ashurst, have succeeded, Reverend. You are to be congratulated."

"Indeed. A stroke of genius, Samuel," added the countess.

Rutter allowed himself a private smile of self-congratulation, although, in truth, he realised he had benefitted largely from sheer good fortune. Captain John Ashurst was from Dalton, only two miles away from Lathom House, and Rutter could scarcely believe his luck when his old school friend had been among the parliamentarian party sent to negotiate with Lady Derby the previous Saturday. During the negotiations, Rutter had managed to secure some time alone with Ashurst, who had been impressed by the show of strength the countess had put on for their benefit. The garrison had lined the walls of the house and the towers, showing their full strength, whilst Lady Derby had given a guard of honour in the courtyard and the Great Hall to the two parliamentarian colonels, Assheton and Rigby, who had been charged with carrying out the negotiations. The two colonels had left that day with nothing more than an agreement that the countess would present a series of counter-proposals.

Rutter, however, had made sure that Ashurst had departed with something that he would remember. Blinded by the pomp, ceremony, and military strength of the countess, Ashurst had been completely taken in by Rutter's claim that a shortage of victuals meant that a siege was what Lady Derby feared most. Rutter had seen from the besieging forces' preparatory work that his ruse had worked.

"This was but a small service," said the chaplain, trying hard to sound humble. "The real success has been your ladyship's success these past days in playing for time."

"This is certainly true," agreed Farrington. "It is nigh on two weeks since the Manchester Committee ordered that the house be reduced by force and fully nine days since Fairfax sent your ladyship a request to listen to his proposals. You have negotiated most skilfully, if I may say so, although I have to admit it is fortunate that Fairfax appears incapable of dealing severely with women who stand up to him. I cannot imagine him being quite so indulgent with the earl, if he had been here."

"Hush, William," said the countess, the faint hint of a warning in her voice. "Sir Thomas is on the wrong side, but he is a gentleman for all that. It is the quality of men he sends here that marks him out for failure. Ralph Assheton is a competent officer, who has shown the necessary level of respect, but I would not have that insolent snake Rigby sully these halls again, and as for the arrogant Welsh dwarf Fairfax sent in his stead-"

Rutter laughed and rocked back on the settle. The countess was referring to an artillery officer named Morgan, who had been sent to the house the previous Sunday with Fairfax's final list of demands, but who had been so peremptory in his manner that Lady Derby had sent him packing with the words that she was ready to receive the parliamentarians' "utmost violence, trusting in God both for protection and deliverance."

"You are right, my lady," said Rutter. "Many of Sir Thomas's men are incorrigible churls, but that does not mean they must not be taken seriously. We will hear from our secret friend soon enough, but, in the meantime, we must prepare to fight, for sooner or later there will be a reckoning here, and we must be ready for it."

Chapter 12

Chester – Thursday March 7th, 1644

As those who know me well will readily testify, being confined within the stinking privy of a Chester whorehouse, whilst trying to prevent myself from being smothered by the breasts of one of the establishment's half-dressed strumpets, is not the kind of situation with which I feel particularly comfortable, nor is it one to which I am accustomed.

And yet that is precisely the position in which Alexander Clowes and I now found ourselves. The effect of fear on the human mind is a curious thing, for as we hid from the hue and cry that had been instigated to track us, I could think of little but the delicious blanc manger that my housekeeper Mrs Padgett had cooked for me the previous week.

Fortunately, the sight of Annie and her ample bosom succeeded not only in taking my mind off the increasingly likely prospect of both Alexander and I being hanged for spying, but also in masking the unremittingly baleful stench that was emanating from the pit below my nether regions; for hanging between Annie's cleavage was a vial of perfume: a small glass bottle encased in metal, carrying the crest of an eagle carrying a child. I smelled rose water, orange flowers, and jasmine, but I was more interested in the motif.

"The House of Stanley!" I breathed.

Annie put her hand across my mouth. "Quiet, you jolt-head," she hissed, her eyes flashing with anger. "You'll get us all killed."

Alexander, for his part, stood motionless, his considerable frame pressed against the wattle and daub of the privy walls, great globules of sweat visible under his tousled sandy hair. My friend nodded to me and put his outstretched finger to his lips, reinforcing Annie's words.

As I sat there, I contemplated the chain of events that had brought us to The Boot Inn and wondered how it had come to pass that a lowly town constable, wich house owner, and part-time cheese vendor could find himself embroiled in such a web of subterfuge and danger. What on Earth could have possessed me to carry out such an ill-advised mission into the very heart of the royalist cause in Cheshire?

Just as I was contemplating this, heavy footsteps approached from across the courtyard, and the door rattled violently.

"Open up!" came a gruff voice from outside. "Who's in there?" It was a voice I knew well and one which filled me with no small amount of trepidation.

I caught a flicker of a smile touch the corner of Annie's lips and realised that she too had recognised the voice. "Jem Bressy," she growled. "Piss off, you pribbling, ill-bred lout. Can't a woman have a shit in peace?"

I sensed hesitation from behind the door and held my breath, expecting the door to be smashed down at any second. Bressy was not a man you would expect to tolerate being spoken to in such a way. Annie, however, as I was later to discover, was full of surprises.

"Oh, it's you, Annie," said Bressy, eventually. "Alright...I'll be back in five minutes, mind. There'll be a guard waiting just by the steps."

All three of us exhaled simultaneously as the footsteps retreated back across the yard and up the stairs towards the first of the bedrooms. I shot Annie a questioning look, but she responded with a nonchalant shrug.

"I'm a whore in a garrison town," she whispered. "What do you expect?"

She had a point, of course, but why she had gone to such risk to protect Alexander and I was beyond me. Outside, I could hear the landlord, Thomas Corbett, being arrested. The sound of splintering wood suggested that Bressy intended for him to pay with more than just his freedom. Annie, I realised, could expect little better. She was a pretty girl, her doe-eyed, freckled face framed by straight brown locks, giving one the impression of her being much more innocent than she was. I shuddered to think what that face would look like once Bressy and his thugs had finished with her.

"You are risking a great deal for us," I whispered, "but I fear it will be all in vain."

"Maybe," she said, pushing herself from my lap, "but that will not be decided today. In a town like this you always need a second plan...and we have plenty. Look behind you."

As I wriggled my body round, a conspiratorial grin spread across her face. A panel in the back wall of the privy slid to one side, and the friendly face of Charles Corbett appeared.

Chapter 13

Chester – Thursday March 7th, 1644

It had not occurred to me to question why Thomas Corbett had built a privy against the side of his house in an enclosed courtyard, rather than in the yard to the rear of the building, where it would have been more accessible to the gong farmers. But now, as I watched his son beckoning me to crawl through the breach in the back of the privy wall, the reason became clear.

"Not a word," whispered Annie. "Just go. I will keep Bressy at bay as long as I can." I would have nodded my thanks had I been able to do so without burying my nose into Annie's bosom. Instead I just smiled weakly, and, extricating myself from between her and the seat, stumbled through the gap into the room beyond, closely followed by Alexander.

To my surprise, I found we were in a ground floor room that had been converted into a bed chamber. A heavy oak blanket chest had been pulled away from in front of the hole in the wall, above which hung a tapestry, displaying three women walking through a wood. On the other side of the room stood a joined oak bedstead, in which lay an indignant-looking old lady, who was staring at me as though I had just robbed her. I turned to Charles Corbett, who was busy trying to manoeuvre the blanket chest back into place.

"My grandmother," he grunted, by way of explanation. "Don't mind her. It's just that they're less likely to want to search the chamber of a bedridden old lady."

"But why go to the trouble of hiding us in the privy?" I asked. "Why not bring us straight here?"

"Sometimes they send people round the back of the building and search our private quarters as well as the tavern," said Charles. "I needed to make sure that didn't happen. Now please make haste, sirs," he urged. "There's no time to lose. We must get you out of here before they raise hue and cry and close all the exits to the city."

Alexander and I helped Charles replace the wall panel and blanket chest before following him along a corridor, through a small kitchen area, and into the scullery, which I could see was located by the back door. I realised that this was not the first time that Charles Corbett had carried out such an exercise, and I marvelled at the young man's courage.

"How do you propose we make our escape?" I asked. "Surely the Eastgate will be too risky?"

"Don't worry about that," said Charles, reassuringly. "I have an alternative method." With that, he reached under one of the worktops and dragged out a wicker basket, from which he pulled two long black robes.

Alexander took one of the garments from Corbett and stared at him in disbelief. "Cassocks?" he said, incredulously. "What are we supposed to do with these?"

"I'll explain on the way," replied Charles, a hint of impatience entering his voice. "Just put them on. We haven't got much time." We quickly donned the plain black garments over the top of our clothes, and, when he was satisfied, Charles opened the door to the small alleyway which led between the rows from Eastgate Street to the front of the cathedral. Once in front of the magnificent red sandstone building, we skirted to the left, past the south tower and cathedral entrance, until we reached the monastic buildings on the northern side of the church.

"We should stay away from the city walls as much as we can," explained Charles. "You will be less conspicuous that way. And stop looking so ill-at-ease," he added, sensing our discomfort. "If anyone asks, you are the new vicar and curate at Plemstall, a village just north of here. I am taking you now to one of our collaborators, a lecturer in divinity here, who will make sure you get out of the city. You will be safe with him, for the church here is a hotbed of royalist support, and he will not attract suspicion, especially as he retains the trust of Bishop Bridgeman himself."

"That does not surprise me," I said. "Sir William Brereton seems to have eyes and ears everywhere."

Corbett ignored my comment and began to lead us through the cloister adjoining the northern part of the nave. "Once you are out of the city," he continued, "you must walk to Mickle Trafford, a small village but three miles from here. Ask for Samuel Challinor. He is a blacksmith and farrier. I will arrange for your horses to be delivered there."

"And what about my brother?" I asked. "We have not seen him since he disappeared into Gloverstone."

"If he shows up at The Boot, we will help him, of course, but, if he has any sense, he will lie low for a while or try to escape across the river to Handbridge or along the banks of the Dee. In truth, he is on his own."

I nodded in resignation and allowed Corbett to lead us across the cloister garth to an imposing building which proved to be the refectory.

"You must wait here," he said. "I will leave you now, but our man will be with you shortly." With that, he disappeared through the door of the refectory, closing it silently behind him. I kept my eyes fixed on the entrance, expecting him to reappear at any moment, so I was somewhat taken aback when I heard a gentle cough from behind me. I wheeled round to find myself face-to-face with a kindly-looking man dressed in a black coat with a white collar. He was almost completely bald but had a look of serenity and calmness about him that immediately put me at my ease.

"My name is William Ainsworth," he said. "If you would care to follow me, I will explain the procedure as we walk." Ainsworth headed off at a brisk pace back through the cloisters, until we reached a slype that cut between the chapter house and the monks' parlour. We walked down the narrow alleyway, emerging outside the cathedral, from where I was able to see the city walls no more than a few yards away.

"You may be wondering why a preacher in a place such as this is willing to help two fugitives such as yourselves," began Ainsworth.

"I confess, it is a mystery to me," I admitted. "You are a divinity lecturer here, I believe."

"That is true, and a city preacher at St Peter's Church."

"Then you have much to lose."

"I am a pragmatist," said Ainsworth, who, I realised, was casting his eyes along the length of the city walls as we spoke. "Now is not a good time to be a parliamentarian in Chester. You have heard of John Ley, I take it?"

"John Ley? The Puritan preacher?"

"The very same. In earlier times, I was his curate. He has held a prebend here for many years and has also held a lectureship at St Peter's. He stands to lose all of that because of his views. I, on the other hand, am not so foolish. I considered it wiser to declare for the King and seek refuge here."

"I see. Do you not feel you dishonour God by preaching what you do not believe?"

Ainsworth gave me a sharp look and opened his mouth as if to rebuke me, but thought better of it.

"I am no follower of Laud and never have been," he said, patiently. "A good thing too, for he will stand trial for his life in these coming days. However, God tests us in different ways and I believe he will be gracious in his judgement on me, when the time comes."

I smiled and decided I would be better advised to avoid questioning a theologian. Instead, I asked Ainsworth to explain how he proposed to get Alexander and myself past the redcoat sentries watching the exits to the town.

"We go over there," he said, pointing to a small postern gate in the sandstone wall, which appeared locked from the outside. "That is the Kaleyard Gate. It leads to the cathedral's vegetable gardens outside the city walls and has been an exit used for centuries by churchmen and monks alike. Just follow me and don't say anything unless spoken to."

Ainsworth marched over to the gate and rapped on it several times. A head briefly appeared over the top of the wall, and a few seconds later we heard the scraping sound of bolts being slid back and a key being turned in the lock. The gate slowly creaked open, and we were confronted by an unsmiling redcoat, who eyed us suspiciously.

"Yes?" he said.

"This is the new vicar and curate of St Peter's in Plemstall," began Ainsworth. "We come directly from the bishop, and I am to accompany them to their new parish."

"Then use the Northgate," said the soldier, "you know that is the proper way out."

"It is shorter this way, as you know," countered Ainsworth. "We need to pass by Flookersbrook. We do not wish to walk further than is necessary."

"Very well," said the redcoat, looking somewhat unsure, "where are your papers?"

"They are still with the bishop. I could go and fetch him if you prefer, although I doubt he will be amused at being disturbed from his work over such a thing."

The soldier looked nervously over his shoulder and lowered his voice, making sure that a pair of other redcoats stood smoking a little further up the wall could not overhear.

"If I let you through, you will not reveal that I allowed you to pass without the necessary permit?"

"In that case there will certainly be no need to inform the bishop," said Ainsworth. It was not what the soldier wanted to hear, but he stood aside anyway.

"And make sure you come back via the Northgate, as you're supposed to," he shouted after us, as we made our way through the potatoes and cabbages towards the turnpike on Cow Lane.

Ainsworth accompanied us most of the way to Mickle Trafford, for which I was grateful. The route led up through another set of earthworks near Flookersbrook Hall, the furthest extremity of the siege defences laid out by the royalists, but once beyond there and out of sight of the soldiers, we were able to discard our temporary clothing. When we reached the turn off for Plemstall, Ainsworth shook our hands and showed us the road we needed to follow to find Challinor the blacksmith.

"May God go with you," he said, as he took his leave of us.

"But what about you?" I asked. "Will suspicions not be raised when you return alone?"

"I have my own papers with me," replied Ainsworth, "and I will return by the Northgate, as the guard suggested. They will not know the difference, nor will they care. The soldiers are poorly paid, and they will not normally wish to cause trouble to a man of the church."

Chapter 14

Mickle Trafford and Lathom – Thursday March 7th - Friday March 8th, 1644

We had been at Samuel Challinor's house for no more than an hour when a flustered-looking Charles Corbett arrived with our horses. The town had been turned upside down in an attempt to find us, he reported, but there had been no news of a third spy being arrested.

"I must not tarry, though," he added, "for my father has been arrested, and I must see him freed."

"Arrested?" I exclaimed, my heart sinking.

"Do not worry yourself," said Corbett, seeing the look on my face. "It is all bluster. Jem Bressy is well known to us, and he is angry because he failed to find what he was looking for. He cannot prove a thing against us. We have all manner of people passing through our doors, after all. My father will be free by the evening, you will see."

I mumbled an acknowledgement, but I cannot say my mind was entirely put at rest. Thomas Corbett had been arrested because of my carelessness, and his son was now being forced to risk exposure himself in order to make sure Alexander and I were able to ride undetected to Lathom. The trail of people whose lives were being put in danger by my ill-advised attempt to rescue James Skinner was mounting by the hour. I decided our best course of action was to ride to Lathom as quickly as possible, deliver our messages to Fairfax, convey our condolences to William Seaman's son and sister, and return as soon as possible to Nantwich, before we caused any more trouble.

After eating our fill of Mrs Challinor's pottage, we set out again, heading north in the direction of Lathom House. We were pleased to be once more in territory controlled by Parliament, and we made sure that we were in possession of the correct passes and paperwork, with our real names on them, in order to get through the garrison town of Warrington.

The afternoon passed without incident, but nonetheless, the light was beginning to fade by the time we arrived in Warrington. We sought out an inn for the night, where we were able to eat and rest in the sure knowledge that we were once again amongst friends.

Keen to reach our goal, we set off again with the first light of dawn and rode with as much haste as our horses would allow; yet it was almost midday before we reached the crest of the higher ground north of Warrington and were able to gaze down across the fields towards Lathom House, which dominated the landscape for miles around.

It was a calm, bright day, cold but clear, and the sun cast sharply defined shadows off the walls of the formidable mansion, emphasising its stature and contrasting with the brightness of the stone. The sight lifted the subdued mood which had plagued us since leaving Chester, and it was with raised hopes that Alexander and I spurred our tired horses towards the promise of food and an afternoon's rest.

Lathom was truly a building the like of which I had never seen before. I counted seven stone towers inside the fortified walls of the house, including one tower in the middle, twice as high as the rest. This, I presumed, was the famous Eagle Tower. The walls of the house, in the middle of which was an imposing-looking gatehouse flanked by two further towers in the form of a barbican, included several more lookout points and appeared to be manned by dozens of soldiers. It was no wonder that the Manchester Committee considered the capture of the house to be so important.

Lathom House was not to be our destination today, though. Our orders had been to ride to New Park House about half a mile from Lathom, where we had been advised that Fairfax had set up his headquarters. New Park was, in fact, a fine, castellated mansion in its own right, with a moat, dovecote, and large walled garden. Fairfax and his leading officers would, I contemplated, not be short of their share of comforts during their sojourn in these parts. I doubted that the same could be said of the regular soldiers camped in the valley a mile or so to the east.

When we reached the drawbridge, we were challenged by a small group of guards armed with swords and halberds, who demanded to see our papers. On the roof I noticed four musketeers with their weapons trained on us.

"What is your business?" demanded a lank, narrow-mouthed sergeant, who appeared to be the leader of the group.

"We are here to report to General Fairfax. Wc have been sent by Sir William Brereton," I said, handing our permits over. The sergeant studied our papers carefully before handing them back.

"And your names?"

"Cheswis and Clowes," I said, "but you know that, for our names are on our travel permits."

"Just making sure you are who you say you are," said the sergeant, reddening slightly. "But you will not find Fairfax here. He left for Yorkshire two days ago. Follow me. You will need to see one of the new commanders."

"*Commanders?*" I exclaimed, not able to conceal my shock. "How many men are in charge, then?"

"At the moment, four," said the sergeant. "This is West Derby Hundred, so in theory, Colonel Peter

Egerton is responsible, but he is currently supervising the construction of the siege works. Then there are Colonels Assheton, Moore, and Rigby. I believe Colonel Rigby may still be here. I will check whether he is available to receive you.

***

Colonel Alexander Rigby was a small, soberly dressed man with a neatly groomed goatee beard and a thin, wispy moustache. He wore his hair short, so that it just touched his collar, and his face displayed a strange lopsided smile, which, I would grow to realise, concealed an otherwise stern and forbidding personality. We found him sat at an oak table in a large private library, his head buried in a jumble of maps and handwritten diagrams which were laid out before him.

Rigby studied our permits, handed to him by the sergeant, and looked us up and down with a frown.

"I thought there were supposed to be three of you," he said, brusquely, dismissing the sergeant with a wave of the hand.

"There were, sir," I said, "but our cover was compromised, and we were lucky to escape from Chester with our lives. My brother is unaccounted for." I briefly explained what had happened in Gloverstone, leaving out the reason why we had ventured into that part of the city.

Rigby clicked his tongue in annoyance. "You were entrusted with the carriage of important intelligence.

154

Do I take it that some of it is missing?"

I nodded glumly. "Yes, sir. Some of it is still in my brother's possession."

"At least we must hope so. I told Brereton it was a mistake to entrust such work to inexperienced men. You have the ciphers?"

"We were supposed to deliver them into the hands of Sir Thomas Fairfax, sir," protested Alexander.

"Well, unfortunately, you're too late for that," said Rigby. "Sir Thomas has been recalled to Yorkshire. You are to release what information you have into my safekeeping. I am now in command here."

We both reached inside our coats and placed the two wax balls on the table in front of the colonel, who swept them up into his palm and deposited them in a small drawer in the front of the table.

"Thank you," said Rigby, gesturing towards a pair of carved oak chairs. "Now please sit down and let us discuss the main reason that you have been dispatched here. You may be aware that I was present with the Lancashire forces at Nantwich and experienced something of your town in the aftermath of that victory. As a result, I came to learn something about your success in tracking down the spies responsible for the treachery that took place at Beeston in December. You did well, I confess, but you were also blessed with much good fortune. I have to say I remain to be convinced of the wisdom of entrusting important intelligence work such as that which awaits you here to a mere town constable, particularly as you may already have managed to let one of your assistants fall into enemy hands."

I could not deny that Simon's disappearance and the loss of the third wax ball did not make us look good, but I could not stop myself from bridling at Rigby's tone. "Colonel," I said, "we are, as I'm sure you realise, not here of our own volition, but because we have been bound into the service of Sir William Brereton. Both Alexander and I have family and business in Nantwich to which we would much rather attend, so if you feel our presence here is no longer required, we would be delighted to leave you to your siege and return to Cheshire on the morrow. I would only ask-"

Rigby raised his hand to silence me and glared through furrowed brows. "That's not what I meant, Mr Cheswis, and I would thank you to alter your tone when addressing me, as you are under my command whilst you are here. Unfortunately, the matter which you were sent here to solve requires urgent attention, and, considering the fact that there is a dearth of alternative intelligencers, and that both Sir William Brereton and Sir Thomas Fairfax appear to have faith in you, I have little choice but to retain your services. How much do you know of the task in hand?"

"Very little," I admitted. "Only that you fear your senior ranks may have been infiltrated by a royalist informer."

"Then let me enlighten you. It is almost a year since Lady Derby was first asked to yield up Lathom House. It was last May, in fact, after the surrender of Warrington. In her stubbornness, however, she has steadfastly refused to yield to the will of the Governor of Manchester, Colonel Holland. Indeed, she has manoeuvred, prevaricated, and been a general thorn in the side of all those who would uphold the propositions of Parliament. What is more, the earl, who has been largely absent in the Isle of Man, has garrisoned the house with three hundred trained men and various ordnance, including several sakers and a couple of sling-pieces.

"As I have said before, these men are a veritable nest of brigands. Despite Lathom having been nominally under siege, they seem able to secrete themselves in and out of the house at will. They harry and worry our men at every opportunity and do everything within their power to oppose the just will of Parliament. Worst of all, they appear to have advance knowledge of our plans at all times, including information on decisions made by the Manchester Committee. This has led us to believe that they have a spy in a senior position within our forces, serving Colonel Assheton, Colonel Moore, or myself.

"The last straw came in January, when one of our captains intercepted a group of men who were attempting to smuggle arms and provisions into the house. However, it appears that the garrison was somehow informed of the arrest and sent out a party to attack our men before the prisoners could be escorted into detention. The result was that the prisoners were freed and some of our men were taken captive themselves."

"And you wish that Mr Clowes and I mingle with your men with a view to identifying who this infiltrator might be?"

"Precisely; but do not think that failure to arrest this traitor will deflect us from our course. As our godly minister in Wigan recently pointed out, the Countess of Derby is herself akin to no less than the scarlet whore of Babylon and Lathom House to Babel itself. As the scriptures so rightly say, God's vengeance must be to throw down her walls, and I have made that my quest. Whatever it takes, we will starve out her men, bombard her with cannon and mortar until she surrenders, and then we shall raze Lathom House to the ground so that it is erased from the face of the Earth."

I must confess that I was somewhat taken aback at the strength of Rigby's emotions as he said this. His face was contorted with barely concealed hatred, and his eyes appeared to be focussed on somewhere indeterminate in the middle distance.

I wondered whether Rigby's motivation in subjugating Lathom House had more of a personal edge than he was prepared to reveal. I pushed these concerns to the back of my mind, though, for my thoughts were on more practical matters.

"Colonel, may I ask how you propose that our true purpose here be kept secret?" I asked. "We will hardly be inconspicuous here."

Rigby nodded and stroked his beard in contemplation. "You are right," he conceded. "Therein lies the difficulty. You see, you were supposed to report directly to Fairfax and were to be presented as members of his own team of scouts and intelligencers. You would not have attracted suspicion so long as Sir Thomas remained here. But since he has returned to Yorkshire, everything is more difficult, and I have been given but two days to arrange alternative cover for you. I must confess, I am at a loss to know how to proceed."

"Could we not simply be recruited as common soldiers, Colonel?" suggested Alexander.

"That would not work," said Rigby. "You would find it impossible to speak freely, apart from which you need to be billeted here at New Park, where all the other officers are housed. The lower ranks are all camped near the main siege works, to the east of here."

Rigby was right, of course, and it was just as well, for the prospect of having to sleep in tents or amongst the trenches in the Tawd Valley was not something which endeared itself to me. I smiled with relief, and

159

as I did so the seeds of an idea began to germinate within my mind.

"If I might make a suggestion, Colonel," I said, "I think I may have a solution which will serve both our purposes equally well." And so it was that I told Rigby about the murder of Katherine Seaman and my promise to her brother that I would impart the sad tidings of her death to his immediate family in Ormskirk. I also mentioned the curious connection with the royalist officer, Chisnall, as well as William Seaman's dealings with Francis Gamull.

"Katherine Seaman was recently present in Ormskirk and was personally acquainted with Edward Chisnall," I said, by way of explanation. "Her brother, William, also has an ongoing business relationship with the Earl of Derby. Despite this, both Seaman and Katherine are clandestine supporters of Parliament. Seaman's son, I am told, even serves under you here at Lathom."

"Yes, that is true," confirmed Rigby. "Lawrence Seaman is an eager young lieutenant in my troop. You will meet him later today."

"Then suppose we let it be known among your men that Katherine Seaman was one of our collaborators and that Mr Clowes and I have been engaged to seek out her killer? That should be easy enough to substantiate, as we are both from Nantwich and are under the direct command of Sir William Brereton, commander of all parliamentarian forces in Cheshire. This way I will be able to ask the kind of questions I need to pose in order to get to the bottom of your security issues, whilst also enabling me to fulfil my personal pledge to William Seaman."

Rigby sucked in his cheeks and stared at me doubtfully. "I'm not convinced of the wisdom of this course of action," he said, "but very well. I'm not sure that I have much option but to co-operate with you. However, let us discuss this more after you have rested. You have ridden a long way, so I suggest you secure yourselves a chamber upstairs – I believe there are still a few that are unoccupied – and please feel free to avail yourselves of some food. The kitchens are well-stocked and our cooks are good. I will look forward to your presence at our briefing this afternoon at four, when I will introduce you to the other officers."

***

New Park House, despite being a fine mansion, was, to my surprise, relatively sparsely furnished, and the spare bed chamber at the back of the house, in which Alexander and I found ourselves, offered little in the way of chattels other than two plain truckle beds, a small table, and a brown chamber pot. It was as though the Earl and Countess of Derby, whose house it was, had foreseen that their property would be sequestered and removed anything of value to the safety of Lathom House before Rigby and his men could seize it.

Despite being rather more spartan than we would

have liked, our room did have the advantage of being quiet. It was therefore with some degree of relief that, after availing ourselves of our share of a very fair and acceptable beef and onion pie, Alexander and I were able to take stock of our eventful two days without fear of being overheard.

"Has it occurred to you," asked my friend, balancing a cup of red wine on his knee, "that the question of who betrayed us is not as clear cut as you would think? It seems to me that nothing that has happened these past two days is exactly as it seems. It is impossible to tell who is dissembling and who speaks the truth."

"You are right," I agreed. "I have been thinking the same thing myself. Yesterday was a very singular kind of experience, and one which I would not willingly repeat." I gave Alexander a wan smile in acknowledgement and winced as I ran my hand along the side of my cheekbone. Until we had reached Warrington the previous evening, I had been so consumed with the necessity of saving my own skin that I had quite forgotten the fearful blow that Skinner had inflicted on the side of my head and had not noticed the stinging tenderness of my ear or the throbbing pain in my jaw. However, the pain, now that I was aware of it, had been bothering me all morning.

"It is true," I conceded, after a moment's consideration, "that we cannot simply assume that Bressy was lying in wait for us because he saw Simon and myself in The Spread Eagle yesterday. There are several people who may have wished to profit from divulging our true identities to the authorities, people of whose loyalties we cannot be certain."

"That's right," said Alexander, warming to the subject. "Take your friend Seaman, for example. He saw straight through your cover. He *says* he is for Parliament, and even has a son fighting under Rigby's command here at Lathom. And yet everything else about him suggests he is for the King. His public front is as a committed royalist, he has remained in Chester, is a close business associate of the man who commands the Chester town guard, and even invites royalist officers to dinner! Can we really be certain he was not responsible for unmasking us?"

"Chisnall could also have betrayed us," I added. "He has been suspicious about me from the start."

"But Chisnall did not know we would be in Gloverstone yesterday morning."

"That is true, but neither did Seaman," I pointed out.

Alexander pondered the point for a moment and took a mouthful of wine, swishing the liquid around the inside of his cheeks before swallowing.

"Fine," he said, "then consider this. Suppose it was Skinner himself who alerted Bressy to our presence? He has already saved your life once. He is under no obligation to do so again."

"Skinner?" I exclaimed, horrified. "Surely not?"

"He wouldn't be the first soldier to turn his coat." Alexander was right, of course; many fighting men had changed their allegiance when it was expedient to do so. Many of the royalists captured at Nantwich had done exactly that. I had also not forgotten Skinner's odd hesitance and initial lack of enthusiasm when Simon and I had revealed our plan to him two days before; and yet something made me doubt that he would have had us arrested as spies. Surely he would have simply told us to leave him to his soldiering and return to our families in Nantwich? It was then that a thought occurred to me.

"There is one other person," I said, "who may have had the necessary knowledge and motive for betraying us to the authorities."

"You mean Annie, the girl at The Boot?"

"Precisely," I said, surprised at my friend's perceptiveness. Alexander was proving himself to be more sharp-witted than I had given him credit for. "Annie portrays herself as a simple whore, but in fact she is more the brothel madam. She is older than the rest of them and enjoys a level of trust from Corbett that the other girls don't. If Corbett and his son were arrested and thrown in gaol, would she not stand to benefit from their misfortune? She is also well-acquainted with Jem Bressy; you heard as much yourself."

"Yes, but then why let us escape with the ciphers, and why weren't we intercepted at the Kaleyard Gate?"

"I don't know," I admitted, with a shrug. "Maybe she didn't know we were carrying the ciphers. Only Corbett himself told us about them." I suddenly felt immensely tired and leant back on my bed, exhaling loudly. "Well, at least we are safe here," I said, closing my eyes, "and we live to fight another day."

As I drifted off into slumber, though, there was one image that remained etched on my mind, one which I felt sure would hold some significance in the days to come. It was the sign of the eagle and child on the perfume bottle that had hung around Annie's neck.

Chapter 15

The military briefing, which took place later that same afternoon, turned out to be a curious affair, in that it eventually became clear which of the four colonels left in command felt best positioned to assume practical responsibility for the completion of the siege works. Colonel Peter Egerton, the man supposedly in charge, was absent for reasons unexplained, whilst two of the other commanders, Ralph Assheton and John Moore, spent most of the time trying to persuade Colonel Rigby that they would be better advised trying to storm the house rather than imposing a potentially lengthy and costly siege.

"There are three thousand of us and only three hundred of them," reasoned Assheton, a muscular, square-jawed man with a confident air. "No matter how strong their defences are, they cannot hold out against overwhelming force."

Rigby, however, argued his case vehemently. "Thanks to Captain Ashurst, we know that the garrison has victuals only for two weeks," he said. "Why risk the lives of good men, when Lathom will be our own before April is out?" Assheton said nothing, but spent much of the rest of the meeting with perpetually raised eyebrows, as Rigby, clearly animated at the prospect of being able to pursue the siege without having to defer to Fairfax, outlined his plans for the coming days.

The besieging force was to be split into three groups, with each being on duty for a day and a night at a time, in order to progress as quickly as possible with the completion of a network of ditches and sconces encircling the entire house.

It was not surprising that Rigby wished to assume responsibility for this, as most of the besieging force, hailing from the Amounderness Hundred north of Lathom, came under his direct command. These included the chief engineer, a taciturn and solemn-looking man called Browne, and a short, arrogant Welshman called Thomas Morgan, to whom I took an instant dislike. Morgan, it was explained, had commanded a troop of dragoons at Nantwich, but was now in charge of Rigby's artillery. There was a Major Robinson and a plethora of captains too – Davie, Duddell, Sharples, and Dandie are names I remember, the latter because he turned out to be the father of the young lieutenant captured by Lady Charlotte's men in the attempted arrest related to me by Rigby the day before. Also present were the aforementioned Captain

Ashurst, a genial-looking officer in his late thirties, and a slim, dark-haired man with aquiline features, who was introduced as William Bootle, Rigby's expert on the interior of Lathom House. Bootle, it transpired, had previously been a porter in the service of the Earl of Derby and hence knew the layout of the house intimately.

When Rigby had finished speaking, there was a momentary silence, as if none of the small assembly of officers dared to be the first to question the colonel. In the end, it was the Welshman, Morgan, who was first to speak.

"Colonel, may I ask what ordnance will be placed at my disposal during this siege and when we will be able to bring it to bear on the enemy? I am supposed to be in charge of artillery here and yet the guns that I do have may as well be in Manchester, for the gun placements are not ready, and we cannot move our cannon into position."

I looked across the room and thought I saw the hint of a smirk on Assheton's lips.

"That, Major, will depend on the progress made during these coming days in completing the trenches," replied Rigby. "All being well, we should be able to get both the cannon and the culverin in position within the next ten days or so. I have authorised Mr Browne to work day and night on the trenches and to recruit more labour from the nearby villages. Both guns will be placed to the south-west of the house, where the ground is best disposed to allow us the maximum chance of creating a breach in their walls, but I repeat, the speed at which we will be able to begin our work will depend on the efficacy of Mr Browne and his men."

"The siege works *will* be ready," said Browne, evenly. If the engineer felt affronted by Morgan's words, he kept it well hidden. "We are building a testudo to protect the workers in the trenches," he added. "This will be ready tomorrow and will allow us to dig during the day."

"That will help," conceded Morgan, "but we need more than just cannon. The angle of the land here means it will be difficult to get the right trajectory to sufficiently damage the walls. We will probably be able to reduce the Eagle Tower to the same height as those surrounding it, but blasting our way through the walls will be a different matter. What we need is a mortar."

"Sir William Brereton has agreed to furnish us with such a piece of equipment," said Rigby, "but it may take some time to procure."

"And ammunition?" pressed Morgan. "We will need more than a few rocks."

I couldn't be certain, but I thought I saw Rigby's eyes flick momentarily towards where Assheton and Moore were sitting, but the two other colonels simply smiled inscrutably back at Rigby.

"Plans are in place," insisted Rigby. "You will have

all the shells you need to reduce this place to rubble."

A low murmur of approval passed around the room and Rigby nodded with satisfaction as he allowed the impact of his words to sink in. "Gentlemen," he said, "if there are no more questions, then I suggest that we pray that God gives us the strength and resolution to complete these works in a timely manner."

"I have a question," came a voice from the back of the room. I looked and saw that the speaker was Captain Bootle.

"What's on your mind, Captain?" asked Rigby.

"How will our new colleagues be employed while we are keeping watch over the trenches and providing target practice for Lady Derby's snipers?" asked Bootle, simply. Immediately, all eyes turned towards Alexander and myself. If the truth be told, when we had entered the room at the start of the meeting, we had attracted a number of curious looks from several of the officers, but Rigby had immediately introduced us as intelligence officers seconded to the command of Sir Thomas Fairfax and entrusted with investigating the murder of one of his informants in Chester. This had caused some puzzled expressions and someone had asked what this had to do with Lathom, but Rigby had not been willing to elaborate, not least because we had not yet spoken to Lawrence Seaman about his aunt's death. That particular task had been scheduled to take place after the conclusion of the briefing.

"I'm glad you asked me that," said Rigby. "Mr Cheswis and Mr Clowes are both proficient with muskets, having served as part of the garrison forces which so bravely came to our aid in Nantwich, so they will serve their fair share of time in the trenches with the rest of you. In fact, they can commence with tonight's watch immediately after this meeting. The rest of the time they are free to conduct their investigations as they see fit."

I cast a glance over towards Alexander and groaned inwardly. Another stint as a musketeer was not what I had expected, but I was not in a position to complain, for I needed to gain the respect of Rigby's officers if I was to make any headway with the task entrusted to me by Fairfax.

Rigby's words seemed to satisfy the officers, one or two of whom nodded to me in acceptance. As they dispersed to their various duties, though, Rigby called William Bootle back.

"Captain Bootle," he said, "you will find Lieutenant Seaman waiting in the hallway. Would you please bring him in? What I have to say to him is for your ears also."

I looked at Rigby, who waited until Bootle had left the room before addressing me. "William Bootle is the brother-in-law of Katherine Seaman's sister, Jane, who resides in Ormskirk," explained the colonel. "It is appropriate that both Lieutenant Seaman and Captain

171

Bootle are informed about their relative's demise."

This was an unexpected development, and my surprise must have shown on my face, because Rigby qualified his statement by adding, "Ormskirk is a small place, Mr Cheswis. Many families are related by marriage. Nantwich cannot be much different." This was true, of course, and there was no reason why Seaman would have necessarily thought to mention the connection, for William Bootle was no blood relative of Seaman's.

I indicated to Rigby that I had no objection to Bootle listening to what I had to say and watched as the captain re-entered the room, closely followed by a young man of medium height with a shock of fair hair covering his forehead and an inquisitive look on his face. Like his father, Lawrence Seaman had a wide mouth, which conveyed a sense of openness, but I detected a sense of disquiet in his voice as he introduced himself.

"You wished to speak to me, sir?" he said, casting an apprehensive glance at Rigby.

"My name is Daniel Cheswis, and this is my associate, Alexander Clowes," I began. "We come directly from your father in Chester. We have some difficult news to impart to you and Mr Bootle concerning your aunt, Katherine Seaman."

"My aunt? But she was here only a few days ago. How can you possibly-"

I raised my hand gently to silence the young man. "I'm

afraid there is no easy way to convey the news I bear, Mr Seaman. Your aunt was most brutally murdered last night, in the courtyard behind your father's house. One of the servants has been arrested, although I am not convinced he is the man responsible."

The young lieutenant stiffened. "Murdered?" he gasped, "but how? And why are you the person bringing me this news? You are not known to me."

"That is true," I said. "I am a cheese vendor from Nantwich, and I was visiting your father on business. However, Mr Clowes and I also work for Sir William Brereton, which is why we are here. I promised to look into the affair on behalf of your father, as well as to pass on the sad tidings to yourself and your other aunt, who, I believe, lives in Ormskirk."

"Aunt Jane? Yes, she is married to William's brother," said Seaman, looking puzzled, "but there is something I don't understand. Colonel Rigby spoke of the murder of one of our informers. Surely he cannot mean my Aunt Katherine; she had no interest in politics. And why would my father ask you to look into this matter?"

I glanced at Rigby and realised that we would have to take Bootle and Seaman into our confidence, at least in part. "I'm afraid I happened to be dining with your parents two days ago, when your aunt was so cruelly attacked," I explained, before giving a brief account of that evening's events.

"But Colonel Rigby gave the impression that you

173

had been specifically sent by Sir William Brereton," interrupted Bootle, who had been following the conversation closely. "If this happened only two days ago, then this cannot have been so, and you say yourself that Lawrence's father asked you here."

I looked again at Rigby, who gave me an exasperated look, followed by an almost imperceptible nod.

"I have other work to carry out here on behalf of Sir William Brereton and Sir Thomas Fairfax, the nature of which I am not at liberty to divulge," I said.

Bootle emitted a brief bark of laughter and looked at me scornfully. "If you are here on behalf of Sir William Brereton and you are an intelligencer, then I'll wager you are here to look into how you might stop information passing into and out of Lathom House. Would that be close to the truth?"

Bootle was clearly no fool and there was little point in denying my role, so I reluctantly conceded the point and left the conversation to Rigby, who stepped in to make sure that both Bootle and Seaman were committed to secrecy. Both agreed readily, and Rigby was just about to draw the conversation to a close when Bootle seemed to have an afterthought and turned towards me.

"For what it's worth," he said, "I don't think you will find any spies around here anymore. They caught one only a few days ago. Isn't that right, Colonel?"

Rigby coughed uncomfortably and glared at Bootle as

though he would like to murder him. "That's right," he said. "A woman by the name of Reade. She was caught red-handed taking messages into and out of the house. Her son is a gamekeeper on the Earl of Derby's estate and is therefore among the men defending the garrison walls. We questioned her to see whether we could get her to reveal the names of any co-conspirators, but her constitution was weak. I'm afraid she was not able to withstand the rigours of interrogation."

I stared at Rigby, shocked. "You mean she died?" I exclaimed.

"That is true," said Rigby. "A most unfortunate outcome. The woman was buried only yesterday."

"It was a tragedy," agreed Lawrence Seaman. "She was a good woman, Mary Reade. A local midwife, she was. A skilled healer too – good with herbs. She was well-respected around here."

"Aye, and she leaves a young family who must fend for themselves," added Bootle. "Her husband's been beneath the sod a few years now; the son, Harry, is stuck inside the garrison; and Jenny, the eldest of the others, is but twelve years old."

"She was a traitor," said Rigby, unmoved, his face betraying no emotion whatsoever. "She got what she deserved. We cannot be responsible for what happens to her offspring. The only person responsible for their plight is Mary Reade herself."

William Bootle and Lawrence Seaman said nothing

more, but I could tell from their demeanour that they did not agree with the colonel, and I had some sympathy with their viewpoint. I had often thought that this conflict, which pitched friend against friend and brother against brother, brought out more evil in mankind than good. I wondered what horrors Mary Reade had been forced to endure, if she had been interrogated so rigorously as to cause her death.

One thing I was already fairly convinced of was that Reade could not have been the only informant. As a mere midwife, she could not possibly have been privy to the kind of military and strategic information that had clearly been finding its way into Lady Derby's hands. Perhaps Reade had been acting merely as a courier. If that had been the case, then perhaps young Jenny Reade had seen something that would help identify the real spy. I resolved to find out more about this woman and made a mental note to seek out the daughter to ascertain whether she was able to tell me anything that might be able to shed light on who else might be responsible for passing information into and out of the house.

First, though, I had another task to complete, and it involved helping Rigby and his men dig the siege trenches around Lathom House. It was something I dreaded, for such labour is hard work indeed, but it was labour to which I was well-accustomed, having done my fair share of digging during the construction of the earthworks around Nantwich the year before.

"You may join us," said Bootle. "We are on duty ourselves tonight. But let us make haste and not keep Mr Browne waiting. Believe me, we do not want to be digging within range of the marksmen on the walls of Lathom House. Those that are not experienced musketeers are all gamekeepers and fowlers who know their business. It will serve us well to be first on hand."

Chapter 16

Lathom House – Friday March 8th – Saturday March 9th, 1644

Viewed from close quarters, Lathom House was even more impressive than it appeared from a distance; especially the defences, which gave off an undeniable aura of impregnability. The house itself stood in a small depression, as though it were lying in the palm of a hand. However, the solid stone outer walls were surrounded by a ditch nearly ten feet deep and forty feet wide, on the outside of which springy moorland turf rose quickly for a few yards before falling away sharply on all sides, making it difficult to see the whole of the building from outside the ditch. This, I realised, was what Browne had meant when he had pointed out the difficulties faced by the artillery that was to be positioned outside the walls. Anyone standing on the downslope of the bank was not only visible to the sharpshooters on the battlements of the house but also within musket range. However, that same person would not be able to see the bottom of the walls, which meant the walls would not be within the trajectory of our siege cannon.

The towers, located at intervals around the walls of the house, also appeared to be well-equipped with ordnance. I observed several pieces on each, including sakers, sling pieces, and murderers: deadly swivel-guns which threatened anyone careless enough to reveal themselves within their range.

When Alexander and I arrived at the main camp in the Tawd valley, we presented ourselves to Major Edward Robinson, under whose command we had been placed. Robinson, a swarthy individual with craggy features and a thick, dark moustache on his upper lip, informed us that there was to be no digging close to the house until dark, when a team of local labourers would arrive.

Alexander was dispatched, grumbling, to help dig a latrine, whilst I, to my relief, was given leave to approach Browne the engineer, who, as a civilian, and therefore not necessarily bound by the loyalties that tie soldiers together, I had earmarked as a potentially vital source of information on the nature of the relationships between the various officers in the parliamentary camp.

I found him near the outermost trenches, where he was instructing a team of carpenters who were sawing and hammering away at a huge wooden frame on wheels with a thick wooden screen on one side, which was still half-completed.

"Our testudo," explained Browne, when he saw me approaching. "The idea is that it will straddle the ditch as it is being dug, with the screen on the side facing the house. The labourers will be able to shovel out the soil on the other side. Unfortunately, it won't be ready until next week, so in the meantime, we will have to make do without."

I complimented Browne on his handiwork and asked him to explain the layout of the siege works that were to be built around the house.

"The aim," said the engineer, "is to build three concentric earthworks around the house – at sixty yards, a hundred yards, and two hundred yards from the battlements. These are to be linked by a series of communications trenches. The innermost trench will be serrated in design so that nobody can shoot down the length of it, and it will be interspersed with a series of small forts and gun placements, which will be protected by stakes and palisades. The second ring will consist of a three foot deep trench protected by an earthwork. This ring will also have eight sconces spaced at regular intervals, strengthened with earthen walls and wicker gabions. The outer ring will be a simple earthen wall."

"I see," I said. "So, in principle, once these earthworks are completed, the ring around the house should be more or less watertight. No-one should be able to get in or out."

"In principle, yes, of course," agreed Browne. "But it is a long way around the house, even with a thousand men per shift, and on a dark night it will be difficult, if not impossible, to guarantee total security. That is, of course, assuming Rigby gives me the men I need to speed up the construction process. So far the building work has been painfully slow. We have been desperately short of manpower, but let us see what happens tonight after the captains have recruited some local labour to help with the digging."

"I get the feeling that you are not impressed with Colonel Rigby," I ventured.

Browne looked at me carefully before he responded. I had taken him for a sardonic sort, but his answer was that of one used to plain speaking.

"I am not sure what your real purpose is here, Mr Cheswis," he said, "but I will speak my mind. Colonel Rigby is a fool in my opinion, a dangerous man, who could put all our lives at risk."

I stared at the engineer in surprise. This was not what I was expecting. "What do you mean?" I asked.

"Rigby is a strict Puritan," explained Browne. "No issue in itself, of course. I hear Sir William Brereton is the same. But Rigby is extreme in his beliefs and unable to temper his prejudices, driven as he is by hatred for the Earl of Derby. He will not stop until Lathom is reduced to dust."

"And you find that to be a problem?"

Browne raised his hands defensively. "Not personally," he said. "I am just an engineer, employed to make this siege a success, but I do value my own skin. A siege needs careful planning. At present, we do not have enough men, the siege works are not built, and there is no ordnance in place. Not only that; if Morgan is to be believed, we will need more than a few cannon to bring this place to its knees."

"But Rigby believes they do not have enough supplies to withstand a long siege."

Browne laughed scornfully. "Do *you* really believe that? That a place as big as Lathom does not have sufficient reserves to withstand a siege? This place has been under threat of attack for nearly a year, and yet it has proved impossible to keep people in or out. Do you really think that the countess will not have made sure in the meantime that their kitchens are amply stocked and that they have enough powder to keep us occupied for a substantial period?"

"And water?"

"There is a well inside the house, although I am looking at ways of diverting the water course so that we can cut off their supply. But it will be no easy task."

I had to concede that Browne had a point. He had said nothing during the briefing that evening, and I was now beginning to see why. I decided to change the subject.

"You know why I am here, Mr Browne," I said.

"I need to investigate the murder of one of our informants."

"I can't help you there, my friend," said Browne. "I am an engineer, not an intelligencer, but I will tell you this. There are many people round here with loyalties to the earl that stretch back generations, maybe even men within our own ranks. Most local people here rely on the earl for their livelihoods and may have friends or relations within the house. There are also many followers of the old faith in this part of Lancashire and although Lady Charlotte is a Huguenot, the King's wife is most definitely Catholic. There are therefore many folk hereabouts who would feel that the preservation of the King's interests in these parts is the best guarantee they will have that they will be able to follow their faith unmolested. No, you will not find it difficult to identify people around here who would happily betray a parliamentary spy, but finding the *right* person… well, you will have your work cut out I believe."

***

That night, spent digging the trenches around Lathom House, was quite possibly the most terrifying eight hours I had ever spent, more frightening than facing Lord Byron's army on the battlefield at Acton or being shot at by Jem Bressy at Hurleston, for in both these cases the enemy was both palpable and identifiable. At Lathom, men lurked on the battlements and in the shadows, an intangible presence, waiting indefatigably for the opportunity to bury a musket ball in the skull of anyone careless enough to make himself visible.

At around seven o'clock in the evening, a number of Rigby's captains presented themselves at the main camp, where Browne was waiting to issue instructions for the night's work. Each officer was accompanied by a team of reluctant recruits, consisting mainly of surly-looking farm labourers, who had evidently been dragged, protesting, from their fields, but also including a few tradesmen and apprentices, as well as any vagrants unlucky enough to be in the vicinity when the captains had come calling.

Once it was fully dark, a number of teams were led silently up the existing network of trenches and positioned at intervals along a fifty yard stretch of ground where new channels were to be dug. Each team consisted of a mixture of musketeers and labourers holding huge wooden screens in place to protect the diggers from being shot. Behind the screens, a couple of musketeers stood guard and watched the rest of the team frantically digging and throwing out the loose earth behind them. Those musketeers involved in digging or holding the screens laid their weapons on the side of the trench. When the diggers grew tired, they swapped position with those holding the screens in place.

After a couple of hours toil, the exhausted team would then crawl back along the trenches to be replaced by a new group of recruits, knowing that before long, they would be recalled for a second shift.

Alexander and I were seconded into one of these teams. It was hard, dangerous work, not made any easier by the fact that it began to rain half way through the night, turning the bottom of the trenches to mud. Every now and then a musket ball thudded into the wooden screen, sending splinters flying everywhere and reminding everyone that to step out from behind the screen was to invite death.

Working on the innermost of the trenches, we were close enough to the walls to hear the constant foul-mouthed abuse being yelled at us throughout the night. Our own musketeers attempted the occasional volley of musket fire in retaliation, but these were inevitably met by a torrent of raucous jeers from the darkness. At one point, a piercing scream came from the team of diggers next to our own, and we looked through the gloom to the left to see a man clutching his arm, which hung loosely by his side. He had obviously been careless enough to step marginally outside the line of the wooden screens and had been picked off by one of the musketeers on the wall, who were by then cheering and yelling in delight. There was a brief commotion as several of the injured man's comrades pulled him behind the screen. One took off his shirt to fashion a makeshift tourniquet. The whole team then backed off slowly towards the outermost earthwork until out of musket range, from where the unfortunate victim was dragged off towards the main camp. When I asked about his welfare later, I was told that the poor man had lost his arm and was clinging desperately to life, having lost much blood during the amputation of his shattered limb.

The night seemed interminable, but just as the faint light of dawn began to appear in the eastern sky, all the teams were ordered to retreat out of musket range and back into the valley, where many collapsed with exhaustion among the trenches and tents of the main camp.

At around midday, Alexander and I tramped slowly back to New Park House, mud-spattered and weary, where I cleaned myself up and fell into a dreamless sleep on my truckle bed. In truth, I could have slept all night, but just before dusk, I was shaken awake by Alexander, who reminded me of my appointment with Lawrence Seaman. I therefore pulled on my breeches and a clean shirt and walked the two and a half miles into Ormskirk, which was unknown to me, but turned out to be a busy and populous market town, straddling the main road to Preston.

The area around the cross in the middle of the town was swarming with parliamentary soldiers, many of whom were billeted in the houses and taverns which lined Aughton Street, the main thoroughfare. Ahead, on a small hill to the west, and silhouetted against a bright red sunset, was the town's curious church, with its western tower and central spire huddled together. It was as though those who had constructed the church couldn't decide which to build, so decided on both.

There was something else unusual about Ormskirk, though, and it took me a few minutes before I realised what it was – an almost total absence of trees, a fact which I found strangely disconcerting. Pulling my coat around my neck, I continued down Moor Street, the road which led into the town centre from the east, and located The Ship Inn, the tavern in which I had agreed to meet Lawrence Seaman.

The alehouse was, as expected, full of soldiers, and as I fought my way through the throng, I was surprised to see Browne the Engineer sat in a corner, playing cards with half a dozen other men. He nodded in recognition and gestured for me to join their game, but I declined politely.

I found Lawrence Seaman propped against the bar, holding a tankard of strong ale. He greeted me with a wave and ordered another beer as well as two mutton pies, which we devoured with gusto. I had almost forgotten how hungry I was.

Lawrence turned out to be a personable young man, uncomplicated in character, but desperate to make a good impression. I explained once again to him the connection between myself and his father and recounted in detail the events of the previous Thursday evening.

"I'm curious to know more about your Aunt Katherine," I began. "You knew her well, I believe."

"Of course," said Lawrence. "She chose the life of a spinster and has always lived in my father's household. I've known her all my life."

"And recently?"

"I've only spoken with her occasionally, but she liked to keep in touch with my Aunt Jane. I've been here with Colonel Rigby's regiment for nearly a year, and she was here perhaps three times, but I very rarely saw her when she visited. My Aunt Jane and I have never been close."

"But you know the Bootles?"

"Of course, but I only have anything to do with William because he happens to be in my regiment. You were well-acquainted with my aunt?"

"I met her for the first time on the day she died," I said, "but she struck me as being of an unusually nervous disposition. Is that an accurate description, would you say?"

Lawrence considered this for a moment, scratching his upper lip in contemplation. "Not really," he said, "although the last time she was here she did seem unusually distracted, as though something were bothering her. I ran into her in the street, but she didn't seem to want to talk. Said something about needing to get back to my father in Chester."

"I see. And when was this exactly?"

"Last Sunday, after church."

This fitted in with the information given to me by William Seaman, but it didn't explain Katherine's behaviour during the afternoon and evening of her death.

"What about Edward Chisnall. What do you know about him?" I ventured.

"Chisnall?" exclaimed Lawrence, the surprise evident on his face. "Royalist gentleman from Chorley. One of Lady Charlotte's captains. I barely know him, but he has a reputation for being brave and straightforward. What does he have to do with this?"

"I don't know," I admitted, "but he turned up at your father's shop when I was there and Katherine appeared stricken to the core when she became aware of his presence. He was also in attendance for at least part of the evening that your aunt died.

Lawrence's eyes widened. "You believe he is responsible for this?"

"Again, I don't know," I said, truthfully. "It's perfectly possible. He was certainly very suspicious of me, and as far as I'm aware, he has no alibi. He left your father's house before your aunt was murdered."

"Perhaps he also held my aunt for an informant," suggested Lawrence.

"Mmm," I said, circumspectly. "That may be the case, but it doesn't explain why Katherine was so disconcerted by the sight of him." I was beginning to realise that promoting Rigby's idea of Katherine as a spy was likely to be more counter-productive than helpful. I decided that I would be on safer ground by asking Lawrence to tell me more about something else which had intrigued me greatly, namely his father's supposed inheritance.

"Henry Oulton has never really been a concern of mine," said Lawrence. "I've never met him, and I was never expecting to inherit anything from him. I do know, however, that he has been a rich and successful merchant and that he has had dealings with my father through his business in France and Spain. I also know that his son and grandson both died young, which is why my father has become the heir to his property. But as a younger son, my plan was never to become a merchant trader. I suppose that now my brother is no longer with us, I will be expected to change my plans, once the war is over. What I do know is that Oulton is now old and ailing, and that my father has travelled recently to Bolton to see him."

"Did you realise that your father has already contracted to sell part of the business to Sir Francis Gamull?"

"No. Why would he do that?"

"I don't know," I said, "that is what I would like to find out."

Lawrence drained his tankard thoughtfully and

gestured to the landlord to serve up two more. "So you think my aunt's death has something to do with my father's business dealings?" he asked.

"It's one line of enquiry," I replied. "I'm merely speculating."

"I see. In that case," said Lawrence, "perhaps we would be better advised to stick to discussing the real reason why you are here."

"You are right," I acknowledged. Until I had spoken to Jane Bootle, there was little sense in more speculation about Katherine Seaman's death. "In that case, tell me what you know about the men under Rigby's command. Let's begin with Browne, the engineer. I spoke with him this afternoon. What is your view of him?"

"Mr Browne? A knowledgeable engineer for sure, but he is lazy and quick to blame others for his shortcomings."

"So something of an outsider, then?"

"Yes, but not just that. There are those that say the tardiness in digging the siege works is as much down to him as anything."

This was a helpful insight, I felt. I had already gained the impression that Browne was not particularly well-liked, and a tendency towards indolence would be a good reason for that, but I was not entirely convinced. "Maybe," I said, "but that doesn't make him a spy. What about the Welshman, Morgan? He is an outsider too."

"Dismissive and peremptory in nature. Arrogant beyond words, but he has the trust of Rigby. He has, of course, been inside the house on his own to negotiate directly with Lady Derby, so he has had ample opportunity to pass on information to her in confidence, but I rather doubt it. He served Parliament loyally at Nantwich and, being in charge of the artillery, he has been openly critical of the siege plans and has been pressing for the availability of more ordnance. Surely that is not the behaviour of someone who would betray us?"

"Alright," I said, "so what about Rigby's captains?"

"Solid Lancashire men, most of them," said Lawrence. "The only one who has any connections inside the house is Captain Ashurst, who is a childhood acquaintance of the countess's personal chaplain."

I considered this for a moment. Ashurst had been among the delegation who had accompanied Assheton and Rigby during the first attempt to negotiate with Lady Derby. It was he who had claimed to have extracted valuable information from her chaplain relating to the countess's ability to withstand a siege. This, I remembered, was precisely one of the doubts that had been voiced by Browne. Could it be that Ashurst was deliberately misinforming Rigby? He was certainly close enough to the command to have had access to fairly high level military information, and may well have had the means to pass information in and out of the house.

The only other member of Rigby's team with connections inside the house was William Bootle.

"William?" said Lawrence. "The earl hates him like the pox. He holds him for a traitorous villain and has sworn to gut him like a fish should he ever lay hands on him. William worked inside the house for three or four years under Mr Broome, the steward, which is why he is of use to Rigby. He left the earl's employment and joined Rigby's regiment when war broke out. I fear the earl took his defection personally."

"And not helped, I imagine, by the express fact that it is Rigby whom he now serves."

"Precisely. There is a certain antipathy between Colonel Rigby and the earl, which is well known."

I was beginning to realise how difficult my task had become. If the truth be told, I could not sensibly rule out any of the officers under Rigby's direct command, but I had the nagging feeling that I had so far only been touching the surface of what was going on at Lathom, and that the true answer to the conundrum lay elsewhere. It then occurred to me that there was one line of enquiry that I had not yet followed.

"What can you tell me about Mary Reade?" I asked. "Colonel Rigby did not seem too keen on talking about her."

"It is a sad story," acknowledged Lawrence. "Mary

Reade was a midwife. There are many folk around Ormskirk of my age and younger who were brought into the world by her. Many also used to go to her for cures and remedies for everyday ailments, for she knew her herbs and potions better than most. Many preferred her to the local physic, but, as is often the case with those who have the ability to heal, she was held in suspicion in some quarters. It appears someone betrayed her to Colonel Rigby."

"But she was carrying messages into and out of the house. Does that not make her guilty of spying?"

"Perhaps so, but it does not excuse what they did to her. It is said she was tortured terribly. Lighted matches were tied to her fingers, so they say, so that the fingers on one of her hands were burned off. I understand she said nothing, but she must have died in excruciating pain. Nobody deserves to die like that."

I sucked my cheeks in and grimaced, listening to the gory details, my mind slipping back to the recurring vision I had of James Nuttall, Simon and Elizabeth's friend, lying dead in the church at Barthomley, his hands having also been mutilated in an attempt to extract information.

Suddenly, I was disturbed from my reflections by a burly man in his sixties, with straggly grey hair and a beard, and who, I noticed to my annoyance, had been listening to our conversation. Seeing that I had registered his presence, he lurched across the tap-room and leant across the bar, swaying slightly. Clearly drunk, he was dressed in a plain white shirt and brown breeches, and stank of beer and tobacco.

"Mary Reade," slurred the man. "She will haunt everyone in this town for the way she was treated. I saw it all myself: rising from her gravestone to persecute those who drove her to her death."

I looked curiously at the old man, but the landlord had moved quickly from behind the bar and grabbed him by the collar.

"You've had too much ale tonight, Isaac," he said. "Leave these gentlemen in peace. They do not wish to hear your pribbling nonsense."

"But I swear I saw her, clear as day."

"Hush, Isaac," the landlord said, a little more insistently this time. "There's those as held Mary Reade for a witch. Talk such as this will not help her memory, nor will it help her children. Apologies, sirs," he added, addressing me directly. "Old Isaac is an incorrigible tosspot and no mistake. Leave him to me. He will not bother you again."

"Let him speak a moment, landlord," I said, trying to calm the situation. "What did you see exactly, old man?"

Isaac shook himself free from the landlord's grasp and stared at me. "Buried her only yesterday, they did, but last night I saw her standing by her gravestone, I swear it. I live near the churchyard, you see. Standing on her own tombstone, she was, all white and pale, but when I approached her she raised her hand as if to threaten me. I ran for my life, I did."

"Bollocks," said the landlord. "Ran straight for the nearest alehouse, more like." With that, the landlord propelled Isaac, stumbling and belching, through the door and into the street.

I was grateful for the landlord's intervention, but, in truth, I had been shaken by the encounter. I decided to finish my beer, then make arrangements to meet up with Lawrence and William Bootle the following morning in order to visit Jane Bootle and her husband.

Lawrence and I left the tavern together, and just as we stepped out into the alleyway, Lawrence shoved me violently against the wall. A split-second later I heard a loud crack and something whistled past my ear, ricocheting off the wall like a handful of gravel. I looked sharply to my left and saw a figure disappear elusively round the back of the inn.

"What in God's name-?" I began.

"A man," shouted Lawrence, pushing himself away from me. "Down the alley. With a bloody big fowling gun." With that, Lawrence charged headlong down the alleyway to where the man had disappeared, and looked tentatively across the backlands of the shops and taverns lining Moor Street. I walked over to join him, but there was little to see. It was clear that the bird had already flown.

"Tell me, Mr Cheswis," said Lawrence, "why would someone want to shoot you?"

"I don't know," I said, although, to be truthful, it had occurred to me that the intended murder victim was just as likely to have been Lawrence as myself. I considered briefly who the gunman might have been – Chisnall, perhaps. He was, after all, the only suspect for Katherine Seaman's murder who I knew to be in Lathom. But how he could have got in and out of Lathom House was not entirely clear.

But supposing the attack was linked not to Katherine Seaman's murder, but to my search for the spy in Colonel Rigby's ranks? After all, every potential suspect in the parliamentary ranks knew me for an intelligencer. It surely would not take long for the guilty person to realise solving Katherine Seaman's murder was not my real reason for being at Lathom.

One thing bothered me though. It was Lawrence Seaman who was in my company when I was attacked. Just supposing, I wondered, there were a connection between my task in identifying Rigby's spy and the murder of Katherine Seaman, and, if that were the case, the gunman was keen on stopping me talking to Lawrence Seaman. Could that be the case?

I had a feeling I was about to find out.

Chapter 17

The Church of St Peter and St Paul in Ormskirk lay on high ground to the north-west of the town, making it visible for some distance. Jane and John Bootle, so I had been informed, lived in one of a row of shabby workers' cottages, which backed onto the graveyard, and so, with convenience in mind, I had arranged to meet William Bootle and Lawrence Seaman outside the church after the Sunday morning service.

I found Bootle leaning nonchalantly against the church wall, sucking on a wooden pipe and blowing billows of smoke into the air. Seaman, meanwhile, had disappeared inside the church, trying to locate his relatives. He emerged a few moments later, accompanied by the vicar, his face lined with worry.

"You look like you are not relishing the prospect of having to tell your aunt about her sister," I commented.

"It's not that which concerns me," responded Lawrence. "It appears neither my Aunt Jane nor her husband attended the service this morning. It is not like them to miss prayer, especially on the Lord's day," he added.

"Master Seaman is in the right of it, sirs," said the vicar, a tall, spindly man, who introduced himself as William Nutt. "John and Jane Bootle are regulars in our congregation, but today I am concerned for John's welfare. He is an honest and pious man, not generally given to ungodly activities, but this morning he was not himself."

"How do you mean?" I asked, with curiosity.

"I saw him in the street," said Nutt, wringing his hands in agitation. "It was about six o'clock this morning, and I was on my way into church to prepare my sermon. He was acting in a manner which was most disturbing."

"How so?"

"It was as though he was the worse for drink, but he hadn't been drinking. His eyes were wide and staring and he was ranting unintelligibly. He said that his mind had been possessed by debauched and unchristian thoughts, that he felt he was flying and feared his mind had been possessed by the Devil. I did not know what to think, so I told him to return to his home and pray that a merciful God would release him from such thoughts."

"More like too much strong ale," contradicted Bootle, scornfully. "He was in The Eagle and Child with me last night. There'll be nothing wrong with him other than a thick head. Let us go and find him."

A gradual feeling of unease began to take me as Alexander and I followed Bootle, Lawrence Seaman, and the vicar back through the churchyard. In the middle of the far wall, overgrown with nettles and other weeds, was another stile, which led into a muddy lane between two small cottages. Bootle led me through the gate, up to the cottage on the right, and knocked on the door. There was no answer, but the door was slightly ajar.

I knew something was wrong as soon as I stepped into the doorway, for there was an odour of evil about the place, a nauseating, sweet aroma of charcoal and roast meat; but there was something else too, a putrid, vile stench, that could only be described as the smell of death.

The vicar took a sharp intake of breath as he entered the house, and put the sleeve of his cassock up to his nose. The blinds were closed in the hall, but as my eyes became accustomed to the light, I found we were looking at a scene of pure horror. Chairs and tables were upturned and a bowl of pottage lay splattered on the floor, but what turned my blood to ice was the sight of a woman's body lying face down, her face buried in the glowing embers of the fire. Her right hand was lying under her face, as though she had tried to protect herself, and the back of her head was bruised and bloody.

Ten feet away, slumped in a chair, was the corpse of a man, which I took to be that of John Bootle. Jammed between his legs and pointing upwards at his throat was a large fowling gun, the butt of which was stained red. There was a gaping hole in the throat and both the back of the cadaver's head and the walls were sprayed with blood and fragments of brain.

There was a moment of silence and disbelief when time seemed to stop, but then I heard the sound of retching beside me and saw Lawrence Seaman bent double, emptying the contents of his stomach onto the floor. I felt the bile rising in my own throat and reached for the back door, vomiting into the alleyway outside.

When I had finished, I went gingerly back inside, to find Alexander and Lawrence sat on the floor, looking as white as snow, whilst the vicar knelt over the woman's body, praying, and William Bootle stood, inspecting the back of the male victim's skull.

"What demons have been at work here, Mr Cheswis?" asked Bootle, his voice shaking with emotion. "What could have driven my brother into such a frenzy as to bring him to slaughter his wife in such a way, and then to take his own life? It is as though witchcraft were at play here."

"Witchcraft?" I said, doubtfully. "I suspect the cause of this evil has more earthly roots than that. What has made you think such a thing?"

"You just have to listen to the townsfolk," said

Bootle. "Hear what they have to say about the widow Reade, who died these past days. Now that she is dead, there are many that have her for a witch."

My mind flashed back to the words of Isaac, the old drunkard in The Ship the previous evening, but I was not one for superstitions of this kind. "Here, help me haul this cadaver out of the fire and we will see what we can find," I said.

Bootle and I each put our hands under Jane Bootle's shoulders and, with Alexander and Lawrence Seaman taking a leg each, we gently lifted the corpse away from the glowing embers and laid it in the middle of the floor, allowing the arms to flop loosely by its side. Rigor mortis, I noted, had not yet set in, which meant that she must have died within the previous three hours.

I rolled the body over onto its side and noticed, with revulsion, that the victim's face was charred to an indescribable black mask of horror, the empty eye sockets still smoking and staring back at me vacantly. Her hair had also been almost entirely burned away, and only a few wisps of brown hair were still visible. The victim's right hand and forearm had also been burned to a crisp. The fire, I reasoned, must have been extremely hot when her death had occurred, for it was as though the hand had been reduced to dust. I put my hand to the back of Jane Bootle's head and felt carefully around the base of the skull. Just behind her right ear, I found an area that was soft and misshapen.

"It would appear that her skull was smashed with the butt of the fowling gun," I said.

"It does not take a genius to work that out," said Bootle. "The solution is obvious. My brother hit Jane over the head with his gun and then shot himself. The question is why."

"So it would appear," I conceded. The solution to the crime appeared straightforward enough, but one or two things did not seem right. The first was John Bootle's strange behaviour that morning, but the position of Jane Bootle's body also concerned me. The upturned furniture and the food thrown on the floor suggested a violent dispute, but, if the Bootles had been arguing violently, it seemed highly unlikely that Jane Bootle would have been so foolish as to turn her back on her husband – unless, of course, she was fleeing from him. If that were the case, though, surely the body would have been facing the door, not lying face down in the fire? There was also a strange smell about the Bootles' house, which went beyond the stench of burning flesh and which I could not quite place.

The other thing which concerned me was that John Bootle possessed a fowling gun, and it was such a weapon that had been pointed at Lawrence Seaman and myself the night before. Could it be that John Bootle had fired the shots at me? And, if so, why? Then it occurred to me that I only had Lawrence Seaman's word for the fact that we had been shot at with a fowling gun. I had not seen the assailant myself. It was, therefore, also possible that Lawrence was lying to me.

It also crossed my mind that Lawrence Seaman and William Bootle had no alibis for that morning. I decided I needed to speak to the vicar, William Nutt, alone, and so I dispatched Seaman and Bootle to find the coroner and a constable. Faced with an apparently obvious solution, the local officials would, no doubt, take the easy option and proclaim that John Bootle had murdered his wife and subsequently committed suicide. As I have mentioned, I was not so sure about this myself, but I figured it would be easier to conduct my own investigations if the coroner and the local constable finished their business with the minimum of fuss and left me alone to my work.

As soon as William Bootle had disappeared, I looked more closely at the body of his brother. I studied the entry and exit wounds on Bootle's throat and skull and smelled the area around the mouth and throat. I then had a closer look at the blood marks on the butt of the fowling gun. Satisfied with my findings, I turned my attention to the vicar, who had finished praying and was beginning to look like he wanted to leave.

"You have been a minister for how long, Reverend Nutt?" I asked.

"Nigh on twenty years," replied Nutt.

"Then you will know the people around here well," I

said. "What can you tell me about the Bootles?"

"I've known them many years," said Nutt. "John is – was the elder brother, honest and hard-working, but not particularly ambitious. He became a fowler and worked for a while on the Earl of Derby's estate. William is the brighter of the two and aspired to greater things. Jane Seaman and William Bootle were close friends when they were younger, and it was he who introduced John to Jane. I married them myself many years ago.

"And there are no children?" I asked.

"None that lived. There was one daughter who died in infancy and another stillborn, but nothing since then."

"And Lawrence Seaman – how well do you know him?"

"Barely. His family is from Chester, but I have known him this past year. John introduced me to him as his nephew. He seems an honest man."

"That is my impression also," I admitted. "Tell me, you said you were concerned about John Bootle this morning, that his demeanour was out of character. Can you think of any reason why that might be so? Anything unusual that has happened to him recently?"

"Not really, except that Mrs Bootle's younger sister was here recently. She was here for a couple of days but departed very suddenly. Oh, and wait a minute, there was another visitor too, a young man of about twenty, a lodger, so I heard. Didn't say much, but he disappeared without a trace too. Only stayed a couple of days. Left immediately after Mrs Bootle's sister, so I heard. Perhaps there was a disagreement of some kind."

"I'm sure you are right," I said, "but do you know where I can find this young man?"

"There's been no sight of him since last Monday, but you might like to ask in the taverns. I understand he was seen in The Eagle and Child on more than one occasion."

I thanked Nutt for the information and was just about to suggest he return to the church when the door burst open and Lawrence Seaman entered with a breathless young constable called Gregson, who immediately jumped to all the conclusions I had expected him to. William Bootle turned up a few minutes later with the coroner, and, after answering a few perfunctory questions and advising both officials where I could be contacted, Alexander and I took our leave, giving the excuse that we did not wish to intrude on the private grief of the Bootles' nearest relatives.

We walked back the way we had come, up Moor Street and past The Ship Inn, where I had been shot at the previous evening, past the mill at Greetby, and on to New Park House. A cooling spring rain had fallen, soaking the fields and reflecting soft rays of sunlight off the imposing walls of Lathom House in the near distance. It was a freshness which was a welcome contrast from the horrors of the Bootles' front room, and it nearly, but not quite, washed away the smell of burned flesh from my nostrils.

"Death has a smell which is hard to shift," I said, as we approached New Park House.

"Aye, that's the truth of it," said Alexander, "but that woman's pottage was fairly pungent too. No wonder her husband saw fit to deposit it over the floor."

I looked at Alexander sharply and then smiled gratefully, returning to my deliberations with satisfaction. He had noticed it as well.

I now knew that John Bootle had not killed his wife. Someone had killed them both. Bootle, perhaps, had died because he knew who his wife's murderer was. Perhaps, I surmised, it was the same person who had killed Katherine Seaman. Logic told me that the murders had to have something to do with William Seaman's business dealings and his supposed inheritance. The Bootles and Katherine must, I realised, have been privy to some kind of information that the murderer could not allow them to have.

But how did Edward Chisnall and William Bootle fit into the picture, I wondered? Bootle was related, at least by marriage, to all three victims, and was hated by the Earl of Derby for what the earl saw as treachery. Chisnall, meanwhile, was a loyal servant to the earl, was clearly relaying information to and from Lathom House, and had been present in Katherine Seaman's company until very shortly before her death. Although he was now presumably installed in the garrison at Lathom House, he had been able to travel to and fro freely at the time the Bootles had been murdered and would continue to be able to do so, at least until the siege works were finished.

I realised that if I were going to solve the mystery of who killed Katherine Seaman and the Bootles, a discussion with Chisnall was going to be imperative. However, with Chisnall in the enemy ranks and showing no small degree of suspicion towards myself, I had no idea how I was going to achieve that. Little did I know that providence would intervene, and the opportunity would come sooner than I expected.

Chapter 18

Lathom House – Monday March 11th, 1644

On the Monday, Alexander and I were both conscious of the fact that we would once again be required to help with the construction of the siege works, and so we rose late and ate a hearty breakfast of bread, butter, smoked ham, and eggs, before making our way over to the main camp.

Taking a route to the north of the house, we walked along a narrow lane, which passed by a small stone chapel, from where we could see that work on the trenches had progressed some way during our absence. Impressive-looking sconces had been built at intervals around the walls and reached as far as the north-west corner of the house, more or less in line with where we were standing. Fortified by earthen ramparts secured with gabions and protected with wooden stakes, the sconces would provide solid placements for the siege guns that Morgan had been promised. However, despite the progress, the trenches and earthen walls still only stretched halfway around the house. With most of the northern half of the siege works still not begun, it was becoming clear that it would take at least a week for Lady Charlotte and her garrison to be completely enclosed.

Most of the construction work, I noted, was being carried out inside the sconces and behind the outer earthen wall, well beyond danger. Some limited work was being done on the ditch and earthen wall that made up the central ring of defences, but because this was located at the edge of effective musket range, workers still took the precaution of carrying wooden screens to protect themselves against any of the practised marksmen stationed on the towers.

As we surveyed the scene, I was momentarily distracted by a sudden movement on the periphery of my vision. I swung round to my left just in time to see a small, waif-like figure disappearing into a copse of trees about a hundred yards away. I could not tell how long the figure had been there, for I had been concentrating on the nearest of the sconces, where a group of men were engaged in trying to transport baskets of earth down a connecting trench for use in the construction of the outer wall. However, in focussing my eyes on a gap in the distant trees, I was surprised to see a black and white sheepdog appear and make its way purposefully through the fields to the left of the partially dug earthworks until it reached a postern gate in the walls of the house. As the animal approached the walls, the gate opened slightly and a furtive-looking figure beckoned the dog inside.

I looked at Alexander in amazement. Was this how information was being passed into the house? And who was the waif-like figure who had disappeared into the woods? We hastened as quick as we could towards the gap in the trees, but, as expected, there was nothing to be seen. By now we were only a few yards from the main camp, so we descended into the valley and sought out Major Robinson, who, to my relief, once again gave me leave during the hours of daylight to conduct my investigations as I saw fit.

I was grateful to Robinson, who struck me as an efficient and understanding officer, which was more than could be said for many of the other officers with whom I spoke. The most interesting, and in some ways disturbing, of these was Captain Ashurst, who appeared strangely naïve, continually insisting that his childhood friend Rutter must have been telling the truth about the garrison's lack of ability to withstand a siege. To be fair, Ashurst appeared somewhat distracted during our discussion, as he had just returned from delivering final surrender terms to Lady Derby, who had, by all accounts, dismissed them out of hand. As he was first choice to be given the task of delivering such a message, Ashurst seemed the officer under Rigby's command who was held in the highest regard by the garrison, which made sense given that Ashurst's report of his conversation with Rutter was the basis for the whole military approach at Lathom – to lay a siege rather than storm the house. If Ashurst's intelligence proved itself to be wrong, then he had to be high among the suspects for the spy in Rigby's ranks.

The other officer who attracted my attention was Captain Dandie, the father of the young lieutenant who had been captured by the garrison in February and subsequently released. He was also disconcertingly evasive in his answers to my questions, to the point where I began to wonder whether the officer's reticence was due to his natural mistrust in me as one of Sir William Brereton's men or whether something more sinister was at play.

The man I most wanted to speak to that morning was Thomas Morgan, the diminutive Welshman in charge of the artillery. I found him in the very sconce which I had been looking at earlier. With no cannon to deploy, he was busying himself by making sure enough gun placements were ready for when the promised siege cannon eventually arrived.

The major, I felt sure, had seen me weaving my way through the trenches, trying manfully to avoid the queues of sweating, cursing labourers hauling bucketloads of earth for use in the outer breastworks, for his immaculately groomed moustache twitched in irritation as I approached. His eyes, however, remained fixed on the team of surly farm hands, who were being instructed in how to level the earth in preparation for the installation of the, as yet, non-existent siege cannon. Several planks of wood had been brought into the sconce and laid next to one of the earth-filled gabions, which would protect the artillery gunners from attack. The planks, I realised, were for the construction of a gun platform, to protect the heavy gun carriages from sinking into the earth.

"Prynhawn da," I said, by way of greeting. It was enough to gain Morgan's attention. The major looked at me with a modicum of surprise, but appeared by no means displeased that I had addressed him in Welsh.

"Ah, Mr Cheswis. Doeddwn i ddim yn gwybod eich bod yn siarad Cymraeg. I didn't know you spoke Welsh."

"Only a few words, I'm afraid," I explained, apologetically. "We have many Welsh traders come to Nantwich and it pays to be able to speak to a man in his own language. I hear from your voice that you are a native Welsh speaker."

"That much is true," said Morgan. "I learned English only in my teenage years. But you are not here to exchange pleasantries with me in Welsh, I'll wager. As you can see, I have a gun placement to construct, so if you have something to ask me, it would be appreciated if you kept it brief. If it is with regard to the murder of Sir William Brereton's informant, then I'm afraid I will be of little help, although I understand you are now seeking a triple murderer."

"News travels fast, Major," I acknowledged.

"You should not be surprised at that. These new deaths are the talk of Ormskirk. The latest victims, I understand, are related to Captain Bootle and Lieutenant Seaman, though. They have nothing to do with me. I fail to see how I can be of assistance."

"I am merely trying to understand the relationships between the various officers under Colonel Rigby's command, to see if I can learn anything," I replied, through slightly gritted teeth. "Tell me, you seem rather dissatisfied with progress so far."

Morgan laughed sardonically. "That would be an understatement, sir. The trenches are being dug too slowly, we have no cannon in place, little ammunition, and even if we did, the terrain here precludes us from targeting the vulnerable part of their walls. What we need is a mortar and there is no sign of that. And if that were not enough, our negotiators are making no progress with Lady Derby. She is playing us all for fools, and all because Sir Thomas Fairfax would not have us play rough with a woman."

"Lady Derby seems a formidable opponent," I agreed.

"Stubborn is the word I would use," said Morgan, in a tone which betrayed more than a hint of malice. "She will not listen to reason, even from her own people. Yesterday, six gentlemen of good standing petitioned her with a view to persuading her to surrender the

214

house for the good of the population hereabouts, but she sent them on their way. She thought their pleas were part of a plot cooked up by Colonel Rigby, so I believe."

"And you say it wasn't?"

"Of course not. The local gentry need no persuasion around these parts. Think about it. Lady Derby has consistently called on the local population for support, not just for manning the garrison but for supplying arms and victuals. That is understandable, for people in Ormskirk have supported the House of Stanley for generations. However, now they are forced to support Parliament also. Local traders are expected to supply us with goods against promissory notes, which may never be honoured, and at the same time they are punished if they sell to the garrison. It is no surprise that local gentlemen wish to avoid a prolonged siege here."

"So what happened?" I asked.

"Lady Derby told them to address their petition to us, the real despoilers of the country, as she called us. That woman will bring about her own downfall with her arrogance, you will see. Unless, of course, Mr Browne continues to play into her hands as he has done so far."

"Mr Browne?" I said in bewilderment. "What do you mean?"

"You mean you haven't noticed?" sneered Morgan.

"If you want my opinion, Browne is either an incompetent, or his loyalties are not quite where they should be. Take a look at these siege works, Mr Cheswis, and what do you see?"

I cast my eye over the scene before me, the serrated trench which sliced through the earth like an ugly scar just yards from the wall, the mounds of earth piled up to create breastworks, and the swarms of soldiers and labourers bent double in the trenches trying to avoid the attention of the sentries and marksmen on Lathom's watch towers. I noticed with interest that Browne's much-vaunted testudo was now in operation: a huge contraption on wheels, spanning the breadth of the inner ditch, which appeared to be providing the workers much better protection as they dug.

"I see a lot of people digging furiously," I said, not quite understanding what Morgan was alluding to.

"Precisely, and all of them having to protect themselves with wooden screens. Browne has built the inner trench far too close to the walls. It lies only sixty yards away from Lady Derby's musketeers, which makes its occupants little more than sitting targets. Many men will die here, mark my words."

I nodded slowly, in realisation that Morgan was right. Even when the earthworks were complete, the marksmen on the towers would be able to bide their time and target anyone careless enough to reveal themselves to the enemy – and for what? In a siege, the primary aim was to keep the defenders in, and that could be done just as effectively from a greater distance.

"And then he talks about draining the moat and their wells," continued Morgan. "Has he not realised that Lathom House sits in a bowl and that water does not flow uphill? Apart from which, their well is deep and the moat is right next to the walls. Any attempt to dig there would be suicide."

"Are you saying that Browne is not all he seems to be?" I asked.

"That he is deliberately working against us, you mean? I cannot say that, Mr Cheswis. I can only say that, so far, his performance does not fill me with confidence. Make of that what you will."

I contemplated Morgan's words with interest. Browne was certainly close enough to the military command to have access to the kind of information that had been passed to Lady Derby. He could have been in league with one of the other officers: Ashurst or Dandie, perhaps. It was then that I remembered that Browne had been present in The Ship Inn the previous evening. If there was a connection between the three murders and the spy within Rigby's camp, did that not make Browne a prime suspect too, along with Chisnall, Ashurst, and Dandie? I did not remember seeing Browne when I left the tavern. He could, I reasoned, easily have been lurking in the shadows outside, waiting to shoot me.

I thanked Morgan for his thoughts and had just begun to walk back slowly to the main camp when I happened to glance across the moor-like ground towards the postern gate. There, padding its way in between heather and bracken, was the same black and white dog I had seen earlier, this time going in the opposite direction.

Quickening my steps, I ran through the connecting trench, climbed the outer earthen wall, and headed directly for the stone chapel from where I had seen the dog earlier that day. Just as I reached the narrow lane, the animal disappeared from sight between two tall alder trees. Heading straight for the copse, I began to wade through long grass, towards a natural clearing in the trees. There was no sign of the dog, but I noticed that the grass and undergrowth around the clearing appeared to have been disturbed.

I could see nothing, but I had the strange sensation that unseen eyes were watching me. I scanned the undergrowth for signs of movement but quickly realised I was wasting my time, and, sighing with exasperation, I turned to retrace my steps. As I did so, I nearly jumped out of my skin, for barring the way was a slip of a girl, aged no more than twelve, carrying a wicker basket laden with herbs and flowers. Next to her was the dog, which nuzzled into the girl's skirts as she stroked the animal on the head.

"Is the dog yours?" I asked, trying hard to smile so as not to unnerve the girl.

"Who's asking?" demanded the girl.

"My name's Mr Cheswis," I said. "I was just walking along the lane-"

"Are you one of the roundheads who wants to kill my brother?"

"I'm no soldier, miss," I said, somewhat taken aback by the directness of the response. "Why would I want to kill your brother?"

"There's plenty as do. He normally minds his own business working in the earl's deer park, but now they want to shoot him, leastways that's what me mam said...an' they killed her too these past days."

A flash of recognition went off in my brain and I took a closer look at the girl. Thin, almost to the point of emaciation, she had long, straggly brown hair, but clear, piercing eyes that betrayed a sharp intellect. She looked and smelled like she could do with a bath, and her faded green skirt and shift looked like they had seen better days, but who was I to judge? If she was who I thought, she needed help, not persecution.

"Your mother?" I enquired. "You wouldn't be young Jenny Reade, by any chance?"

"Aye, that's me, mister. How do you know that?"

"Let's just say I heard what happened to your mother. I'm sorry about that. What are you doing in the woods, Jenny?"

"Gathering herbs and foraging for what food I can," said the girl, who now looked at me with suspicion. "Why are you asking me this?"

"No reason," I said, "but here's a shilling. Go and buy your family some food."

Jenny's palm closed on the coin but she didn't move. "Why would you give me this, mister?" she asked. "I don't know you."

I didn't answer, but I wasn't given the chance to either, for Jenny immediately pocketed the money and headed off out of the clearing, back onto the roadway, closely followed by the dog. Just before she disappeared behind a clump of trees, she stopped as though she had forgotten something.

"An' just in case you were wondering, the dog isn't mine," she shouted over her shoulder. "It just likes following me."

Chapter 19

Lathom House – Monday March 11ᵗʰ, 1644

It was four in the morning when they came. It was a dark night, cloudy, overcast, and with a hint of drizzle in the air. Those of us positioned in the inner trench were finding it a struggle to keep our matches dry and wishing we had carbines or pistols to fall back on. It was nearing the end of our watch, and most of us were hunkered down with our backs to the inner wall of the ditch, waiting for the signal that would allow us to swap places with the next group of musketeers tasked with guarding our defences. An occasional glance through the loop holes towards the moat revealed nothing. There seemed to be little activity on the walls of the house, although, in truth, it was too dark to see clearly.

I had considered myself fortunate in avoiding digging duty that night. Rigby's captains had performed miracles during the afternoon, and what seemed like hundreds of locals had been pressed into action, most of them labouring in the trenches, which were slowly and inexorably creeping their way around the northern perimeter of the house. Having been trained as a musketeer, I was allocated a position in the inner trench to the south-west of the house, not far to the left of the main gates. Alexander was positioned a few yards to my left, and so, in between checking the loop holes for signs of movement, we were able to discuss what we had found out during the course of the day.

My friend, it turned out, had been fortunate in that he had been seconded to help deal with the influx of labour brought in from Ormskirk and the surrounding countryside, which meant that he was able to carry out brief discussions with the remainder of Rigby's captains, as well as with a number of local farmers and tradesmen.

Particularly useful was the confirmation that Captains Davie, Duddell, and Sharples were all from the Amounderness Hundred north of Preston. This meant they had few, if any, contacts locally and less opportunity to gain access to strategic information than the colonel's other officers. This, in my view, made all three unlikely candidates for the spy in Rigby's ranks.

What concerned me above all, though, was that I was faced with two ostensibly separate tasks, which appeared to becoming intertwined, perhaps unnecessarily so. On the face of it, there was no firm evidence to support the theory that there was a connection between Lady Derby's informant and the murderer of Katherine Seaman and the Bootles, and yet

I was being drawn inexorably towards that conclusion. How could that be so, I asked myself. Whether it was mere intuition that was drawing me in this direction, I did not know.

However, there were, I reasoned, several links connecting the two cases. The first of these, quite obviously, was the royalist officer Edward Chisnall, who knew the Seaman family and was present in Seaman's house until very shortly before Katherine Seaman's death. Chisnall was quite clearly relaying information to and from the Earl of Derby and was even now ensconced behind the walls of Lathom House.

The second connection was the Bootle family. Both William and John Bootle had been employed in the Earl of Derby's household and Katherine Seaman had been staying with her sister, Jane Bootle, until a few days before her death. But William Bootle, now in the service of Parliament, was considered a traitor by the Earl of Derby. So how, if at all, were they connected?

And then there was the unproven status of William Seaman, friends with Chisnall and a close business associate of Sir Francis Gamull, himself a leading royalist, and Robert Whitby. What did William Seaman's expected inheritance from Henry Oulton's business in France and Spain have to do with this affair? I was at a loss to know.

One thing, however, was certain. Until the siege

works around Lathom House were complete, it would be relatively easy to smuggle information into and out of the house, as proven by the ease with which Chisnall was able to move around, and by the case of Mary Reade, whose daughter, Jenny, even now appeared to be communicating with the house with the help of her dog.

Assuming that the four main parliamentary commanders, Assheton, Egerton, Moore, and Rigby could be eliminated from suspicion, there were, I reasoned, nine officers and civilians with close enough connections to Parliament's military command to be considered potential suspects for the role of informant. These were the two majors, Morgan and Robinson, the engineer Browne, and the six captains: Ashurst, Bootle, Dandie, Davie, Duddell, and Sharples. Assuming that the last three and Robinson were unlikely candidates, that left five; Ashurst, well known in the area, trusted by the royalists and responsible, at least in part, for the strategy of besieging rather than attacking the house; Bootle, erstwhile servant of the Earl of Derby, knowledgeable about the layout of the house but considered a traitor and hated by the earl's household; Browne, the unpopular engineer, accused of constructing the siege works too slowly and of building them too close to the house; Dandie, father of the lieutenant who had been captured by the garrison and who had, therefore, had access to Lady Derby, and Morgan, the small, arrogant Welshman, head of artillery and overly critical about the siege plans.

The issue of the murders was even more complicated. All I had to go on was a plethora of unanswered questions. How were Sir Francis Gamull and Robert Whitby involved, and how important was Henry Oulton's will? Why did Katherine Seaman go back to Chester from Ormskirk, and, if Katherine and the Bootles had died because of it, why specifically choose to kill them – people who were relatively low in the line of inheritance? Why was Katherine so shocked to see Chisnall in Seaman's shop in Chester? Why did the murderer of the Bootles try to make it look as though John Bootle had committed the murder and subsequently committed suicide? Who was the mysterious guest staying with the Bootles, and why had he disappeared? And finally, was the person with the fowling gun outside The Ship Inn aiming at me or at Lawrence Seaman?

It seemed an impossible series of conundrums, a profusion of dead ends leading only to more questions, but it was a puzzle on which I would have willingly dwelt a little longer, were it not for what happened next. I was watching Alexander, who was sat a few yards away, his head drooped over his knees, seemingly asleep. I picked up a small stone from the floor of the trench and was about to toss it in my friend's direction, when he jerked awake, shaken from his reverie by an outburst of angry shouting not thirty yards away. Almost immediately, I heard the unmistakeable crack of musket and carbine fire, multiple shots, one after the other, accompanied by screams and more frenzied shouting. I jumped to my feet and peered through my loop hole. What I saw chilled me to the bone.

Through the gloom, I could make out at least twenty glowing matches and many more shadowy figures creeping their way across the ground to my left. A good many of them were stood by the edge of the trench and were firing into it.

"God's teeth, Daniel," rasped Alexander. "We are under attack. There are scores of them!"

In truth, it was too dark to see exactly how many royalists were approaching our lines, but it was clear that they had skilfully used the advantage of surprise to panic the mixture of labourers and guards gathered further down the trench. I glanced over the rear of the trench and saw that a number of men had jumped out of the trench and were fleeing towards the outer breastworks. Several of them had forgotten that the central ditch lay between them and safety, and at least two of them clambered over mounds of earth only to plummet into the darkness, howling with pain as they landed awkwardly in the three foot trench. They were the lucky ones.

A rumble of hooves signalled the arrival of a small troop of horse, perhaps ten strong, who entered the fray from around the side of the house, having clearly exited from the postern gate, passing in front of the stone chapel. Those men who had been foolhardy enough to escape from the trench on the inside froze in their tracks, and I watched in horror as one after the other was cut down with swords and carbine fire.

Through the melee, I heard a harsh Scottish voice barking orders at the rows of royalist attackers, and for a brief moment it reminded me of Major Lothian, the parliamentary officer who had been captured by Lord Byron's forces near Nantwich during the previous winter's siege.

Suddenly, Alexander and I were spurred into action by the sight of four men fleeing towards us down the trench.

"Quick, run for your lives," yelled one of them. "They are trying to kill us."

I glanced back over my shoulder at two musketeers further down the line gesturing to us to follow them.

"Don't get out of the trench," said one. "That's what the bastards want. Keep your heads low and follow us. We'll escape down the connecting trench the other side of the main gates."

Stumbling after him, we weaved our way through the darkness along the trench, which veered off every few yards, first to the left and then to the right. One of the labourers ignored the musketeers and clambered out of the trench, aiming to run towards the outer breastworks. He had barely gone five yards when a flash and a crack from among the swirling horsemen was followed by a guttural scream, and the man fell forward onto his face, remaining motionless.

Ahead of us, the two musketeers led the way silently through the trench, the sound of gunfire receding behind us.

"They don't want to venture too far," hissed one of the musketeers. "We'll be safe now, if we keep-"

It was the last word he ever spoke, for, as he rounded the next turn in the trench, there was a sharp volley of gunfire, and his head jerked suddenly back, strangling his final word. A soft wet spray spattered against my face as the man fell backwards into Alexander, almost knocking him over. My shoulders tightened as I fought back the panic rising in my stomach. Ahead of us in the trench was a group of four musketeers, two kneeling and two standing, all with their weapons trained on us. On the edge of the trench stood several more. We were trapped and there was no way of escape. There was only one thing to do.

"Quarter," I yelled, at the top of my voice, and, sinking to my knees with my hands in the air, I entrusted God with the task of deciding whether I lived or died.

Chapter 20

Chester – Thursday March 7ᵗʰ – Monday March 11ᵗʰ, 1644

*S*imon hobbled down the alleyway towards the glover's workshop belonging to Jack Taylor, pain shooting through his ankle like red hot daggers. Behind him he heard the sharp report of musket fire. He thought briefly of Daniel and Alexander, but he had no time to stop. Staggering into Taylor's yard, he crashed like a dead weight straight through the door of the workshop and collapsed in a heap on the floor.

"Help me, Jack," he breathed, through gritted teeth. "I think I've broken my ankle."

Taylor rushed over to where Simon was lying and hoisted him to his feet. "What happened?" asked the glover, breathing heavily as he supported Simon's weight.

"We've been betrayed. Never mind how. We've no time. Where can I hide, Jack? If the bastards find me, they'll shoot me, and that's the truth of it."

Taylor gestured towards a murky corner of the workshop, where a pile of hides was being stored against the wall.

"Over there," he urged. "Lie down against the wall, and I'll cover you with hides. But whatever you do, don't move. I'll come and get you when the coast is clear."

Meanwhile, inside a workers' cottage on Bunce Lane, Roisin Byrne was saying a quiet prayer in thanks for her good fortune. Jem Bressy had recognised her from The Boot, but fortunately he had not seen her with Simon. To her surprise, she had been able to persuade Bressy that she had sent the two parliamentary spies packing.

"They're away across the fields towards Black Friars," she said, "and good riddance too. If you're quick you may catch them, but then again, you might not."

"They will not get far," said Bressy, his piercing eyes studying Roisin for any hint of treachery. "There is little point to them leaving by the Watergate. Their horses will be being kept somewhere on Eastgate or Foregate. They will need to leave the city by that route in order to return to Nantwich, so we will simply wait for them by The Boot."

Roisin bit her lip in concern. She had no inkling that Bressy and his men had been watching Simon's brother and his friend, but there was little she could do about it now. She had helped them the best she could, and they would have to rely on their own stealth and *cunning to escape Bressy's clutches.*

Roisin waited patiently until she heard the sound of the eleven o'clock bells from the cathedral. When she was sure that Bressy and his men were no longer around, she tucked her auburn hair inside her coif, crossed herself, and marched out of the front door, down Bunce Lane and into Jack Taylor's yard.

As it happened, Roisin's moon-shaped, freckled face was the first thing that Simon saw when the thin layer of calf skins was removed from above his head. It was a sight he would see much of during the coming five days. Simon's knees had begun to stiffen up due to his cramped position, and his ankle was throbbing painfully. Nonetheless, Roisin, with the help of a stick provided by Jack Taylor, managed to push and cajole Simon back up Bunce Lane to her cottage, where she fed him and provided him with shelter and protection while his ankle healed.

Roisin, he learned, had come over from Ireland with her family several years previously to sell skins and hides to the leather trade. Jack Taylor had been one of the family's first customers. However, her mother had died in childbirth and her father and two brothers had succumbed to the sweating sickness not six months previously. Left alone, with no means to support herself, becoming a whore, she explained, was the only way to earn a living.

Simon had felt a pang of guilt when she had told him

231

her name that night in The Boot, but he found himself strongly attracted to her. He had to lie low when she left every day to work in The Boot and was surprised to experience feelings of jealousy and disgust when she came back smelling of other men.

"You don't need to be a whore, Roisin," he said, one evening.

"Who do you think you are?" she replied, venomously. "It's my life. You have no right to sit in my house and tell me what I can and can't do." For some reason, he didn't tell her about Rose Bailey.

Simon's ankle, it transpired, was not broken; he had merely twisted it, and so within a few days, once the swelling had subsided, he was able to get about the house unaided.

Simon was half-expecting Jem Bressy to pay Roisin another visit, but by the time the weekend had passed, it was becoming clear that he was not returning, having assumed that Simon had escaped across the Dee. To his relief, Roisin, despite asking in all the right places, had been unable to report any arrests on the previous Thursday, and so he was fairly certain that Daniel and Alexander had also managed to evade capture.

By the following Monday, Simon was able to walk without limping and was becoming impatient to be on his way. Having endured five days of Roisin's company, the novelty was beginning to wear a little thin. Her mood had become increasingly grumpy, and when he had asked her why she was helping to conceal him from the royalists, he had received little more than a sulky shrug in response. Therefore, when he heard on the Monday morning that Prince Rupert was due to ride into town, he took the opportunity to escape the claustrophobic confines of Roisin's cottage in order to see the legendary Prince Robber for himself.

Before he left the house, he shaved and cut his hair short in the Puritan style, as a precaution against being recognised. He then walked up towards the cross, where he found the streets crammed with curious onlookers and lined with respectful soldiers. In front of the Pentice, a number of civil dignitaries stood patiently awaiting the prince, all dressed formally in the robes of their various offices: the justices of the peace in red, the town aldermen in mulberry. At one point, a coach drew up in front of the building and the portly figure of Randle Holmes, the mayor, stepped out and hobbled up to the entrance.

Rupert had taken a week to march from Shrewsbury. After winning a small skirmish at Market Drayton, defeating forces under the command of Sir William Fairfax and Colonel Mytton, he had marched on Chester, bringing three hundred horse and six hundred foot with him. Dressed in black armour with black and gold shoulder plates, a white necktie, and sporting a crimson scarf fastened at the shoulder with a gold clasp, he cut an impressive figure. Next to him rode

Lord Byron, and perched in front of the prince, on the back of his horse, was the unusual sight of Rupert's white poodle, Boye.

"They say the dog is bewitched," whispered the man stood next to Simon in the crowd. Simon turned to his left and recognised one of the shoemakers he had visited the previous week.

"Aye, that would not surprise me," whispered Simon.

When Rupert arrived at the Pentice, he dismounted and was addressed by the mayor, who gave a welcoming speech.

"Your highness is welcome among us to enjoy what poor entertainment we are able to give," announced Holmes. "This is not what your highness deserves," he added, "but it is all we are able to muster given the reduced state of our city. With this in mind, we would beseech your highness to ease the burden placed on our citizens due to the free billeting of soldiers in our houses, which has become very burdensome to us-"

"He speaks well," said the shoemaker. "The city cannot afford to support so many men without adequate recompense."

Simon nodded in agreement. "There is no doubt about that," he said, "but do you really think that will happen? Is it not more likely that the prince will strip the city of men and victuals and then march away somewhere else without a second thought?"

If Simon regretted his words, he had little time

to think about it, for no sooner had he spoken than several pairs of arms fastened themselves around himself and the shoemaker, and both were hauled unceremoniously through the crowds and out of sight down a side street.

"Those are the words of a traitor," spat a voice from behind him as he was thrust up against a wall. Simon glanced over his shoulder and realised that he and the shoemaker had been accosted by a captain and three well-built redcoats, who were now eyeing him with suspicion. He was about to defend himself, when his attention was distracted by the sight of a red-haired female figure, which suddenly appeared, as if out of nowhere, and launched herself at the captain, catching him on the side of the face with a glancing blow, which left an angry scratch on his cheek.

"You leave my brother Conor alone," screamed Roisin, her arms wheeling like a windmill. "He's done nothing to you."

"Sweet Jesus," hissed the captain, putting one hand to his cheek and defending his face with the other. "Someone grab a hold of this mad fucking strumpet, would you?"

The two men holding the shoemaker promptly let go of their captive and grabbed Roisin by the arms, pinning her against the wall. The shoemaker, meanwhile, took advantage of the confusion and disappeared promptly round the corner and into the crowds.

"So the whore is your sister?" asked the captain, once Roisin had been subdued. Simon thought about this for a moment, but only for a second, for to deny it would only have resulted in more questions.

"Aye, sir," he replied, in his best Irish accent.

The captain looked at Simon with a contemptuous smile. "What do they call you, Irishman?" he demanded.

"Conor Byrne, sir," he replied. There was no going back now.

"Well, Conor Byrne," said the captain, "you are coming with us and you can find out at first-hand what it's like to serve your king and your prince with respect."

"No, you bastards," screamed Roisin, struggling and aiming a kick at the shins of one of the redcoats. "You can't take him."

"I think you'll find we can," replied the captain. "Now get you home before we find a secure gaol cell for you instead."

"Go home, Roisin," urged Simon, as he was marched down the alleyway. "It will be alright." Straining his neck, the last view he had of Roisin was of her sprawling in the dust and howling disconsolately where the redcoats had thrown her. Simon did the hardest thing he had done since his arrival in Chester. He turned his back on Roisin and marched into the service of Prince Rupert of the Rhine.

Chapter 21

Lathom House – Tuesday March 12th, 1644

"I find it difficult to believe you are here quite by accident, Mr Cheswis," said the corpulent, balding cleric, who had introduced himself as the Reverend Samuel Rutter. With a thin smile, he moved closer to the chair to which I had been tied and put his face close enough to mine so that I could smell his breath. "Perhaps you would care to elucidate."

I was sat in a strong room half way up the Eagle Tower. There were two other people in the room besides Rutter and myself: a distinguished-looking gentleman with grey hair called Farrington had positioned himself by the door, whilst behind Rutter, by the far wall, stood the familiar figure of Edward Chisnall, wearing a thinly disguised expression of contempt.

It was Chisnall who had picked me out from among my fellow prisoners as we were being led across one of Lathom House's many courtyards by my captor, a young captain named Ogle, who had treated us with civility, stopping his men from shooting us on the grounds that he had received similar courteous treatment at Kineton Fight, where he, himself, had been taken prisoner. He was, he explained, anxious to return the favour.

Chisnall, on the other hand, promptly separated me from the others and had me marched directly to the cell in which I now sat.

"As Mr Chisnall is perfectly well aware, I am a long-time acquaintance of a Chester merchant named William Seaman," I said, exaggerating the extent of my relationship with Seaman somewhat. "I am here as a personal favour to represent him in a family matter. I suspect your captain is also aware of the matter of which I speak."

Chisnall snorted with incredulity. "Do not dissemble with us, sirrah," he said, coldly. "I advise you to speak the truth. How can it be that a Nantwich man with limited credentials can be seen dining in Chester with prominent royalists one day, only to be found encamped outside Lathom House, miles from his home town, only a few days later?"

"I am here to report the death of Katherine Seaman, as you well know," I retorted. "I should perhaps be asking you what you did after leaving Mr Seaman's house last Wednesday. As for why you find me in the trenches, I was pressed into service by Colonel Rigby and his officers, as were many other people hereabouts; people, I might add, who you appear to have no compunction about killing indiscriminately."

The effect of my words on Chisnall was wholly unexpected. The expression on his face had been instantly transformed into one of confusion. "Miss Seaman is dead?" he enquired, disbelievingly, running his hand nervously through his hair.

I had no knowledge as to the extent of Chisnall's acting skills, but his reaction, I had to admit, seemed perfectly genuine.

"She was found murdered in Mr Seaman's courtyard shortly after you left, strangled with a cheese wire. You mean you were not aware of this? I had assumed that you might have something to do with it. Miss Seaman seemed both surprised and shocked to see you in Chester."

"Why in the name of God would you think that? I had no idea that such a crime had been committed. But that does not explain why you would travel-"

At this juncture, Chisnall was interrupted by Farrington, who had been looking at me curiously. "Edward, I think you are being distracted from the matter in hand," he said. "There is no evidence that this man is anything other than he says he is."

I noticed that Rutter did not seem entirely convinced, but I breathed a little easier nonetheless. Chisnall merely gave Farrington an angry glare, which the latter judiciously ignored.

"Mr Cheswis," said Farrington, "you say you had been pressed into service by Colonel Rigby, but it was Sir Thomas Fairfax who was sent to starve us out of here. I had thought he was in command."

"He was," I confirmed, "but he left several days ago. Command of the siege is now in the hands of Colonel Egerton, in conjunction with Colonels Rigby, Assheton, and Moore."

My three captors exchanged glances with one another, and I realised that this was news to them and therefore significant in that it meant that Lady Derby's spy had not been able to update Rutter on events for at least the last six days. It also showed that, prior to that, the same informant had managed to communicate to Lady Derby that Parliament planned a lengthy siege rather than an all-out assault.

What, I wondered, could have kept this person from communicating with the house for a whole week? The increased activity in building the siege works, perhaps? Or something else?

Farrington, Rutter, and Chisnall spent another hour interrogating me, asking me questions about the layout of the siege works, the relations between the commanding officers and other such things. Fortunately, the fact that I had only been at the camp for a few days allowed me to plead ignorance on most counts.

Once they had finished with me, I was led out of

the Eagle Tower, back across the courtyard, and into a room in the main building, where Alexander and the four other prisoners were being held under armed guard. Over the course of the day, all five were led away to be questioned individually. The one soldier among us, a sergeant called Greenwood, was gone nearly two hours. At one point I thought I heard a familiar male voice, which I could not place, coming from outside the room, but I thought nothing more of it and focussed instead on thoughts of Elizabeth, young Ralph, Mrs Padgett, and Amy, and wondered if I would ever find my way back to them. I wondered about Simon and whether he had been able to escape from the clutches of Jem Bressy and his thugs. I wondered about James Skinner and whether he had managed to persuade Bressy that he had not intended to flee back to Nantwich. I wondered about Thomas Corbett, arrested trying to protect me from being apprehended as a spy, and I wondered about the servant, Gibson, arrested, I was sure, for a crime he did not commit.

I suddenly realised how tired I was from a day and a night in the trenches. Amidst such thoughts, and in the certain knowledge that I would not be leaving Lathom House that day, I gave up pondering about what might yet prove to be pointless, and fell into a deep, dreamless sleep.

Chapter 22

We were freed on the Wednesday afternoon, much sooner than anticipated. The three local labourers were allowed to leave first and were told in no uncertain terms to return to their farms and their families. My suspicion that Reverend Rutter was still not sure what to make of us was confirmed by the fact that Alexander, Sergeant Greenwood, and I were made the subject of a prisoner exchange, the three of us being led out under a flag of truce and exchanged for three members of the garrison taken prisoner a few weeks previously, when Rigby's men had captured earthworks at a place called The Stand, a strategic high point a few hundred yards to the south of the house.

I was not convinced of Rigby's wisdom in agreeing to include Alexander and myself in a trade of prisoners, for it amounted to a tacit admission that we were in Rigby's employ. My fears were confirmed, for there was something about the look on Rutter's face as we were led out of the front gate that told me I would be unwise to risk capture a second time.

Upon our release, we were immediately summoned to New Park House, where we found not only Colonel Rigby waiting for us, but Assheton, Egerton, and Moore as well.

"I told you that this siege is exactly what Lady Derby wants," said Assheton, on hearing that the inhabitants of the house did not appear to be suffering unduly from a shortage of victuals. "Your man Ashurst has been duped. There is little doubt of that."

"Nonsense," said Rigby, dismissively, "but even if this were true, the cost of a direct assault on the house would be prohibitive. Hundreds would be killed. Would you want that on your conscience? No, Colonel, we may not be able to starve them out, but we will besiege them and pound them into surrender."

"Pound them with what? We do not have enough ordnance, and even if we did, we do not have the funds to purchase the powder and ammunition that we need. How do you propose we solve that?"

"I believe we have discussed this before. It is common knowledge, and I see no reason why Mr Cheswis and Mr Clowes should not hear it also," said Rigby, his voice rising a notch.

"You mean the great tax that is to be levied on the people of Lancashire to pay for this leaguer?" cut in Moore. "There are those of us, Colonel Rigby, who believe that this is illegal both in matter and manner."

"Illegal?" scoffed Rigby. "The tax has been passed by the committee, as you well know, and it will pay for the mortar shells that will reduce Lathom House to rubble. Be thankful for that, Colonel Moore."

"That is not strictly true. The money is supposed to pay for extra soldiers, and we already have ten times as many of those as they do. Why do we need more? Secondly, the tax is being raised on the whole of Lancashire with the exception of Lonsdale. I would argue that this, in itself, is illegal. A leaguer in West Derby Hundred should be paid for by West Derby alone."

"And one thing further," added Assheton. "The amount you propose to raise with this tax is almost exactly the same amount raised by Lord Derby himself under similar circumstances during the Bishops War, and you tried to have him impeached for that. What, pray, makes this tax more legal?"

The muscles in Rigby's neck twitched involuntarily with anger, and I could see him struggling to keep his emotions in check. The colonel was clearly furious, not only, I suspected, because he had disagreed with his colleagues, but because they had dared to venture their opinions in front of Alexander and myself.

It was Egerton, who seemed an altogether calmer type than his three colleagues, who stepped in to stop the argument. "Gentlemen, this is neither seemly nor constructive," he said. "I am in charge here, and my judgement is that we should continue to persecute this siege along the lines proposed by Colonel Rigby. The ordnance will be in place soon. Let us see what mood Lady Derby is in once she has felt the full weight of what our cannons can throw at her."

Assheton and Moore raised their hands in submission, but Assheton was unable to resist a final comment. "Of course you would wish to follow Colonel Rigby's proposals," he said. "You are the commanding officer of West Derby Hundred. It is in your interest that the rest of Lancashire pays for this folly. You will receive much opposition to this, I warn you," he added.

I own that I was in no small degree astounded at this open display of squabbling between the four senior officers, not just because they were not of the same mind, but because of the level of scorn I detected in Assheton's voice and the anger in Rigby's that bordered on malice. Things did not bode well for the rest of the siege, I realised, if these men could not work together.

With Egerton having asserted his authority, the talk turned to more practical matters, particularly the nature of the chain of command within the house and anything that might lead me towards identifying the informer within Rigby's ranks.

I had not forgotten the strangely familiar voice I had heard from behind the door of the room where I had been kept, but I did not mention it to Egerton. I might well have been mistaken after all, I reasoned. I was, however, able to pass on some information about the nature of command within the house, most of which, I guessed, Rigby would already be aware of as a result of the negotiations he had carried out.

Farrington and Rutter, it appeared, were Lady Derby's chief strategic advisors, although military command was in the hands of the 'Major of the House', a Scotsman named Farmer, who it turned out owned the voice I had heard barking commands to his men during the attack on our trenches. There were five other captains in the house, one of which was Chisnall, and each of these captains had a junior officer underneath him. The captains tended to alternate roles relating to the defence of the house, with the exception of one Rawsthorne, who was in charge of manning the towers and battlements and hence was in command of a number of fowlers and gamekeepers from among the house's domestic staff, as well as his own musketeers.

The defenders of the garrison were clearly both well-trained and superbly organised, and yet over the next two days they were unable to press home the advantage that they had accrued from the successful attack on our trenches. It became clear that the defenders' strategy was merely to harry and worry our own force and the labourers, who by now had worked their way around most of the northern side of the house. Like ourselves, Lady Derby's forces also seemed to be conserving their stock of powder and ammunition and were relying heavily on the skill of the marksmen on the ramparts, who were causing a steady stream of casualties among soldiers and labourers alike. The skill of Lady Derby's men was becoming ever more apparent, particularly when it became clear that Rawsthorne's musketeers were deliberately targeting the loopholes in the inner trench. Unable to see inside the trench itself, they were simply waiting until they saw someone looking through the loopholes before shooting directly into the gap. By the Thursday night, when Alexander and I were once again on duty, several musketeers had already died this way, and the feeling of nervousness among those manning the trenches was palpable.

By Friday lunchtime, however, I was once again able to turn my mind to the issue of solving the murders of Katherine Seaman and the Bootles and was somewhat irked to find out that the funerals of John and Jane Bootle had taken place whilst Alexander and I were languishing inside Lathom House. This was a shame, for I would have liked to have studied the reactions of those who had turned up for the burial.

There was, however, one resident of Ormskirk who I particularly wished to speak to. On the Friday evening, therefore, I left Alexander to his own devices and walked once more into the town. It was a bright evening, with a hint of spring in the air. Daffodils lined the edges of the woods, close to the roadside, and blossom was beginning to show on some of the trees, between which squirrels darted. Despite a lingering chill in the air, it felt as though the landscape was about to come alive, the perfect antidote to the death, mud, and misery I had left behind.

As I passed the mill at Greetby, I caught sight of a small figure half-concealed behind one of the hedgerows, and I realised it was Jenny Reade. She hid herself a little more from my gaze when she realised I had seen her, but I smiled and waved at her. The dog, I noticed, was still by her side.

The Ship Inn, meanwhile, was again full of off-duty soldiers drinking in relief that they wouldn't have to face the trenches for another two days. The tap-room was crowded, but, as expected, the person I sought was propping up the bar, emptying the dregs from a large pewter tankard.

"I remember you," said Old Isaac, as I deposited another beer in front of him. "Now why, I ask myself, would someone like you wish to ply the likes of me with ale?"

"Information," I said, with a wry smile. "My guess is that you know rather more of what is going on around you than you let on."

The old man rubbed his grubby sleeve across his mouth and chuckled. "That is shrewdly observed," he said. "Sometimes it pays to appear drunker than you really are."

"Quite so," I agreed. "You said you saw a strange

sight in the churchyard these past days. How drunk were you then, would you say?"

"At Mary Reade's grave, you mean? I were sober enough for the experience to fair loosen my bowels, I'd say. I've stayed well away from there at night since."

"You have reason to walk that way often?"

"Aye. I live up that way myself. But I've taken to walking by the road since then."

"So, if you live up that way, you will presumably have known the Bootles?"

"John and Jane Bootle?" asked Isaac. "They were no great friends, but I knew them to pass the time of day with. I were proper shocked to hear about them."

"In that case," I asked, "were you aware of a young man who was staying with them maybe a couple of weeks ago?"

Isaac nodded and took a mouthful of ale. "The French lad, you mean?" he said. "Aye, I remember him all right. He weren't here very long – a couple of nights perhaps."

"French?" I said, with surprise. "Are you sure?"

"Aye, leastways that's what he said. He was in here one night. Drunk as a lord he was, but he seemed agitated, proper worked up, like. Talked about settling a score or something like that. I didn't think much of it at the time. I couldn't understand him properly anyway. His voice were all slurred an' that."

"And what happened to him?"

"Dunno. John Bootle came in and dragged him back home. I never saw him again after that."

I was dumbfounded. Why, I asked myself, would a Frenchman, a stranger to Ormskirk, be staying with the Bootles? Could he perhaps have had some connection to Lady Derby, herself a Frenchwoman, or was he connected in some way to Seaman's business in France? Katherine Seaman had, after all, being staying with the Bootles at the same time. And what was this unspecified score that needed to be settled? There were only three people I was aware of who might know. One, William Seaman, was still in Chester, but the other two were close at hand. With a smile of determination, I thanked Isaac for his help and resolved to task Lawrence Seaman and William Bootle about the strange foreigner at the earliest possible opportunity.

Chapter 23

Lathom House – Saturday March 16th – Monday March 18th, 1644

Nothing had prepared me for the tedium of conducting a siege, not even my experience at Nantwich in January. Digging and waiting. That's all there was, save for dodging the occasional musket ball, and occasional they certainly were, for the men defending the garrison at Lathom House were not foolish enough to waste their shot. They were intent on conserving as much of it as they could.

Defending Nantwich had been different, for at least then I had had my daily business to concern me. I imagined my current situation was much as it must have been for Byron's men, camped in the snow-covered fields for days on end. At least I had my comfortable billet in New Park House to return to when I was not on duty.

On the Saturday, it rained a thin, steady drizzle that drenched the soul as well as one's clothes, and so I stayed indoors. I had heard that a messenger would be riding to London and stopping at Nantwich on the way, so I prepared a letter for Elizabeth, but found it impossible to write anything that offered any hope. Simon was missing, presumed dead, I had been dragged into investigating two murders, the perpetrator of which had tried to shoot me, I had been nearly killed in the trenches and imprisoned, there was no indication how long the proposed siege would last, I was no nearer completing the task I had been sent to Lathom for, and, as if all that were not enough, everyone who mattered either knew me for a spy or held me for one. In the end, I simply told Elizabeth that I missed her and would return as soon as I could.

Alexander, in contrast, appeared to be relishing the freedom his new role gave him. Being of a sociable disposition, he spent much of his time talking to the officers billeted at New Park House as well as trawling the taverns in Ormskirk. His time was not totally wasted, for he learned a lot about the officers under whom we served and gathered a wide range of opinion about Rigby's siege plans – much of it negative. However, he learned nothing of consequence that would aid me in our investigations.

More soldiers began to arrive, including a company from Fylde under a captain called Patterson, full of raw recruits, still wet behind the ears. Billets were increasingly hard to come by in the vicinity, and it emerged that soldiers were being housed miles away and being asked to march into Lathom every three days to complete their watch. It was no wonder that morale was low.

Colonel Rigby, meanwhile, was becoming increasingly impatient about getting the siege works completed and seemed to be constantly preoccupied with his own thoughts. Assheton, what I saw of him, was also looking more and more frustrated. He and Moore had removed themselves to Ormskirk and appeared to be slowly reducing their involvement in the whole business. Egerton was still around, ostensibly in charge, but I was getting the impression that this was Rigby's siege and its success or failure would depend on him.

Despite the boredom, Sunday evening and our next duty watch soon came around. Night alarms from Rawsthorne's musketeers were now commonplace, and, to our dismay, we once more became the target of a night raid. In fact, I was beginning to wonder whether the garrison was deliberately arranging sallies every third night in order to demoralise one of our watches. If they were, it was certainly working.

At around three in the morning, someone in the forward trench spotted burning match cord across the ground towards the stone chapel, and it quickly became apparent that a company of musketeers had exited the house by the postern gate and was attempting to surprise us. Although this time the attackers were identified before they got too close, the effect was very much the same. General panic ensued and we were forced to flee into the nearby woods, where we tried to hold our ground. The royalists mostly halted before they reached the trees, unwilling to risk being caught too far away from safety. In the gloom, I thought I saw the muscular figure of Edward Chisnall leading the raid. Several of his men fired shots into the trees, and to my right I heard a dull thud and a howl of pain as one of our men collapsed to the ground.

"Quick, get behind the trees," shouted one of our sergeants, "or they'll shoot our arses all the way to Preston."

Chisnall was busy trying to prevent his men from charging headlong into the woods, and with most he succeeded. However, I noticed that a few yards to my left, three men had failed to heed the warning and had lumbered, swords drawn, into the undergrowth, and were now bearing down on a group of four labourers, who, as far as I could see, were unarmed.

"Shoot the bastards," screamed the sergeant, aiming his carbine at the foremost of the three soldiers, who I noticed with shock was a young ensign who could have been no older than seventeen or eighteen. A volley of shots followed, most of which buried themselves in the trees or sent splinters flying through the air. One shot, however, caught the ensign on his sword arm, wheeling him round and sending him sprawling on the floor. His colleagues immediately realised they had come too far and turned on their tails, heading back towards Chisnall. The young ensign, however, struggled to his feet and stumbled off through the trees away from the house, leaving his sword in the grass where he had fallen.

"Get after him," the sergeant yelled to Alexander and me.

The young royalist sprinted between the trees, holding his arm, whilst Alexander and I lumbered after him. He was hard to catch, for he was young and fit, and we had run a good hundred yards through the trees when the young man tripped over a tree root in the dark and fell head first into a pile of nettles, landing with a groan. He pulled himself immediately to his feet and made to continue his escape, but we were already on him. Realising he was trapped, he backed himself up against a tree and held his hands in the air. I noticed that blood was seeping through his coat and down his right arm.

"Quarter," he said, breathlessly, his chin slumping onto his chest.

"What's your name, Officer?" I asked.

"Edward Halsall," said the young man. "Ensign of Foot to Captain Chisnall's company. Are you taking me for a prisoner, sir?"

I don't know what made me do it, but I shook my head and gestured towards the postern gate, which was just visible through the trees.

"Get yourself some treatment, Mr Halsall," I said.

Alexander stared at me open-mouthed. "Daniel, have you taken leave of your senses?" he breathed. "You'll have us arrested."

Alexander was right, of course; if anyone found out about this, we'd likely be in serious trouble. But there was something about the young officer's face that stopped me from changing my mind.

Halsall, however, needed no second bidding. He looked me in the eyes for a few seconds before nodding at me in gratitude and disappearing through the trees into the night.

"He was not much older than Skinner," I said to Alexander. "I couldn't shoot him or have him subjected to interrogation by Rigby. We will just have to say he was too quick for us."

Chapter 24

Lathom House – Tuesday March 19th – Wednesday March 20th, 1644

The officers' meeting at New Park House on the morning following Chisnall's night raid was a sight to behold. Assheton and Moore both remained steadfastly tight-lipped but wore faces like thunder, whilst Egerton nervously tapped his leg on the side of his chair throughout. Rigby, for his part, looked as if he were about to explode. His face had taken on a striking shade of crimson, and, finally losing patience with Browne, he commanded the engineer to redouble his efforts to complete the encirclement of the house.

As a result, for the next two days, as many labourers as he could muster were pressed into action. Despite the use of the testudo, Rawsthorne's snipers were a constant worry and the teams of exhausted diggers suffered many casualties.

By the Tuesday evening, however, the trenches were complete, and Morgan began to drag his heavy artillery into position, the first of which was a demi-cannon, which was located at the gun placement at the south-west of the house, opposite the main gates.

During this time, Alexander and I had hardly spoken. My decision to let the young ensign escape through the trees to the safety of Lathom House seemed to have shaken Alexander to the core, and for two days his demeanour was of a kind I had not seen from him before – the rigidity of posture, the anxious frown, the sideways glances – all appeared as if I had broken a bond between us that I had thought would last our whole lives. The idea that I had disturbed my friend to such an extent saddened me beyond words, but when I asked myself if, given a second chance, I would have acted differently, I found I could not swear to that.

To my relief, by Wednesday morning Alexander's behaviour seemed to be returning to normal, and so we walked over to the siege works together to report for duty, approaching from the south-west by the shortest route. When we arrived, we were met by a very strange sight indeed.

In the lee of the outer breastworks, directly in line with the gun placement, where the demi-cannon was now located, a crowd of perhaps a hundred people had gathered, mostly women, the majority of whom appeared to have dressed up for the occasion and were chattering and giggling, eyelashes fluttering. Some had even brought baskets of food with them and mats to sit on. A curiosity took hold of me and a closer look revealed that in the middle of the crowd, an animated

Colonel Rigby was holding court, flanked on either side by Browne the engineer and Major Morgan.

"Ladies and gentlemen of Lathom," boomed the colonel, "you are about to witness the downfall of the House of Babylon. In the coming days, if God is just, you will see towers fall and walls crumble. You will see the whore herself brought to her knees, and the rats and vermin who inhabit her world will come crawling out to meet God's judgement. One day, you will be able to relate to your children the fact that you bore witness to this day."

Rigby was clearly in his element. He puffed out his chest with impressive haughtiness and spoke with a zealous conviction that had his audience hanging onto his every word. I could have sworn some of the ladies in the crowd were about to swoon.

"Zounds, Daniel," said Alexander, with a look of astonishment on his face. "The man can certainly talk."

"That he can," I agreed. "The question is whether he can deliver. I'll wager we are about to find out."

"These fine earthworks," announced the colonel, sweeping his arm in a wide arc, "are the creation of our talented engineer, Mr Browne, aided by you, the people of West Derby Hundred. You can be sure that, thanks to his unrivalled engineering skills, nothing will now be able to pass into or out of Lathom House." A ripple of applause passed through the crowd, and a beaming

Browne stepped forward to receive his acclaim.

Rigby waited a few moments to allow Browne his moment of recognition before summoning Morgan to deliver his part of the sideshow.

"People of Lathom," said the Welshman, "today you will see our ordnance begin to go to work on Lady Derby's defences. On the gun placement in the inner ring of the earthworks you will see we have mounted the first of our two major guns, a demi-cannon."

Necks spun round towards the three-strong team of gunners a hundred and fifty yards away, who saluted in response to a raised arm from Morgan.

"Our demi-cannon," explained Morgan, "is a six and a half inch calibre piece weighing six thousand pounds. It has a ten foot barrel and can fire a twenty-four pound cannonball. As you can see, the gunner has two assistants. On his right, the first assistant is responsible for handling the ladle and the sponge, used for inserting powder into the barrel and for cleaning it. He is also charged with preparing the shot. The assistant on the left is in charge of the wadding, the rammer, and also fetches the budge barrel containing the powder."

I was not sure how many of Morgan's audience understood the technicalities of what the Welshman was saying. Nevertheless, they all looked over to where the team was working rapidly to prepare the gun for firing. The first assistant began by inserting the sponge, a long rod with a sheepskin head moistened with water in order to put out any remaining embers and prevent premature explosions. He then filled the ladle with powder and inserted it into the barrel. Once this was done, the second assistant used his rammer to push the powder to the bottom of the gun barrel. He then put in one of two wads of straw, which he had tied behind the wheels of the gun carriage to stop them blowing away in the wind.

The shot was then checked by the gunner and the first assistant before being inserted carefully into the barrel. Finally, the second assistant inserted another wad, before thrusting it home with the rammer.

"The gunner must now gauge his piece," continued Morgan. "That is to say he must make sure that the gun is aligned correctly. Once he is satisfied, he will fill up the vent with priming powder and check there is a clear line to the main charge."

After a minute's pause, the gunner stepped back and raised his hand in the air. Suddenly, there was a blinding flash, followed a split second later by a resounding boom. Women squealed and put their hands over their ears. The cannonball flew at a low trajectory towards the house and buried itself into the wall with a crunch, sending a huge cloud of dust flying into the air.

Raucous cheers emanated from the forward trench. Fists were shaken and insults hurled at the snipers in the towers and on the walls. A few stones crumbled, but once the dust had dissipated, it became clear that the cannonball had done precious little damage.

"That's strange," said Alexander. "I thought cannonballs that size were supposed to break up walls like these."

"They are," I said, "but the walls are so old that the rock will probably only crumble. Only new stone will crack in the way you mention. Apart from which, Lady Derby's men will have been building up earth banks behind the walls. It will take more than a few cannonballs to break through them. Look at Browne," I added, "he is an engineer. He knows it."

In fact, both Browne and Morgan had noticed the problem and were trying to attract the attention of Rigby, who seemed oblivious to the lack of damage caused by the first cannonball and was continuing to play to the crowds. Eventually, though, Browne managed to draw the colonel away from his audience for a moment. When they had finished talking, Rigby addressed the crowd.

"Ladies and gentlemen," he announced, "Mr Browne and Major Morgan wish to provide you with more sport and a more spectacular outcome. Our gunners, therefore, will now target the towers, so there will be a brief pause, whilst our gunner resets the angles on our demi-cannon."

"I knew it," breathed Alexander. "Browne and Morgan have been saying all along that the slope of the hill prevents them from getting the right trajectory to target the wall where it matters. The best they can hope for is the sight of some falling masonry."

And so it proved. By the time the demi-cannon had been reset, Alexander and I were back on duty in the forward trench and were therefore able to get a much closer view of the damage caused by our ordnance. The gun was fired twice more, this time the balls arching upwards and hitting the stone towers inside the walls. It certainly made for a more spectacular sight, as both cannonballs sent substantial amounts of masonry crashing into the courtyards below, and sent the snipers scurrying for cover, which inevitably provided much entertainment for the spectators. The damage, however, was merely cosmetic, and there was no sign that Rigby would be able to make any further impression on the walls.

Fortunately for him, Rigby was able to save himself from further embarrassment by the appearance of a messenger from York, where Fairfax was now encamped. Sir Thomas, it appeared, had received word that the Earl of Derby, still in Chester, and thinking to save his wife from unnecessary danger, had been persuaded to agree terms for the surrender of the house and wished to convey this message to Lady Derby.

Having received this missive from the earl, Rigby immediately ordered Morgan to cease bombarding the house with shot and sent his personal chaplain, a man called Jackson, into the house under a temporary flag of truce, in order to convey this information to her ladyship. Lady Derby received the chaplain with all due courtesy and thanked Fairfax for the same, but nonetheless chose to reject the offer.

All this I heard from Colonel Rigby's own mouth when he summoned me to his field command base in the Tawd Valley as soon as Jackson returned.

"I need a rider to take Lady Derby's response to her husband," said Rigby, by way of explanation. "You are the most obvious candidate."

I was not sure why this should be so, but any opportunity to escape the purgatory of the trenches was welcome, and it would give me the opportunity, once in Chester, to conduct some further investigations into the murders, as well as to seek out William Seaman and pass on the news of what had happened to Jane Bootle. I therefore readily agreed to Rigby's request.

"That is good," said Rigby. "It is too late to depart this evening. You can be on your way at first light tomorrow. In the meantime, you are excused from duty tonight. I suggest you go back to New Park House and get some rest."

"Thank you, Colonel," I said, "but what of Mr Clowes. Will he accompany me?"

I looked up to see Rigby's constant lopsided smile; only I knew he was not smiling.

"I think not, Mr Cheswis," he said, eyebrows

furrowed in disapproval. "You do not need a chaperone to deliver a message. If Mr Clowes asks where you are, I will make sure he is duly informed."

Chapter 25

I walked back to New Park House by the northern route, through the sprawling parliamentary camp and onto the track past the woods where I had seen Jenny Reade a few days earlier. As I climbed out of the valley and onto the track, I noticed that Morgan had positioned the rest of his limited ordnance, consisting of three sakers, at the gun placements on the northern side of the house. For the present, they were pointing at the postern gate, from where both of the night attacks on our position had originated.

As I considered this vista, I was amazed to see the postern gate open slightly, allowing Jenny Reade's dog to emerge and trot lazily across the open ground towards the trees where I had seen it disappear before. This time, however, it did not vanish into the copse but turned left, bypassed the chapel, and headed off towards Ormskirk.

Forgetting all thought of returning to New Park House, I picked up my feet and ran after the dog, desperate not to let it out of my sight. Fortunately, the animal kept stopping to sniff at the ground and to relieve itself against walls and posts along the way, and so I was able to keep it within my sight right to the edge of Ormskirk, close by the windmill at Greetby. There it slid off to the left of the road and entered the garden of a small cottage set slightly apart from a row of workers' houses.

As I approached the cottage, though, I was forced to duck instinctively behind a stone wall, for a male figure suddenly appeared from around the back of the cottage, leading a horse by the reins.

It was a figure I knew well, but not one which I had expected to see. How, I asked myself, had Edward Chisnall managed to get out of Lathom House undetected? The house was now fully surrounded, so I could only assume he had managed to distract the guards watching the various sally ports around the house.

I crouched low behind the wall and watched as Chisnall mounted his horse and rode away across the fields to the south. There was, I realised, only one place that he could conceivably be heading.

I considered briefly whether I should be asking the grooms at New Park House to ready Demeter for a night ride to Chester in order to reach there before Chisnall, but decided, on reflection, that there was little point. If Chisnall himself decided to ride in the dark, I would have no chance of catching him.

At that moment, a second figure, small and waif-like, appeared from around the rear of the cottage. Jenny Reade was singing to herself, and her dog was running round her heels, but she came to an abrupt halt when she realised I was watching her. Behind her, two young children, a boy of about eight and a younger girl, stood sullenly and stared at me.

"Jenny!" I said. For a moment it looked as though the girl was about to take to her heels and flee, but she thought better of it.

"You will not tell, will you, sir? If Colonel Rigby should find out my brother is still sending out messages with the dog, they will kill me, as they did my mother."

"Then why allow it?" I asked.

"I have no choice. The earl sends one of his men from Chester to pick up messages. I can hardly refuse."

"I suppose not," I said, "but what is Edward Chisnall doing here?"

Jenny looked at me in resignation. "Mr Chisnall merely keeps his horse here," she explained. "My mother looked after it for him and I have continued to do this. I receive a small consideration in return. If I did not do this, our family would starve."

I thought about this for a moment. That messages for the Earl of Derby were being passed out with Jenny as an intermediary were one thing, but they did not throw any light on how Lady Derby was receiving information from the parliamentary commanders.

Neither did it explain how Chisnall had managed to leave the house undetected. I could easily have stopped the trafficking of secret messages by hauling Jenny off to Rigby's interrogators, but I could not see what that would achieve other than to condemn Jenny to death and her siblings to destitution. I made a decision and chose the more subtle option. Gaining this girl's trust, I considered, might prove to be more valuable than betraying her to the colonel.

"Jenny," I said, "I have little interest in what messages your dog is smuggling out of the house, but I would like to know how Edward Chisnall manages to escape the attention of our guards."

Jenny looked at me in bewilderment. "That I do not know," she said. "He will not say for fear of his secret being discovered. He has told me this himself."

"But you will tell me if you find out?"

"I don't know, sir," she said, uncertainly. "You will not betray me, will you?"

"I do not wish to cause you trouble," I said, truthfully. "I promise you, if Colonel Rigby finds out about this, it will not be me who has told him. But I may need your help on another matter. You are knowledgeable on the subject of herbs and remedies, I understand."

"I learned a lot from my mother," replied Jenny, a touch of suspicion in her voice.

"Then I will return," I said, reaching inside my pocket and giving her another shilling. "In the meantime, you must have a care and keep Chisnall away from here as much as you can."

Jenny hesitated for a few seconds but eventually reached out and snatched the coin, a broad smile breaking out across her face.

"You are a good man, Mr Cheswis," she said, before turning on her heels and shepherding her younger siblings around the back of the house.

Chapter 26

Lathom House – Thursday March 21st - Friday March 22nd,1644

The next morning brought with it a stiff breeze and squally showers, but the changeable weather did not deter me from my business. I woke early, having not seen Demeter for several days, and was gratified to find that Rigby's grooms had already prepared her for the ride. My bay mare whickered in recognition and nuzzled her nose into my neck as I led her out into the courtyard. Her ears stood erect and alert, as though she too was elated at the prospect of putting some distance between herself and Lathom.

Despite having to negotiate muddy and rutted roads, we made good time, and by late Friday morning I was in Mickle Trafford, banging on the door of Challinor's forge. Knowing that, as Rigby's messenger, I would be kept under close watch whilst in Chester, I arranged for messages to be taken to Annie at The Boot and to William Seaman at his shop, requesting each of them meet me at Challinor's later that afternoon. I stayed only long enough to make sure Demeter was fed and watered, and before long we were in sight of the outer earthworks at Flookersbrook. To my surprise, I found the earthen banks and palisades to be completely abandoned, whilst all that remained of Flookersbrook Hall was a burned out and empty shell.

"Destroyed on the order of Prince Rupert," explained a farmer, who I encountered coming the other way. "A monstrous display of wanton destruction, if you ask me," he opined, "but the prince reckoned it would make the inner defences more secure. You'll need to show your papers at the toll booth at Henwald's Lowe."

"Prince Rupert was here?" I asked, surprised.

"Aye, that he was," said the farmer. "Came with a whole load of soldiers and left with a few more. Ate our food, drank our ale, burned down half the houses hereabouts and then buggered off back to Shrewsbury."

I thanked the farmer and rode on to the toll booth, where I was stopped by a burly redcoat. The look of suspicion he greeted me with turned into one of contempt when he saw my papers.

"Bloody roundhead, are we?" he growled.

"I have an important communication for his lordship, the Earl of Derby," I said, trying to sound as self-important as possible.

The redcoat sniffed and deposited a large globule of spittle on the ground at my feet. "Aye, that's as mebbe," he growled, "but you're going nowhere without an escort in and out of the city. And I would recommend that you don't try any funny business, either. There's plenty here would give their eye's teeth for the chance to shove a red hot poker up your traitorous arse and feed your miserable pizzle to the dogs. Is that clear?"

I indicated to the redcoat that I understood his warning and waited fifteen minutes while an escort of four dragoons was organised. Once they arrived, they led me down Cow Lane, past the Kaleyard Gate, through which I had escaped but a few days earlier, and into the city via the Eastgate. From there, I was escorted past The Boot, around the Pentice, and down Watergate Street, until we reached the fine gabled town house that belonged to the Earl of Derby. As I rode past The Boot, I glanced upwards to row level and caught sight of Thomas Corbett, who was busy sweeping his stallboards. The youngster caught sight of me momentarily and stared quizzically at me before disappearing through the door into the tap-room.

Outside Derby House, the dragoons dismounted and ordered me to do the same, one of them taking hold of Demeter's reins. Two of them escorted me to the front door and were just about to announce their presence by tugging the bell that hung at the end of a rope outside the front door, when the door was flung open and out strode Edward Chisnall, clutching a small leather satchel. When he saw me he came to an abrupt halt, his eyes widening in astonishment.

"You!" he croaked, in strangled tones, a vein

throbbing prominently in his neck. "Am I to believe you have had the nerve to follow me here, sir?"

The dragoons looked at each other in puzzlement. Behind me, Demeter reared nervously.

"I am the bearer of correspondence from Colonel Rigby in response to his lordship's letter to Sir Thomas Fairfax, but my services as a courier would appear to be surplus to requirements, for I see you have beaten me to it."

Chisnall glared balefully at me and opened his mouth to speak, but then seemed to think better of it. Instead, he simply wagged a gloved finger in my face and glowered at me for a brief moment, before snorting loudly and disappearing up the street towards the cross.

The leader of the small group of dragoons, a craggy-faced sergeant with tanned skin that looked like leather, rubbed his hand through greasy black hair and regarded me with a look of new-found respect.

"I don't know who you are, mister," he said, "but he seems mortal fed up with you."

I thought to tell the dragoon that Chisnall was merely a hasty and judgemental fool, who had taken a dislike to me from the start, but by this time a footman had appeared in the doorway and bid me enter a spacious and well-appointed reception room.

To the right, a fireplace was supported by a large ship's timber, a reminder of how close we were to the port of Chester and that the Stanley family remained the custodians of Watergate, attracting an income from all goods landed there. The walls themselves were covered in plain wood panelling, the ceiling cross-beamed, and to my left, a wooden staircase led to the upper floors. I was allowed to sit on a chair next to the hearth, but the two redcoats positioned themselves ominously by the door.

After a few minutes, I heard voices, accompanied by the sound of leather boots on the stairwell, and three figures descended into view. The first of these was a man of medium build with a long, straight nose and dark hair that lay flat over his forehead, but tumbled in curls over his shoulders. Clean shaven, but with a thin, wispy moustache on his upper lip, he wore dark clothing, un-extravagant in style, and exuded an air of authority. I realised at once that I was in the presence of James Stanley, the seventh Earl of Derby.

"So, you have been sent by that treacherous dog Rigby, have you?" exclaimed the earl. "I fear your efforts have been wasted, for I already have news from my wife."

"So I have seen, my lord," I said, struggling to my feet and bowing hastily. "I apologise for my tardiness. I set off from Lathom at first light yesterday, but I'm afraid I was not as fast as Captain Chisnall."

Lord Derby looked at me sharply and took the small leather pouch that I proffered to him. He opened the pouch and took out a sealed envelope. Carefully breaking the seal, he extracted a sheet of paper, which he read carefully.

"Tell me," began the earl. "I am curious. How is it that you know Captain Chisnall?"

"I think I can answer that, my lord," said one of the two men behind the earl. I had been so transfixed by being in the presence of the Earl of Derby that I had taken only scant notice of his two companions. I noticed, with a start, that the man who had spoken was none other than Robert Whitby, who, it seemed, was just as shocked to see me.

"Am I to understand, sir, that I dined with a man in the employ of Parliament's rebel forces?" he demanded, a hint of steel in his voice. "I might have known a Nantwich man was not as loyal as he made out."

"Who is this cur, Robert?" asked the third man, stepping out from behind the earl. Dressed ostentatiously in a striking blue doublet with gold trimmings, he was about the same age as the earl, but carried the beginnings of a paunch and a slightly florid complexion that suggested rather more of a liking for good French wine than was strictly healthy.

"This is Cheswis, the man I was telling you about, Francis," said Whitby. "A friend of William Seaman. He was present when poor Katherine was so cruelly murdered."

"And now he presents himself on his lordship's doorstep bearing communications from Parliamentary High Command. I would say he has some explaining to do."

"Things are not quite as they seem, Mr Gamull," I said, realising the identity of the third man.

"Then pray enlighten us," invited the earl, with a smile. "We have all day."

I needed to think quickly. As long as I was Rigby's messenger, I had a certain amount of immunity from arrest, but I was loath to put that to the test. Sooner or later it would occur to Chisnall to tell Whitby or the earl that I had been captured in the trenches at Lathom and had been the subject of a prisoner exchange. If he chose to tell either that he held me for a spy, then I was in serious trouble.

However, an idea occurred to me, which I fancied might just help me change the subject enough to get me off the hook, whilst also securing me valuable information in my hunt for the murderer of William Seaman's relatives.

"I am an acquaintance of William Seaman, as Mr Whitby well knows," I began. "A cheese merchant, who would expand his business. As Mr Whitby is also aware, I am one of the town constables in Nantwich, and I recently enjoyed some success in solving a series of murders that took place in our town. Mr Seaman knows this, and when his sister was so brutally murdered herself, he asked me to travel to Ormskirk, not only to convey to his relatives the sad tidings of his sister's demise, but also to see whether I could be of assistance in tracking down her killer. I naturally agreed, for I wish to gain Mr Seaman's trust. When this war is over, I wish to expand my cheese business, and he has the contacts, which will enable me-"

"Yes, yes, go on," cut in Gamull, impatiently.

"When I arrived in Ormskirk, I was pressed into service by Colonel Rigby and his men, made to dig trenches around Lathom House. Then, when I tried to deliver my news to William Seaman's other sister, I found that she had also been murdered, together with her husband; a fowler called Bootle."

"Bootle?" exclaimed the earl, his face darkening. "I know a Bootle, a treacherous canker blossom of a man, who once had the trust of my household, but now betrays that trust by helping that common churl Rigby, who threatens my wife and family and seeks to destroy my property."

"You speak of Captain William Bootle, my Lord," I said. "The dead man was his brother."

It took a couple of seconds for this to register, but when it did, the effect was exactly as I had hoped.

"You mean William Seaman is related by marriage to Bootle?" he exclaimed, turning to Gamull and Whitby. "How can this be so? Why was I not informed?"

"W-we did not know, my lord," stuttered Whitby,

looking worried. "There was no reason for us to know this information. We knew Seaman had a sister in Ormskirk, but he has not been there for years, to our knowledge. Why would we be aware of this connection?"

I smiled to myself. I had guessed that Lord Derby would be unaware of Seaman's relationship with the Bootles. It also meant that it was highly likely that he was unaware of the fact that Seaman's son, Lawrence, was serving under Rigby and encamped in the trenches outside Lathom House. I decided I was not going to be the one to reveal that particular piece of information.

Gamull, meanwhile, had not been deflected from his understanding of the more significant implications of what I had told them.

"Murdered, you say?" he said, slowly, scrutinising me intently, his eyes boring into mine. "So two of Seaman's sisters have died within a week. Is that why you are here, Mr Cheswis?"

"Not entirely," I said. "I am here because I volunteered to deliver Colonel Rigby's message as a means to escape the trenches. I am a cheese merchant, sir. Not a soldier. However, I admit that I needed to return to Chester in order to continue my investigations. I had learned that Mr Seaman stands to inherit some business interests in France, particularly in the calfskin trade, and that he has committed to sell these interests to you before he has even inherited them himself. Your close confidant,

Mr Whitby, was present when Katherine Seaman died, and now a second close relative of William Seaman has been murdered. I was wondering whether this inheritance was connected in any way-"

"I would be very careful what you say, Mr Cheswis," warned Whitby, his lip curling in indignation, but Gamull quietened him with a wave of the hand.

"If you are suggesting that I would become in any way involved in any kind of impropriety that involves purchasing shares from someone who has no right to sell, or that Mr Whitby or I are in some way involved in these murders-"

"You misunderstand me, Mr Gamull," I said. "I suggest no such thing. I merely wished to ascertain whether this inheritance was of some import in this whole matter. You have being dealing with William Seaman a long time, sir?"

"Yes, of course, over many years. I can't remember how many."

"And he has helped facilitate the export of your calfskins through Henry Oulton's company in St Jean de Luz."

"You are well-informed, sir," said Gamull. "Then you will understand why it is important for me to secure this outlet for when Mr Oulton is no longer with us."

"I do," I conceded, "but you have signed a contract with William Seaman, whilst Henry Oulton still walks on this earth. Money has exchanged hands. Is this strictly ethical, sir? Or even legal?"

"That's none of your damned business," snapped Gamull. "Odds bodkins, you are an impertinent fellow."

"Then I apologise," I said, sensing that I had overstepped the mark. "Nonetheless, I understand Katherine Seaman did not approve of this arrangement."

"So I'm told," said Gamull, "but that does not mean either I or Robert Whitby had anything to do with her murder."

"That, of course, is true," I said, "and I make no such suggestion. Tell me, though, how much do you know about how Henry Oulton's business is operated today? Both Henry Oulton's son and his grandson are dead, I understand."

"That's correct," said Gamull. "When the grandson, George, died, his wife remarried one of the warehousemen there, a man called Le Croix. He is still there and now runs the business on Oulton's behalf."

"And George had no children?"

"No. He died young, of a fever, I believe. Le Croix had children of his own, but I do not know what happened to them. You really need to be speaking to William Seaman about this."

"I would be happy to do this, Mr Gamull," I said. "However, I doubt your dragoons will allow me to do that, unless, of course, you order them to accompany me there before I leave."

"That I would do willingly," said Gamull, "if it meant you were to leave me to conclude my business without you poking your nose into my affairs. However, there is one problem with that course of action. Mr Whitby has returned from Mr Seaman's residence not one hour since. Apparently, Seaman did not return home last night, and his wife is frantic with worry. William Seaman, it appears, has vanished without trace."

Chapter 27

Lathom House – Friday March 22nd, 1644

It was with a troubled mind that I rode through the gates at Henwald's Lowe, the area of common pasture to the north-east of Chester. Although I had managed to deflect the attention of the Earl of Derby, Francis Gamull, and Robert Whitby from exploring the real reasons for my presence in Chester the previous week, my investigations had, once again, produced more questions than answers.

For example, why had my presence at Seaman's house been considered important enough for Whitby to have informed Gamull about me? How had Chisnall escaped from Lathom House, and why was he so antagonistic towards me? There seemed to be connections everywhere but no common thread. The Earl of Derby, Gamull, Whitby, Chisnall, Henry Oulton, and the various members of the Seaman and Bootle families were all interconnected in a way that had resulted in the deaths of Katherine Seaman, Jane Bootle, and John Bootle. That much was clear, but the one piece of information that would draw all these connections together into one cohesive picture still eluded me.

The disappearance of William Seaman was even more worrying. Where was he, and why had he vanished without telling his wife, Isabel? Could it be that he was the murderer, and that he feared being exposed as such? Whatever the answer, I knew that I must find him.

Gamull's dragoons escorted me as far as Henwald's Lowe, not allowing me to speak to any passers-by, but as soon as we reached the toll booth, they bid me on my way, and I was able to ride with increased speed towards Flookersbrook and Mickle Trafford, the earl's response to Rigby safely stowed inside my shirt.

The strip of land that led to Flookersbrook Hall was almost deserted, all houses and barns in the vicinity having been destroyed and burned to the ground. A couple of hundred yards to either side of the road, the line of the abandoned earthworks snaked through the landscape, partly hidden by hedgerows and trees. The whole area had been deliberately laid to waste by the royalists, in order to make it unattractive to any parliamentary force which fancied it might find cover there.

As I passed through this no-man's land, I became increasingly uneasy, as though someone were following me, an unseen presence lurking in the hedgerows. I turned Demeter round to scour the path from whence I had come, but could see nothing. At one point I thought I caught a movement in a copse about a hundred yards away, but I couldn't be sure. Perhaps, I reasoned, the desolate environment was playing tricks with my mind, so I dug my heels into Demeter's flanks to encourage her to quicken her pace.

As we reached the gates to the burned out remains of Flookersbrook Hall, a female figure, dressed in a plain brown dress and carrying a basket, darted out from behind a stone wall and hailed me. I noticed, with surprise, that it was Annie.

"I thought we were to meet at Mickle Trafford," I said, somewhat flustered.

"Yes, but you have already been to Chester. Thomas Corbett saw you. You may well be being followed, and I cannot risk compromising Challinor's safety. If he is unmasked as a parliamentary collaborator, they will hang him."

I dismounted and tied Demeter to the gatepost. "Then let us talk here," I said. "We should be safe enough."

How wrong I was! At that precise moment, I heard a gentle click and swung around to see the triumphant and grinning face of Edward Chisnall, who was pointing a carbine at my chest. I realised with dismay that he must have been tracking me through the trees and hedgerows on the side of the road. He must have doubled back through the remains of Flookersbrook

Hall, for he had emerged from behind the thick stone wall which marked the boundary to the house. I cursed to myself, for I had not thought to inspect all potential hiding places properly before dismounting from Demeter's back.

"At last," sneered Chisnall, menacingly. "Now I have you, Cheswis. Now I will find out what you are really about."

It was then that an awful thought occurred to me. I remembered the vial of perfume around Annie's neck bearing the Earl of Derby's eagle and child crest. I had suspected Annie before, but had given her the benefit of the doubt. Now I realised how foolish I had been to do so. Annie had betrayed me, deliberately accosting me in a place where there would be no onlookers and where Chisnall could hide effectively and ambush me.

"Annie," I said, disappointment hanging from my every word, "I would have thought better of you."

Annie's eyes widened, and she looked at me in panic.

"Shush, Daniel. No!" she hissed. "You have me all wrong."

"I think not," I said, in anger. "You have led me here intentionally."

Chisnall, meanwhile, was staring at the two of us in bewilderment. It was good that he was, for my words were just enough to distract him from the charging figure which emerged from the trees behind him, pulling him down behind the wall and out of sight.

"Quick, help us," urged Annie, picking up her skirts and running through the gate towards where Chisnall had disappeared. Hesitantly, I walked over to the wall and glanced over it; with relief, for on the other side, Edward Chisnall was flat on his back, cursing loudly, while straddling his chest and brandishing Chisnall's carbine was my friend Alexander Clowes.

"Would somebody care to tell me what is going on?" I demanded, once Chisnall had been securely tied with his back to the gatepost. We were sat on a grassy hump a few yards down the main path leading to where Flookersbrook Hall had once stood, out of earshot, but within sight of Chisnall, who glowered at us through knotted eyebrows, a look of pure hatred on his face.

"Rigby told me that you had been sent to Chester as a messenger," explained Alexander, inspecting Chisnall's carbine with interest. "I figured that you might need my assistance, so I managed to steal away from the main camp, back to New Park House, and rode after you. I guessed that you would use the opportunity to pass by Challinor's on the way, but when I got there, you had already left. I realised that I would not be able to catch you before you entered the city, so I decided to use the abandoned earthworks as cover to wait for your return. There is a good view from up there and plenty of cover among the ruins of the hall."

"And so what happened?"

"Annie was the first person to arrive. I knew you

would want to speak to her and guessed that she might be on her way to Challinor's, so I went down to meet her and we waited for you together."

"So you weren't waiting here instead of at Challinor's in order to betray me to Chisnall?" I said to Annie, who responded with a perplexed look.

"Of course not, you jolthead," she said. "Whatever has made you think that?"

"Around your neck," I said. "The vial of perfume, it carries the earl's crest. I thought you might have been behind our betrayal to Jem Bressy."

"God's bones, Daniel," she breathed, throwing her hands in the air in exasperation. "Such a beef-witted clot-pole as you I have seldom come across. Is it so difficult to see? You are very well aware of the trade I practice. Who do you think gathers so much information on the Earl of Derby, and how do you think we get it? How, for that matter, do you think The Boot manages to stay open? Mr Corbett is now out of gaol. How do you think we would manage that if we didn't have influence? The earl is a grown man. How do you think he manages after weeks in the Isle of Man and with his wife besieged at Lathom?"

I stared at Annie in disbelief.

"So you are the Earl of Derby's lover?" I said.

"If that's what you want to call it."

"But what about Bressy?" I asked, nonplussed.

"Bressy has no influence with the earl or with Francis

288

Gamull for that matter. He is one of Byron's men. Bressy was acting on his own when he tried to have you arrested. Fortunately for you, he did not mention your real names to Gamull or the earl, and you were registered at The Boot under your assumed identities."

I slumped onto my back. I had been such a fool. Were it not for Alexander's presence, I would have probably ended up getting Annie killed as well as myself.

"So what do we do now?" I asked.

"You must first go to Challinor's," said Annie. "The boy Challinor sent as a messenger said you had asked to see William Seaman, a merchant whose sister was murdered last week. You wouldn't have anything to do with that, by any chance?"

"I was a dinner guest at his house on the night she died," I admitted.

Annie whistled. "Well, Seaman, by all accounts, has vanished, but his wife wishes to speak with you. You'll find her at Challinor's house. First, though, we must make sure that this fellow cannot follow you." Annie looked over to where Chisnall was sitting, still staring intently at us with murder in his eyes. "Come with me," she said to me, getting to her feet and strolling over towards Chisnall.

"Captain," she said. "We will now be taking leave of you. Unfortunately, for our own security, we cannot afford to untie you."

"You can't leave me here on my own," seethed

Chisnall. "No-one will find me."

"Yes they will," said Annie. "I will now return to Chester and will leave word as to where you can be found. I'm sure someone will come and get you by nightfall."

"If I ever find out who you are, madam, I will make sure you feel the end of a rope. You can be sure of it."

"We shall see," said Annie, with a smile. "In the meantime, my friends will be taking your horse, which I assume is tied up somewhere in the woods the other side of Flookersbrook Hall. Would that be correct?"

Chisnall gave Annie a murderous glare. "You would steal my horse, Cheswis?" he snarled, addressing me.

"Don't worry," I said. "I am no thief. I will leave it for you at the Reade's house, where it has been stabled these past days."

Chisnall looked at me with loathing. "You mean you knew where I kept the horse? Is this Jenny Reade's doing?"

"No. I followed her dog there yesterday afternoon. You just happened to be there. She did not betray you. I will not steal your horse, Captain Chisnall, but I cannot vouch for anyone else within the parliamentary army on that score. I suggest that when you get back to Lathom, you retrieve your horse and do not bother the Reade family again."

***

Challinor was ready and waiting for us when

Alexander and I arrived in Mickle Trafford. I could hear the rhythmic clanging of hammer on anvil as we approached, but as soon as we entered his yard, he stopped what he was doing and ushered us into his house.

Inside, I found Isabel Seaman already settled at his hall table. She looked slightly dishevelled, as though she had left home in a hurry. Her coif was slightly lopsided, and red rings around her eyes betrayed the fact that she had been crying. She tried to rise to her feet when I entered the room, but I gestured for her to remain seated.

"Mr Cheswis, I don't know what to say," she began. "We have put you to so much trouble."

"It is no trouble, I assure you," I replied. "I only wish I had better tidings to report. I am afraid I am the bearer of bad news, but it seems you have enough on your mind."

Isabel took a handkerchief and dabbed her eyes. "It is true," she said. "William has disappeared and I know not where. I have not seen him since yesterday. But you speak of more bad news?"

"Indeed," I said. "It concerns Mr Seaman's sister Jane and her husband." I proceeded to recount the story of my arrival at Lathom, the attempt on the life of myself and Lawrence Seaman, and the horrific murders of Jane and John Bootle.

To my amazement, Isabel did not gasp or register

surprise at the news. Instead, she merely nodded sadly. "It is as I feared," she said. "Yesterday, a messenger arrived from Ormskirk. He bore a letter from Lawrence. William would not say what was in the letter, but I guessed that the news was not good, for he went white and left the house without a word. Later, he returned saying that he had been with Robert Whitby and Francis Gamull, and had persuaded them to postpone the trial of Gibbons, the poor man accused of Katherine's murder – that he had promised to provide them with evidence that would clear Gibbons' name."

This was interesting news, for if Gamull and Whitby were involved in Katherine Seaman's murder, then surely it was in their interest for Gibbons to be found guilty. If Gamull and Whitby had agreed to Seaman's request to help Gibbons, did that not suggest that they were innocent of any involvement in the murders? I wondered whether Seaman had told Gamull and Whitby that there had been a second and a third murder and that Gibbons must, therefore, be innocent. If he had, Gamull and Whitby had betrayed no knowledge of it earlier that day.

"And what happened next, Mrs Seaman?" I asked.

"I wish I knew. William simply went out again and never returned. I am at my wit's end. What in God's name has he got himself involved with? Where can he possibly be?"

"I think I have a good idea," I said. "Please do not

worry yourself. Now I have spoken to you, I believe your husband to be innocent of any serious wrongdoing. He is guilty only of foolishness. I promise I will find him, and with God's will bring this whole sorry episode to a conclusion for the benefit of us all."

And with that, I shook Isabel by the hand, thanked Challinor for his hospitality, and with Chisnall's horse in tow, Alexander and I climbed wearily back into our saddles and made our way northwards, on the long ride back to Lathom.

Chapter 28

*S*imon Cheswis lay flat on his back in thick undergrowth, just below the crest of Beacon Hill, and stared at the stars. Fifty yards above him he could hear the chattering and joking of Sir John Meldrum's parliamentarian army echoing across the top of the escarpment. They were the voices of confident soldiers, men who knew that the royalist stronghold of Newark, stretched out in the valley below them, could not hold out for much longer, that the mixture of young royalist gentlemen, beautiful young ladies, and militant churchmen who had gathered in the town would soon be at their mercy. Meldrum, it was said, had already turned down one attempt by the besieged to negotiate a surrender, but the canny Scotsman had refused, knowing that the town was full of plate, money, and good plunder to keep his troops happy.

Sir John had arrived outside Newark no more than two weeks previously with two thousand horse, five thousand foot, and an artillery of thirteen siege guns, and although he had not quite kept his promise to *reduce Newark within the space of a week, he had made significant progress. He had stormed Muskham Bridge to the north-west of the town and taken control of the island, a large tract of land enclosed by two branches of the River Trent and lying immediately opposite Newark Castle. Meldrum had set up headquarters in the Spittal, the burned-out remains of a manor house to the north-east of the town, and now also occupied the high ground to the east.*

What he did not realise, however, was that Prince Rupert was on the march and, by the following evening, would be encamped at Bingham, only eight miles to the south-west of Newark.

Simon longed to get to his feet, to announce his presence to the soldiers above him and warn them of Rupert's impending arrival, but knew that he couldn't, that he would probably be arrested and held as a royalist scout, especially wearing the green coat he had been given, which identified him as a soldier of Henry Tillier's regiment. He would have dearly liked to ditch the coat, but the sharp March weather precluded such a plan, for it was far too cold to be riding around the countryside dressed only in a shirt and breeches. Simon, therefore, decided to bide his time and, clutching his carbine to his chest, prayed that God would prove to be merciful and keep him concealed.

The horse he had stolen, when he had absconded

from the royalist camp the day before, stood out of sight and tethered to a tree half a mile down the hill to the east. From there he had waited until the hours of darkness before proceeding by foot and keeping to the shadows to avoid detection. As he lay among the bushes and the grass, awaiting his chance, Simon considered what he had been forced to endure during the past week.

Six miserable days he had spent with Prince Rupert's army, pretending to be an Irishman. He had been marched to Shrewsbury, then down the Severn to Bridgnorth, and finally across country to Ashby de la Zouch, by which time the prince's force had swollen to three thousand five hundred horse and three thousand foot.

James Skinner had remained elusive during the hard marches. The royalist force was large, gathering strength as it moved, and Simon had no wish to draw unwelcome attention to himself. He therefore spent several days keeping himself to himself and speaking as little as possible, lest his imperfect Irish accent be unmasked as fake. Skinner, however, had noticed Simon's presence amongst Tillier's men and had thrown several quizzical looks in his direction.

By the time they reached Ashby de la Zouch, Simon realised that time was running short. In two days they would be before the gates of Newark. If he wished to effect Skinner's escape and avoid having to risk his own life fighting for the King's party against Meldrum's men, he had little time to lose.

That evening, after they had eaten, Simon picked his way through the sprawling encampment and sought out Skinner, in order to outline his plans to escape to parliamentary lines and thence back to Nantwich. What he heard from his brother's erstwhile apprentice, though, was not what he had wanted or expected to hear.

"I will stay here, Simon," said Skinner. "My place is to remain with my regiment and fight for the King. I will not betray you," he added, "but you must make good your escape and leave me here."

Simon was dumbfounded. "You wish to fight for Prince Rupert?" he exclaimed. "But you were kidnapped and pressed into service. Daniel, Alexander Clowes, and I have all risked our lives trying to release you."

"But I didn't ask you to do that," retorted Skinner. "Master Cheswis knows that I wish to be a soldier for the sake of adventure. I have no feeling one way or the other about the rights of Parliament. London is a long way from Nantwich – it is beyond my knowledge, but I do know I could never be disloyal to the King, so I am happy to fight for him."

"But what about your brothers, who have tried so hard to persuade us to help free you? They will be distraught."

"There is no need for them to be so," said Skinner. "Please tell them they are in my thoughts and they should not worry about me."

Simon sat quietly for a few moments before exhaling loudly is exasperation. "So you are to be my enemy, then?" he said.

"You are not my enemy, Simon," replied Skinner, "not until the day you stand before me with sword in hand. Now go, before you attract attention to yourself and while you still have the opportunity to do so."

Simon's mind had been in turmoil as he rode the forty miles from Ashby de la Zouch to Beacon Hill. How on Earth had he managed to allow himself to be dragged into such an enterprise? He had nearly got himself killed trying to rescue this ungrateful wretch, and all because Daniel felt he owed the Skinner family something. Now he found himself in enemy territory with a stolen horse and weaponry, having to find his way to the nearest parliamentary unit and persuade them he was no royalist scout, but an intelligencer under the command of Sir William Brereton. Fortunately, he still had possession of the pass he had used to enter Chester and the wax ball with the encrypted message given to him by Thomas Corbett, which might, he hoped, lend some credence to his story.

Gritting his teeth with resolve, he had ridden to within a couple of miles of Beacon Hill and waited for it to go dark. From there he had proceeded to *the bottom of the slope before leaving his horse and walking up through woodland, which hugged the slopes of the escarpment. Now, he lay silently, at the mercy of Meldrum's sentries, wondering whether he had lost his mind.*

Eventually, he heard the sound he was hoping for, and he became instantly alert. The clump-clump of footsteps on the steep slope, the whistling of a popular tune and then the steady stream of liquid as the soldier relieved himself on the grass a few yards away.

Simon rolled over onto his front and pointed his carbine at the man.

"Don't move," hissed Simon, "identify yourself."

The man looked over his shoulder and continued to spray the hillside with urine. "Just having a piss, my friend," he said. "I'll be back up there in a minute."

"I said identify yourself, unless you want a bullet in your leg," insisted Simon. "What's the field word?"

"The field word? Religion. For God's sake, man, I just need a piss, that's all."

The soldier finished urinating, shoved his member back inside his breeches, and stomped back up the hillside, grumbling, without even bothering to look at Simon, who waited until the soldier was out of sight before slipping silently back into the trees and creeping stealthily down towards the clearing at the foot of the hill, where his horse was tethered.

***

Simon waited until it was light before venturing into the open. After eating some bread and cheese that he had bought the previous day, he reluctantly removed his green jacket and left it at the foot of a tree. Rubbing his shoulders to stop himself shivering in the sharp morning air, he mounted his horse and trotted up the side of Beacon Hill, taking care to keep to the narrow roadway to make sure that he was in full view of the sentries on top of the ridge.

By the time he reached the crest of the hill, a substantial group of soldiers was waiting to receive him, some with primed muskets aimed at him, others looking on curiously from a distance.

"For King and Parliament," he called out, as he rode the last few yards, raising his arm in greeting.

A slightly-built officer stepped out from the crowd and addressed him. "You know the field word?" he called.

"Religion," replied Simon, with confidence.

The officer squinted in the early morning sunlight and gestured for a couple of his men to hold onto Simon's horse to allow him to dismount. Clean shaven, with delicate features dominated by a prominent, pointed chin, he cut a somewhat incongruous figure. He wore his hair short in the Puritan style, just covering his ears, the top combed forward to conceal a slightly receding hairline.

"Who are you, sir?" he called.

"My name is Cheswis. I am engaged under the personal command of Sir William Brereton," replied Simon.

"Brereton, the Cheshire man? Then what are you doing in Nottinghamshire, may I ask?"

"It is a long story, but I have news of Prince Rupert's army, with whom I was most recently pressed into service. He marches on Newark as we speak under orders to relieve this siege. By now he can be no more than twenty miles from here. I would speak to Sir John Meldrum, in order to impart what information I have."

A murmur of interest passed around those soldiers near enough to be within earshot, but the officer raised his hand to quieten them.

"I take it you can prove your identity?"

"I have paperwork bearing Sir William's seal and other items that will support my story, although I would not wish to share this information with the whole of your company."

The officer nodded. "In that case I will accompany you personally. Sir John will be found in the Spittal. It is but a short ride from here. I will have someone ready a horse for me. In the meantime, I will get one of my men to procure a coat for you. You have ridden all this way without one?"

"I left it in the trees at the foot of the hill," admitted Simon. "It was a green coat from Tillier's Regiment – highly recognisable. I would not have had you mistake

301

me for one of his men."

The officer nodded and smiled wryly. "Just one more thing," he added, lowering his voice so that no-one else could hear. "If you have come directly from Prince Rupert's army, how is it that you know our field word? Or is that a pointless thing to ask of an intelligencer?"

Simon grinned. "I think you have just answered that question, sir," he replied.

***

The Spittal had once been a fine family mansion with extensive gardens, owned by the Earl of Exeter, but now its beams were blackened with soot and the roof had caved in on one side, giving the house a strange, lopsided look. The stone walls, however, remained strong and provided excellent protection for Meldrum and his senior officers. The Spittal had the added advantage of being located within sight of the city walls as well as being close to the River Trent, where Meldrum had constructed a bridge of boats over to the island, thereby allowing him to maintain close control of the siege from the most strategically advantageous position.

Meldrum, a jowly, round-faced man with large eyes and downturned lips that made him look more severe than his character actually deserved, stroked his goatee beard and looked at Simon doubtfully. He had read the false papers provided by Sir William Brereton and had broken open the wax ball to reveal the

302

encrypted message intended for Sir Thomas Fairfax.

"Well, Mr Cheswis," he said, "you have what appears to be genuine paperwork and a tale to tell me, which, if not true, makes you a storyteller of particular skill. You say you are from a group of three of Sir William Brereton's men tasked with delivering secret information to Sir Thomas Fairfax at Lathom House in Lancashire, and yet you allow yourself to be captured and enlisted by Prince Rupert of the Rhine. This smacks of a carelessness that does not lie easy with everything else you say about yourself."

"You are right, Sir John," said Simon, honestly. "It is true we were careless. We were attempting to rescue my brother's apprentice, who himself had been kidnapped and pressed into the King's service after January's battle at Nantwich."

"I see. And where is this apprentice now?" asked Meldrum, eventually.

"He remains with Rupert's army," admitted Simon. "It was a great disappointment to me. He has turned his coat and prefers to fight with Rupert's band of papists and malignants."

"Then you have risked your life and come close to losing important correspondence for no gain?"

"So it would appear, sir. It is a cause of some embarrassment to me."

Meldrum clicked his tongue in irritation. "And your aim now is-"

"To ride to Lathom, report to Fairfax, and rejoin my colleagues, sir. I will then take further orders from Sir Thomas."

"As things stand, you will be fortunate indeed to achieve those aims," said Meldrum. "Sir Thomas Fairfax has returned to Yorkshire and you, sir, need to be properly equipped before you ride any further. If what you say is true, Rupert will be here very soon. You would do best to stay with us and help us defend our position here. Newark is on its last legs, and if we can rebuff Prince Rupert, we will have given very worthy and commendable service to Parliament. How long do you suppose before they reach here?"

"They will be here tomorrow, sir, earlier if they march non-stop."

"In that case," said Meldrum, "they will be tired and may be easily picked off by our own forces. We will invite the prince to take the high ground at the top of Beacon Hill and persuade him to follow our own men down into the valley, where he will be within range of our artillery. There we will destroy him with our guns. In the meantime, I will call a council of my senior officers and you, Mr Cheswis, can take up arms with one of our companies.

Simon glanced across at the officer who had brought him to Meldrum. "You are welcome to join us, Mr Cheswis," he said. "I will have someone find you a musket. I presume you can use one?"

"Of course," said Simon.

"That is good," said Meldrum, who then hesitated and looked at Simon for a moment. "Tell me," he said, "you are a distinctive type of individual, not the usual kind we get here. Why is it that you chose to fight for Parliament?"

"That is easy, Sir John," said Simon. "For me this war is not just a conflict between a rightfully elected parliament and a stubborn and arrogant king, but an opportunity for every man in this land to have a say in how England is governed, an opportunity to create a country where every man is truly equal, where men can rise to prominence on merit, not by inherited right."

The officer was looking at Simon with renewed interest, but it was Meldrum who spoke first.

"Hah!" he exclaimed, "I thought so. This is new-fangled politics, which is not of my liking, but I suspect you and Major Lilburne are of a like mind."

It was then that Simon realised the officer's identity. "Lilburne," he said. "You are not John Lilburne, by any chance, author of The Work of the Beast and Come out of Her, My People?"

"The very same," said Lilburne, with an approving smile. "Well met, sir. I can see that you and I will have something to talk about whilst we await the arrival of Prince Rupert and his men. Come, let us return to our post and we can discuss this in more detail."

Chapter 29

Lathom House – Thursday March 21st – Thursday April 11th, 1644

It was not until several days after our return to Lathom that Alexander and I received news of Prince Rupert's startling victory at Newark. At the time, of course, I was entirely unaware that both Simon and James Skinner had been present at that particular encounter, fighting on opposing sides, and it wasn't until several months later that I began to realise the role that particular event would have in determining the direction my brother's life would take, and the impact it would have on our own relationship.

On March 21st, Rupert, after a march by moonlight through the Nottinghamshire countryside, had taken Sir John Meldrum's force by surprise, leading his cavalry to the south-east of Newark and attacking Meldrum's men at two in the morning. When the rest of the royalist cavalry and foot arrived some time later, Meldrum's horse was forced back over the bridge of boats onto the island, leaving his infantry stranded.

At the same time, the prince had sent a detachment of men to capture the bridge at Muskham on the far side of the island, Meldrum's only possible escape route. Trapped and surrounded by royalists and with no more than three days provisions, Meldrum had been forced to call a parley, and, although he and his men were given free passage off the island, he had been obliged to surrender all his artillery, firearms, and ammunition, consisting of over 3,000 muskets, two mortars, and eleven artillery pieces.

It was indeed a comprehensive victory, the significance of which was not lost on Colonel Rigby and his fellow commanders, for they understood that, with the siege of Newark lifted, Rupert would now be free to direct his attentions elsewhere, and that addressing the issue of Parliament's superiority in Lancashire would be high on his list of priorities.

Rigby himself had begun to look increasingly troubled, for it had become patently obvious that Lady Derby's various attempts at negotiation had been little more than a pretence to waste time, and she clearly had no intention whatsoever of surrendering her house. The colonel's behaviour had become progressively more erratic, ranging from periods of solemn introspection to moments of seething rage, as he contemplated ways in which he might achieve his ultimate goal of reducing Lathom House to rubble.

The fact that Rigby's force was not adequately

financed did not help either. Ammunition was in short supply, men were forced to walk miles every day to serve in trenches they were not familiar with, and pay was in arrears. To add to the problems, communication between Assheton and Moore on the one hand and Rigby and Egerton on the other had begun to break down.

I had assumed that the antipathy between the commanders was due to their difference of opinion on how to manage the siege. Assheton and Moore, it was clear, were of the view that we should use our obvious numerical superiority and storm the house, whereas Rigby favoured a more patient approach, using artillery to bombard the garrison whilst simultaneously starving it into submission.

But there was more to it than that, as the engineer, Browne, pointed out to me on the Monday morning following my return.

"It is the tax that Rigby and Egerton wish to levy in order to pay for this siege," he explained. "More than four thousand pounds to be paid for by people who can ill afford it – and by more or less the whole of Lancashire too. Assheton believes the proposed tax is illegal."

"Illegal? How so?" I asked. "Someone has to pay, surely? We have no ammunition."

"That is true," conceded Browne, "and it is said much of this money will be used to buy the mortar shells we will need. After all, our cannon is useless in this terrain. Rigby, however, claims the money is for extra soldiers, not ammunition, and what do we want with more soldiers when we already have ten times more than they do? Furthermore, Assheton argues that only West Derby Hundred should be paying for the siege, not the whole of the county."

"I have heard these arguments before," I said, "but is it true that the legality of this may be in doubt?"

"Who can say?" said Browne. "I am no lawyer, but this is not the only point of contention between the two parties. Firstly, Assheton believes that this siege is an irrelevance and that we should not be here at all. Lathom, he says, is of little import in this war. Lady Derby offers no threat to our forces, and, in truth, taking the house would be little more than a symbolic victory. And there is more. The Earl of Derby raised a similar tax himself during the Bishops' War, almost the same sum, in fact, and Rigby had the earl impeached for that particular action."

I understood the point immediately. "So Assheton holds Rigby for a hypocrite?" I said.

"Precisely, and Moore is with him on that. In truth, it is no surprise that Assheton and Moore hold the Manchester Committee in such low regard. They question not only the military skill of Rigby, Egerton, and Colonel Holland, but their honesty and motives too. Things cannot carry on in this manner for much longer," he added. "Mark my words."

As it happened, the observant Browne was right, and over the following week things came rapidly to a head, starting, oddly enough, on the very same day I had spoken to the engineer.

On that afternoon, Morgan's artillerymen decided to give some action to their demi-cannon and culverin and fired several rounds at the gatehouse. One of these shots ricocheted off the ground in front of the house and crashed through the sturdy oaken gates, sending shards of wood flying in all directions. The little Welshman was jubilant as he and his artillery team watched the garrison men rushing to stop up the gates. The scene was made even more impressive by the fact that Rigby had once again assembled a crowd of onlookers to enjoy the show.

Ever the cynic, Browne, who was also present, was suitably unimpressed. "You lucky bastard," he said to Morgan, instantly wiping the smile from the Welshman's face. "You fired seven shots at the gates and missed six because you can't see properly what you're aiming at, and the one you got lucky with you nearly buried in the fucking ground."

Morgan, haughty and intolerant of criticism at the best of times, exploded in anger. "And you, sirrah," he snapped, "do you suppose you have much room to talk? You, who took forever to build these siege works and who dug the trenches so damned close to the walls that our men are in constant danger of being shot? Are you sure you are not on the side of the King? It would not surprise me."

A full-scale brawl between the two men was only avoided by the swift intervention of Rigby himself, who had overheard Browne's words and reprimanded both him and Morgan for their behaviour. The tone for the following days, however, was set, and men began to openly discuss whether Rigby and Egerton were in the right or whether Assheton and Moore's approach was more likely to succeed. It should have come as no surprise, therefore, that when Rigby and Egerton were called away to Manchester on Thursday March 28th, an attempt would be made to alter the course of the siege.

On that day, Assheton and Moore announced a change of strategy, stipulating that, henceforward, all focus would be on the main gates and the turrets around the gatehouse, in preparation for storming the house. Morgan, I was told, fired two cannon shots in the air in defiance, and reiterated his support of Rigby's strategy, but ultimately had little option but to comply with the orders given by the two senior commanders.

On the following morning, artillery and musketeers alike focussed their efforts on the gateway and, to my surprise, they met with some success. In the morning, an over-confident marksman on the battlements was shot dead by one of our musketeers, and in the afternoon a series of cannon shots was aimed at the guns on the turrets around the gatehouse, one of which scored a direct hit, killing a cannonier outright.

Such insubordination could clearly not last, though, for ostensibly Egerton was in charge, and when he and Rigby returned from Manchester two days later, they immediately reversed the orders given by Assheton and Moore. I was, of course, not privy to the subsequent meeting held between the four commanders, but it must have been a lively affair, because from that date we did not see Assheton and Moore again.

We did not find out what had happened until nearly a full week later, when Assheton and Moore issued an open letter to well-wishers in the vicinity, the content of which is still etched in my mind.

To all Ministers and Parsons in Lancashire, well-wishers to our success against Lathom House, these-

For as much as more than ordinary obstructions have, from the beginning of this present service against Lathom House, intersposed our proceedings, and yet, still remain, which cannot otherwise be removed nor our success furthered, but only by divine assistance, it is thus our desires to the ministers and other well-affected persons of this county of Lancaster, in public manner, as they shall please, to commend our care to

God, so the Almighty would crown our weak endeavour with speedy success in the said design.

Ralph Assheton
John Moore
Ormskirk Apr. 5, 1644

So that was it. Assheton and Moore had departed in exasperation and left us to our fate. The inference of their letter was that, with Egerton and Rigby in charge, only God could help us now. Browne, I noticed, read the letter with a cynical chuckle. I suspected he was of the same view as Assheton and Moore, but, as a civilian, and with Rigby and Egerton paying his fees, he took great care not to show this to his paymasters.

Rigby, for his part, was a changed man with his main detractors off the scene, and, displaying renewed energy and enthusiasm, he lost no time in pursuing his own strategy of causing maximum damage to Lathom House and its occupants without actually storming the building.

On the day following Assheton and Moore's departure, he had Morgan fire two cannon shots into the upper rooms of the house. By the following day, however, it had become clear that one of the main reasons for the upturn in Rigby's mood was the fact that the long-promised mortar had arrived from Sir

313

William Brereton and had been positioned in the gun battery outside the main gates. To find room for the mortar, Rigby needed to relocate the demi-cannon and culverin, so he spent all day on Monday April 1st showering the occupants of the house with chain shot and iron bars in order to keep them quiet, whilst he completed the repositioning of his big guns.

By the Wednesday, the mortar was in position, secured in a location about eight feet higher than the ditch surrounding the house.

"Now we shall see what Lady Derby is made of," said Morgan, with unrestrained glee, once he had Rigby's approval to start firing on the house. It was certainly true that the mortar threatened to change the whole course of the siege. With cannon, Morgan could only shoot at the walls, which were bolstered on the inside with thick turves. However, with the mortar, he could now fire stones and grenades over the walls and into the house. The only question was how quickly Morgan could get the necessary supply of mortar shells to enable him to bring the siege to a conclusion. For the time being, he only had a limited supply of grenades, so Morgan began by firing showers of stones and rocks over the walls at the house. Even without grenades, the effect of the mortar was mesmerising. The awe-inspiring machine threw rocks so far into the air that they almost disappeared from view before crashing down onto the towers and buildings inside the walls.

Morgan used his grenades sparingly, and fired the first one on Thursday 4th April. However, he promptly wasted it by sending it sailing right over the house, having failed to recalculate the trajectory properly. Despite this, the feeling amongst our ranks was clear. So long as Morgan was supplied with enough mortar shells, Lady Derby's days in Lathom House were numbered.

Whilst all this was going on, I tried to use my spare time constructively by cultivating relationships with those I felt might ultimately help me get to the bottom of what had happened to Katherine Seaman and the Bootles. In particular, I found I was spending an increasing amount of time in the company of Lawrence Seaman, who I judged to be a most personable and interesting young man. As the spring weather started to improve, I found welcome respite from the growing squalor of the encampment by exploring the villages around Ormskirk – Burscough with its mill and ruined priory, Newburgh, and Parbold. Lawrence, being of a similar disposition, joined me on many of these expeditions. Alexander, whose preferences in terms of entertainment and diversion tended to be of a somewhat baser nature, preferred to stay within the confines of New Park House or the alehouses in Ormskirk.

Not that I was averse to a tankard of ale myself, of course, and I did take care to visit some of the taverns in search of Old Isaac, who, when he was not blind drunk, provided good conversation himself and proved especially useful as a source of information as to what was going on in and around the town. Despite his weakness for drink, he was an observant and inquisitive character, and not much of the day-to-day business of the inhabitants of Ormskirk escaped his notice.

I also took the opportunity to talk more in depth with William Bootle, who, after the death of his brother, had lost no time in clearing and cleaning up the empty cottage and installing a tenant.

"I cannot leave the house empty and abandoned in the knowledge of what happened within those walls," he told me one morning. "A house does not easily forget such horrors. 'Tis better a new family live there to help erase the memories of what was here before." The new tenant, a recently married baker's son called Fitch, provided Bootle with a selection of cakes and pastries on moving in, which the captain generously shared around his fellow officers at New Park House.

Bootle, although affable and easygoing enough, was somewhat elusive outside the confines of New Park House, where he stayed occasionally. From what I could tell, he rarely went drinking in Ormskirk, but, having told us he possessed a cottage of his own in Burscough, I left him to live his life in private. One thing I did notice, though, was the fact that, despite the relationship by marriage, he and Lawrence Seaman had little to do with each other. Indeed, as time went by and I spent more time with Lawrence, I realised that they barely knew each other, although, with Lawrence having grown up in Chester and with Bootle related to his aunt only by marriage, there was, I supposed, no reason why they should.

My walks through the lanes and fields around Lathom also brought me more into contact with Jenny Reade, who seemed to have the uncanny knack of remaining concealed and then suddenly appearing in amongst the trees or behind some wall with her basket of herbs. In fact, I saw her so often around the woodland and hedgerows that I began to suspect she was following me around, although I could not blame her if she was, for I regularly asked after her welfare and occasionally gave her a penny or two to help feed her and her siblings. She seemed pleased that Chisnall had removed his horse from her cottage, and I gradually began to gain her trust.

One day, she noticed a graze on my hand and my swollen wrist, sustained when I had tripped and fallen in the trenches that morning, so she invited me back to her cottage, where she applied a comfrey poultice, and to my delight, within a couple of days, my injured wrist was entirely healed.

A couple of weeks after my return to Lathom, Alexander and I also received letters from Nantwich, which both delighted us and brought us to the brink of despair at the same time.

My heart jumped when I opened my letter and realised it was from Elizabeth. The town, she wrote, had been peaceful since our departure. Jack Wade was now almost fully recovered and was working hard in the wich house under Gilbert Robinson's instructions. A kindling had already been carried out since my departure and had been completed successfully, thanks in part to the help of John and Ann Davenport, who, still grateful for my help in clearing John's name after the murders in December and January, had seconded many of their own workers to my wich house for the duration of the kindling, which they had managed on my behalf.

Wade had also been collecting cheese from local farmers, but it was Elizabeth herself who had managed our stall, ably helped by Amy Padgett, who, according to Elizabeth, spent every Saturday morning accosting shoppers in the square and along Pepper Street, offering them samples of cheese and leading them to Elizabeth. All my growing adopted family, however, especially young Ralph, were missing me, and it tore at my conscience that I was not able to tell them when I would be able to return.

Worse still was the news that word of Simon's disappearance had reached Nantwich. Rose Bailey, of course, was frantic with worry, but with no news one way or the other, she was, like me, holding out hope that he would make an unannounced appearance before long, as he had a habit of doing. Simkins had apparently also showed some concern, although I suspected that had more to do with the loss of his horse and a cartload of shoes than any particular concern for Simon's wellbeing.

When I saw Alexander after we had both read our letters, I saw from his face that the news from Marjery Clowes was of a similar kind. I realised that Alexander and I would have to engineer a way of escaping from our duties at Lathom and securing a return to our loved ones in Nantwich. But how were we to achieve this? I was at a loss to know.

However, as is so often the case when spirits are at their lowest ebb, just as we had reached the depths of despair, over a three day period beginning on Wednesday 10th April, things began to happen which reinvigorated my fading hopes that events at Lathom would at last come to a conclusion of sorts.

Shortly after 11 in the morning on the Wednesday, just before the soldiers in the trenches were due to end their twenty-four hour watch, William Bootle burst into the courtyard at New Park House to report that our siege works were under attack. According to a later report by Major Robinson, who was present during the assault, Farmer and his men left by the postern gate and, protected by snipers on the battlements and directed with flags by a captain at the top of the Eagle Tower, marched under the line of fire right up to our gun positions and drove out our gunners. Farmer's men then proceeded to nail up the guns and charge through the trenches, driving out all our soldiers and killing them indiscriminately. They would have nailed up the mortar too if they had been able, but its mouth was too wide. They therefore tipped it over and tried to hammer the bore out of true.

Afterwards, I thanked God that I had been at New Park House at the time, waiting to walk up to the trenches to relieve the men who had been there all night. If Farmer had left his attack another hour, I would certainly have been caught right in the middle of the fray. As it was, we lost fifty men, numerous arms, three drums, and a flag. Only one of their men was killed.

As we marched through the Tawd Valley to relieve the dispirited and battered troops, a steady stream of dead and injured was being stretchered through the trenches into the makeshift infirmary. Those that could walk staggered, wide-eyed and vacant, into the encampment, their faces etched with the shock of their experience.

I saw one pale-faced individual clasping his arm to his chest, his wrist shattered by a musket ball. Another held a bloody rag to his eye, removing it momentarily to reveal a shattered eye socket and an ugly gash the length of his cheek. Yet another, who had slipped and fallen in the melee, was being supported by two comrades, his knee jutting out at a bizarre angle.

The next shift was carried out under a cloud of nervous tension. A fearful silence was broken only by occasional jeers and taunts emanating from the towers by the gateway. At one point, the flag the royalists had captured was draped over the battlements, where it hung all afternoon.

Morale among our men could scarcely have been lower. Many of us were anticipating another raid once it got dark, but to our relief such an attack never materialised, and I began to realise that this was because the royalists, like ourselves, also needed to conserve their ammunition. Their strategy was not to utterly defeat us, simply to wear us down, bit by bit.

With Assheton and Moore gone, the royalists were clearly winning the siege. Watching Morgan and his men right the mortar and check its bore for damage, I realised how much depended on this weapon. If Farmer's raiding party had been able to drag away the heavy piece of equipment, they surely would have, for it was clear that with such a weapon under parliamentary control, even the most inept commander would surely prevail, so long as he was adequately supplied with grenades. No wonder Farmer had tried to disable it. I began to realise that the coming days would be crucial in deciding the course of the leaguer of Lathom, and I prayed Alexander and I would survive it.

The following day, Alexander and I arrived back, exhausted, at New Park House, to find an unusual disturbance taking place. As we crossed the moat and entered the courtyard, I was surprised to find Lawrence Seaman and William Bootle engaged in a heated argument. From his demeanour, I could see that Lawrence was apoplectic with range, whilst Bootle was calm, but vigorously defending himself.

"Whatever is the matter?" I said, striding up to them and interrupting Lawrence, who was hurling a torrent of invective at Bootle.

"My father is in Ormskirk," said Lawrence, struggling to stop himself from shaking. "He sits under lock and key in the town gaol. William has had him arrested for my aunt and uncle's murder."

"What?" I exclaimed, turning to Bootle. "Is this true?"

Bootle shrugged. "The Fitches found him inside their house, poking around in the cupboards. He had broken in. He told them who he was, so I was called to investigate. What was I supposed to do? Lawrence had not told me he was in town."

"I did not know that he was," countered Lawrence, "but that is no reason to have him arrested."

"You forget," said Bootle, his voice hardening, "that house is mine now and he was caught ransacking the place like a common criminal. Not only that; he is a prime suspect for the murder, not least because he was also present when his sister Katherine was killed in Chester."

"But he was also in Chester when John and Jane Bootle died," cut in Alexander.

"Can you be sure of that?" said Bootle. "You were at Lathom yourself that night. Can you vouch for his presence in Chester? Could he not have been here already?"

"You are talking nonsense, William," spat Lawrence, making as though he were preparing to strike Bootle. Alexander took a step forward and placed himself between the two of them.

"Lawrence," I said. "I think you would be best advised to hold your counsel. I will come with you now to the gaol house, and we will see what your father has to say about this matter."

"You're wasting your time," said Bootle. "Seaman is a murderer. He will hang for this."

"And you, Captain," I warned, "had also best hold your tongue. You and your tenants have every right to protect your property from intruders, but I will be the judge of his guilt or otherwise."

Bootle smiled and held up his palms in mock deference. "I think you'll find that it is down to the constable, the bailiff, and ultimately the courts," he said, matter-of-factly.

Bootle was right, of course, but nevertheless I gave

the captain an impatient look and led Lawrence by the arm, leaving Alexander to try to find out more from the captain as to exactly what had happened in the Bootles' home.

The gaol house in Ormskirk reminded me of the small, dark, and dingy building that I was used to in Nantwich. Like many such places, it stank of dirt, sweat, and despair. The town's gaoler was also of a type that was familiar to me, and it did not take much bribing to gain access to William Seaman, who we found sitting on the floor of one of the cells, looking sorry for himself. He had an angry-looking swelling under his eye from where he had struggled with his captors, and his shirt was torn at the shoulder.

"I fear you are in trouble, William," I said, after allowing Lawrence to embrace his father. "William Bootle has you for a murderer. What are you doing here?"

"I would have thought," said Seaman, after a moment's pause, "that my purpose would have been self-evident. Like you, I was looking for clues."

"And where have you been these past days?" I continued. "Your wife worries herself greatly. She says you have disappeared."

"You have been back to Chester?" asked Seaman.

I briefly explained the purpose of my recent visit to Chester and described my short meeting with Isabel Seaman. "Where have you been all this time?" I demanded.

"I have been to Bolton," admitted Seaman, somewhat sheepishly.

"Bolton?" said Lawrence, with a frown. "Why would you need to go there?"

Seaman grimaced as he altered his position to make himself more comfortable. "When I heard that Jane had been killed, I realised, like Daniel, that the reason for her death must be linked with Henry Oulton's inheritance, so I went to confront him."

"And you found out something?" I enquired.

"I did. I found out that I am not the main beneficiary of his will as I originally thought. That honour belongs to one Marc le Croix."

"What? A Frenchman?" said Lawrence, incredulously.

"Aye, he is the son of Oulton's grandson, now dead. He was brought up by Le Croix, the manager of Oulton's import business, when he married the widow of Oulton's dead grandson. It turns out that when the boy was about ten, he was shipped over to Bolton to continue his education and was raised by a local family, one of Oulton's most trusted employees, with the express intention that he would inherit when the time was right. Henry Oulton just didn't bother telling anyone on my side of the family about him. I suppose we are to blame for being more distant relatives than we should have been."

I nodded. "And where is Le Croix now?"

"That," said Seaman, "is the conundrum. Oulton said he went to visit my sister Jane and secured lodging with him for a while. However, he failed to return to Bolton and has simply vanished into thin air."

"That makes sense," I said. "The Bootles' neighbours spoke of a visitor – a young man, who stayed with them for several days. They also say he vanished without trace. However, Katherine was here at the same time. She said nothing to you?"

"No," said Seaman, "but you saw for yourself. Something was troubling her when she returned to Chester from her visit. I'll wager this had something to do with it."

"And is it possible Francis Gamull or Robert Whitby know anything about this?"

"No…I don't know. Katherine could have said something to them, I suppose. Why do you ask?"

"Because you have sold Gamull a share in the business, of course. Le Croix's existence means that agreement is invalid as things stand. It also gives them both a motive for all three murders and may explain Le Croix's disappearance."

Seaman blanched as the implications of what I had said began to sink in. Lawrence, however, was frowning and looking confused.

"William Bootle said nothing about such a visitor," he said. "Is it also not possible that this Frenchman could be the murderer?"

"I think not, Lawrence," I said, patiently. "Le Croix is the main beneficiary. There is no reason for him to murder anyone. And there is no reason why William Bootle should necessarily have been aware of his visit. He was not that close to his brother."

Lawrence looked at me and exhaled deeply. "So what do we do now?" he asked. "We are no nearer the truth, and my father sits in gaol."

I have to admit, I was also running out of ideas, but then William Seaman spoke. "There's one thing I haven't told you," he said. "Le Croix has a sister, a most charming young lady. Her name is Beatrice and she travelled with me from Bolton to help find her brother. You will, I think, find her in our lodgings on Aughton Street. She is travelling as my daughter."

Chapter 30

Beatrice Le Croix was not difficult to locate. Dressed soberly in a plain maroon bodice with a white lace collar and a matching maroon dress, she was sat demurely on her own in a corner of the tavern, eating a plate of mutton, onions, and potatoes.

"You friends of hers, then?" asked the landlord, with suspicion. "Because if you are, you can pay for her food, because the fellow she arrived with has buggered off and left her with no money."

"Her father, you mean?" I said, remembering the pretence under which Seaman had secured lodgings for them both.

"Aye, if you wish," said the landlord. "If you settle her debt, she can be whoever you like, although, to be honest, if she's that fellow's daughter, then I'm Prince Rupert. The fellow who disappeared was a local man, she's a bloody frenchie! I don't blame the man for pretending, though," he added. "She's a comely enough lass, if the truth be told. I've spent the last hour fending off these drooling bastards. Like bees to a honey pot, they are."

The landlord indicated to a table not far away, where a group of leering soldiers sat, glancing over occasionally at the girl, who looked up as she realised she was being talked about.

The landlord was certainly right. Beatrice was an attractive young woman. Olive-skinned, with full lips and dark brown eyes, she wore her straight black hair parted in the middle and tucked just under her coif. Lawrence was also not slow to notice the girl's charms and, before I could react, he had bounded off to her table to introduce himself.

I settled for paying Beatrice's unpaid bill for food and lodging and ordering two more plates of food and tankards of ale for Lawrence and myself. The room was not cheap, but that was not surprising, for the inns and taverns were full to bursting with soldiers and officers. Indeed, I was surprised that Seaman had managed to find accommodation at all. Some poor junior officer, I guessed, would have been removed from his quarters so that the unusual couple could be accommodated.

By the time I sat down, Lawrence had already introduced himself as William Seaman's son, and Beatrice's face had taken on a less worried expression.

"So, I am your cousin," she said, shaking Lawrence's hand. "Enchantée, monsieur."

"It would appear so," said Lawrence, "one that I did not know I had until a short time ago."

"Indeed," said Beatrice, in an apologetic tone. "Your father told me you were not aware of my existence, or that of Marc, my brother. And you," she added, turning to me, "must be Mr Cheswis. William said you are a good man, skilled in solving problems such as ours. He is confident that you may help us find out what has happened to Marc and why William's close relatives are being murdered."

"I am flattered that Mr Seaman holds me in such regard," I said, truthfully. "His trust is based on hearsay, I assure you. I'm afraid I have been able to solve very little as yet to justify such confidence, but I will endeavour to do my best. Perhaps you should begin by explaining how you come to be in Ormskirk. I hear from your accent that you cannot have been here very long."

Beatrice smiled and pulled her chair closer to the table. "It is true," she admitted. "In fact, I have only been in England for a matter of weeks, since I heard of my great uncle's illness."

I looked at Beatrice with interest. "Great uncle?" I said. "I thought Henry Oulton was your great-grandfather?"

"No, that's not true," replied Beatrice. "Marc is only my half-brother. He is two years older than me and is a direct descendent of Henry Oulton. My father, on the other hand, is Guillaume Le Croix, who married the widow of Henry Oulton's grandson after his death. My father raised Marc as a son, but when he was twelve, my Great Uncle Henry sent for him in the knowledge that he would become heir to his fortune one day. He wanted him brought up in the English way and had him raised by a local family in Bolton. However, my great uncle told no-one; until now, that is."

"I see," I said, "but that doesn't explain why you came to England."

"It's quite simple," said Beatrice. "My father was concerned for his livelihood – all he has worked for. Marc wrote to us to say that Great Uncle Henry was gravely ill, so I thought to travel to England to represent our interests. But when I arrived in Bolton, I discovered Marc had left to visit his cousins in Ormskirk."

"Have you any idea why he would do that?"

"Despite many years in England, Marc still has a French accent; or at least so he says, for I have not heard him speak for eleven years. Marc confided in me that he was concerned at the way things were going in Bolton, which was becoming a Puritan stronghold. We are Catholics from the south-west of France, and Marc wished to move somewhere where he would be less likely to be persecuted for his faith. He had heard that this might be possible in Ormskirk. I believe there are many who still follow our faith in this area."

"That is true," I conceded.

"I had not expected Marc to return to Bolton until

things became easier there," said Beatrice, "but I had not heard from him and needed to find him urgently."

"And then William Seaman turned up and told you that not only had Katherine Seaman and Jane Bootle been murdered, but your brother had vanished too."

"That is the truth of it, Mr Cheswis," said Beatrice, dabbing the corner of her eye with a handkerchief. "Do you think you will be able to find Marc for me?"

"I cannot be sure of that," I admitted. "Things are becoming clearer than they were, but there are still several aspects of this case which confuse me. One thing is certain, though. Time is no longer on our side, for unless we can find the real murderer, William Seaman will hang for crimes he did not commit."

Chapter 31

Lathom House – Sunday April 14th – Saturday April 20th, 1644

The next three days passed by quietly. Were it not for the constant passage of officers in and out of New Park House, one would have been forgiven for thinking that the siege had ended. The temporary calm gave Alexander and myself the opportunity to spend more time with Lawrence and Beatrice. The Frenchwoman, it seemed to me, was the key to the solving of both murders. Her missing half-brother, Marc Le Croix, was at the heart of everything, and Beatrice was the only person I knew who had a direct connection to him. She would, I hoped, prove to be the catalyst that set me on my way to identifying the perpetrator of both crimes. Time was of the essence, though, not only due to William Seaman's predicament, but because Lawrence, Alexander, and I had been obliged to fund Beatrice's board and lodging, something we could not afford to do forever.

On the Sunday afternoon, after we had completed our shift, Alexander and I took advantage of the warmer spring weather and strolled into Ormskirk, where we called on Lawrence and suggested that we accompany Beatrice on a walk through the nearby countryside. This would, I told him, give Beatrice the opportunity to escape the confines of her quarters in the tavern and provide a more relaxed environment in which to question her about the relationship between her family and the Oultons.

Lawrence, as I expected, readily agreed, for I had not failed to notice the way he was looking at the young Frenchwoman. Beatrice herself was less keen on the excursion, for she was fearful of becoming too noticeable in and around the town. Nevertheless, we managed to persuade her, and after a brief lunch in the tavern (added, of course, to my rapidly growing debt to the landlord) we set out intrepidly along lanes to the north of the town until we reached the small village of Burscough, a couple of miles away. Here we explored the remains of the small priory, destroyed the previous century by King Henry. Nearby stood a mill, apparently disused but probably still serviceable. It was here that we were witnesses to a very strange occurrence.

As we came within a hundred yards of the building, the door opened and a man stepped carefully out, looking around assiduously, before striding purposefully over towards the ruined priory, where he disappeared behind a wall. This episode could only have lasted a few seconds, but Alexander, Lawrence, and I all looked at each other with astonishment, for we were all thinking the same thing.

"God's teeth, Alexander," I said. "Tell me that was not William Bootle, because it looked for all the world like him."

"It certainly *looked* like him," confirmed Alexander, "but why would he be here?"

"I don't know," said Lawrence, "but he does live not so very far from here. Perhaps he knows the mill owner. Come, let us find him and ask him ourselves."

All four of us quickened our pace and marched over to where we had seen the figure disappear, but there was no sign of Bootle at all, and no obvious path which he might have taken, where he would have remained out of our sight.

"Strange," said Alexander. "But perhaps we were mistaken."

"Maybe," I agreed, "but even if it was not Bootle, that does not explain what happened to the person we saw."

I would have thought no more about this episode, were it not for what happened during the course of the following week.

On the Monday morning, Colonel Rigby recommenced his bombardment of Lathom House with increased intensity. During the day, the mortar was fired five times with stones. However, on the sixth occasion, Morgan used one of his grenades, which sailed over the walls, landing close to the Chapel Tower and exploding with a mighty boom. We could only imagine the damage caused to some of the flimsy wood and plaster buildings within the walls, but the amount of shrieking and shouting which we heard confirmed that the shell had produced the desired effect.

The next morning, the cannon, now unspiked, was used to bombard the battlements and tower walls, and this was followed by thirty minutes of heavy musket fire. At eleven in the morning, Morgan ordered his artillery team to fire the mortar, initially charged with stones. When the first shot landed accurately in the middle of the house, the Welshman ordered his men to fire another grenade, which landed inside the walls, but seemed to explode in mid-air, causing a huge blast which sent shrapnel and clay flying in all directions.

It was clear that the tactic of using the mortar was starting to succeed. The only dampener on the morning's activities was the fact that one of Morgan's men climbed up onto the earthworks surrounding the mortar, in an attempt to see where the grenade had landed, and was promptly shot dead by one of the marksmen positioned on the towers.

Flushed by two days of success, one might have expected Rigby to have continued the bombardment, but he didn't. On the Wednesday an uneasy quiet reigned, and with the days after that being Maundy Thursday and Good Friday respectively, Rigby appeared to have left the garrison to consider the damage Lathom House was likely to sustain after Easter, although many suggested the ceasefire had more to do with the fact that the colonel was still waiting for his long-awaited delivery of mortar shells.

It was during these three days of relative calm that my attention was once again drawn to the curious movements of William Bootle, and, predictably, it was my friend Alexander Clowes who unwittingly opened my eyes to that which I might otherwise have missed.

On the Wednesday, just after noon, we were walking back, heavy-legged and exhausted from our shift, when Alexander suddenly grabbed me by the arm and gesticulated towards the gateway of New Park House a hundred yards away. I glanced over to where Alexander was pointing and saw that William Bootle had left the house by the main gateway, had skirted round the front of the buildings, and was heading through the gardens where the dovecote was located, towards a track which led through the fields to the north, towards the road to both Ormskirk and Burscough.

I would have considered this of little significance, were it not for the fact that Alexander said, "You know, I could have sworn he did this last Thursday, and we know for a fact he went to Burscough on Sunday afternoon too."

I slowed my pace to a dawdle and thought about this for a moment. I had the strange feeling that Alexander had said something of critical importance, but I could not work out what it was.

"Remind me," I said. "On which day does Bootle do his shift in the trenches?"

"He usually does the day before us," said Alexander, "but because he is Rigby's only expert on the interior of the house, he is at the colonel's beck and call whenever his services are required. As a result, he is afforded some flexibility. If the colonel needs him to be on hand for certain operations, he is allowed to rest at certain other times."

Again, I considered this for a short while, and slowly, a pattern began to emerge.

"Wait a minute," I said. "Over the course of the last ten days, there have been only four days on which Bootle was both free and on which there was no bombardment. Three of those days were Thursday, Sunday, and today. The other day – Saturday – we were on duty ourselves, so he may well have been on the march on that day too."

"And on the days when Morgan was peppering the house with his artillery, he stayed put."

"Exactly. And there's one other thing. On Wednesday morning, when the garrison launched their attack, Bootle should have been on duty, facing the attack, but he was not, at least not the whole time, for it was he who alerted us to the attack. Presumably he received special dispensation from Rigby to stand down and take that time off."

"So when we attack the garrison or when the garrison attacks us, Bootle is safely tucked away in New Park House, but when things are quiet, he sneaks off to Burscough at a similar time each day."

"So it appears," I said, "but perhaps it's just a coincidence. Let us keep watch over the next couple of days and see what transpires."

I said little more that day on the matter, but I did take note that it was five in the afternoon before Bootle reappeared inside the courtyard at New Park House. The next day was also without activity from our artillery, but Bootle was on duty himself, so the first day that we were able to test our theory was on Good Friday.

As it happened, Rigby kept his guns quiet for a third day in succession. Unfortunately, we were on duty ourselves, so I slipped a few coins to one of the ostlers with whom I had become friends, and, on our return to New Park House at midday on the Saturday, he was able to report to us that Bootle had indeed crept surreptitiously out of New Park House the previous afternoon and made his way through the garden and onto the track towards Burscough.

As luck would have it, Good Friday was also significant in that on that day, Colonel Egerton was recalled to Manchester, leaving Rigby as the sole commander of the siege.

"Ah, now the cat is well and truly out of the bag," commented the ever-cynical Browne on hearing the news, and, in my judgement, he was not mistaken, for on the Saturday morning, the colonel ordered Morgan to move the demi-cannon and the culverin to the north-east gun placement opposite the postern gate and begin bombarding the tower next to it.

This, in itself, was not a bad idea, for, as the tower protruded beyond the moat, it offered one of the more likely ways of breaching the walls. However, Rigby's haste once again became his undoing, for he had miscalculated the lie of the land, which sloped away too steeply from the gate. The best Morgan's gunners were able to do, therefore, was to damage a small section of wall high on the battlements, which the garrison was able to make good within the space of a couple of hours.

I felt sure Morgan had realised Rigby's mistake, but he said nothing. Nonetheless, his mood cannot have been helped by the fact that one of his gunners was killed by one of Lady Derby's marksmen, shooting through a pothole in the tower.

That afternoon, Morgan switched his attention from the postern gate to the main gateway, using his mortar five times to good effect. The growth in intensity of the bombardment was palpable, and there was a feeling of anticipation among our troops that at long last a reckoning was due, and that it would be Lady Derby who would be counting the cost.

For my part, I stayed well away from the action, not just because I was tired from the previous night's exertions, but because I wanted to keep a watch over Bootle, who maintained an uneasy presence at New Park House and seemed to become increasingly disconcerted as the day progressed. He tried to affect a certain nonchalance, but I was not fooled, and I caught him several times staring through the windows in the direction of the siege works.

With Morgan continuing to bombard the house with mortar fire, albeit still restricted to the use of stones and boulders, I was not expecting any movement from the captain, but suddenly, at around three in the afternoon, out of the corner of my eye, I watched him sidle out of the drawing room. A few moments later I heard the crunch of footsteps on the stones in the courtyard as he marched towards the main gate.

I gave Bootle a few moments' start, then made my way across the courtyard myself. As I did so, I signalled to Alexander, who had been sat in a corner of the yard, out of Bootle's line of vision.

"You stay here and get some real sleep," I said, "we need at least one of us to be awake later in order to maintain a watch." My friend nodded gratefully and stumbled off in the direction of our chamber.

Once outside the house, I made my way through the gardens, past the dovecote, and out onto the track through the fields. Bootle, I noted with satisfaction, was still in sight, a couple of hundred yards ahead. Keeping to the hedgerows so as to avoid discovery, I followed him as far as the fork in the road, where the main route headed west into Ormskirk, leaving a smaller, narrower track heading north in the direction of Burscough. As I suspected, Bootle took the northern route, heading straight for the mill.

Two miles later, concealing myself as best I could behind a hedgerow, I watched the captain enter the mill buildings by a wooden door to what looked like a storeroom, before vanishing from sight. Thirty minutes after this, he reappeared, and, to my amazement, he did exactly as he had done the previous Sunday, heading straight for the ruined priory before disappearing from sight behind a wall.

I leapt from my hiding place and ran across towards the tumbledown ruins, but I was confused to find that Bootle had once again completely vanished, as if by magic. I walked slowly around the area where I had seen Bootle last, examining the walls for potential hiding places, but was disappointed to find nothing.

As I did so, however, I began to feel a strange prickling sensation on the back of my neck, as though I was being watched. I looked over my shoulder and nearly jumped out of my skin as a small figure appeared from behind the wall.

"Sweet Jesus," I breathed, exhaling in relief as I recognised the scrawny shape of Jenny Reade. "Jenny, what the devil are you doing here?" I exclaimed.

"Same as you, Mr Cheswis, I s'ppose. He's a strange fellow, that one. Disappears regular like, inside the mill, then vanishes like a ghost."

"You've seen him before, Jenny?"

"Oh, aye, I notice things like that. Out of the ordnery, you see. He's been up and down here regular as you like. Every few days, for sure, but nearly every day recently."

"Any idea where he goes to?"

"Dunno, Mr Cheswis, but there's some folks as say there's a tunnel from here that leads to the house. P'raps that how Mr Chisnall managed to escape-"

Jenny got no further, for I grabbed her by the shoulders and planted a kiss on her forehead, transforming her face instantly into one of astonishment. Of course! Why had I not thought of that before? It was the obvious solution. All of a sudden, things started to fall into place. I cast my mind back and realised, suddenly, that the strangely familiar voice that I had heard from behind the door whilst imprisoned inside the house had been that of Bootle himself.

"Jenny," I said, reaching inside my purse for a shilling and pressing it into her palm, "you don't know how helpful you've been."

Jenny's face, on sight of the coin, slowly changed back into a grin, although it was clear that she had no idea why she had been so richly rewarded.

"Aye, well," she said, "I'm happy to help you, Mr Cheswis. You're always kind to me."

So William Bootle was Rigby's spy, I mused in wonder. Operating a sophisticated double bluff, he had been able to join Rigby's forces as an informer, whilst all the time informing Lady Derby about Rigby's own plans. I realised I had to report back to the colonel in order to effect Bootle's arrest as soon as he returned to New Park House.

It was then, however, that I realised there was more to it than this, that my work was not quite done, and that Bootle could not be arrested just yet. There were still a few answers that I needed in order to complete the whole picture of what had happened during these past weeks. Bootle, I realised, would have to be afforded his freedom for a few days yet; but I knew exactly what to do. I had several tasks to complete, and for one of those tasks I needed the help of the young girl who was looking at me expectantly.

"Jenny," I said. "There is one thing you can help me with. Do you know the house where John and Jane Bootle used to live?"

"The people who were murdered?" said Jenny. "Aye, their house backs onto the church."

"That's right," I said. "Meet me outside the church

344

after tomorrow's service. I have something I need you
to do for me."

Chapter 32

"Let me get this straight," said Alexander, when I related my findings to him later that evening. "We have been sent to this hellhole for the sole purpose of identifying the spy within Rigby's ranks. Against all odds, we have achieved that. If we have Bootle arrested today, we will be feted as heroes, and we will be allowed to return to our families in Nantwich in one piece and with our reputations enhanced. And yet you are proposing that we conceal our findings, running the risk of Bootle escaping justice and ourselves being arrested, all in order that you might solve three murders that neither took place within your jurisdiction, nor which you have any real obligation to solve. Have you taken leave of your senses?"

The logic of my friend's argument, of course, was unimpeachable. I thought about Elizabeth, young Ralph, Mrs Padgett, Amy, Jack Wade, and all the others who depended on me, but then I considered the plight of William Seaman, who would surely hang if

I were to abandon him. And, I had to admit it, there was also something within my nature which forbade me from leaving a job half done, an obsessiveness borne from perfectionism, which told me that it was my duty to unravel the mystery that was tearing the Seaman family apart. Mrs Padgett would have called it pig-headedness, and I could see from Alexander's expression that he felt the same.

"You are like a dog with a bone, Daniel," he said.

"I confess it," I replied, "but if we do nothing, we are condemning William Seaman to death; besides which I believe I know how these murders were committed."

"You do?" said Alexander, giving me a searching look. "How?"

"These killings are not related to Bootle's activities as a spy," I explained. "The murderer's motives lie somewhere in the relationship between the four families of Bootle, Le Croix, Oulton, and Seaman, the exact nature of which I have not yet ascertained. This is partly due to the fact that we have not yet established where Marc Le Croix sits in all of this. He was simply here one day and gone the next. So is he an accessory or a victim? I have some theories, which I need to test, but I need a few days to prove them, and to do this, it is best if Bootle remains at large."

"A few days?" exclaimed Alexander. "We don't have that much time."

"Perhaps that is so," I conceded, "but I believe we *do*

347

have a few days. Firstly, Bootle does not yet know that we suspect him. Secondly, tomorrow is Sunday, and from midday onwards, Bootle will be on duty in the siege works. From Monday till Tuesday, it is our turn in the trenches, but if I am right, Rigby will intensify his bombardment, at least for the early part of the week. We have, therefore, at least until Tuesday by my reckoning, perhaps a little longer. Let us be patient; we have no other option. If I reveal what I know now, Rigby, who as you know, doesn't much care for either of us, will send us on our way."

Alexander sighed in acquiescence. "And are you going to reveal your suspicions to me?" he asked.

"Not yet," I said. "I have one or two people to speak to first. Most important, though, is that you do not breathe a word of this to Lawrence or Beatrice. They must act naturally. We cannot tolerate either of them inadvertently alerting Bootle to what we know."

***

Jenny Reade was waiting for me when I emerged from Reverend Nutt's sermon the following day. I found her sat on the church wall, swinging her legs to and fro and humming a tune to herself. Her dog was sleeping quietly in the grass beneath her feet.

"Don't you attend church on a Sunday, Jenny?" I asked. "I find it relaxes the mind."

"No point," muttered the girl, moodily. "If God exists, he ain't done me no favours, that's for sure. An' the folk round here don't seem too mithered about me staying away, either. Best to keep myself to myself, if you ask me."

I smiled in sympathy. Jenny's viewpoint was understandable. Life had not dealt her a particularly advantageous hand. "I see you prefer your own company," I said, "but nonetheless, it's best if you show up every now and then. People are afraid of what they don't know. You have a secretive nature, and you are known to be knowledgeable about herbs and remedies. You would not be the first woman to fall foul of such a set of circumstances."

"You mean they'll have me for a witch?"

"That's what I fear," I admitted.

Jenny smiled and put her hand on my arm. "Your concern for us is strange, Mr Cheswis," she said, "but it is welcome. What is it you want of me today?"

"The benefit of your knowledge," I replied. "I believe Mr Bootle may have been poisoned. If I describe the symptoms, would you be able to hazard a guess at the cause?"

"I can try."

"Good," I said. "Wild, staring eyes, hallucinations, ranting speech, a feeling of flying. What can cause that?"

Jenny looked at me curiously for a moment and then took me by the hand. Leading me through the churchyard, she headed straight for the wall which backed onto the Bootles' house and gestured towards a clump of ugly-looking plants with sticky, hairy stems and triangular, pointed leaves.

"Henbane," she said. "Many also call it stinking nightshade because of its smell. In small quantities it has a strong calming effect. Good for the nerves, so my mam used to say. She used to mix it with other herbs to make ointments and poultices. It's dangerous, though, if you don't know what you're doing. If you take too much, it will send you into a sleep from which you will not wake. It could be something else, but, as you see, it grows here aplenty."

I stepped up to the plant and caught a whiff of its strong, putrid aroma, which I immediately recognised as the stench I was unable to identify in the Bootles' kitchen on the day of their death.

"Thank you, Jenny," I said. "That's all I need for now, but there is one more thing you can do for me. Keep an eye out at Burscough Mill for me, and if the fellow we saw the other day puts in an appearance, be sure to let me know. I will return to New Park House at noon on Tuesday."

Once again, I put my hands in my pocket to extract a couple of coins, but this time Jenny stopped me. "Not today, Mr Cheswis," she said. "Today it's my turn to do something for *you*." And with that, she turned on her heels and skipped down the road, her dog barking at her ankles.

Chapter 33

If there had been any doubts about the vindictiveness of Colonel Rigby's intentions now that Egerton had been recalled to Manchester, or about his ability to stage a public show, these were rapidly dispelled the following morning, when the extent of the colonel's planning became clear.

It was Easter Monday, and, with the prospect of free entertainment, the populace of Lathom, Ormskirk, and the surrounding villages had flocked in their droves to see Lady Charlotte, the Countess of Derby, brought to her knees. It was like a public hanging. It never ceased to amaze me how folk could derive pleasure from someone else's misfortune in this way.

Hundreds of people had gathered on the land to the north-east of the house, where the artillery was now located. Many had turned up in their Sunday best and had brought baskets of food and flagons of ale with them to last the whole day. Those who had left sustenance at home were amply served by an army of traders and peddlers, who, with an eye for business, had brought all manner of bread, pies, cakes, fruit, and beer for sale to those who could afford it. The aromas of cooked meat and baking filled the air. There was also a fair smattering of jugglers, minstrels, jesters, and other entertainers, as well as the usual collection of beggars and vagrants who showed up at every public gathering.

Rigby, for his part, was doing his best to ensure that he was the main attraction, strutting through the crowds, shaking hands, bowing to the ladies and ruffling the hair of children. His strange, lopsided smile was wider than ever, but on this day the expression on his face was genuine.

"Today," he had told us, at a briefing held in the main encampment before the crowds arrived, "is the beginning of the end for Lathom House. Gentlemen, it is entirely just that God should choose a time when we celebrate the resurrection to impose his judgement on the whore of Babylon herself and the hordes of cavaliers, traitors, and papists that follow her. By Friday," he added, "we shall have the grenades we need to teach Lady Derby's men a lesson, once and for all. For King and Parliament!"

"For King and Parliament!" echoed the dwindling group of officers. Now that Assheton, Moore, and Egerton had left Lathom, taking their officers with them, most of the remaining men were loyal to Rigby, and the majority responded with renewed vigour.

Morgan, in particular, puffed out his chest and pulled himself up to his full height, which, admittedly, was not very much, before marching with determination in the direction of the gun placement opposite the postern tower. Browne, on the other hand, cast a knowing look in my direction and made circles with his index finger, pointing towards his temple to indicate what he thought of Rigby's state of mind.

"He is mad with hatred and power," said the engineer, once the crowd of officers had dispersed, "but it seems the colonel is determined to have his day."

And so it proved. Orchestrating arrangements for maximum theatrical effect, Rigby made sure that the onlookers were kept entertained all day. Firstly, he had his best team of musketeers spend half an hour firing at Lady Derby's sharpshooters on the battlements. Not that they had any effect on those inside the garrison, for muskets were as good as useless against the well-protected men inside the house, but they did provide a great deal of noise and entertainment for the spectators, who cheered every shot enthusiastically.

Morgan then moved his artillery team into place and ordered his cannon to dispense eight or nine shots at the battlements and the towers. He then marched round to the mortar placement opposite the main gate and fired two lots of stones deep into the house. The crowd gave prolonged cheers as the rocks disappeared high into the air before crashing down violently on the roofs of the buildings inside the walls.

By this time, I was sat in the trenches myself and was amazed at the bloodlust of the local population. Many of these people, I realised, had friends and relations inside the house, but still they cheered.

"War does strange things to mankind," I said to Browne, as I watched a shower of rocks fly over my head.

"You are in the right of it, Cheswis," said the engineer, "but it is ironic, would you not say, that our hate-driven colonel has created a sideshow here for the entertainment of the good folk of Lathom? It is an entirely appropriate response, for this siege is little more than a sideshow in the grand scheme of this war, believe me. The trouble we can cause, if we are successful – and, of course, there is no guarantee of that – is barely worse than a pimple on the King's arse. Even if we do take this place, Rupert will be here before long, and the whole rigmarole will start again. I ask you, what the devil are we doing this for?"

I was warming to Browne, someone who, like me, who had been dragged into the conflict against his will, in his case because of his particular skill in construction techniques. I would have liked to discuss things more with him, but realised I could not, for there was one person I urgently needed to seek out, and, during my first break from duty, I took the opportunity to locate him among the spectators. He was exactly where I expected to find him, less than five yards from a beer seller, propped up against a bank of earth and supping from a pewter tankard.

"Good afternoon, Isaac," I said, purchasing two more beers from the trader and handing one to my companion.

"Ah, Mr Cheswis, good health to you," said Isaac, trying to get to his feet, but succeeding only in falling back down on his rump and spilling a good proportion of the beer I had just given him. Isaac, as usual, was in his cups, but I was hoping he would be lucid enough for my purposes.

"Don't get up," I said, sitting down next to him. "I'll join you. I just wanted to ask a couple of questions."

"Oh, aye?"

"Yes. Nothing of great import, I assure you. I just wanted to make sure I was not mistaken about something and make some use of your local knowledge."

"Well, I'll try," said Isaac, slurring his words slightly.

"The first thing is this," I said. "On the night you said you saw the ghost by Mary Reade's grave, how much had you drunk?"

"Oh quite a bit, Mr Cheswis, but I weren't that drunk. I saw what I saw, and I'll stand by it."

"How much?" I persisted. "About the same as you've drunk today?"

"Oh aye," he said, "that's for sure, but I can see you now all right. Just as I saw the ghost of Mary Reade that evening. What was the other thing you wanted to know?"

"Burscough Mill," I said. "You've been here a long time. What can you tell me about that place?"

"The mill?" said Isaac, with a confused look on his face. "Why would you want to know?"

"Let's just say I have an interest in who might be living there."

"Living there?" Isaac snorted with laughter. "No-one to my knowledge. A few rats mebbe, that's all. I think it's still used from time to time, but not the whole year round. The buildings are half-derelict, although I believe the grain store is still secure and is used at certain times of year. But I can't imagine anyone wanting to live there, proper like. It's not much better than a cowshed, if you ask me."

It was then that I had a thought. "Tell me," I said, "do you know who owns the mill?"

"Oh aye," replied Isaac, taking a large swig from his tankard, drops spilling down the front of his shirt. "Everyone knows that. But you won't get to speak to him too easily, mind, for he's the personal chaplain to the Countess of Derby. Rutter is his name, Samuel Rutter."

Chapter 34

I was not afforded much of an opportunity to consider the revelation that Isaac had presented me with until the following morning, for during the hours of darkness the garrison kept us well-occupied. Having already inflicted considerable losses on our forces during the previous nocturnal raids, Lady Derby's men had developed an enviable degree of resourcefulness in creating alarms and diversions to cause panic within our ranks, for which I conceded them some grudging respect.

One of their favourite tricks was to fix a length of slow-burning match cord into a ball of clay and throw it over the battlements towards our trenches. This inevitably caused gales of laughter as our musketeers shot at thin air or scattered in disarray like chickens being chased by a fox.

At one point, two of their marksmen ventured out of the postern gate with matchlock muskets with the aim of causing a diversion, attracting a massive volley of fire from our trenches. The royalists quickly retreated

357

back inside the walls with little risk to their safety, and we gradually began to realise that Lady Derby's men were treating us like playthings, engendering fear, creating nervousness, and making us waste our ammunition.

Once dawn broke, however, the pendulum began to swing once again in our favour. No longer were the royalists able to use the protection of the darkness to conceal surprise attacks on our positions, and Morgan was able to make full use of his artillery to strike terror into the hearts of the besieged.

By nine in the morning on Tuesday, it was becoming clear that everything was set perfectly for Rigby to achieve what he had in mind. It was a bright spring morning, clear and fresh with fleece-like clouds scudding across the sky, encouraging even bigger crowds to assemble in front of the house than on the previous day, in the hope of seeing an even more spectacular show.

Rigby and Morgan once again took prime positions close to the gun battery to the north-east of the house. However, this time I noticed that they were accompanied by a reluctant-looking Captain Bootle, who I could see, from where I was standing, out of range and behind the outer breastwork, was in deep conversation with Morgan and appeared to be pointing towards the Eagle Tower. The reason for this soon became clear once the diminutive Welshman began his bombardment.

Over the course of the next two hours, Morgan aimed shot after shot at one particular corner of the tower, about halfway up, until eventually a breach was made in the wall, and the gunner was able to send a cannonball clean through the hole into the interior of the tower, sending plumes of dust billowing out into the air.

"That," announced Morgan, with pride and to enthusiastic cheers from the assembled onlookers, "was the private chamber of the countess herself. Tonight she will be sleeping in less comfortable surroundings than those to which she is normally accustomed."

"No wonder Bootle looks worried," whispered Alexander, who was standing next to me. "I would not wish to be in his position, having to explain to the countess why he has revealed the location of her ladyship's private quarters."

"He could barely refuse," I said. "Giving false information to Rigby would have brought him under suspicion."

Having commanded Morgan's artillery to cease their bombardment of the Eagle Tower, Rigby now stepped forward and delivered the words that I knew were coming, but which I had been dreading.

"Ladies and gentlemen of Lathom," he announced, his face betraying the manic triumph of one who is convinced his destiny is about to be achieved. "Today you have seen some fine sport, but now the serious business begins. Tomorrow and Thursday we will give Lady Derby the opportunity to reconsider her continued defiance of the will of Parliament, but on Friday our patience runs out. Then, I invite the officers and gentlemen of the Manchester Committee and all the people of Ormskirk and Lathom to attend this place, when I pledge that Lathom House will be destroyed and removed from the face of the Earth."

I cast a glance across to the group of officers standing behind Rigby. Morgan's face bore the broad grin of the supremely confident, but Bootle, standing next to him, had blanched noticeably. He was trying manfully to force a smile, but I was not fooled.

"Alexander," I said. "Time is of the essence. We have but two days to complete our work here. We need to find Lawrence and Beatrice, for I need their help."

"Beatrice is here," said Alexander. "I'm sure I saw her amongst the crowds this morning. Rigby's show must have been too much to resist. And if Beatrice *is* here," he added, with a knowing smile, "Lawrence will not be too far away."

Alexander was right. We found them holding hands on a grassy mound a few yards away from the milling throng of spectators. Beatrice saw us coming and treated me with a smile from ear to ear. I could see what Lawrence saw in her.

"Bonjour, Monsieur Cheswis, Monsieur Clowes,"

she said. "It is good to see you are all safe."

Lawrence, who had been staring at his feet, looked up and nodded affably in my direction. "Morning, Daniel," he said. "Are you any closer to working out how to get my father out of gaol?"

"I think so," I said. "I have a theory, but there is one thing which still troubles me. I cannot fathom what role Marc plays in all of this. Old Isaac said he heard him talking about a score he had to settle. What on Earth did he mean?"

Beatrice suddenly sat up straight and looked at me earnestly. "Au secours," she said, simply, "is the French for help. Marc was simply asking Isaac to help him."

I clasped my left hand to my forehead as the meaning of the words sank in. If only I had possessed some French!

"Then that means Marc is in danger," said Lawrence, "...or worse."

Beatrice gasped at the implication, and Lawrence instinctively put his arm around her shoulder.

"We will find him, Beatrice," he said, softly, before turning to me. "So what do we need to do?"

"In the first instance, I suggest all three of you return to your lodgings in Ormskirk and try and get some sleep, for we have a busy night ahead. In the meantime, I need to spend some time with Jenny Reade. I will meet you outside the church at two in the morning."

"The church?" exclaimed Alexander. "At what time?

What on Earth do you have in mind?"

"I will enlighten you later," I said. "Just one thing though. Make sure you bring a lantern and a spade."

***

Jenny was waiting for me when I arrived back at New Park House. She had been observing my approach from within the walled garden and stepped out to greet me when she was sure she could not be seen by anyone else. I noticed her dog was not with her and remarked as such.

"Are you daft?" she said, scornfully. "'He's with my brother and sister. I can't bring him here. The soldiers would shoot him as soon as look at him."

This was true, of course. The dog's errands to and from the postern gate had recently begun to be noticed by others within our ranks. Bored musketeers hungry for sport had recognised the degree of status that would be accrued by the person who managed to stop the dog in his tracks and had begun to take pot shots at him as he scurried across the moor-like ground between the house and our siege works. Slowly but surely, he had become a marked target. I had found myself secretly hoping that one of the musketeers would succeed, for it was only a matter of time before Rigby tasked me with the responsibility of identifying the animal's owner, and that, I knew, would spell serious trouble for Jenny.

I had it in mind to explain this to her, but I bit my tongue and forced myself to leave the lecture for

362

another time. I was not her father, after all. Instead, I focused on the matter in hand.

"So, did you keep watch for me at Burscough Mill?" I asked.

"Yes," replied Jenny, her face brightening. "He came back, the man we saw, just as you said."

"And when was that?" I asked.

"Yesterday afternoon, about four o'clock. He did the same as before. Went inside the mill for a while and then disappeared amongst the priory ruins. Who is he, Mr Cheswis, and why are you so interested in him?"

I gave Jenny a serious look. "His name is Bootle," I said. "He is a captain under Colonel Rigby. He is also the brother of John Bootle, the man who was murdered with his wife in the house by the church." I watched Jenny's eyes widen at this. "As for his significance," I added, "I think you probably have some idea of this. Am I right?"

Jenny pouted and said nothing, so I persisted.

"Am I correct in thinking you have seen him several times already, that you have been keeping watch on the mill for some time, and that is why you saw me there the other day?"

Again Jenny kept silent, but I could tell that I was right and that she was contemplating whether her best option was to come clean or run.

"Listen, Jenny," I said. "I will not betray you, but you must help me. Would this have something to do with Edward Chisnall, perchance?"

Jenny nodded. "He told me to go there," she said. "When he took away his horse, the last time I saw him. He said he could no longer visit my house and told me to deliver any future messages to the mill at Burscough. Someone, he said, would pick 'em up from there."

"And messages going the other way?"

"There's a water butt round the side of the mill. I was to look behind there for messages."

"And then send the dog over to the house, I suppose? Jenny, you must be careful, you will get yourself arrested."

"But what am I to do?" she retorted, her voice angry now, eyes flashing dangerously. "My brother Harry is inside the house, trapped. Until this siege ends and he's free, I have to look after my other brother an' sister myself, an' as you can see, we have little to call our own. I have to go outside to earn or scavenge what I can. My brother an' sister are too young for this, so they stay at home an' look after the house."

"And they can do that?"

"They are young, but I've shown 'em what to do. How to clean, cook, make a fire. When you have nobody else, you learn quickly. But I repeat, we wait for Harry to come home. The house is now his, and he'll look after us once he's free. Until then we must wait."

"Harry has told you this?"

"In his messages, aye, of course."

I stood in silence for a moment and looked at Jenny in pity. She was truly trapped, with no option but to do her brother's bidding, regardless of the risk to herself.

"Very well," I said, eventually. "So tell me, you have been keeping watch on the mill for a while. Is Bootle the only person you have seen there?"

"No, there've been others. I've seen Mr Chisnall a couple of times. I believe his horse may be kept there now."

"And how does Chisnall get there? The same way as Bootle? From somewhere in the priory?"

Jenny nodded. "But there is also someone else," she said, "someone inside the mill. I couldn't see her properly, but she opened the door for the others a couple of times."

I looked up sharply. "Her?" I said. "You mean there's a woman in there?"

"Aye. As I say, she keeps in the shadows, away from view."

I smiled at Jenny, gratefully. Little did she know it, but she had finally helped me fill in the final piece of the puzzle. I now saw the whole picture.

"Jenny," I said. "I am going to need your help. Let me explain why."

And so I took this twelve year old girl into my confidence. I told her the whole story. I recounted how I had been recruited to identify Lady Derby's spy within Rigby's inner circle. I explained how this was connected to the murders in Chester and Ormskirk. I described how and why the killings had been carried out and by whom, and I gave Jenny my pledge that if she helped me, then I would make sure that Rigby knew about it, but that news of how she had helped would go no further than that. Finally, once she had taken all this in and her stupefaction at my story had subsided, I arranged to meet her outside her house at one-thirty in the morning, from where we would walk to the church together.

***

It was a dark night, thick rolling cloud having drifted in during the course of the afternoon. The air was still and heavy and, as Jenny and I sat on the wall by the lych gate, the brooding presence of the church spire and tower watched over us, the structures looming like twin sentinels. I could almost feel their disappointment at what we were about to do. The town was silent at two in the morning, which was just as well, for discovery was not to be contemplated.

Presently, I spotted a light bobbing its way up the slope to the church, and, out of the gloom, the figures of Alexander, Beatrice, and Lawrence began to take shape. Beatrice, I noticed, was carrying the lantern, using her hand to shield the light source, in order to reduce the risk of being spotted. Alexander and

Lawrence both had spades slung over their shoulders.

"Courtesy of Mr Browne," explained Lawrence, as the little group reached me. "Taken without his knowledge, of course. We will return them in the morning."

It was Alexander who first noticed Jenny sat on the wall beside me. "What is she doing here?" he asked, his features gradually freezing as realisation dawned. "God's blood, Daniel. I hope I have this wrong. Please do not tell me you mean for us to dig up the body of this girl's mother."

"Do not concern yourself, my friend," I said. "We will just be digging up her grave. There is a difference, as you will see."

"Good God, man. They will burn us for this," hissed Lawrence, as Beatrice stifled a squeal.

"Only if they catch us," I said. "Come, this will not take long. Let us get it over with. Jenny, please lead the way."

Jenny pushed herself nimbly off the wall and beckoned for us to follow. Unlocking the lych gate as gently as possible, she led us down the path towards the church entrance before veering off to the left through rows of gravestones, until we arrived at a recently dug plot fronted by a plain headstone. We were, I noted, no more than fifty yards from the rear of the Bootles' house and therefore directly on the route Isaac would have taken to return home.

"Here we are, Mr Cheswis," whispered Jenny. "Let us

hope you're right."

I nodded at Jenny and beckoned for Alexander to give me his spade. I started digging quickly at the loose soil, piling it up in a mound by the grave. After a few seconds, Lawrence shrugged and joined in, digging furiously and creating his own pile of soil.

"If someone comes now, we are all in the shit together," he said, by way of explanation. Beatrice grimaced and placed the lantern behind the gravestone, so that the grave was still illuminated but so the lantern was not visible from the roadway.

"Very well, Daniel," said Alexander. "You win, give me the shovel. I am stronger than you."

After a few minutes digging, I heard the soft clunk of metal on wood and a gasp of exclamation from Lawrence.

"The coffin lid is loose," he exclaimed. "Are you going to tell us what is going on, Daniel?"

"In a moment," I said. "Scrape away the rest of the loose earth and see if you can remove the coffin lid."

"That shouldn't be too difficult," came the reply. "The wood has been smashed down one side." Squinting, I peered into the hole and realised that Lawrence was right. Alexander quickly shovelled away the remaining loose earth and prised off the shattered coffin lid. Five pairs of eyes focused simultaneously on the contents, of which there were none. As I had anticipated, the casket was completely empty.

Chapter 35

Lathom House – Thursday April 25th, 1644

Samuel Rutter dragged his portly frame across the cobbles of the main courtyard and clicked his tongue in irritation. Now he was in his late thirties, he was finding it less easy to move freely about the house than he used to.

"You will have to temper your appetite, Samuel," her ladyship had remarked on several occasions. "You are becoming fat."

Concerns of such a vain nature would have to wait, however, for more pressing matters were at hand. He looked around himself, and his heart sank. Several of the flimsier outbuildings – servants quarters, stables, and workshops – had been levelled by Rigby's grenades. There was a huge hole in the side of the Eagle Tower, exposing a staircase, and the clock on the Chapel Tower had been destroyed, leaving debris scattered around the courtyard. Worse still, unease had begun to develop among the regular soldiers. Those housed in the lath and plaster upper storeys of the main building had refused to remain there unless the officers joined them, and it did not take an expert artilleryman to deduce that the team operating Rigby's mortar was becoming more accurate as each day passed.

And to top it all, a drummer boy sent by Rigby was waiting at the main gate with the rebel cur's latest ultimatum. No officer, mind – just a slip of a drummer boy. The studied insult was not lost on Rutter, who growled quietly under his breath as he approached the nervous-looking youth, who was holding a small leather satchel. The boy could not have been more than fifteen years old.

"My, have you drawn the short straw, young man," said Rutter. "I cannot begin to hazard a guess as to what you have done to upset the colonel so."

"Sir?" The boy, clearly terrified, proffered the satchel to Rutter, who shook his head.

"That is not for my eyes," he said. "You may deliver your colonel's latest dose of poison directly into her ladyship's hands. Follow me."

Rutter led the boy, flanked by two guards, back across the courtyard, in through the door of the main house and into a drawing room, where Lady Derby and William Farrington were stood waiting.

"So," said the countess, drawing herself up to her full height. "You are the best messenger Rigby could muster, are you? Parliament's elite, so to speak?"

"Y-yes, my lady," said the boy, fumbling with the satchel. "The colonel has correspondence for you. He would have me convey your response to him."

"I'm sure he would," she snapped. "Well, let me have it, then. I haven't got all day."

The youth handed the satchel to the countess, who drew out a sealed letter, which she opened and read slowly, her expression becoming gradually more strained as she did so. Eventually, she uttered a low, spluttering sound and exploded in anger.

"Such insolence!" she spat, tearing the message in two and tossing it at the boy's feet. "That man will yet feel the force of my wrath in return for his treachery. As for you, my boy, a due reward for your pains would be to be hanged from our gates. Guards! Secure him, and lock him up."

The boy gave a brief moan of terror as the two guards grabbed hold of him, one thrusting his knee into his back and forcing him to fall backwards in pain. William Farrington, who, until now, had remained silent and stony-faced, stepped forward and raised his hand.

"My lady," he said, calmly, "I would caution you against this course of action. He is but a boy, and making an example of him will serve no purpose other than to enrage the colonel even further.

The countess stared at Farrington for a moment before exhaling in resignation. "Very well, William," she said. *"Your counsel is always wise. You are right. The boy is simply the foolish instrument of a traitor's pride. I will instruct the boy to carry back our answer and save our anger for another day."*

"Thank you, my lady. I think that would be the most prudent response, under the circumstances."

"As for you," said the countess, turning to the petrified youth, *"you may tell that insolent rebel he shall have neither persons, goods, nor house. When our strengths and provisions are spent, we shall find a fire more merciful than Rigby; and then, if the providence of God prevents it not, my goods and house shall burn in his sight, and myself, children, and soldiers, rather than fall into his hands, will seal our religion and loyalty in the same flames. Guards!"* she added. *"You may show this boy the way out."*

Without a word, the two soldiers manhandled the boy roughly out of the house, across the courtyard, and ejected him with a shove out of the gate from whence he had come.

"Gentlemen," said the countess, once the room had emptied, leaving only Farrington and Rutter present. *"It has come to this. How should we respond to this latest provocation?"*

Rutter glanced briefly at Farrington, who nodded imperceptibly, allowing the chaplain to speak.

"My lady," he said, *"the men of this garrison have conducted themselves with skill and bravery, but the*

time has come when this is no longer enough. Yesterday, one of the enemy's grenades exploded close to where you and your daughters were at dinner. Today, you are safe, but the next time it may be different. Furthermore, we have it on good authority that Rigby received a full delivery of grenades yesterday, so he no longer needs to ration his mortar fire. If we do not do something tonight, then this place will become Hell on Earth."

"So what do you propose?" asked the countess.

"I say we must summon Captain Farmer and make our plans without delay. The time has come to kill or be killed...but, above all, we must capture that mortar."

Chapter 36

Lathom House – Wednesday April 24th – Thursday April 25th, 1644

Once we had restored Mary Reade's grave to something approaching its former state, we extinguished the lantern, and all five of us walked together, in silence, to Jenny's cottage. None of us wished to raise suspicion by returning to our respective lodgings at such an unearthly hour, for fear that somebody else underway at that time had happened to notice the strange activities taking place in the churchyard.

Jenny offered Beatrice the use of her brother Harry's empty truckle bed, which she gratefully accepted, but the rest of us passed an uncomfortable night huddled on the floor near the hearth in the hall.

Before Beatrice retired for the night, I used the opportunity to explain what I had told Jenny the day before. The most difficult aspect was clarifying why it was necessary to prove Bootle a spy before doing anything about the murders.

"Firstly," I said, "we need to discover how Bootle

and Chisnall have been getting in and out of Lathom House – that is the main priority. If we simply arrest Bootle, we can prove nothing, and the captain will deny everything. We have to catch him in the act; red-handed, as it were."

"I understand that," said Lawrence, "but if Bootle did not commit the atrocities that took place in his brother's house, why can we not simply reveal what happened there, secure my father's release, and reveal Bootle's status as a spy later?"

"That," I explained, "is self-evident. If Bootle is given any hint that we are close to solving this matter, both he and the murderer will abscond, your father will not be able to prove his innocence, and there will be little point in us revealing what we discovered in the graveyard; unless, of course, we wish to explain to the authorities what we were doing digging up Mary Reade's grave in the dead of night. Indeed, it is likely that we will be accused of stealing her body."

"And then there is the issue of Marc," added Alexander, helpfully.

"That is correct," I said. "We still don't know where Marc is being kept, or indeed whether he is alive or dead. If we wish to ascertain this, then we have but one course of action that is open to us."

And so it was that we were forced to stake everything on the belief that Bootle would need to consult his paymasters within Lathom House at least one more time before Rigby launched a final attack with his beloved mortar.

This proved more difficult than at first thought. On the Wednesday, Bootle was kept busy all day by Rigby, who needed him to help Morgan's artillery team direct mortar and cannon fire at the most vulnerable places within the house.

When a full shipment of grenades was delivered to a beaming Morgan during the course of the morning, I began to be worried, and when, early on Thursday, Rigby sent over an ultimatum to Lady Derby and announced a twenty-four hour truce to allow her ladyship to digest the colonel's offer, I realised that time was running short. Nonetheless, with the guns guaranteed to be silent that afternoon, and with Bootle granted leave in advance of whatever Rigby had planned for the morrow, I guessed that if the captain planned one last visit to the house, he would do it that afternoon.

The difficulty, of course, was that Alexander, Lawrence, and I were due to be on duty from midday onwards. Shortly after breakfast, therefore, I drew the engineer Browne to one side and asked him to inform Rigby that all three of us were on urgent business relating to my primary responsibility at the camp and would return as soon as events would allow.

Alexander and I then made our way through the garden, past the dovecote, and out onto the path that led northwards from New Park House. However, instead of heading directly to Burscough, we walked down the lane to Ormskirk, in order to find Lawrence, and located him in the tavern where Beatrice was staying, where he was making short work of a breakfast of bread, butter, and salted bacon. Beatrice, who was with him, looked pale and was eating nothing.

I quickly explained our plan to Lawrence, who nodded eagerly and gulped down a few more chunks of bread, before gathering up his pistol and gesturing to us that he was ready to leave.

"I would come too," said Beatrice, more in hope than expectation, but I shook my head.

"It is too dangerous," I said, "and besides, you will serve us better if you wait here. If we have not returned by first light tomorrow, you may go to New Park House and raise the alarm."

Beatrice was reluctant to accept my suggestion. However, she understood my reasoning and eventually acquiesced, giving each of us a hug, which naturally attracted curious looks from those at the adjacent table, before allowing us on our way.

Forty minutes later, when we arrived in Burscough, we split up. Lawrence positioned himself in a copse of trees, which overlooked the narrow track coming from the direction of Lathom, whilst Alexander found a suitable location near some bushes a couple of hundred yards along the Ormskirk road, just in case

Bootle approached from that direction. I, for my part, picked my way through the ruins of the priory until I found a good position behind one of the crumbling walls, from where I had acceptable views both of the spot where I imagined Bootle had disappeared a few days previously, and of Alexander and Lawrence's respective positions.

And there we sat, for what seemed like an eternity. But eventually, sometime during the late afternoon, I was roused from my thoughts by the sight of Lawrence, who had stepped out from behind a tree and was waving frantically in my direction. I cast my eyes to the left of where he was standing, and, sure enough, weaving his way in between the hedgerows, was the unmistakeable figure of William Bootle.

The plan Lawrence, Alexander, and I had devised was that the two others would wait until Bootle had entered the mill, at which point they would join me, and we would wait together for Bootle to make his way over to the priory.

If Bootle had behaved exactly as he had on previous occasions, there is every likelihood that what happened next could have been avoided. However, to my consternation, the captain, instead of making for the mill, made a beeline directly for where I was crouching. I could see Lawrence in the distance, looking earnestly in my direction and then setting off at pace towards me, but he was too late. Bootle, who, I noticed, was carrying a lantern, stepped over a stile and ploughed through thick undergrowth until he reached a stone alcove a few yards from where I was positioned. There he bent over, opened a trapdoor in the middle of the pathway, and disappeared from view.

Astounded, I leapt from my hiding place and sprinted over to where Bootle had vanished into the earth and inspected the ground closely. No wonder I had not been able to find the tunnel before. On the face of it, the trapdoor was completely invisible. However, close inspection revealed a small metal ring lying in an indent between two of the flagstones. I lifted the ring and saw that it was attached to the adjacent stone. Hooking my fingers through the ring, I pulled hard, and, sure enough, the trapdoor sprung open. It was narrow, no more than two feet square, but heavy nonetheless, for stone had been laid on top of the wooden trapdoor, underneath which were two iron grips to open and close it, depending upon whether you were entering or leaving the tunnel.

I glanced quickly down into the hole and noticed there was perhaps a three foot drop, from where steps led downwards into near-darkness. I caught the sight of a faint light receding down the tunnel. Above ground, I looked into the distance and saw that Lawrence was still a hundred yards away. I had a decision to make. I had no lantern, so if I waited for Lawrence, then Bootle would be out of my sight and therefore out of my reach. On the other hand, if I entered the tunnel, I would be too far down it for Lawrence and Alexander to follow me, especially as I would have to close the trapdoor, lest Bootle turn around and realise he was being followed.

I contemplated my options for a moment, and then I lowered myself carefully down the hatch, closed the trapdoor over my head, and headed off down the stairs towards the fading and flickering glow of Bootle's lantern.

**

Although the trapdoor itself was narrow, the stone steps were much more accommodating, wide enough, in fact, for two people to sit side by side. I slid down the staircase on my posterior until I was able to stand, and, after twenty steps or so, I emerged into a long tunnel, perhaps six feet wide. Unused and decaying sconces hung from alternate walls, suggesting that the tunnel had been much more widely used in the past. It was also absolutely straight, which was just as well, for Bootle was marching at a fair pace, and his light was already little more than a pin prick in the distance. Squinting heavily as I tried to become accustomed to the darkness, I set off as fast as I could in an attempt to close the gap. I had lost all sense of direction, and it occurred to me that, if there were any bends in the tunnel, I would be pitched into complete blackness.

We seemed to be walking for ages, which was

unsurprising, for Burscough Priory was over a mile from Lathom House. I marvelled at the feat of engineering it must have taken to construct the tunnel. Browne, I mused, would have been most impressed.

I tried to stay about fifty yards behind Bootle, not least because it was proving difficult to remain absolutely silent. At one point, after I had tripped over a stone, Bootle stopped and swung round, holding his lantern in the air and peering directly towards me. Fortunately, I realised he could see nothing more than ten yards ahead of him, and I breathed a sigh of relief as he turned round and continued on his way.

Eventually, the small point of light stopped bobbing to and fro, and after a few seconds it started moving slowly upwards. I strained my eyes and realised that Bootle had reached the end of the tunnel. Turning round to face me, he pushed himself slowly up the steps, holding one of his hands above his head to feel for the metal handle that would allow him to open the trapdoor. I felt a pang of fear dart through my chest as I realised the tunnel was about to be flooded with light, and pressed my body hard against the wall of the tunnel.

Bootle must have heard something, for he stopped his shuffling and held the lantern up to his face, staring in my direction and moving the light from side to side.

Eventually, he lowered the lantern once more, placed it on the ground, and pressed upwards with both hands, sending the trapdoor flying open. I exhaled in apprehension, but, fortunately, the light entering the tunnel was relatively dim and Bootle stood up without looking any further in my direction. Instead, he grunted and heaved himself through the trapdoor before closing it again and transforming my world into pitch blackness.

It was precisely at this point that I realised my eagerness in chasing my quarry had led me to make a serious error of judgement.

I had, it occurred to me, left myself with only three courses of action. I could attempt to walk over a mile back down the tunnel in absolute darkness, I could sit in the tunnel until Bootle returned, or I could open the trapdoor myself and see where it emerged.

The second option, I considered, was pointless, for I would surely be discovered as soon as Bootle opened the hatch. Option one was possible in theory, although having come this far, the idea of walking all the way back down the tunnel without having achieved anything did not appeal to me. Not only that; my senses, I realised, were already beginning to play tricks with me, and I was concerned that I would eventually become confused as to which way was which.

As for option three, the dangers were obvious, but at least I would be doing something. It struck me that the area above the trapdoor was dark and hence probably not located in an area of the house heavily frequented by those who might take an interest in my presence.

I therefore started to shuffle my way tentatively in the direction of the trapdoor, running one hand along the wall and holding out the other in front of me. Of course, this did not stop me from stubbing my toe on the bottom step when I reached it. However, I then felt for the third step to sit on and started moving my way upwards a step at a time, feeling above my head for the trapdoor handles.

Once I was directly under the trapdoor, I listened carefully to see if I could ascertain any sounds from above, but I could hear nothing other than a deathly silence. Taking a deep breath, I pushed upwards slowly and found myself staring into a dark underground chamber.

"Of course, the crypt of Lathom House's chapel," I thought to myself. "Where else would a tunnel from Burscough Priory lead to?"

It was then that I heard a slight movement from behind the raised trapdoor, and I spun round to find myself face to face with a pair of leather bucket-top boots. I looked upwards to see the barrel of a pistol, behind which lurked the grinning, triumphant features of Edward Chisnall. At his side, dressed entirely in black, stood Lady Derby's chaplain, Samuel Rutter.

"Ah, Mr Cheswis," said the cleric, his face betraying a hint of a smirk, "do come and join us. We were beginning to get worried. We were wondering whether you might have got lost in the dark."

Chapter 37

Lathom House – Thursday April 25th – Friday April 26th, 1644

And so, for the second time in a little over a month, I found myself being led at gunpoint across the central courtyard of Lathom House.

From inside the extensive and forbidding outer walls of the house, the effects of Morgan's cannon and mortar fire were much easier to appraise than from behind our own siege lines. There was a sizeable crater in the courtyard next to the damaged clock tower, behind which I could see several wooden outbuildings damaged beyond repair. In the main courtyard itself, holes were visible in the upper storeys of the main building, where cannon shot had sailed right through the fabric of the house. Even the damage to the Eagle Tower looked more shocking when viewed from close quarters.

"I know what you're thinking," said Rutter, "and you are right in that we have sustained some damage from your artillery, but this is to be expected, and, believe me, we are well-prepared to defend this place. We have made our plans, and tonight you will have the opportunity to see what we are made of. Rigby has pushed us to a point where we are being forced to show our hand, and tonight that hand will smite him brutally."

"You mean you plan to attack? Tonight?"

"Yes, of course. What do you expect? You have a new shipment of grenades, so we hear, so we have no option but to attack your positions and capture the mortar piece that has caused so much damage."

"You intend to take our mortar? How do you propose to achieve that?"

"By stealth and good organisation," smiled Rutter, "but also by making use of the arrogance of your commanding officer. He plans to rain fire and brimstone on us tomorrow, but I'll wager he has made no particular plans for a counter attack by us. Am I right?"

I stared at Rutter, who studied me for a moment, and then chuckled.

"I thought so," he said. "Rigby truly is an imbecile. Watching him flounder these past days has given her ladyship no little amusement, I can assure you. He is more interested in putting on a show for the public and his committee men than in securing the victory he seeks."

It had not occurred to me before, but Rutter was

absolutely right. Perhaps my own judgement had been clouded by Rigby's triumphalism and showmanship. All of the colonel's focus had been on the fact that he now had the grenades he needed to achieve his ambition of destroying Lathom House. There had been no preparations at all for the eventuality that Lady Derby would make a last, desperate roll of the dice and attempt an all-or-nothing assault on our positions. Rigby's mind, it seemed, had been befuddled by his unexplained personal hatred for Lord Derby. I began to wonder whether I might actually be safer that night imprisoned somewhere inside Lathom House rather than having to defend the trenches against a highly motivated attack by the men of the garrison.

Whilst I was contemplating this, Rutter and Chisnall marched me directly to the foot of the Eagle Tower, where we were met by a group of six soldiers, one of whom I noticed was Edward Halsall, the young ensign whose life I had spared during the night attack several weeks previously. The young officer, his arm now fully healed, looked at me quizzically, but said nothing.

"Lock him up," ordered Rutter. "Keep him secure in one of the rooms at the top of the tower. I will be back for him later."

I was marched up a staircase, which wound its way around the perimeter of the tower, past the exposed section which looked out towards Morgan's gun position, and up to a sparsely furnished room almost at the top of the tower, which appeared to serve as a kind of rest chamber for those soldiers manning the battlements. It had six chairs and a table, on which stood a couple of tankards, an empty trencher, and somebody's Montero cap. There was also a small window, which looked out towards the north-west. In the foreground I could see the small chapel from where I had first spotted Jenny Reade's dog and, beyond that, in the distance, the buildings of Burscough, the ruins of the priory standing out against the green of the trees, and the darker stone of the mill. I wondered whether Alexander and Lawrence were still waiting for me there, or whether they had returned to the encampment to raise the alarm.

I was pushed unceremoniously into the room, and the tankards and trenchers were removed, although for some reason I was left the Montero cap. The door was then locked behind me, and I was left to my own devices.

I remained locked in the room for hours. Shortly after dark, I was attended by a self-important-looking man, who introduced himself as Broome, the head steward. His sole purpose, it seemed, was to feed me with a hunk of stale bread, some cheese, and a tankard of weak ale with the words, "Never let it be said that the Countess of Derby does not show hospitality to those who stay in her house, even if they are her enemies."

I ate the food and drank the ale gratefully, but then,

as it seemed I was there for the night, I curled up on the floor and tried my best to sleep.

I was eventually woken sometime in the middle of the night by the sound of the key turning in the lock. Seconds later, Samuel Rutter was standing in the doorway bearing a lantern and a large bunch of keys.

"Good morning, Mr Cheswis," he said. "I trust you slept well. Please come with me. There is something I would like you to see."

"What time is it?" I demanded, trying to wipe the tiredness from my eyes.

"It is three-thirty in the morning. A time when most good men are in bed. But tonight there is work to be done. Please," he added, stepping to one side and gesturing to the open doorway. "After you. Up the stairs, if you please."

I slowly struggled to my feet and brushed myself down. Rutter, I noticed, had changed out of his cassock, but was still soberly dressed all in black. If it had not been for the circumstances, he could, I realised, have easily been mistaken for being of Puritan inclination.

At the cleric's bidding, I climbed a couple of flights of stairs until our way was blocked by a solid oak door. Rutter produced a large metal key from the bunch dangling from his waist, inserted it into the lock, and pushed the door open.

I stepped through the doorway, and suddenly we were outside, at the very top of the Eagle Tower, looking out over the whole of Lathom House and the fields and villages of Lancashire beyond. It was a clear, moonlit night, and so I was able to make out our siege works clearly. On the walls and towers, musketeers, gamekeepers, and fowlers stood ready with their weapons, whilst below in the main courtyard foot soldiers and servants alike stood ready for action. A similarly large detachment of men also stood waiting in a small courtyard next to the postern gate. What struck me above all, though, was the absolute silence of it all. Every one of these men understood the value of surprise and had assumed their positions quietly, efficiently, and with the minimum of fuss. I could not help but be impressed by their resolve.

Rutter stood behind me and let me take in the view. "A magnificent sight, Mr Cheswis," he said, the pride unmistakeable in his voice. "The silence lends a certain grandeur to the proceedings, does it not?"

I nodded slowly, for I could not disagree. "Perhaps, Reverend, you would care to explain exactly what is happening here," I said. "I presume that is why you have brought me to this viewpoint."

"Indeed," said Rutter. "You will notice that the majority of our regular soldiers are positioned inside the postern gate to the north-east of the house. There you will find Captain Chisnall, who you already know. His task is to capture the fort where your cannon and culverin are housed. With Chisnall is Captain Fox, who has the most important task today. His role is to attack the trenches to the east and then work his way around to the south-west of the house, in order to attack and capture the sconce that houses the mortar.

"The other men you see are essentially playing support roles. Captain Ogle is in command of the main guard at the south gate. He will secure the retreat through that gate, Captain Rawsthorne is standing guard at the postern gate, and Captain Ratcliffe is in charge of the musketeers and other marksmen on the walls. Last but not least, Captain Farmer is positioned in the main courtyard and will stand in reserve to support anyone who needs help."

"And the servants?" I asked, looking down into the courtyard at the mixture of footmen, grooms, and stewards armed with clubs, buckets, spades, and a large flat contraption, the purpose of which was unclear.

Rutter smiled. "They're not there to fight," he said. "Their task will become evident in due course."

"You and Lady Derby appear to have it all planned out, Reverend," I said. "Her ladyship is showing herself to be a soldier of some substance, but tell me, why are you showing me all this?"

The cleric sighed and sat down on a ledge behind one of the crenellations. "That," he said, "is a very good question, and one which I cannot definitively answer. Perhaps I perceive something within you with which I sympathise. I have the feeling perhaps that you are a person of middling social standing like me, who has caught the eye of his patrons. But, like me, I feel you are not, by instinct, a man of war, rather a man of peace and insight, who has been dragged into this conflict by circumstances rather than by will. Does that strike a chord with you?"

You are very perceptive, Reverend," I said, sitting down next to the cleric and determining to make best use of this unexpected turn of events. "What is your story, may I ask?"

"My family," said Rutter, "as I am sure you have already ascertained, are owners of the mill at Burscough. It is now only in intermittent use and semi-derelict, but in its day it was a successful enterprise, and my parents were comfortably well off. However, I am, when all is said and done, only a mill owner's son and my future would undoubtedly have been in that trade, were it not for his lordship, the sixth earl."

"How so?" I asked.

"As luck would have it, I am the same age as the present earl, and when we were small we had some contact with each other. His lordship must have seen some aptitude in me, for he took a shine to me and was generous enough to sponsor my education. His patronage allowed me to attend Westminster School and Christ Church College in Oxford. You see, I have much to thank the earl for.

"As it happened, my ordination coincided with

the earl's decision to step back from the day-to-day management of the estate, and so the current earl immediately employed me as his personal chaplain. As you see, though, I fulfil other roles besides."

"So I have noticed," I replied. "Then you truly have a reason for your loyalty to the earl and the countess."

"And for your part, Mr Cheswis, how is it that a man like you ends up as an intelligencer serving the likes of Rigby?"

"Rigby?" I exclaimed. "In that respect, you have me wrong, Reverend. I have no allegiance to Rigby. I serve under the command of Sir William Brereton of Handforth, and, as you rightly guessed, I am not here by choice."

Rutter looked at me with surprise and scratched his head. "Brereton?" he said. "He is in charge of the forces in Cheshire. So what are you doing here?"

And so against my better judgement, I told Rutter about how I had ended up at Lathom. I told him the story of the murders I had solved in Nantwich, about my wich house, my cheese business and about my betrothal to Elizabeth. I told him about Brereton's identification of myself as a potential intelligencer and finally I told him about Brereton's offer to arrange for me to be released from my duties as a constable should I undertake to help identify the spy in Rigby's inner circle.

Rutter nodded in understanding and smiled, before

clapping me on the shoulder.

"I had an inkling that you might have such a story to tell," he said, and I thought I detected a hint of sadness in his voice. "You see, you leave me with something of a dilemma."

"A dilemma?"

"Yes. You see, you know about the existence of the tunnel between our chapel and Burscough Priory. I cannot allow you to go free, for fear you will betray its location. By rights, I should either keep you prisoner here until the siege is over, or have you cast from the top of this tower, a simple death, easily explained. You tried to escape, fought with us, and were pushed over the edge in self-defence. Your side would think no worse of us for that."

I frowned. The proceedings had taken a rather unpleasant turn.

"You would do that?" I asked. "I guarantee it would serve little purpose if you did, for I have two colleagues waiting for me at the priory, who saw me enter the tunnel. I fear they will reveal the location of the tunnel regardless of what you do with me."

Rutter smiled and said nothing for a moment. Instead, he got to his feet and walked towards the door, laying his hand on the handle.

"Enjoy the show, Mr Cheswis," he said. "I will return for you later."

He then disappeared down the stairs, closing the

door behind him, his feet echoing on the steps as he descended into the courtyard.

I sat and stared at the door for a moment in disbelief, for despite the chaplain's words, it had not escaped my notice that he had left the door to the only exit route unlocked.

I was now faced with a dilemma of my own. Did I take my chances and attempt to escape immediately down the stairs, or did I stay where I was and watch the battle in the hope that the door would still be unlocked later? On balance, considering the likelihood that Rutter had placed a guard at the entrance to the Eagle Tower, and in the knowledge that the courtyard was swarming with soldiers and servants eager for parliamentarian blood, I decided in favour of a cautious approach and elected to wait at least until the men of the garrison were more fully occupied.

I still had plenty to think about though. Had Rutter left the door unlocked intentionally, and, if so, why? Was he supremely confident that I would not be able to make it past the guard on the tower gateway, across the network of courtyards to the chapel and then into the crypt? Or was it just possible that, in a bizarre display of understanding and kinship for a man with whom he felt a certain affinity, he had offered me a sporting chance? Could it have been the knowledge that others were waiting at Burscough for me to emerge from the tunnel that was the deciding factor? One thing was certain. I did not relish the prospect of waiting long enough to see whether Rutter's threat to have me thrown from the battlements was real or just bluster, but I accepted that I would need to show patience, so I sat back down and concentrated on the scene developing below.

Chisnall and around eighty of his men had filed silently out of the postern gate and, keeping low, to avoid being spotted by our sentries, had fanned out across the rough terrain and were edging their way towards the ramparts that protected the gun placement where our cannon and culverin were located. I thought to shout a warning, but realised that such an action would have been pointless, for Chisnall and his men were already under the cannon's line of fire.

A shout went up from the trenches, but it was already too late. The royalists charged, capturing the gun placement after a brief skirmish. Most of those positioned behind the ramparts did not, it seemed, have the stomach to fight, and fled in order to save their own skins.

Whilst this was happening, Fox, the other captain waiting by the postern gate, followed Chisnall out and attacked the siege works to the right of the gun placement, quickly enveloping those caught in the trenches and pushing them back along the inner trench towards the south-west of the house, where the mortar was positioned.

By now, everyone in the parliamentary camp was aware that a full-scale attack was underway, and I could see soldiers filing up from the Tawd Valley towards the connecting trenches, rushing to come to the aid of those caught in the middle of the encounter. The battle was curiously devoid of gunfire, for, apart from an initial volley of musket fire as Fox's men approached the trench, neither side was able to use their muskets effectively. There was an occasional pistol shot, but the narrow confines of the trench and the speed needed to reload meant that the fighting was of the hand-to-hand variety, with swords, musket butts, and any rock or stones on which hands could be laid. The raucous screams and guttural moans of men killing and being killed echoed across the ground, clearly identifiable and made somehow more poignant by the lack of musket fire.

Fox's men fought their way to the sconce containing the mortar, and, after fifteen minutes of hurling stones at the occupants, they scaled the ramparts in a single energetic push, scattering the defenders in all directions and swiftly overwhelming those who were unwise enough to resist.

There was a brief counter attack, and I thought I recognised the shape of Major Robinson in the midst of the fray, but the resistance soon petered out. The battle was already won. Chisnall and Fox had secured both artillery placements, and any parliamentarians manning the trenches had fled for their lives.

At this point, I began to notice activity in the central courtyard. Captain Ogle and several others opened the main gates, allowing the multitude of servants and other household staff to flood out into the open and head straight for where the mortar was located. The same was happening at the postern gate.

It was then that I noticed the head steward, Broome, organising his men into teams. Some dug away at the ramparts to flatten them and create a gap through which the mortar could be manoeuvred. Others shovelled the loose earth frantically into the ditch, in order to create a flat surface leading all the way to the main gate.

Meanwhile, another team of men hauled the strange, flat contraption, which I now realised was a sled, out of the courtyard and up to the half-dismantled sconce. The mortar was then manhandled onto the sled and hauled back to the gate amidst whooping and cheering, like a slain stag after a hunt.

I was astounded. The organisation and planning required to achieve such an overwhelming and comprehensive success was something to be truly admired, and the whole operation had taken less than an hour.

The only failure was that Captain Rawsthorne, who had left the postern gate in order to try and drag back the rest of the heavy artillery, had been forced to give up due to the excessive weight of the cannon and culverin and the width of the trench at that point. Instead, he nailed both pieces and retreated to safety.

It was not long after this that my mind began to turn once again to how I might escape from the Eagle Tower. A glance down into the courtyard revealed that celebrations were in full swing. Servants and soldiers alike were climbing and fooling around on the captured mortar as though it were a plaything. Others were dancing around it in a manner akin to some kind of pagan ceremony. Bagpipes were being played, and someone had produced a barrel of ale. If there was ever going to be the chance that I might be able to evade the attentions of Rutter's guards, it was now.

However, just as I was about to put that theory to the test, the door to the staircase sprang open and Edward Halsall appeared.

"Follow me, sir," he said, holding the door open for me.

I gave the young officer a curious look, for he was unarmed and on his own. "Where to?" I asked.

"Don't ask me to answer that, sir," said Halsall, whose eyes, I noticed, were darting from side to side as though he were agitated. "We don't have much time."

On the assumption that I was better off trusting Halsall than taking my chances with the cleric, I nodded gratefully to the youth and followed him down the stairs.

As we emerged into the courtyard, I noticed that

there were no longer any guards watching over the entrance to the tower. Anyone who had been there was now engaged in the revelry taking place in the middle of the courtyard.

"Remember, you are my prisoner," hissed Halsall. "Just act as such, and nobody will say a thing. We have taken several of your men captive during the fight, and people will assume I am just escorting you to where they are being kept."

Instead of taking me across the courtyard, Halsall led me behind the Eagle Tower and through a narrow alley, which led between the main building and a bakehouse. This led into a smaller courtyard, which was quite empty. Beyond that, we passed through an archway dividing some of the soldiers' quarters and emerged in front of a pile of fallen masonry and twisted metal. I realised I was looking at the remains of the Chapel Tower clock. Halsall, I realised, had led me back to the chapel by an alternate and obviously underused route.

"Why are you doing this, Mr Halsall?" I asked. "You are taking some risk."

Halsall smiled, nervously. "You spared my life," he said, simply. "I am now saving yours. If her ladyship finds out you are here, your life will not be worth living, especially if Mr Chisnall knows about it. Now let us make haste, before we are discovered."

I followed Halsall into the chapel and down into the

crypt, where I saw that the trapdoor still remained open from earlier.

"I wish you good fortune, Mr Halsall," I said, as I lowered myself into the tunnel. "However, I would ask one more thing of you. I have no lantern."

Halsall looked at me, and for a brief second I thought I saw a flash of irritation pass over his features, but he quickly regained his composure.

"I'm afraid we have no time for that," he said. "However, the tunnel goes only in one direction. You cannot go wrong. I wish you well, Mr Cheswis."

Raising his right hand in salute, he closed the trapdoor over my head, and once more I was plunged into a blackness that seemed darker than death itself.

Chapter 38

Lathom House – Friday April 26th, 1644

It is truly amazing what the human mind and body will endure if given no option. Little more than twelve hours previously I had chosen to risk discovery by Rutter and his men rather than face the ordeal of walking the length of the tunnel in the dark. This time I had no choice but to walk to freedom, so I simply gritted my teeth and got on with it.

As before, I stumbled forward uncertainly, placing one hand on the wall for guidance and the other in front of me to intercept anything untoward that might be hanging from the ceiling of the tunnel. I progressed slowly at first, but then more quickly as I gained confidence. The rhythmic movement of my stride was almost hypnotic in effect, and more than once I fancied I saw figures or orbs of light in the dark, although I knew that could not be true, for not one shaft of light was able to penetrate the darkness.

I had descended into this almost dreamlike state of mind when my right foot caught the bottom step at the end of the tunnel, and I pitched forward, cracking my knee against one of the other steps. Cursing loudly, I turned over into a sitting position and shuffled up the staircase until I could feel the metal handles above my head. For one awful moment, the trapdoor refused to move, and I felt the panic rising like daggers within my guts, but then I gave the metal bars a hefty shove and exhaled with relief as light once more entered my world.

Pulling myself up out of the tunnel, I landed in a heap on the grass and inspected my knee, which had begun to throb ominously. I rolled up my breeches and noticed that I had grazed the skin, causing a few blotches of blood to appear. Satisfied that the damage was only minor, I sat up and looked around me.

Over towards the mill, the first hints of dawn had begun to touch the eastern horizon. The stars were still prominent in the sky, and it looked as though it was set to be a bright spring morning.

Suddenly, a lantern illuminating a tuft of sandy hair appeared from behind the wall, over where I had concealed myself from Bootle the previous afternoon.

"Ah, Alexander," I cried. "Greetings. You are indeed a sight for sore eyes." At the sound of my voice, Lawrence Seaman's face also sprang into view.

"So that's where the tunnel is," said Alexander, stepping out from behind the wall and inspecting the trapdoor. "We spent hours yesterday searching every inch of these godforsaken ruins without success. It is well-hidden, that has to be said."

"So you have been here the whole time?" I asked.

"Yes. When you disappeared, we thought to raise the alarm but decided it would make more sense to wait until either you or Bootle came back out."

"By that, I assume Bootle has still not emerged?"

"Clearly not, or we would have known where the trapdoor was," pointed out Lawrence. "However, we have heard a good deal of noise coming from the direction of Lathom House. What has been happening?"

I explained to Alexander and Lawrence about the garrison's stunning attack on our trenches and the capture of the mortar. I also recounted my experiences in the Eagle Tower and the manner of my escape.

When he heard Halsall's name, Alexander's eyes widened, and a degree of contrition entered his voice. "Then I fear I owe you an apology," he said. "If you had not shown mercy to that young ensign, there is every chance you would not be here now. I should have trusted your judgement."

"No matter," I replied. "It is forgotten, and, in truth, I have to admit that my good fortune has little to do with the quality of my judgement. We have been lucky today. In particular, we are fortunate indeed not to have been caught in those trenches. From what I could see, many men lost their lives there."

My friends nodded grimly. "So what now?" asked

Alexander.

I glanced over towards the mill and smiled. "I suspect Bootle will not be long," I said. "Time is short, so I suggest we take a look and see what he has hidden in there."

As Lawrence was the only one of us carrying a firearm, he took up the rear, with Alexander in the middle and myself leading the way. Taking care to make as little noise as possible, we crept over to the front door of the main building and tried to turn the handle. To my surprise, the door opened. Alexander handed me the lantern, and I stepped warily inside.

The interior showed more signs of habitation than I was expecting. There were two main rooms, the first of which, a large, sparsely furnished, rectangular space, contained a single oak table and chairs, positioned in a rather isolated manner in the middle of the floor. In one of the corners, rushes had been laid out, as though someone had been sleeping there, although there were no signs of any personal effects. I walked over to the table and inspected an empty trencher with food remains on it: crumbs of bread and cheese, by the look of them. The room smelled of tallow, and, sure enough, there was also a candle, which had clearly been very recently extinguished.

The room had two doors. One, which was locked, I guessed led to the cellars. The other led to a smaller room at the rear, where Alexander and I found a fireplace, a cooking pot, another table, and a small, thinly stocked larder. In the corner, strangely enough, was a bundle of women's clothes. It was as though they had been stored there, in order to hide the obvious signs of habitation elsewhere in the building.

"Hello," I called, "is anybody there?"

At first there was a deathly silence, but then, suddenly, I heard a slight scraping sound coming from the front room. Initially I thought it was Lawrence, for he had hung back when Alexander and I had entered the larder, but then there was a shout, followed by the sharp crack of pistol fire, the sound of a brief struggle, and the heavy clump of a body hitting the floor.

Alexander and I burst through the doorway, but it was too late. Standing with his back to the table and brandishing a fully loaded carbine was William Bootle. Sprawled at his feet, groaning and holding his head, was Lawrence.

"That was very careless of you, Cheswis," said Bootle, his teeth flashing white in triumph. "You should have known I would follow you down the tunnel. Halsall will be dealt with later, but first I have to deal with you."

My first thought was that Lawrence had been shot, but, glancing over towards the cellar door, I spotted a neat bullet hole and realised that the shot had actually come from Lawrence's pistol. I glanced behind Bootle and saw that the pistol was lying on the other side of the

405

table, too far for one of us to reach without being shot. There were, however, three of us, including Lawrence, who was slowly coming to his senses.

"You cannot possibly get away with this, Bootle," I said, with rather more bravado than I was actually feeling. "You do not have time to shoot more than one of us. The best you can hope for is to make good your escape or return to Lathom House."

Bootle smiled the smile of one who knew he had an ace up his sleeve. "I believe you may have miscalculated," he said, with a hint of a sneer.

At that precise moment, the door to the cellar crashed open and in strode a well-built, dark-haired woman, who, before any of us could react, walked over to where Lawrence's gun was lying and picked it up. The woman, I noticed, was already holding a pistol in her other hand, and I realised that, in the space of a heartbeat, our odds of survival had reduced dramatically.

"Ah, Mrs Bootle, I presume," I said, wearily. "I wondered whether you might put in an appearance at some juncture."

Ten minutes later, all three of us were bound by our hands and feet, with our backs propped up against the wall. William and Jane Bootle each took one of the chairs and sat cradling their weapons in their laps as though contemplating what to do with us.

Jane Bootle regarded me with curiosity. She looked

at lot like her sister Katherine, I thought, but with a touch of hardness around the corner of her mouth.

"You do not seem surprised to see me here, Mr Cheswis," she said, angling her head as if to challenge me to explain.

"No, of course not," I replied, gratefully accepting the opportunity to play for time. "I have known for a long time that you were not dead and that the body we found in your fireplace was that of Mary Reade. It was not until we dug up Mary's grave and found an empty casket that I could prove it. It was only then that Colonel Rigby was informed."

Bootle stared at me with incredulity. "You lie, Cheswis," he spat. "If you had told Rigby about this, he would have had me arrested."

"That would have served no purpose," I said. "We needed to find the tunnel and determine the whereabouts of Mrs Bootle. Only you could lead us to both."

"We shall see in due course whether you are telling the truth," said Jane Bootle, doubtfully. "In the meantime, you can begin by explaining how you knew I was still alive."

"What alerted me to the fact that something was not right," I said, "was the curious positioning of the body, head first in the fire, with one arm in the fire also. It was too precise. You hit Mary's cadaver over the back of the head with the butt of your husband's fowling

407

gun, but, truthfully, if she had been alive when you had done that, it is very unlikely that she would have fallen in such a precise manner. The only explanation was that the body was placed that way for a reason, namely to burn her face beyond recognition and to disguise the fact that Mary had lost some of her fingers under torture.

"To begin with, I was confused by the fact that the body was not yet stiff, which made me think at first that it was only a few hours old. But then I remembered that the state of rigor mortis does not last for long. By the time Mary's body was exhumed, her limbs would no longer have been stiff."

"That is very perceptive," said Jane Bootle, "but how did you realise it was Mary's body?"

"I did not know for sure, but I guessed. To begin with, the grave is very close to the back of your house, making it relatively easy to access without disturbing anybody, but more specifically, Old Isaac saw you digging the body up. Of course, he was far too drunk to realise what was happening, so you frightened him away by standing on the gravestone and raising your hand to him. He thought he was looking at Mary's ghost."

"Very impressive," said William Bootle, sitting down on one of the wooden chairs. "Nothing much gets past you, Cheswis, I will grant you that. But how did you work out that I was involved in this?"

"There were a number of clues," I said, "but it all begins with Mrs Bootle, I think. She was the instigator of this whole series of events, am I right?" Jane Bootle said nothing, but continued to stare at me through furrowed eyebrows. "Very well," I said, "then let me explain how everything happened. It all began when Marc Le Croix turned up at your house out of the blue. Like William Seaman, you were not aware of Marc's existence, but he carried supporting documentation from Henry Oulton requesting you to give him accommodation and sustenance, which, as a good cousin, you naturally agreed to do. At some point, however, Marc explained to you that he was the sole heir to Oulton's fortune and that Oulton did not have long to live.

"It was at this point that you cooked up the scheme to inherit Oulton's money yourself. It involved eliminating all the other four people in front of you in the list of potential heirs, namely, and in order, Marc Le Croix, William Seaman, his son Lawrence, and Katherine Seaman. You told your husband, John, about this in the hope of soliciting his help, but he was justly horrified and promptly told Katherine, who happened to be staying with you at the time, thereby sealing both their fates. Katherine returned, still horrified, to Chester, her mind in turmoil as to whether to tell her brother, William Seaman, or not. John presumably thought little more of the matter and got on with his life. At this point you needed another collaborator, so you approached your brother-in-law, William Bootle.

"It took me a while to work out that William was the collaborator in question, but then I remembered Old Isaac telling me that your brother-in-law had long held a torch for you. Who better to choose as a partner in crime than someone who thought he stood to gain your undying love if he helped you?"

"Thought he stood-?" cut in William Bootle, shuffling uncomfortably on his chair. "I can assure you that Jane and I-"

"I cannot speak for you and Mrs Bootle," I said. "All I can say is that you were tempted by the offer of untold riches and the love of a woman you had long lusted after."

Bootle said nothing, but gave me a surly stare and sat back onto his chair.

"Please carry on, Mr Cheswis," said Jane Bootle. "You amuse me greatly."

"Very well," I said. "The first task was to remove Marc Le Croix from the scene. His body has not been found, so my guess is that the original idea was not to murder him, but to kidnap him in the hope that you might be able to frame him for the various murders you were about to commit. Since then, of course, William Seaman has aided you immeasurably in this regard by getting himself arrested, thereby fulfilling that role.

"Marc was drugged one night in the tavern. He knew

what was happening to him because he asked Isaac for help. However, he was ushered away from the tavern by your brother-in-law. Unfortunately, Isaac was, once again, very drunk, and across the crowded tap-room mistook your brother-in-law for your husband. Having access to a disused mill due to your brother-in-law's connection with Reverend Rutter proved to be most opportune here. I am not sure what exactly has happened to Marc Le Croix, but I suspect if we were to inspect the cellars of this place, we might find out."

"It is a pity you will not get that opportunity," said William Bootle, acidly.

I ignored the captain and continued. "The next task," I said, "was to dispose of Katherine Seaman. The plan was to have poor John Gibbons blamed for the murder, as Katherine had already told you about his obsession for her. You persuaded your new collaborator to carry out this killing and sent him to Chester. The intention was to arrange a meeting with Katherine and strangle her with a stolen cheese wire, but first Captain Bootle had to purloin such an item from Seaman's shop. To his horror, however, when he arrived there, not only was Katherine Seaman in the shop, but so too was Edward Chisnall, who also knew him, so he had to disappear quietly into the crowds. Although, even now, he probably does not realise it, I was also in the shop at that time, and I noticed the horrified look on Katherine Seaman's face, although, at the time, I mistook this for surprise on her part at the presence of Chisnall.

"Captain Bootle returned to the shop sometime later and talked to William Seaman, who he did not know. He managed to distract him and steal one of the cheese wires used in the shop. He also somehow managed to make contact with Katherine and persuaded her to meet him in the courtyard later that evening. From her he perhaps learned of the intention for the Seamans to host a dinner that evening, which meant that Gibbons would be on duty. He couldn't believe his luck.

"The captain returned later that evening after Katherine had excused herself from dinner. Katherine let him into the courtyard via the rear gate and, once he had ascertained that she had not yet told William Seaman about the plan, garrotted her with the cheese wire and made good his escape by climbing the gate.

"It took me a while to work out all the connections here because I was confused by the presence of Edward Chisnall and Robert Whitby, as well as by William Seaman's apparent calmness when faced with the murder of his sister. At first I thought Chisnall might be responsible for Katherine's murder because he left shortly before she died, but despite the connection between him and your brother-in-law, Chisnall had nothing to do with the murders. The same applies to Robert Whitby and Francis Gamull, who, despite having an interest in Henry Oulton's business, had no involvement in this wickedness either. As for Seaman,

I eventually began to realise that his lack of emotion was simply his own way of reacting to the shock of finding Katherine murdered in such a brutal manner."

"Most impressive, Mr Cheswis," said Jane Bootle. "Pray continue. So what happened next?"

"Captain Bootle," I said, "returned to Lathom in order to carry out the next stage of the plan, which was to kill Lawrence Seaman. That would no doubt have been successful, had he been a little more accurate with his brother's fowling gun, but he missed, almost killing me in the process. If he'd succeeded, of course, it would have been John Bootle, as owner of the gun, who would have been the prime suspect for the murder.

"Failing to kill Lawrence was a setback, but you figured, with him serving in the trenches, it would be easy enough to arrange for an accident when the time was right. That time might have been yesterday, had we not decided to come here and find you instead. In any case, dealing with Lawrence had to be put on hold when the opportunity arose to dispose of your husband and simultaneously make yourself temporarily disappear, by which I refer to the death of Mary Reade.

"You hatched a plot to make it look as though your husband had gone mad, murdered you, and then committed suicide. You used the henbane that grows against the wall at the back of the churchyard and used it in a pottage, which you fed to your husband. The effect was his strange behaviour on the morning of the murder and accounts for the smell in your kitchen when I found the bodies. The henbane eventually did its work, and when your husband had fallen into a stupor on his chair, you procured the help of William here, who helped you move Mary Reade's body. You then positioned your husband's fowling gun between his legs and shot him through the throat. Once this was completed, you immediately made for this place, where you have remained ever since."

Jane Bootle stared at me for a moment before bursting into laughter. "Congratulations," she said, "you most certainly have a singular talent for unravelling puzzles of this kind. It is a pity that it must go to waste, for you realise that we cannot afford to let you live. William will now depart, and when he is far enough away, I will dispose of the three of you. I know of a perfectly good tunnel not far from here, where your bodies can be easily disposed of. If someone from the garrison discovers them when leaving the house, it will be assumed that William came across these three interlopers and was forced to kill them to protect the integrity of the tunnel. Then, once my brother has been convicted and hung for the murder of my husband, we will present ourselves to Henry Oulton in Bolton and claim my inheritance."

I looked at Jane Bootle in confusion. "That's all very well," I said, "but how will you account for the fact that the world thinks you are dead?"

"That is easy. I will claim that my husband had an affair and that I returned to Bolton to escape him. He then went mad and murdered his mistress and killed himself. The latter part of this story is already believed and there will be nobody left to contradict my account. And, by this time, my brother will already be dead."

I nodded slowly. It all fitted in perfectly. "You are a clever woman, Jane Bootle, and an evil one. One day you will be held to account for this by a higher authority."

"That may well be," she smiled, "but come, I am growing weary of this. William, it is time you were on your way."

Bootle nodded meekly and got to his feet, making me realise to what extent Jane Bootle was the key protagonist in these events. Bootle was merely her lackey, driven by lust.

I watched, sickened, as the two of them embraced. The captain then went back into the kitchen and closed the door behind him, with a view to leaving the building by the back door.

"We have spent enough time talking," said Jane Bootle, a grim smile touching the corner of her mouth. "It is now time for you to meet your maker." In perfect calm, she reached for the carbine and pointed it directly at my chest. In anticipation of the shot, I felt as though my heart was about to burst, so I closed my eyes and held my breath.

Suddenly, there was a loud crack and then nothing, save the sound of footsteps retreating at pace into the distance. I felt no pain. At first I thought I was dead, but I opened my eyes and realised I was still alive. Had she shot one of the others first? I looked to either side of me, but no. Both Alexander and Lawrence were staring ahead to where Jane Bootle was slumped backwards over her chair, a huge hole in her chest, from which pumped a river of dark, red blood.

I struggled onto my side and there, standing by the door, was the most beautiful sight I ever saw. Wearing a face betraying both hatred and grim determination, was Beatrice Le Croix. She was holding a matchlock musket, still smoking, the cord glowing red and angry in the light of the dawn.

Chapter 39

Lathom House – Saturday April 27th – Monday May 13th, 1644

Colonel Alexander Rigby's shame was complete. The following afternoon at two o'clock, Colonel Holland and the rest of the Manchester Committee arrived at Lathom House expecting to view Lady Derby's final surrender and Parliament's triumphal march through the gates. Instead, all his superiors were able to view were scores of dead bodies and Morgan's nailed-up ordnance. Brereton's mortar had been lost to the enemy, as had three drums and numerous arms. If that were not enough, five prisoners had been taken, including one of Browne's assistants, which meant that Lady Derby would have gained full knowledge of the engineer's construction designs, including his, as yet, incomplete plans to drain the house's water supplies.

There was no getting around it. It was a disaster of monumental proportions, and any chance that Rigby thought he might have had of persuading the committee to renew the tax that had paid for his grenades lay broken, twisted, and dismantled in the middle of the main courtyard of Lathom House.

The only thing which gave Rigby some grounds for cheer, and caused me some sadness, was that on the afternoon prior to the attack, one of the colonel's musketeers shot dead Jenny Reade's dog attempting one trip too many to the postern gate. Rigby never did discover who the dog belonged to, but I made a mental note to seek out Jenny and comfort her when the opportunity arose.

For my part, things could barely have gone any better. We found Marc Le Croix starved and emaciated in the cellars of Burscough Mill, or rather it was he who found us. After the timely arrival of Beatrice, we had heard a crashing sound emanating from the cellar, so we searched Jane Bootle's body for the key and unlocked the door. As we did so, a whirling, screaming ball of wood and fists flew towards us, striking out in all directions. Fortunately for us, Marc chose Alexander as his initial target, and, as most people who know us are aware, items propelled in Alexander's direction tend to bounce off him, rather than knock him over. In this instance, my friend merely grabbed Marc by the throat, put one foot behind his right leg and pushed, sending him flying onto his back. At the same time, Beatrice cried out several times in French and wrapped her arms around the now-floored prisoner.

"Beatrice?" said Marc, confused at the sight of Jane Bootle's corpse as well as three people he didn't know and the half-sister he hadn't seen for years. There followed several minutes of hugging and earnest conversation in French as Beatrice calmed her brother down and explained what had transpired.

Of course, we told Rigby the same afternoon about Bootle, but by that time Lady Derby's spy had long since made himself scarce. Browne and a team of labourers were immediately sent over to Burscough to block up the entrance to the tunnel, which was filled up with enough earth and boulders to keep the whole of the garrison at bay. The pile of rubble was then levelled and secured with mortar and stones from the ruined priory. The engineer later told me that Rigby had briefly considered launching an assault through the tunnel but baulked when the further potential for disaster was pointed out to him.

Securing the release of William Seaman took rather longer to achieve, not least due to the obstinacy of the local constable, Gregson, who refused to believe our story about William and Jane Bootle and even threatened to arrest Beatrice for Jane Bootle's murder, when he examined the scene at the mill. The hanging of a Frenchwoman, he said, would be sure to draw the crowds.

I called him a disgrace to his office, but he was unmoved, and it eventually took the personal intervention of Rigby himself to secure Seaman's freedom. He thanked Alexander and I profusely for our efforts, and within a couple of days he was back on the road to Chester in the knowledge that the killers of his sister and brother-in-law had, at least, been identified, if not all brought to justice. The one thing he now had to come to terms with was how to explain to Francis Gamull and Robert Whitby that the option he had sold to purchase Oulton's import business was worthless.

Meanwhile, the siege persisted, and although Rigby was able to restrict the liberty of the men from the garrison reasonably effectively, without his mortar and heavy artillery he was able to do little else. Indeed, with the royalists devising ever more inventive ways of causing us night alarms, such as hanging strings of matchcord in the trees or sending dogs and even horses loose with burning matchcord attached to them, it felt at times like it was becoming difficult to tell who was the besieger and who was the besieged.

None of this was helped by the fact that the weather had turned, offering day after day of rain, which turned the trenches to thick, clagging mud. The water soaked our shirts, made our hats droop, and got into our boots. It even felt like it had found its way into our souls, for it reduced the morale of our men to a level of despondency not yet seen during the siege.

And then, amidst it all, Simon turned up, all of a sudden and unannounced, as was his wont. One day in early May, about a week after the rains started, he simply rode into New Park House and asked to see me.

I was overjoyed, of course, to discover that my brother was still alive, as was Alexander, although I was less pleased to discover that he had been encamped with Parliamentary forces outside York for over a month without him sending us word of his safety. In the event, Simon had volunteered to carry a message from Sir Thomas Fairfax to Rigby. Sir Thomas, it seemed, had been made aware of Simon's presence in Yorkshire and had given his personal approval for Simon to ride to Lathom.

Simon related how he had escaped from Jem Bressy and how he ended up being recruited into Prince Rupert's army. He described the long march to Newark, Skinner's decision to remain with Rupert's forces, his own escape, and his involvement in the damaging defeat at Newark.

He also explained how he had met John Lilburne, the man he most admired, and under whose command he now served. Lilburne, said Simon, had lost most of his possessions at Newark, but still possessed his political integrity. Now that he had found someone who he could follow, Simon intended to stay with Lilburne and fight for his political ideal of freedom and equality. Finding Lilburne in the manner he had was, he claimed, nothing short of destiny.

I was far from convinced of the wisdom of Simon's plan, but knew better than to contradict him, for I was sure it would get me nowhere. Nonetheless, I would have been failing in my duties as a brother had I not drawn his attention to two things in particular.

"But what about your apprenticeship?" I said, "and Rose Bailey? She is no doubt waiting for you to return in Nantwich."

"I have written to Rose," said Simon. "I have told her I will not forsake her and that I will return for her as soon as my work is complete, but I must follow the path God has laid out for me. As for Simkins, even if he were to have me back after losing his horse and a cartload of shoes, I don't think I am cut out to be a shoemaker, do you? I will follow my fate, whichever way it takes me."

And so that was that. Two days after riding into Lathom, Simon departed again, with no promise of when we would see him again.

As it turned out, my brother's brief visit was the catalyst for our own departure. With the siege floundering and Bootle gone, there was little need for us to remain.

"Our work here is done," I said to Alexander, one morning towards the middle of May. "Marc, although not fully recovered from his ordeal, is at least fit enough to travel, and Rigby has no need of our services anymore. If we are to complete our task, there is but one place for us to go. We must ride to Bolton."

Chapter 40

Bolton – Monday May 27ᵗʰ, 1644

*C*aptain Edward Rawsthorne lowered himself *into the trench opposite the postern gate and scratched his head. He had risen just before first light, expecting to lead the assault that would finally break the siege of Lathom House. He had envisaged a glorious rout of the enemy and a triumphal march through the rebel siege works, but it was not to be. Instead, he felt deflated and cheated, for the trenches that surrounded the house were completely deserted.*

Bending down, he picked up a discarded powder flask and inspected it, before flinging it in frustration at the side of the trench.

"Have a care, Edward," said a voice from behind him. "There is little to be gained from that. They are gone, slunk away into the woods like foxes in the night."

Rawsthorne turned round and looked upwards, to see the familiar figure of Captain Henry Ogle, behind whom stood a group of musketeers, perhaps thirty strong, their weapons at the ready as they cast careful eyes along the length of the trench. They had been sent out to protect the two officers, lest the apparent absence of besiegers in the trench turn out to be little more than a ruse designed to catch them unawares.

"Aye, that is the truth of it, Henry," said Rawsthorne. "Just what you would expect from a man like Rigby."

On reflection, Rawsthorne had to admit it was hardly surprising that Colonel Rigby had decided to terminate the siege. After all, for the past week the signs had been evident that the colonel had been angling for a withdrawal.

On the previous Thursday, Rigby had sent over a captain called Moseley with a demand for Lady Derby to vacate the house. No vindictiveness – no negotiating points – just a simple demand. When she refused, Moseley had immediately offered her the very same terms she herself had demanded of Fairfax at the start of the siege. It was then that she knew she had won, and simply instructed Moseley to tell Rigby to negotiate directly with her husband.

Her stance had been vindicated that very same evening, when one of her messengers got into the house by shooting the sole sentry standing in his way. The earl, she was told, was in Cheshire with Prince Rupert, whose army was poised to cut a swathe through Lancashire on its way to relieve Lathom. It was no wonder that Rigby had made himself scarce.

On the Sunday, during the midday change of watch,

the lookouts atop the Eagle Tower had noticed that the new watch was much reduced. Lady Derby had taken this as a sign of weakened morale, and so plans had been set for a final assault to end the siege. The men of the garrison had expected to win, but they had not anticipated that the besiegers would cut and run in the middle of the night.

"It is indeed a shame," said Ogle, "that we cannot teach that cowardly dog a lesson once and for all."

"You are right," replied Rawsthorne, with a smile, "but have no fear, he will get what is coming to him. In the meantime, we have but one task left to fulfil. Lieutenant Key," he called, beckoning over a junior officer. "It is time for her ladyship to inspect her property and enjoy this day of triumph. Have Mr Broome prepare her carriage forthwith."

Chapter 41

Bolton – Tuesday May 28th, 1644

Henry Oulton's house, Green Acres, was a fair brick mansion with a walled garden and orchards. It stood next to an even bigger property called Private Acres, which was located at the end of Deansgate, the narrow lane which led west from the iron cross at the centre of Bolton.

We arrived there on 15th May and were immediately welcomed by Oulton's steward, a serious-looking man called Horrocks, and his wife, who clearly saw Marc as their future master and treated him as such.

Oulton himself was a jaundiced, bedridden fellow, who clearly did not have long to live, but his eyes possessed a clarity and steeliness which helped to explain how he had survived so long after Marc's disappearance. It was as though he had refused to die until his inheritance was secured.

Alexander and I were welcomed into the household as Marc's rescuers and invited to stay until such time as Bootle was apprehended. Beatrice, having made it clear that she had fallen in love with Lawrence, was also offered accommodation until she was able to be reunited with him. Marc, meanwhile, who continued to recover slowly from his ordeal, was simply delighted to have regained his half-sister as a companion after years of separation.

As it turned out, Bolton, or Bolton le Moors to give it its full name, had little in common with Nantwich other than its approximate size and its reputation as a magnet for all manner of Puritan sympathisers and the overtly godly. In retrospect, I have no idea why I had thought otherwise.

The most obvious difference to two men from the milder climate of Cheshire like Alexander and myself, was that the town, situated in a valley surrounded by open moorland, seemed to be perpetually freezing cold, lending its inhabitants a hardiness and individualism which had stood it in good stead over the years.

The town centre stood on a high bank situated on the inside of a bend in the River Croal. The main street, Churchgate, was a jumble of timber houses, jutting out over a narrow, muddy thoroughfare. At one end, overlooking the bend in the river, was St Peter's Church, which was being used as a warehouse for storing military equipment. At the other end was the iron cross, next to which stood a large coaching house called The Swan.

From the cross led the town's three main roads. To the north, the road led down a steep slope called

Windy Bank, past a dungeon, to a bridge over the river and the hamlet of Little Bolton. To the south was Bradshawgate, the main road to Manchester, and to the west, Deansgate. Most people lived along these four main thoroughfares, although to the south-west of the cross, between Bradshawgate and Deansgate, was a large area of lanes, thatched houses, and crofts inhabited by Bolton's poorer townsfolk, many of whom worked in the trade for fustians and cotton wool, for which Bolton had become renowned.

The local people, I quickly learned, were justifiably proud of the fact that they had repelled an attack on their town the previous March. However, I soon realised that the town's defences, damaged at that time, had not been adequately repaired. A large sconce to the south of the town was completely unusable, whilst the defensive walls and ditch, despite surrounding the vulnerable south and west sides of the town, were nothing like the huge earthen banks and wooden walkways that we had built at Nantwich, and which had become so instrumental to us surviving our own siege. The end of each of the main roads was protected by little more than a series of posts and heavy chains.

Apart from this, the town was only defended by around five hundred local militia and a troop of horse, so it was difficult to see how it would be possible to repel a determined attack by a large army. When we heard that Prince Rupert was on the march through

Cheshire, I began to fear the worst.

***

As luck would have it, Alexander and I spent two full weeks in Bolton before things came to a head, but when they did, they did so with a vengeance.

Early on the morning of Tuesday 28th May, Colonel Rigby marched into the town with around two thousand men. The colonel, it transpired, had abandoned the siege at Lathom the previous Sunday, as soon as he became aware that Prince Rupert was on the march. Some of his forces had gone with Colonel Holland to Manchester and others with John Moore to Liverpool, leaving Rigby with only his own units raised from the Amounderness Hundred. The colonel had marched to Eccleston Green near Chorley, and from there, with a view to avoiding Rupert's much larger force, he had headed towards the perceived safety of the nearest garrison.

Although many of the townsfolk of Bolton cheered and ran to shake the hands of Rigby's men as they marched past Green Acres towards the cross and the taverns on Churchgate, I began to wonder whether Rigby's presence might not actually be a portent of disaster. After all, five hundred clubmen could do little against the might of Rupert's army, and a quick surrender would have been no disgrace, but two thousand five hundred men? Would they not be inclined to fight? And would a town protecting the likes of Rigby not be a certain target for the worst kind of retribution?

The only advantage as far as I could see was that we were able to seek out Lawrence again. We managed to spot him as he passed Green Acres and were able to offer him and some of his men billets for the night.

The next thing that happened – the very next morning, in fact – was that William Bootle turned up. After having waited for him for two whole weeks, Alexander and I had almost begun to wonder whether, in fact, he had found out about Jane Bootle's demise and had made good his escape.

However, sometime during mid-morning, just as Marc, Lawrence, Alexander, and I were leaving the house, in order to stroll into town, we saw him, as plain as day, walking down the street towards us. Perhaps he had been on his way to Green Acres to ask for an audience with Henry Oulton, but we never found out, for Bootle spotted us at exactly the same moment, and bolted in panic before we could reach him, escaping through one of the gardens on the south side of Deansgate and into the orchards beyond.

"Don't worry," said Lawrence, calmly. "Let him run. He won't get far. The town is full of Rigby's men. Someone will recognise him."

Chapter 42

Bolton – Tuesday May 28th, 1644

*J**ames Stanley, the seventh Earl of Derby, rode over the crest of Great Lever Moor and cast his gaze down the broad valley of the River Croal, towards Bolton. It was raining steadily, and large globules of water dripped from his hat onto his thigh, seeping through his breeches. It was a filthy day, but on this particular afternoon, he would not allow such a trifling matter to dampen the brightness of his mood. He could scarcely believe his luck.*

That morning, Prince Rupert had sent Colonel Henry Tillier and his greencoats forward to scout the route into the place known as the Geneva of the North. They had reached the moorland overlooking the town but had been astounded to find the place crawling with roundheads – and not just any old group of roundheads. With the exception of around five hundred clubmen and local militia, the men defending Bolton were none other than Colonel Alexander Rigby and his men from Amounderness, the very same force, who, until recently, had not only persecuted and

431

besieged the earl's wife and family, but also caused great damage to his ancestral home at Lathom.

In truth, things had not gone perfectly for the earl since his return from the Isle of Man. To his disappointment, Rupert had refused his request to be given a command of his own, but at least he had been given the honour of riding as a gentleman volunteer in the prince's own troop of horse, who, it had to be said, were in enormously good cheer.

Wiping the water from his face, he looked down towards the town and liked what he saw. The enemy had formed a solid line around the earthen defences, but the mud walls thrown up a year ago were less than a pike's length in height and clearly not designed to keep out a force of the likes of that which approached the town now. The great sconce to the south of the earthworks, in disrepair since Derby's own failed attack the previous year, lay deserted and broken, and the force manning the walls, he knew, consisted largely of raw recruits, demotivated from their experiences at Lathom.

Derby watched with a smile as a troop of horse – from a distance it looked like Shuttleworth's – began to move bravely out towards them, in order to vex the prince's own blue-coated regiment of foot – for the earl knew that Rupert would soon order his own horse to engage them. The moment he had waited for was finally approaching. This was not just about *vindication for his failure to take the town a year ago, but the opportunity to make Rigby pay dearly for a year of persecution.*

All he needed now to make his day complete was the presence of the traitorous porter who had gained his trust and then turned his coat, advising Rigby on the layout of Lathom House, so that the colonel could bombard it with stones and grenades. Yes, he mused, the sight of William Bootle among those defending the town would make vengeance all the sweeter

Chapter 43

The first we realised for certain what that fateful day would bring was at around two in the afternoon, when Rupert's forces were spotted traversing the high ground to the south of the town. The thin drizzle that had fallen for most of the morning had turned into a more solid downpour, transforming the already sodden streets into a morass of mud, but as soon as the shouts and alarms went up, men began to appear from their houses to join Rigby's forces. Some had guns of their own, but most were armed with pikes, axes, and clubs. Marc was still too weak to fight, so he stayed ensconced inside the house, but when Lawrence went to join his unit, Alexander and I followed Horrocks to a shed, where we found an assortment of weapons. Alexander, being of substantial bulk, chose a pike, whereas I made do with a dagger and a club similar to that with which I used to dispense my constabulary duties at home. All three of us then headed down Deansgate to the cross, and then south down Bradshawgate towards where most of the men were heading.

On the horizon, I could see a mass of bodies moving across the crest of the ridge at Great Lever. It was like watching a colony of ants, although somebody else likened it to a cloud racing across the sky. Presently, though, the mass began to form itself into individual units, each searching for ways in which to approach the town.

Alexander and I followed Horrocks to the end of Bradshawgate, where we lined up along the inadequate-looking earthworks and waited for the charge. I noticed that our own troop of horse, under Colonel Shuttleworth, had already issued out of the town with a view to intercepting the royalist foot, but Prince Rupert's cavalry reacted quickly and charged itself. In amongst the melee, I thought I caught sight of Rupert's famous dog, Boye, barking and yapping at the men and horses. Then, out of the crowd, appeared a figure I had seen before, heading straight for our own cornet. I watched, transfixed, as the Earl of Derby cut down the junior officer with his own sword and retreated amongst raucous cheers with Shuttleworth's colours in his possession. Our horse, having lost shape, tried to reform itself, but, left with the option of being overwhelmed or living to fight another day, Shuttleworth called for an orderly retreat and sped off over the moorland to the west.

Once the field was clear of horses, we were able to see exactly what units of foot were lined up against us. Immediately opposite us to the south were Prince Rupert's own bluecoats, alongside Henry Warren's Irish regiment, who I recognised from Nantwich. To the west of the town were two further regiments, including a great crowd of redcoats, who I later found out were under the command of Sir Thomas Tyldesley.

And then, all of a sudden, they were upon us. Firelocks and musketeers with matchlock muskets fired at us to keep us at bay, whilst teams of pikemen attacked us directly, these in turn shielding groups of men with ladders.

The fighting was much more intense than what I had experienced at Nantwich, but our men stuck manfully to the task and repulsed their first attack at considerable loss to the enemy. Quite a few of our men lay wounded and dying, but there must have been at least a hundred dead royalists lying in the sodden ditch or on the side of the earthworks.

To the west, the royalist red-coated regiment had managed to break through our lines into the town, but they too had eventually been overwhelmed and forced to retreat through the pouring rain.

I was astounded. Considering that our forces consisted largely of Rigby's battered recruits from Lathom, our men had fought valiantly and had been able to achieve a result beyond all expectations. Our good fortune could not last forever, though. New royalist units were now being brought forward to replace those regiments who had taken a mauling, and I was beginning to wonder how Alexander and I would be able to extricate ourselves from the situation with our skins intact.

It was then that our forces made a fatal mistake. A group of Rigby's men, flush with success, dragged forward an Irish prisoner they had taken and decided to hang him as a papist in full view of the royalist forces. An eerie silence descended on both sides as the man was led screaming to his fate, but then, when his struggling had stopped, an angry roar erupted from the royalist ranks, rising to a crescendo of noise as the enemy charged again. To the west, Tyldesley's red-coated regiment was still in the field, and, as I glanced towards them, I was surprised to notice Lord Derby, who was leading them in person. Facing us to the south, however, was a new opponent, Rupert's bluecoats having been replaced by a fresher-looking regiment wearing green tunics.

I looked round for the nearest officer and caught sight of Major Robinson a few yards away, who was trying hard to get his musketeers to reload and hold their positions.

"Who are they, Major?" I shouted.

Robinson glanced over his shoulder and nodded in recognition. "Broughton's," he called back. "Battle-hardened veterans from Ormonde's army in Ireland. Flushed with success from Newark too. They will be no easy proposition, that is for sure."

As they approached, I could hear them chanting rhythmically. It sounded almost hypnotic. At first I could not make out their words, but then I caught them: "Kill dead, kill dead," repeated again and again, not just mechanically, but spat at us with fury. Alexander looked over at me and nodded back up Bradshawgate towards the cross.

"This is not a good place to be, Daniel," he said. "We should try and make our way back to Green Acres. It may be safer there."

I turned round to Horrocks and grabbed him by the wrist. "Alexander is right," I said. "Let us head back to the house. There are women and sick people to protect there."

Horrocks shook his wrist free and stared at me in anger.

"You would run from these papists? Are you a coward, sir? We must fight here. If we stand firm, we will repel them again."

Horrocks spoke well – and bravely. However, it was, unfortunately also the last thing that he ever did, for at that precise moment a musket ball ripped through his neck, sending him tumbling to the floor. The servant's eyes bulged, his legs convulsing as he held his hand to his throat, thick red blood pouring between his fingers.

"God have mercy," I breathed, before stumbling off down the road after my friend. Looking around me, I quickly realised that many others had the same idea. With Broughton's men breaking through our defences in several places, a number of men, many of whom I recognised from Lathom, had already turned to run. Captains Duddell and Davie, I noticed, had already begun to lead their units backwards and were heading down a lane, which ran parallel to the river bank and ultimately led to the church. I made to follow them, but a local clubman grabbed me by the arm.

"Not that way, mate," he warned. "Not if you want to see tomorrow, that is. There's a wall down there that runs the whole length of the river bank. Even if you get over it, the slope is too steep. You will be trapped."

I hesitated momentarily, but then nodded my thanks and ran due north, up Bradshawgate, back towards the cross. As I did so, I caught sight of Captain and Lieutenant Dandie disappearing under a mound of greencoats, father and son, standing together to the last.

Within the space of a few minutes, the tide had turned. Obstinate resistance had given way to self-preservation, and the battle had turned into a full scale rout. Men, fuelled by panic, were slipping in the mud and falling over each other in their haste to escape.

Rigby, who had been commanding the defence from horseback fifty yards or so further up Bradshawgate, had also begun to look uncertain, his horse stamping nervously as fleeing men began to run past him. His mind was made up when a company of royalist horse broke through the wall to the west and began to trample their way across the fields and between the crofts to try and cut off the escape route back to the cross.

"Fall back," he shouted. His strange smile, still visible through the visor on his helmet, now looked more like a grimace, but he wheeled his horse round and spurred it in the direction of his fleeing men. Next to him, a trooper grabbed his chest and fell forward over the neck of his horse before slumping like a rag doll to one side.

At that moment, one of the fleeing soldiers charged past me, almost knocking me off my feet, grabbed hold of the horse's reins, and dragged the dying trooper from the saddle.

"Sorry, friend," he said. "This is more use to me than you now." I looked into the man's face and realised with a start that it was Lawrence.

"Daniel," he shouted, recognising me in the same instant. "What are you doing here? Get yourself somewhere safe and throw away your weapons. As an unarmed civilian you have half a chance. As an armed soldier you are a dead man."

"But what about you?" I asked.

"I will take my chances with Rigby," he said. "Please look after Beatrice for me. I will be back." With that he mounted the horse and rode after Rigby towards the cross.

Alexander and I were somewhat slower. The main street was now full of royalists, both greencoats and redcoats, so we jumped over a fence and headed off through a row of back gardens and yards until we reached the rear of the stables belonging to The Swan, the coaching house on the corner of Churchgate.

The gate to the stable yard was locked and was made of solid oak, but there was no time for hesitation, for the field behind us leading to the river bank was the scene of unremitting horror, swarming with screaming, dying men, as the green-coated royalist regiment rampaged along the line of the wall, cutting men down indiscriminately, many asking for quarter, but none being given. Alexander launched himself shoulder first at the gate, which gave a splintering crack and fell inwards. Behind it stood two nervous-looking grooms wielding pieces of wood from an old beer barrel. However, as soon as they saw that we were not royalists, they beckoned us over.

"Quick," said one, "get inside and keep low."

"And get rid of your fucking weapons," said the other. We needed no further bidding. Alexander tossed his pike back through the gate, and I did likewise with my club, although I thought better of throwing away the dagger and stuffed it down the side of my boots.

We were led through a corridor into the tap-room, which was crammed with people, mostly old men, women, and children cowering against the walls, but also several others, who had escaped the fighting. Tables had been upturned and used to barricade the doors.

I ventured over to one of the windows and looked out at the scene in Bradshawgate, which was a melee of horsemen and royalist foot soldiers, many wearing crimson scarves around their waists, slashing wildly at anyone who was still unwise enough to be outdoors. I watched in horror as one woman, heavily with child, was dragged out into the street, where her husband was being held, and she was forced to watch as he was cut down before her very eyes. The street was littered with bodies, and not just menfolk. There were women and children too. One old woman had been run through with a sword because she had nothing to give the plundering royalists. They were truly out of control.

However, in amongst the swirling mass of horses, men, and cold steel, I caught sight of one man who was making his way very purposely forward. Alexander Rigby, having discarded his tawny-coloured scarf, was mingling with the royalists. Somehow he had managed to get hold of their field word and was manfully pretending to be one of their number.

"A scorn on your roundhead God," I heard him shout, with convincing venom, as he passed by our window, closely followed by Lawrence, who was gritting his teeth grimly and trying to keep as close to the colonel as he could. It was ironic, I thought. Rigby had spent weeks being outthought and humiliated by Lady Derby, but now, in extremis, the colonel was showing an intuition and coolness of thought that I could not, hitherto, have expected of him.

As he passed the window, I could have sworn he looked me straight in the eye and smiled at me, but then he spurred his horse through the crowd and rode off with Lawrence in his wake down Windy Bank towards the bridge over the River Croal.

By this time, royalist horsemen were coming from all directions. Rigby's men and the local militia had resisted well, but there was nothing left to fight for except oneself. A troop of horse was making its way up Deansgate, having broken into the town by Private Acres, and at its head was the unmistakeable figure of the Earl of Derby, jaw set, hatred still etched on his face.

It was then that William Bootle appeared. In my desire to assure my own survival, I had almost forgotten about the captain, and so I was somewhat taken aback when he sprinted out from between two houses and approached the earl's horse.

I was too far away to hear what was being said. However, the earl, spotting Bootle, calmly dismounted, walked over to him, and then, after a brief conversation, drew his sword and ran Bootle through in cold blood. The captain staggered backwards, a look of pained surprise on his face, grimaced, and fell backwards against the cross at the end of Churchgate. The earl simply wiped his sword against his breeches, remounted, and rode away. Perhaps I was imagining it, but, as he did so, it seemed as though he was clenching his fist in triumph.

I was shocked, not because of the brutality, for I had seen plenty of that already that day, but because of the unfathomable nature of this act and the coldness with which it had been executed.

It was then that the horrible truth dawned on me. The Earl of Derby did not have the slightest idea that Bootle was working as a spy for the countess. He had been recruited after the earl had left for the Isle of Man and Chester, and his status, for security reasons, was probably known only to Rutter, Farrington, and the countess herself. To the earl, Bootle was no more than an ex-servant who had betrayed him.

I tore myself away from the window and sat down on the tap-room floor, my back propped up against the bar. I had seen enough for one day. Poetic justice is the term many would have used to describe William Bootle's death. I did not care for such justice myself, for I would not have wished such a death on anyone. But I could not deny it. The irony was overwhelming.

Chapter 44

Bolton – Wednesday May 29ᵗʰ, 1644

It was the middle of the following afternoon by the time the royalists got around to searching Green Acres. We watched them approach from the window of Henry Oulton's bed chamber, a great column of exuberant triumphalism leading an equally despondent line of prisoners, defeated and downcast. Hundreds of them, shackled together in twos. In truth, Alexander and I were fortunate not to be among their number. It was a day for sadness and reflection, but, as Alexander put it, at least the rain had stopped.

We had spent a tense evening with half a dozen others cowering in the cellars of The Swan, although it has to be said, the availability of so much free ale made our stay rather more comfortable than it might otherwise have been. We had realised that staying in the tap-room was not advisable, for the victorious royalists were bound to want to drink their fill once they had tired of looting and plundering the town, and trying to escape through the streets would only have been possible once the victors' bloodlust had receded.

Beatrice initially looked shocked to see only two of us return to Green Acres, but I was able to put her mind at rest by telling her about Lawrence's escape with Rigby. I did not need to say anything to Mrs Horrocks, though, for she already knew of her husband's fate.

"He died bravely, urging us to hold our lines," I said. "He can have felt very little."

"He was a fool," said the widow, bitterly. "He was a civilian. He had no need to fight Prince Rupert. He should have remained concealed here with the rest of us."

I said nothing, for there was nothing adequate that could have conveyed my feelings at that moment. During the previous evening, the scale of the slaughter that had taken place on both sides had become painfully apparent. The royalists had lost over two hundred men during their first assault and as many again during the rest of the action. It was little wonder that they had seen fit to take such retribution.

The number of defenders and townsfolk who had perished was impossible to gauge, for many had fled into the countryside and had been pursued for miles around. Some said upwards of a thousand men, women, and children had died, and who was I to argue? Many of Rigby's men had been cut down in the area known as Silverwell Bottoms, which lay alongside the bank of the River Croal, which I had seen Captains Duddell and Davie fleeing towards. Those lucky ones who had escaped the carnage had sought refuge in the church and had been taken prisoner.

As the convoy of prisoners filed past Green Acres, I noticed a group of greencoats break away from the line and head purposefully for the entrance to the house.

"They are checking every building," said Marc. "They are looking for anyone who would still resist them. We would be best advised to remain passive and sit in my uncle's dressing room. Mrs Horrocks will try to divert them."

I had little energy left to resist any more, and so sitting in the dressing room is exactly what we did. We were resigned to having to explain our presence in the house and half-expected to be dragged off with the hordes of prisoners filing down Deansgate, but we were totally unprepared for what happened when the soldiers entered Henry Oulton's chamber.

I could hear Mrs Horrocks remonstrating angrily with the men, her voice loud and shrill. "Have you not caused enough misery in this town?" she said. "You are in the chamber of a sick old man, there is no need for this."

"I will be the arbiter of that, goodwife," snapped a gruff voice. "Jim, take a quick look in that dressing room and make sure there's nobody in there."

My heart sank, and I prepared myself for the inevitable. However, when the door opened, I found myself staring with amazement at the slim, perpetually

447

downcast-looking features of James Skinner.

The youngster's jaw dropped momentarily as he took in the three figures stood huddled in the corner of the room, but he quickly pulled himself together, gave a wry smile, and nodded at me.

"There's no-one in here, sir," I heard him call, as the door shut behind him.

Chapter 45

Marston Moor, Chester, Ormskirk, Nantwich –
Tuesday July 2ⁿᵈ, 1644

O n a warm Tuesday evening in July, two months
after he had ridden away from Lathom, the
young soldier collapsed on a tuft of grass and wiped the
sweat and grime of battle from his face. His recently
re-grown blond hair, normally loose and flowing, was
matted with mud and rain from the thunderstorm that
had accompanied Parliament's initial charge.

It was almost completely dark, but a full moon cast a
ghostly light across the landscape. In the distance, he
could still make out the sight of bodies strewn across
the open fields, some still moving and calling for help.

In between them, figures lurched in and out of the
ditches that criss-crossed the moorland, but these
were not all soldiers. These were looters, come to strip
the dead bodies of their clothes and any valuables they
could lay their hands on. These people did not waste
their time, he thought, and he thanked God for his
deliverance from such a fate.

What had he been thinking of, committing himself

to this? Today was his brother's wedding day, and he should have been in Nantwich with those he loved and who loved him, rather than risking his life in some godforsaken Yorkshire field.

But he had survived, as had several others he had recognised, including many from the unit he had fought with in Newark. He had also seen the colonel his brother had served under at Lathom and the personable young lieutenant he had been introduced to at that time. The latter had carried his arm in a sling, but at least he was not lying amongst the corpses that were being robbed and desecrated on the battlefield.

And, most importantly of all, Parliament had won the day. The royalists had been routed, and thousands of their number had perished. Even Prince Rupert's diabolical white poodle was dead, and with the King defeated, the soldier's dream of an England where all men could be equal was still alive and still worth fighting for.

No, he had done the right thing. His brother and his flame-haired sweetheart would understand. He would return to Nantwich, but not until he had achieved his dream.

Meanwhile, on the edge of the village of Tockwith, a young musketeer in a green coat sat under armed guard. Like many in his regiment, including his commanding officer, he had been taken prisoner, but he was not downhearted. His limbs still buzzed with the

450

adrenalin of the fight, and his captors were treating him with respect. He would have a few uncomfortable days ahead, but he knew he would eventually be returned home or given the opportunity to fight for Parliament, and, if the truth be told, he didn't mind who he fought for, so long as he could continue to learn his craft, that of a professional soldier.

At the same time in Chester, a footman summoned his master and mistress to dinner in their substantial merchant's house on Eastgate Street. He was grateful, for not only had he been freed from gaol, where he had been held for weeks on end on unfounded murder charges, he had also been promoted to head footman, his predecessor having been dismissed for pilfering from the kitchens. Several items had been found in his possession, including food and various kitchen tools, including, oddly enough, a cheese wire.

He had been devastated at the death of the woman he loved, but he was no fool. He realised that his infatuation would have come to nothing in the end. The recently widowed cook, Martha Woodcock, however, was a different matter. Perhaps he was imagining it, but had she not been particularly attentive towards him since his reinstatement? And did she not make the very best pies he had ever tasted?

"Yes," he thought, as he showed his master and mistress to their table. "Things were looking up." He might even mention it to Martha herself. In fact, if he *played his cards right, wedding bells might even be in the offing.*

Meanwhile, in Ormskirk, a young girl was cooking a meal of much more meagre rations for her older brother and two younger siblings. She was delighted to have Harry back at home. He had served his mistress well during the siege, but now he had been given leave to stay at home and look after his younger brother and sisters. He would not be expected to man the walls of Lathom House again, even if the roundheads were to return, especially now the family dog, such a useful and obedient courier of messages, was dead.

Not that the Lady of Lathom herself had much of a view on the matter anymore, for she had left for the greater comforts of Knowsley, leaving the defence of the house in the hands of Captain Rawsthorne.

It seemed to the girl that, with the siege finally over, the worst chapter in her life had come to an end. The only thing she missed were the attentions of the kind Parliament man, who had helped her when she most needed it. She had not seen him since the day the mortar was captured, and she wondered what had become of him.

In Nantwich, the very same man, grateful to have been relieved from his onerous position as town constable, blinked in the moonlight and kissed his new wife as he emerged from the Red Cow on Beam Street. Townsfolk had spilled out of the tavern onto the street.

The wedding feast was long since over, but many had stayed until the newly-wed couple had decided to retire.

The best man, a tall-built fellow with sandy hair, rang the bell, which was normally used for very different purposes, to propose a toast to his friend, while a young girl and an even smaller boy ran wildly between the knees of the revellers. The groom's apprentice waved a tankard in the air and cheered, nearly falling on his back, for he was still having trouble getting used to his wooden leg. Even the guest of honour, a slim, severe-looking man, who exuded an air of authority and commanded the respect of all those present, especially those who knew him as Sir William Brereton, Commander-in-Chief of the Parliamentary forces in Cheshire, appeared to be enjoying himself.

The only people whose smiles appeared slightly strained were the soberly dressed colonel sat at Brereton's side and the auburn-haired young woman who was standing on the periphery of the group. The young officer, responsible for the recruitment and payment of Brereton's army, would have been pleased to join in the celebrations – he considered himself a sociable type. However, his good mood had been tempered by his knowledge of the contents of the letter Sir William had received from Sir Thomas Fairfax that morning. The third wax ball provided by Brereton's spies in Chester and taken from the bridegroom's brother by Sir John Meldrum, had finally found its way into Sir Thomas's hands. Once decrypted, together with the two balls passed on by Colonel Rigby, it had revealed details of a plot involving a royalist intelligencer by the name of Bressy. Brereton had made it clear that urgent action would need to be taken and that the bridegroom's services would be required again, very soon. The young colonel did not relish breaking this news to the groom the day after his wedding, but duty was duty, and in this regard he would not be found wanting.

As for the young woman, she had willingly attended the celebrations, but was finding it hard to join in, for wedding bells should have been ringing for her too. Her betrothed, however, had followed a different path to the groom. He had chosen to follow his political conviction rather than marry her. He had promised to return for her, but was he to be believed? She honestly did not know any more.

At that moment, she looked across the road and caught the eye of the young tanner's apprentice, who had been showing her so much attention recently. The youth smiled at her and beckoned for her to come over.

The young woman looked down to her feet and hesitated for a moment, but then she sighed, took a long lingering look at the bridegroom, and crossed the road.

Author's Note

Considering the dramatic nature of Lady Charlotte de Tremouille's valiant defence of Lathom House with only three hundred men against a vastly superior parliamentary force, it is a wonder that the story is not more widely known today.

Certainly, up until the end of the 19th century, the tale of Lady Derby's exploits retained a much more prominent place within the national consciousness, spawning a number of books and poems, the best known of which is William Harrison Ainsworth's novel *The Leaguer of Lathom*. Even at the time of the siege, Lady Derby was eulogised by those on the royalist side, the *Scottish Dove* newspaper, for example, famously pointing out that she had 'stolen the earl's breeches'. Over the last hundred years, however, the details surrounding the First Siege of Lathom House (there were, in fact, two sieges) have gradually drifted into the backwaters of history.

This is a shame, because the events which took place between March and May 1644 make up a captivating adventure story. Given the abject incompetence of the parliamentary forces at times, they would also, in my opinion, form the basis for an engaging comedy film – but that is another story. In any case, I make no apologies for purloining this piece of history as the basis for *A Soldier of Substance*.

Historically, it suited many of those writing about the siege to portray Lady Derby as a defenceless woman, who loyally defended her husband's house against evil and heartless oppressors. It is, however, clear that Lady Derby was nothing of the kind. In his excellent 1991 book *To Play the Man*, Colin Pilkington describes her as being 'as devious as Elizabeth I, as inflexible as Mrs Thatcher and with the physical presence of an Amazon,' which just about sums her up. Lady Derby, who was a granddaughter of William of Orange (William the Silent) and a cousin of Prince Rupert, was most certainly not a woman to be trifled with.

There are three main contemporary sources for the siege, all of which were written by people who make an appearance in *A Soldier of Substance*.

The first of these is a comprehensive siege journal written by Edward Halsall, who was a seventeen year old ensign at the time. Halsall, who, incidentally, *was* injured in the raid on March 18, wrote the siege journal two or three years after the event. Following the siege, he followed an interesting career as a royalist spy. In 1650, he become implicated in the murder of Anthony Ascham, the Commonwealth Ambassador to Madrid, and was later involved in a plot to assassinate Cromwell himself. He survived the Protectorate and by 1663, he was Equerry to the Queen.

The second source is the writing of Samuel Rutter, chaplain to the Countess of Derby. Along with William Farrington, he was one of Lady Derby's main advisors during the siege. A protégé of the Stanley family, he came from the family which owned the mill at Burscough. Rutter was responsible for a major piece of disinformation early in the siege, when he managed to persuade one of the parliamentary captains, probably Captain John Ashurst, that the countess was terrified of a siege, thereby changing the whole course of Rigby's strategy. In later life, Rutter became the Bishop of Sodor and Man and died in 1663.

The other major source, and the only one from the Parliamentary side, is *A Discourse of the Warr in Lancashire,* written in 1655 by Major Edward Robinson.

In describing the course of the siege within the context of the novel, I've kept faithfully to the time scale of the historical siege, including all the key events, such as the various attacks on the besiegers by the garrison, Assheton and Moore's departure, the effort by Stanley to intervene, Rigby's bizarre sideshow over Easter, etc.

I've also taken the liberty of incorporating Daniel Cheswis into some events; for example – six men *were* taken prisoner by Captain Ogle on March 12 and were later the subject of a prisoner exchange.

The murder plot involving the killings of Katherine Seaman and John Bootle, however, is invented. Both of the murder victims in the story are invented characters, as are the majority of the Seaman, Bootle, Le Croix, and Oulton families. However, there *was* a spy in Lady Derby's ranks, referred to as her 'secret friend,' who passed important strategic information to her during February and March.

This person, however, most definitely was not William Bootle, and was most probably a senior officer in the ranks of either Assheton or Moore, because the information available to the countess fell away when Assheton and Moore withdrew their support for the siege.

William Bootle was a real person, and my apologies are due to him for how I have portrayed him in *A Soldier of Substance*. He had been a servant in the earl's employ and was engaged as an advisor to Rigby on the layout of Lathom House, but he was not engaged as a double agent – that part of the story is a product of my imagination. Bootle, who was probably from Bolton, was an active officer on the parliamentary side during the Bolton Massacre and lost his life during the battle. The manner of his death is open to conjecture. In his siege journal, Halsall has him dying 'by his Lord's hand', although other royalist sources say the Earl of Derby happened upon Bootle during the conflict, refused to kill him, but said he could not save him from others. Parliamentary sources, on the other hand, have Derby killing Bootle after quarter had been given. Whatever the truth, Derby was convicted of Bootle's murder, and, as every Boltonian who has an interest in the town's history knows, he was executed on Churchgate on 15th October, 1651. The earl is said to have spent his last few hours in Ye Old Man and Scythe, an inn opposite the cross, which to this day contains a chair that the earl is supposed to have sat on before being led outside to be beheaded.

During the siege, the defence of Lathom House was entrusted to six captains, all named in the novel. Each of these had a trusted lieutenant (who I deliberately haven't named for fear of unnecessarily adding to the already long list of characters in the book). In charge of the garrison was William Farmer, a Scotsman and a professional soldier with extensive experience fighting in the Low Countries. Farmer died at Marston Moor.

Of the others, Chisnall is particularly interesting, having been considered at one time to be a candidate for being the author of the siege journal, due largely to the fact that he penned a book of his own, *A Catholike History*, several years after the siege. Chisnall, clearly a brave and skilful soldier, was promoted after the siege to the rank of colonel and served at Marston Moor. He died in 1653 at the early age of 35. The storylines relating to his presence in and around Chester during the siege are invented.

The siege was a personal disaster for Alexander Rigby, who not only had to explain his failures to the Manchester Committee, but was forced to pay his men out of his own pocket. His escape from the carnage at Bolton was exceedingly fortunate. As described in the novel, he is said to have mingled with the royalists and managed to flee with one of his colleagues down Tonge Moor Road to the north-east of the town, eventually reaching Bradshaw Hall, where he received shelter. Local tradition has it that he took the wrong turn when he got to Turton Road, and, realising his mistake, turned down a lane to the right and crossed Bradshaw Brook, in order to get back on the right path. This lane is still called Rigby Lane.

A lawyer and MP for Wigan, Rigby was said to have been an able and learned man, but severe in nature and lacking in humour. The exact nature of his hatred for the Earl of Derby is unknown, but exist it did, and it was certainly a driving force for him throughout the siege. Rigby died in 1650 at the age of 56, after contracting gaol fever whilst on circuit in the south of England.

One person whose career prospects were not damaged by the disaster of the siege was Thomas Morgan. The Welshman rose to the rank of major general and was eventually knighted. Towards the end of the Protectorate, he became associated with

General Monck and played an important part in the Restoration, eventually becoming Governor of Jersey in 1665. Unfortunately for him, his place in history has been somewhat overshadowed by his more illustrious nephew, Henry, the famous buccaneer, whose memory has been immortalised in the name of a brand of rum.

Less is known about Browne, Rigby's chief engineer during the siege. Portrayed in the novel as a cynic, but essentially loyal, there were, at the time, questions both as to his competence as well as to his loyalties.

Jenny Reade is an invented character. However, there *was* a woman called Reade who died under torture after being caught receiving smuggled messages from the house. She is reported to have lost some of her fingers during her ordeal. The message-carrying dog is also documented in more than one account, with some having the dog belonging to Reade. As related in the story, the dog lost its life, being shot by a parliamentary musketeer after trying one trip too many. The other dog mentioned in the novel, Prince Rupert's famous poodle, Boye, didn't fare much better. He died at Marston Moor.

The existence of tunnels from Lathom House to outside locations has never been proven, although there have been plenty of rumours and stories that such tunnels did exist. Burscough Priory is one of the places mentioned.

At this point, it is worth saying something about

461

Nantwich, Chester, and Bolton during early 1644.

Nantwich went quiet after the battle on January 25th. Sir William Brereton left for London but he was clever enough to manipulate the committees of local government to such a degree that he was able to maintain total control of local decision-making during the conflict to the detriment of members of the county elite, such as George Booth. Thomas Croxton was one of Brereton's leading cronies and was responsible for the payment of Brereton's field army. He eventually ended up as Governor of Chester.

As for the characters in Chester, Francis Gamull is possibly the best known. He was a leading merchant and founder of the town guard. His house on Bridge Street still exists. Robert Whitby was also a real person. As mentioned in the story, his uncle married Gamull's mother. The divinity lecturer William Ainsworth was also a real historical figure, although his role as a parliamentary collaborator is entirely invented.

As previously mentioned, most of the Seaman family are fictional characters. However, William Seaman *was* the name of the merchant who organised the first recorded major shipment of Cheshire Cheese to London in 1650. Somehow, Daniel Cheswis's role in this event has escaped historical record!

The Boot still exists on Eastgate Street and was indeed a new tavern and a brothel in early 1644. The layout inside the tavern as described in the novel, however, has been largely invented by me, in order to fit in with the plot. Thomas and Charles Corbett, Annie, and Roisin are all fictional characters.

The massacre which took place at Bolton on 28 May 1644 was shocking by any standards, and it was certainly one of the most horrific events of the whole civil war. The amount of people killed is open to debate, but it was certainly several hundred and perhaps over a thousand. Ironically, the presence of Rigby and his men in the town contributed to the slaughter, partly due to the strong resistance put up by the small parliamentary force, but also because of the grave error made by the defenders in executing one of the royalists after the first assault.

Many of Rigby's officers who were present at Lathom died here, including Captains Davie, Duddell, and Dandie, as well as Dandie's son. As I have suggested, a large number lost their lives at Silverwell Bottoms after fleeing into Silverwell Fields during the royalists' second assault. Those that escaped fled to the church, where they were taken prisoner. Legend has it that there is a mass grave at Silverwell Bottoms.

It is also certain that a great many atrocities took place in Bolton Town Centre in the immediate aftermath of the battle. The two such events mentioned in the novel were real, documented events. The man killed in front of his pregnant wife was called William Boulton, and the old lady cut down because she had nothing to give her killers was named Katherine Seddon.

Finally, a word about the novel's most important character – Lathom House itself. In the aftermath of Marston Moor, it did not take long before the house was under siege again, although this time Lady Derby was not present. In command was Captain Rawsthorne, who, under much more difficult conditions than during the first siege, managed to keep Parliament at bay until December 1645, when he was forced to surrender.

Today, not one trace remains of the original house, considered, according to an old ballad, 'so spacious that it can receive, Two Kings, their trains and all.' After the Restoration, the house fell into ruin and the Lathom Estate was eventually sold by the Stanleys in 1724, believe it or not to a man by the name of Bootle (Sir Thomas Bootle of Melling), who built a new Palladian mansion on the site, which was finished in 1734. There are not even any contemporary paintings of the old house – only a painting created from the descriptions left by the likes of Halsall and Rutter. It is as though the place never existed, a bitter irony of which Colonel Rigby would have wholeheartedly approved.

Acknowledgements

Thanks are once again due to Matthew, Tom, and Vanessa at Electric Reads, whose expert advice, editing and design skills helped make this book immeasurably better than it otherwise would have been.

Thanks also to Colin Bissett of the Sealed Knot for helping to iron out the historical errors in my first draft. Any remaining mistakes are entirely down to me. I'm also grateful to Ed Abram, David Casserly, and Kevin Winter for their expertise on Chester, Bolton, and Newark respectively.

I have to give an extra special thank you to Steve and Denise Lawson at the Nantwich Bookshop who have offered me fantastic support ever since the launch of *The Winter Siege*.

And above all, thanks to Karen, Richard, and Louisa for their love and support throughout.

Bibliographical Notes

In compiling the research for *A Soldier of Substance*, I referred to a multitude of different books and online resources, the most significant of which I have listed below.

For information on Nantwich, my main source, as always, was James Hall's *A History of the Town and Parish of Nantwich or Wich Malbank in the County Palatine of Chester* (1883). For specific details of local politics in Nantwich I used JS Morrill's *Cheshire 1630-1660 – County Government and Society during the English Revolution* (1974).

For information on the Siege of Lathom House, in addition to the contemporary accounts written by Edwrad Halsall, Samuel Rutter, and Edward Robinson, I referred mainly to four books, these being Stephen Bull's *The Civil Wars in Lancashire 1640-1660* (2009), Colin Pilkington's *To Play the Man* (1991), MB Williams and MJ Lawson's *The Better Soldier* (1999) and David Casserly's *The Storming of Bolton* (2011). Casserly's excellently researched book was also my primary source for the Bolton Massacre, although I also used James Clegg's *Annals of Bolton* (1888).

For information on Chester, my main sources were John Barratt – *The Great Siege of Chester* (2003), Simon Ward – *Chester – A History* (2009) and CP Lewis and AT Thacker – *A History of the County of Chester* (2003).

Of particular help for information on Newark was Stuart B Jennings' *These Uncertaine Tymes – Newark and the Civilian Experience of the Civil Wars 1640-1660* (2009).

Glossary

Awning   Staring

Bonesore   Tired, weary

Canker blossom   An insult, derives from a
                      term for an infectious skin
                      disease

Clot-pole   Idiot

Corviser   Shoemaker

Fou drunk   Very drunk, mad drunk

Gallas   A Cheshire dialect word
                      used to describe someone
                      who is always getting int
                      scrapes

Goody good een   A familiar greeting

Heckle-tempered   Short-tempered

Mithered	Bothered
Pribbling	Drooling
Scranny	Thin, scraggy
Slype	A covered walkway way between a cathedral transept and the chapter house
Tosspot	Drunkard

Printed in Great Britain
by Amazon.co.uk, Ltd.,
Marston Gate.